IN HER CHEST HER LITTLE SPIRIT GROWLS, BUT THERE'S NO TIME TO CALL AND RELEASE HER.

The Dog bites at the back of her heart, making it leap.

Kill him.

She yanks the knife free from his belt and sticks it up below his chin. Through the skin and muscle, deep into his skull.

There is the sound he makes as the blood flows out, following the pull of the blade.

Her family shouts in dismay. The dogs bark in fury, scenting the blood. Soon the Kabliw men will hear it and come.

But through it all she hears his dying. Her Dog falls silent, appeased. The Kabliw man collapses to the snow beside her. His cries are strangled and wet, like a baby born with the cord around its neck.

Sjenn drops the army blade into the snow, where it leaves a streak of red on the white, like a scar.

BY KARIN LOWACHEE

Warchild

Burndive

Cagebird

The Gaslight Dogs

THE
GASLIGHT
DOGS

KARIN LOWACHEE

www.orbitbooks.net

Copyright © 2010 by Karin Lowachee

Excerpt from *The Drowning City* copyright © 2009 by Amanda Downum

All rights reserved. Except as permitted under the U.S. Copyright Act of 1976, no part of this publication may be reproduced, distributed, or transmitted in any form or by any means, or stored in a database or retrieval system, without the prior written permission of the publisher.

Book design by Giorgetta Bell McRee
Cover art by Sam Weber

Orbit
Hachette Book Group
237 Park Avenue, New York, NY 10017
Visit our website at www.orbitbooks.net

Orbit is an imprint of Hachette Book Group. The Orbit name and logo are trademarks of Little, Brown Book Group Limited.

Printed in the United States of America

First edition: April 2010

10 9 8 7 6 5 4 3 2 1

To the Inuit of Canada, whose unique and beautiful culture was, and is, my inspiration. I've taken creative license, but my experience in the Great North sowed the seeds of this tale.

THE
GASLIGHT
DOGS

THE LAND

From the black ship spilled all manner of tall Kabliw—men from the South land, men from a world past the barrier of stunted trees that Sjennonirk's people called the Hackles of the Dog. That stick barrier was a warning laid by the spiritual ancestors of the *ankago:* no Aniw should venture farther than their tundra plain and frozen seas. Instead the People stayed to the ends of the rivers that flowed below the beginning of the sticks.

But the Hackles of the Dog couldn't stop the Kabliw of the South from sailing to North shores. These Kabliw, these people of the boats, went where they would and did as they pleased. Through late winter ice and the onset of spring their dark ship forged a passage, some great black whale to blot out the blue and white of her home.

Sjennonirk, an *ankago* of her people, named after her grandfather, stood on the small rocky hill overlooking the inlet where the Kabliw ship had anchored and watched these tall men unload their long wooden crates upon the

Land. They'd rowed ashore with their load in smaller boats that still sat twice the size of her people's kayaks. One of the men, bundled in black and brown wolf pelt, pried open the lid of the nearest crate to reveal the steel contents glittering within. She knew them to be guns. Father Bari from the South, a priest of his Seven Deities, had told her grandfather long ago about Southern hunters and their guns.

Now, it seemed, he had brought them to the Aniw. She recognized Bari's thin silhouette in his heavy gray robes, standing just to one side of the rougher-shaped men and their determined task.

Sjennonirk turned and fled down the opposite side of the hill, sealskin boots scratching over the crust of hard snow. She did not stop until she reached her family's camp.

In her mother's snowhouse they gathered, a small tribe of nomad Aniw that traveled together to hunt and fish. Sjennonirk sat upon the wide sleeping platform made of packed snow, the stone lamp by her side burning seal oil into the close quarters, creating a warmth she did not feel inside. All around her the white walls of their winter home glistened, narrow light glowing from the lamp. She saw many shadows.

"What has your little spirit seen?" her mother asked, kneeling on a bed of tan caribou skins and white bear fur. All of her family and the other Aniw they traveled with, her small tribe here at the corner of their Land, gazed up at her for answers and direction. Her father Aleqa, before he'd been killed by the great white bear, had been her tribe's *ankago,* and his father before him. They traced her ancestry of the little spirit straight back to the First Female, the great Dog that now resided in her and paced in the pit of her chest. She felt the paw steps behind her ribs, beating softly like a drum, like a heart.

She was the *ankago,* and she had no answers.

In the middle light, where her little spirit roamed, she had seen nothing but the smoky depths of the Kabliw world. They moved against the wind lines of the winter tundra, and the direction they pointed was nowhere she wanted to go.

"I will speak to the priest," she said to broad hopeful faces and dark fearful eyes. Though they'd traded with the Kabliw since the spring season of her birth, some Southern deeds weren't wanted on the Land.

When she was a child, Father Bari had talked of war.

The priest met her at the feet of the rocks, some distance from the men, who paid her little attention. They knew the Aniw—she was nothing spectacular to them anymore. The captain from that black ship had sat among her people, and captains before him, and eaten of seal meat with the Elders. Through all of these changing Kabliw, Father Bari had remained, the first of them. He kept a notebook and scratched in it often. He'd taught her with books from the South, and from these things she'd learned of war.

She looked up at him and the black freckles on his dark cheeks. His eyes were pinched. "Why do you bring guns?" she asked him.

"They say they've come to protect the Aniw. The people they fight with, the Sairlanders from across the ocean, they say the Sairlanders might come to the Land."

"Why would they come?" She knew the only reason the Land was not flooded by Kabliw was that most Kabliw couldn't sustain in the weather. They were too warm-blooded against the gouging cold and knew no way to navigate the terrain. They had no little spirits to guide them, and their gods were snowblind.

Father Bari shook his head.

"We trade," she said. This was a fair arrangement made long ago. What reason would any Kabliw have to bring force of arms?

"I'm sorry," the priest said. "I couldn't stop them. I tried. My church tried. But these are army orders."

She stared at the men and the crates. More of them treaded on the shore, and they weren't the sailors she knew. They wore black uniforms beneath their furs, and from their belts hung long blades and short guns.

She heard them singing even with the tundra and the jagged hill between their camps. The Northern air carried the boisterous male voices, and she spied a glow of orange fire over the bumpy cranium of snow-dusted rocks. The dogs whined, restless, and two of them pulled at their leashes in the direction of the noise, curious and wary. Sjennonirk stroked the lead dog's white ears, calm for them both.

Her cousin Twyee stuck his head out from the low entrance of her family's snowhouse and whistled to her. "You're going to stand there all night? These Kabliw don't sleep."

Twyee loved to laugh. He loved to laugh mostly at the lumbering Kabliw and their odd Southern ways. Sjenn patted the dog's ears once more, then crawled into the house as Twyee scrambled back. Inside was warm from the burning lamp and the clutch of bodies of her family: her mother, her aunt and uncle, and Twyee's little sister, Bernikka.

"They make a lot of noise," her mother said, sitting cross-legged on the sleeping platform, sewing up one of Twyee's mittens.

"What are they celebrating?" her aunt asked. She was stroking Bernikka's hair of knots with an ivory comb, and the little girl winced. Uncle was already asleep on the spread of caribou skins, snoring. He was older than her father had been when he had died, and not even a horde of Kabliw could keep her uncle awake.

"Celebrating? I don't know," Sjenn said. She didn't want to scare them with talk of guns, not now when sleep pulled at them. Tomorrow would be a day to consider these Kabliw. The dogs outside began to settle; she felt their bodies burrowing into the snow, tails over noses. Her little spirit twitched her own tail in response, a feather tickle in the curve of her ribs.

"Sleep," her mother said, looking up with pointed insistence, the sinew thread between her blunt teeth.

Sjenn may have been the *ankago* of her tribe, younger than all but Bernikka, but she knew to still respect her Elders. She set her parka down and curled up onto it, beside her mother on the platform of snow.

Her dream was a black expanse, like the tundra in the dead of a winter night. Moonlight and wind made the landscape moan. The Land's spirit grew restless, like her dogs were, and on the long horizon line stood the silhouette of a black Dog. Aleqa's little spirit.

"Father," Sjenn called.

He threw back his head and howled.

Breath pushes against her cheek, rank with hours of alcohol. "The tattoos on your face." The voice scratches against her skin.

Awake and the snowhouse is still, as quiet as her dream before her father spoke. Quiet except for the Kabliw bending over her, his large hand pressing into her stomach. In his other hand is a gun. Her family are shadows by the white walls, and Sjenn breathes up against the man's touch. Across from her, the snow entrance lies obliterated. This big Kabliw broke through the blocks and let in moonlight. Outside the dogs bark. There is no more singing, no noise but this.

The dream had pinned her and she hadn't heard this man come in. Now his gun waves around like the horn of a narwhale above gray waves. The gun shines above the shadows and keeps her family at bay. The Kabliw jabbers, every other word in a language she can't understand. His chin tilts up, blue eyes like shards of sea ice reflecting a sky only he can see.

In her chest her little spirit growls, but there's no time to Call and release her. The Dog bites at the back of her heart, making it leap.

Kill him.

She yanks the knife free from his belt and sticks it up below his chin. Through the skin and muscle, deep into his skull.

There is the sound he makes as the blood flows out, following the pull of the blade.

Her family shouts in dismay. The dogs bark in fury, scenting the blood. Soon the Kabliw men will hear it and come.

But through it all, she hears his dying. Her Dog falls silent, appeased. The Kabliw man collapses to the snow beside her. His cries are stangled and wet, like a baby born with the cord around its neck.

Sjenn drops the army blade into the snow, where it leaves a streak of red on the white, like a scar.

"You must go!" Twyee hisses, catching her trembling arm. "Run, Sjenn, before they get here!"

So she scrambles from the broken mouth of her snow-house. The night stands clear above her, looking down upon her with countless glittering eyes. "Father." The shadows on the snow could be the form of a black Dog. But they begin to break apart as light from the Kabliw camp, voices, and the clatter of steel break above the rocky hill and rumble closer like a storm.

CIRACUSA

They were three days' ride from Fort Girs, at the squatting end of a thundering rain that did nothing to drown Captain Jarrett Fawle's dreams. The day knew no acquaintance with the sun, had not shaken hands or tipped a hat to any but dark clouds. The farmers called this spring, but nature was a moody bitch, no less than an alley dog or a wanton wife. With the rain came a bite of cold. He'd been dreaming of rabid dogs now for five nights running. And for five nights he ran in the dreams but could never get away.

Ten rode in his patrol, all ahorse, hooves squishing through the flooded grass. They made obscene noises in their going, in between ear-splitting cracks and shards of light in the sky, some god up there rattling a saber upon all who dwelled beneath. Jarrett hadn't slept more than three hours in the past three days in the field, so the shadows weren't all beneath his eyes. In every corner of his vision they hung and billowed, like funereal drapery at an open window, calling his attention. But he had no desire to look out at the world. His bones felt as creaky as a spinster's, or like a rocking chair left too long to bleach, dried out by nightmare despite what the waking world poured on his head.

His men had not commented the entire way about his mood, but he knew their whispers when they thought him asleep in bedroll. And perhaps their three days of going and coming, unmet by savage vengeance like Major Dirrick had predicted, had tightened enough to squeeze out some voice. Because now Sergeant Malocklin edged up beside him, another shadow on a black horse. This one spoke.

"The weather is passing strange, cap'n."

Jarrett stared at the matted blond hair of his own mount. The mare's mane looked like the bedraggled locks of a drowned old woman. It had been raining all day. "There's nothing *passing* about it, sergeant." His thoughts held no barrel through which to fire idle conversation. His gaze remained fixed ahead, and he clamped his jaw tight.

Malocklin tried again. "The Soreganee's too wet to fight."

"Revenge isn't fairweather," Jarrett said. Luck did not often accompany the absence of an abo warband. More likely they were lying in wait. "The Crawft farm should be a grim reminder of that fact."

Malocklin grunted. Two days ago they had come upon the unfortunate family and what remained of their fetal homestead. The Soreganee warband had made a bloody abortion of the grounds, and his men had spent the day gathering and burning what remained of the dismembered dead. Three had been barely past their mother's skirts, but abo warriors did not distinguish between Ciracusan children and the adults. The grudge went deep and beyond a single generation.

"That beady demon's worse than his grandpa," said Malocklin.

"You won't hear me debate it." Jarrett had seen old Chief Qoyoches before the battle at Four Pin Ridge forced the war leader through a quick exit from this world. A wily bush fox, he'd fallen with a corporal's severed head in one hand and a rifle bayonet in the other, its point embedded in his chest.

The grandson and beady demon, Qoyotariz as he was called by his people, was the wolf to the wrinkled chief's fox, reared on tougher meat. He had developed a taste for war that knew no season. Stories about the first clash between the early settlers and the Soreganee tribe more than two hundred years ago had been passed down in blood from his grandfather.

If it came down to a choice between fighting their backward ancestors from Sairland and the hostile tribes of the Nation, Jarrett would take up arms against the Sairlanders and call it a day. That war bobbed and flailed into recession sometimes, but no respite followed the trail one shared with the abos.

Respite wasn't his task or his choice on this patrol. Instead they attempted to track Qoyotariz after the Crawft discovery—while the rain pelted down. He thought of turning back, but the raids were a menace, encroaching closer to Fort Girs. So Major Dirrick had ordered this venture, and the gods help any hapless farmers who stood in Qoyotariz's way. The abo bastard was bold and some said a little mad.

"Tracks're long gone," Malocklin apparently felt a need to point out. Working wetly through the fields on a hunt for that warrior didn't sit well with the men.

Jarrett rose in his saddle momentarily and looked over his shoulder, stretch and assessment of the glum and disgruntled faces of the eight behind him. One was their abo tracker, and he motioned the man forward with a flick of his fingers.

Not Soreganee, of course. A quiet Whishishian with a gaunt face, skin stained black around the eyes in the savage way. But so far he'd proved dependable, his tribe a well-worn ally; a sunny disposition was not required in army company.

"Well?" Jarrett asked him, though he knew the answer from the downturn of the abo's mouth.

"River's flood up," was the short pronouncement, which was the tracker's way of saying one step farther and they were in threat of a drowning. Damp-curtain weather, some dark caul across the landscape, made tracking difficult and ambushes likely. Trees aplenty stood soldiering against the horizon and from their ranks many a vileness could spurt. Qoyotariz was known for his fleetness.

Jarrett didn't favor returning to Fort Girs with a spectral report, all ghosts of dead settlers and no enemy to show for it. But three days of this and the dampness of his despair made his muscles ache and his will retreat. His horse had stopped already, shivering in the driven rain, cued by the shifting of his weight if not the tug of the reins.

"All right," he said, beneath a sudden racket from the sky. The men watched him out of drenched gazes with childlike hope. "All right," his voice, louder. He tipped his hat back in an attempt to shoo the shadows, but to no avail. Whipped air made a mark across his skin, and the rain poured upon his shoulders from the brim, sliding down coated arms, sogging his trousers. They were all overrun by misery. "We go home. The bastard will live another day."

They set a picket that night while the storm subsided to a low growl, all barking at bay for now. Jarrett took first watch with young Corporal Grabe, as he'd noted the boy sleeping in his saddle with a fascinating ability to stay upright. The other men needed the shut-eye, and Grabe was fairly fresh from his nap. Jarrett knew he wouldn't sleep and so put himself to use in the dark, clammy and restless, one hand on his gun. The fire burned low and too distant from his position to provide any warmth, and the far landscape rooted the sky like an upside-down hole— no light in or out of the trees and their cousin bushes, no light upon the sodden field. Rainclouds obscured most of the moon, forcing a squint as he looked out upon the darkness and shivered.

Too easy to dream, even standing. The peep, hoot, and rustle of every nocturnal critter pulled his senses to a paranoid point on which he balanced precariously. Blue night bled into black and made bruises of his sight. Thoughts wandered, no matter how much he tugged their leashes, drifting toward memories of headless babes and limbless longer bodies. Though only in his grim imagination, blood soaked the earth beyond rain spatter, made red pools in which he saw his own hollow-eyed reflection.

Such things had damaged his attempts to sleep in

previous nights. He thought himself cursed, for even before they'd come upon the unfortunate Crawfts, blood had tracked him into the slumbering hours. Four paws and long fangs, pointed ears and a gimlet gaze, a slow blink manifested the creature out of the shadows and he gasped himself awake. The night progressed in staggered breaths and taut twitches until he nearly reeled from the buffeting of it.

There came a battle cry.

Sudden gunfire spat around him as the dark fields erupted, popping up abos upon their camp. Weapon in hand, he saw no ready target past his nightmare reverie and panicked in the jolt, spewing wide all bullets from his chamber. Heart fled up his throat, an uncommon feeling when steadiness tended to grab hold and shake loose some action sense. He choked on it just as a demon cast him to the ground.

It sat upon his legs, copper shining eyes in a face beset by tiny red beads. Droplets of blood solidified on skin. The demon said, "I see you now," in the trade language of the Nation tribes. It seized his jaw and leaned forward as if to kiss.

The long, warm tongue of the creature pasted a line right across his mouth, then shoved between his teeth. The exploration drove in, heedless to his hand finding desperate life to gouge at muscle and skin. Some wild scent like burning grass and stale smoke surrounded his head from the banner of dark hair grazing across his cheeks. "Dog," it said as it withdrew, and laughed. "You shine like the moon. I mark your men by you."

Shock pushed for residence against his ribs, elbowing with fear. The struggle kept him pinned as the demon bent low again, grazing its face against his cheek, into the side of his hair. Breathing him in as his own breaths stopped. "Soon," it said into his ear, then gave a shove on his shoulders and launched back into the dark.

Rain pelted anew into his upturned eyes.

"Qoyotariz!" one of his men yelled from up and behind where he lay. "Captain, the abo's running!"

The abo ran and he couldn't move. Qoyotariz had kissed him with the flavor of blood, drawn from the gods knew what. It would not leave his tongue, and it drowned out even the rain.

Sleepless, they trotted back to Fort Girs, four men short. One was his Whishishian tracker; of course the Soreganee went for the other abo first, blood enemies as they were, and yet Qoyotariz had spared *him*. He told no one of the night-obscured encounter, and they buried the dead in the field, in silent grief. He managed some mumbled form of false comfort, but his troopers knew—no gods were listening, and the blessed trees did not truly salute. His nightmare had allowed this living terror to wreak havoc on his patrol, and he sat with the guilt behind his teeth, mud and smoke in every corner of his mouth.

A day closer to the fort and luck or the gods bestowed on them a boon. Not the warband they sought, but six straggled Soreganee youths, out on a forage or an animal hunt. Pups by the looks of them and, as such, easy pickings. Jarrett had the flame of humiliation and some stifled fear from his unprepared intimacy with the bastard

Qoyotariz—they burned through his sleepless state and he drew his gun and fired.

Pups grew into dogs, after all—that was the steady strain of any soldier's thoughts. There was no excitement to it. The troopers remembered their freshly dead comrades; it was in the sudden silence of their ride.

So Jarrett led his men in a furious gallop and cut the abos down.

He was not one for church of any kind but found himself in the wooden wonder, waiting on the garrison priest—a man of single score and five years, spry faith, Father Timmis. The chapel sagged from weather and smelled of incense and candle wax. No smiling sun shone down upon it or through its dirty blue windows. The Seven Deities bestowed no favor on this chapel any more than they did out in the field, and that equanimity perhaps was what drove him here at last. Some funeral moment would be held in the near future, but for now Jarrett sat on one of the hard pews, hoping for respite against shadows and mad abos. He held his gun in his hand and gazed down upon its sheen as if it could tell his fortune. It had told the fortunes of those he shot.

Father Timmis sneaked up on him from the rear door, and Jarrett turned and nearly aimed that gun at him.

"Easy, captain." The father's voice was of northern lilt, some deep ancestry from Ioen Aidra. He slipped into Jarrett's line of sight, a gray falcon in his long robe, though his face was more pleasant owl. "You're here late, I see..." Voice trailed and Jarrett stared back.

He knew how he looked. Death had more lively dancing partners on the battlefield.

"I lost men," he said. Not outstanding news in his business and the father knew it, two years in service to the frontier fort. The man sat one pew ahead, gaze heavy as Jarrett caught it, and it caused his words to stumble. "You...you worked a little with the abos, yeah?"

"In schools, early in my clergy studies," Timmis replied. He was not a priest of bombast oratory, but rather waited upon others in conversation. A rare enough quality in some men, and it made him tolerable to those who weren't as faithful and likable to those who were.

Jarrett lost the live end of what he wanted to say and flailed in silence.

"Rough patrol?" the father prompted.

It made him laugh. Not the most logical reaction in a holy house after the week he'd endured. His voice sounded hollow as it rose to the pointed ceiling. The rafters tittered back, some hill mouse scampering in the dusk. Jarrett gestured up toward the unseen rodent with his gun—that wasn't logical in a holy house either, but he didn't care. Fatigue ran respectful concern into the ground, even as the priest's eyes tracked the weapon warily.

"The abos are like those furry things," Jarrett declared. He was drunk on sleeplessness.

"How so?"

"Well," he said, "do you ever understand the intentions of a mouse? Occasionally they slip into your bed and bite your toes."

"Surely the warbands do more than bite your toes."

"No. No they don't." He leaned forward, arms on

the back of the father's pew, gun pointed down between them. "Have you ever seen a man try to walk without toes? Don't underestimate the intelligence of a mouse. The little furry bastard can bring down an army just by nibbling away at its toes."

Father Timmis didn't reply, but his stare took on a cast of concern. He said eventually, "Have you been sleeping, Captain Fawle?"

Jarrett laughed and stood. He shoved his gun into the holster at his hip and turned his back on the priest and the altar. His stride grew long as he made for the double doors at the rear of the church, calling to the ceiling: "The spirit of sleep has found better bodies to haunt than mine."

As if the gods could hear him.

THE KABLIW

Sjenn saw the priest from the corners of her eyes, a rib bone of a man standing on the opposite side of black iron bars. His long robe blended with them in shadow, his dark hands too. He looked in at her as she lay on the deck, called her name, offered water and words. She didn't reach out, and soon her eyes shut. The rocking motion of the great wooden ship was one she'd gotten used to, though this prison still retained the sharp edges and relentless unease of something dark and foreign. Like guns and gods. She was well-worn, kin to the slats of wood she lay on, well-worn like her hands and her clothing for how often she picked and clawed at the sealskin wrapped around her body. These they hadn't taken, at least, though they had taken *her*. These, at least, still held a scent of home.

*　　*　　*

"But you killed a man," Father Bari said, as if the dry red stain on her parka did not exist, as if she could not see it with every cant of her chin.

Looking out at the priest from behind the iron bars she said, "You brought them to my people. His death is on *your* head."

Yes, she had killed a man, but she still protested this prison, this inability to see sky or sea or to ground herself in the long horizon. The waves beneath her resisted anchor, but they were vast like the tundra. She wasn't fond of water, not these black depths that sounded like groans from inside the ship's belly, but she would trade the sight of the skinny priest for the sight of crashing waves. Or sky. She'd pleaded for it and they had laughed, the men of this ship. They thought her breathlessness a ploy. It had taken despair to chase her panic, to find herself curled to the wall.

She didn't know walls like this, scarred and gouged, giving splinters to the touch and black dust at every scrape; on the land the walls were white. They were snow, and in the evening light they sparkled like stars. The cold she knew had a smell of open air and it was not this; this was Southern cold, suffocating and stinking and hemmed in by waste. She felt it now steeped in her skin, and she hated these men for it. She didn't used to speak harshly and think violent thoughts. But she remembered once when her uncle had made the mistake of hitting one of their sled dogs, and the dog had bitten his leg in answer. Who was to blame for the injury?

The yellow lamp swayed behind the priest from its ceiling hook, and the light made his dark cowl and ebony skin seem deep-ice black. "I tried to stop them," he murmured, over and over. "I tried to stop those army orders." And with those orders, violent men. She used to see this priest's regret. But days and nights had rubbed down the bristle of her attention—and her care. What were his words worth when everything he had exchanged with her grandfather and her father had been disregarded in favor of barreling whale hunters or raucous soldiers, and their deep imprints in the giving green of her tundra spring? They trod without heed or caution, when once there had been care.

So once she'd had care for the well-being of this priest. Once she had followed the tracks of her father and led this priest to the other tribes, invited him into the great snowhouses, shared with him the rituals of the *ankago*. Father Bari, who was no kin of the Aniw. Yet the People had welcomed him. Now no more. *Kill the priest,* rattled the urge. It bit her thoughts.

"I did not know it would come to this," he said.

The wild Dog in her raised her eyes.

There were things Father Bari did know, in those heavy open books that he set before her when he came to visit every day on this ship. He carried a squat wooden stool and charcoal pencil. He talked of laws and told her words like "murder" and "trial," and showed her, in his book, crowded black lines that created pictures of men with large noses and sagging clothes. They stood before a shadowed door made of bars. There were the shapes of women too, Southern women, bent over and bloated like pregnant ring seals, heavy-laden with babies or baskets. They walked to the iron bars, too. Bars much

like the ones that separated her from the priest and held
her in. "This." He jabbed the pencil to the image on the
wrinkled brown page. "Sjenn, this is where you may end,
if you don't listen."

He talked. In her dreams her father talked too. The
timbers of the ship creaked deeply in the cold water like
the disgruntled groan of a narwhale far from home. She
didn't understand why they wished to punish her when
the man she'd killed had attacked her people, had broken
into her house and held a gun to her family. An Aniw
called his death justice, the stab of his own blade into his
throat. Threat from other people could not be tolerated
on the Land, and once the threat was removed, dealt with
somehow, that was the end of it. Why this paper, these
words, the tedious turning of the light from shadow to
deeper shadow? She was no longer in her world, not even
in the middle light where her Dog prowled.

"I never killed a man before," she said, and Father
Bari slowly closed his leather-bound book. "As woman
or Dog."

He shook his head twice. "You can't talk about your
Dog, Sjenn." He rose to his feet, gathered up his stool,
and tucked the charcoal pencil into the layers of his gray
clothing. His feet disappeared beneath the long robes,
and he swayed to catch his balance on the uneven deck.
"They don't understand such things," he said.

She turned away, pressed her shoulder to the wall, and
dug her cracked fingernail into the grooves on the wood.
The priest said she would have to tell what happened, yet
now he said that she could not tell the truth. He taught her
his language, but he could not explain his thoughts.

So this wasn't thinking. These were lies.

*   *   *

In her dream her father, Aleqa, stood beside the bear
that had killed him. It had been the spring of her first
tattoo when he'd been mauled. She now knew a mark of
time the priest called years, and she'd been maybe fifteen
of these years. All her life to that point she'd been the
daughter of her tribe's *ankago*. Spiritwalker, the priest
had called Aleqa.

Sjenn knew her father in the middle light, as well,
when he would walk with her, four-footed and amber-
eyed in the ancestral Dog form of his little spirit. He'd
taught her the arts of the *ankago*. He was a black Dog
in the middle light, full fur, long-legged and long-nosed,
and though he showed no teeth or tongue she understood
his words.

Here in this dream his words seemed to echo from
shard ice to night sky. And the bear, subdued in the
dream in a way he would never be in life, yawned with
a show of fangs. They were light and shadow, the white
bear and the black dog, in the dusk and glow of this
dream. This was not the familiar terrain of the middle
light, where the *ankago* walked. Only dream surrounded
her in this prison, waking or asleep, only dream. Here
Aleqa and his bear were memories, his voice a tiny whisper of his little spirit.

"Sjenn," her father said, with a twitch of pointed black
ears. The voice in her mind seemed to echo with the
drumbeat of their ancestors, those first who had stood
on four and hunted as one. "Sjenn," her father said. "You
must wake up. You must kill the priest."

"It's too late." This was not the first time she'd said

it, and she was weary. She stood before the bear and her father on two legs, as a woman, and the dark ship on the violent sea had routed the ferocity she hoped to conjure. Her little spirit was asleep, muffled and tied. She could see the agitation in her father's eyes. His Dog eyes were open, and hers were shut. He walked around her, tail flicking, soft growls at the back of his throat. They were *ankago;* they were born of the wild Dogs. They walked in the middle light, and yet it had been months since she had met him there. And so the dream.

Here Aleqa did not fear the yawning bear, did not feel the cold, did not accept her tired replies. The bear was a warning, her threat animal to balance the light of her father. He sat in wait. As Sjenn turned in a slow circle to watch her father pace, the bear raised his head and stared straight at her, unblinking black eyes in a deceptive, serene white face. He could not speak their language, but she felt the threat. Even here. She feared him.

"You must kill the priest," her father repeated, with a darker growl and a snap at the tips of her fingers.

She yanked her hands up to her chest. "Sjennonirk brought him to the people!" Sjennonirk her grandfather, her father's father, when he was yet alive. He had clasped arms with the priest when both were young, when the priest brought them nothing but words and handcraft. The priest had smiled so white at her grandfather Sjennonirk, and they had sat in the great snowhouse just at the break of spring when many of the tribes gathered, and burned seal oil and ate seal meat. Peaceful times. The time before the priest had brought other men to the Land, and those men had brought guns. Grandfather Sjennonirk was long dead, and she bore his name and now his burden; what he had invited to the Land had stolen her from it.

And her father was dead, killed by this bear that accompanied him in her dreams and yawned at her as if her state made him sleep when she could not. And she could not reason with the black Dog, not as a woman. It was always a struggle to tame the little spirit, in or out of the middle light, and in the airy weight of a dream she had no control. Brittle-boned and bare-skinned, she was as thin as dawn. Dreams were the mischievous little brothers of the middle light, the domain of men, and she could not tame her father here. He bore the strength of all their ancestors, and she could not even muster her Dog.

And Aleqa had one purpose to visit upon her, every night since she'd been taken from the people, so many nights that she'd lost count.

So many nights in the belly of this Southern ship, in the center of the creak and groan of its timber bones, in the dark echoes of its occupants and their language and their laughter. They stank of black oil and old smoke, and warm places without air. They stank of leather goods and puppy fur, salt-wet from the sea, and the blood and fat of the whales they killed. The priest came often to speak with her, like he had when she was young, telling kindness and showing books. He had taught her of the South, and when she was young she had thought it all a fine fantasy. Such detailed drawings, such odd words. He'd made her laugh with the descriptions and the tales. Now he came even though she pretended to sleep. Though she wished to kill him and could not.

The priest came in the day and night, to warn her of

what was to come, and her father came in the thin veil of dreams to warn her of what had passed.

And the white bear's gaze was baleful, and she had no rest.

He said his name was Captain Mackenzi and he visited her once, a short man compared to the other Southerners she saw, Aniw height, with round dark eyes like the snow hare. He was wrapped in a heavy wool coat, and Sjenn couldn't take her gaze from the golden buttons at his collar. They were like the reflections of his eyes as he peered in at her, hands tucked up beneath opposite armpits. He hadn't met her before, but she'd seen him speaking with Father Bari when his hunters and a couple army men had brought her onboard. In the dim light the shadows made caves of his cheeks, and he rubbed repeatedly at his nose as he spoke.

"The men say you tore out Stoan's throat."

Stoan, the dead Southern man. She sat against the wall with her arms inside her sleeves for warmth. She was used to the cold, but this briny chill that seemed to seep through the wooden deck made her skin itch. It had bothered Father Bari that he could not see her arms, and she wondered if it bothered Captain Mackenzi. Without arms she could not strike out. This should have been a comfort, but he stared at her with a certain suspicion.

"I didn't tear out his throat. Why do they lie?"

"One or two of the men say you have witch magic. If it weren't for their upset I would've left you in that gods-forsaken place."

They liked to invoke their gods for idle things. Sjenn

said nothing. She knew the word *witch,* and knew it did not describe her, but these Southerners called things what they would and seemed unshakable about them. They wrote books and drew pictures about the things they knew. Father Bari had said they weren't supposed to know about the Dog, but these whale hunters visited Aniw shores every spring and summer. They'd heard stories from the tribes just as Father Bari had, even if they hadn't seen anything. Even if they hadn't seemed to care. But one dead army man and suddenly they saw.

"Do you have witch magic?" the captain asked.

Perhaps Father Bari would caution her to lie. She didn't think she was lying when she said, "No." That wasn't what her people called it. The *ankago* were taught the dark light. Father Bari called it magic, but she didn't know that word. Her ancestors were born from the dark light. She, an *ankago,* walked the middle light: the domain of her Dog, her little spirit. How could these Southern men understand? They dealt only in dreams.

The captain stared at her and she sat very still, looking back. She thought he might speak again with the way he opened his mouth and pulled in the air between his teeth. He rubbed his nose; it made her want to rub her nose against the pervading stink of this ship and these men. Though all but Father Bari stayed away she still smelled them, leaking through the walls like dripping fat through a skein.

Captain Mackenzi had not been cruel to her, yet he had brought the whale hunters and the army and the guns to the Land. Boxes stacked on the rocky shore, and she did not know what would become of them, or the Aniw. Most of the army men had remained behind, and she was too far to see now, too far to go back. In the beginning, when she'd first been brought aboard, she'd pleaded with the men to return to the Land. But they were deaf to her.

Now the captain turned away just as the other men had, just as Father Bari did every day, and started for the steps that would lead him to the top deck. Up above where one could see the horizon. And the bones of his knees creaked like his ship.

The bear. In her dream Sjenn watched him pace, lumbering strides so thick his white flanks shook from the movement. Yet if he wanted to run he could cut down a man in no time at all. He ignored her now, though she stood on a floe only two leaps away, balancing effortlessly. The dream was different this time. As she stood there she thought of games played with her cousin Twyee, hopping from floe to floe, daring each other not to fall between the cracks and into the cold water. They traveled from island to shore that way, breathless with danger, before they finally collapsed to the packed snow on the Land, immersed in giggles and warmth. Sometimes they saw the bears far off, sometimes a mother with her cub fished with her great paws dipping into the water. Swipe, swipe.

Sjenn watched the bear, the bottom of his fur spiky from wet, some pale ends already crystalline with icicles. He'd been swimming and paused now on his floe to shake his head and blink, glancing to the side. Away from her. Even when she was in her ancestral Dog form she could not speak to him, not in a language he would readily understand, but here was a mutual awareness and respect. Animal to animal. Sometimes the bears were shy, especially the cubs, and hid behind snow mounds in camouflage, so the only way one noticed them was by their blinking black eyes. Her father always cautioned her to stay away, even in Dog form, not to be deceived by the fluffy fur and the round ears. They were not sled dogs. Even the cubs could be vicious. "They've been here since the time of our ancestors," he'd said. They were as old as the Land and just as wild.

As a woman she did not approach, only watched. The bear dipped his chin to the gray water and pawed the surface for a second, perhaps spying a fish or a little seal. Sjenn crouched on her own floe with the leisure of a dream. She wanted this vision, if she could not be there in the middle light. Even when she awoke, at least she would have this tingle of a memory, well-worn. This was a vision of home.

The bear poked at the top of the water again, moved his great head from side to side as if he watched the quicksilver blur of a fish beneath the surface. His paw lifted, paused. He stood frozen for a moment and didn't look at her, perhaps because he knew she was there. This great hunter of the Land that even her four-legged ancestors had revered. She felt herself smiling, yearning to reach out and touch the wide white flank, if only for a blink, to feel the bear breathe. Home.

His large paw struck at something in the water, and Sjenn set her hand to the ice floe, balancing against a reflexive recoil. The bear growled, stepped back, then again, dragging a form from the sea. Gray and bedraggled from the water she thought it a seal at first, but then the bear tossed the body beside him on the ice. It was her father, Aleqa. He raised his arms to ward off the descending blow of the bear's claws, but she heard the muffled crash of the animal's power come down on his chest. She watched, bone-stiff, as the bear grabbed at her father's head with his other paw. The claws dug, then pulled, dragging along Aleqa's scalp.

Aleqa had told her once that the great white bears killed the people much like they did the seal. With their long black claws they skinned their prey.

But this wasn't quite how her father had died. He'd been hunting, he had put up a fight. His brothers had managed to kill the bear with their spears after it had killed him. He had not lain on the ice, docile and waiting.

Here, blood spread on the white beneath her father's body.

She cried out, a sound of warning. The bear's dipping muzzle and bared teeth flashed up toward her. She looked into the upswept black eyes of the beast and took a step back. She must run to safety, run to her cousin Twyee so he might watch over her body. She needed her Dog. She could fight this bear as her little spirit. She could protect her father.

She began the words, the incantation, the song from her throat in rapid breaths and pointed growls, piercing the cold air. With every exhale she felt herself lowering to her knees, body weakening. No time to run. She heard the bear's steps on the ice coming toward her, a hollow drumbeat. His hollow animal heart. Her eyes shut and soon she lay flat on her back. No running now, this dream held her down. Yet she still sang, pushing the air in her lungs and the words of her Call up toward the darkening sky. Shadow moved across the sun, she felt the warmth and light recoil.

The bear's hot breath puffed against her cheek, and she awoke with fangs.

The prison opens. Her Dog rises from beneath the cover of sealskins and bear pelt. There stands the priest, in light and shadow.

She catches his fear on her tongue. It tastes like the hunger of her Aniw form.

So she leaps toward him. Paws collide with chest and they both crash to the deck. He's a skinny thing, his long arms and open mouth do nothing against her. Behind her she senses another man, but he doesn't matter, he cannot hold her. Only the priest matters, only his soft form below the weight of her bones, her muscle and fur. She crushes the human form into the wood of this ship, seizes him by the throat and bites down.

It's as easy as chewing snow. She jerks her head away, ripping her fangs from his neck. The flesh tears.

Sound snaps in her sensitive ears, a man shouting. A heart dying down. The scent of wet iron fills her nostrils, its taste at the back of her throat.

✦ NEV ANYAN

Wet and decay, Jarrett had thought upon waking in the dawn. Wet and decay, like some drowned soul was breathing on the city.

The rank smell swept in from the ships and the sea and hit the raw edges of bloated Nev Anyan. It rubbed sore the morning air, from the House of Correction in Ironstack Fields down to the string of dilapidated buildings along the dockside. Dun life regurgitated over windowsills and stoops, into gutters and alleyways, and there was just no getting away from it, not farther inland on hills where churches loomed, nor in blue gardens blooming with powdered women in petticoats. Deterioration and refuse sank deep into every old stone fluting and shaded patio, and Jarrett couldn't go far enough within Nev Anyan's confines to be rid of it. So instead he sought the edges, where fish and rotting wood collided, where bodies trawled the expanse of the Lower Roog, hoping for a catch. At least here on the edge of Nev Anyan, sometimes, there was a breeze…but he still hated the city by the sea.

He hated the sea, too, the noisy gulls and brackish water that piled and licked the legs of the piers, leaving dregs of gangrene weeds and suspicious sludge on the worn columns and planks of wood. The only thing that stank more than the sea were the sailors off the ships. They were aplenty on the dockside, rolling in their curious gait from brothel to pub to gods knew where. His army soul didn't much like the navy either, or any of its brother kin: merchants, pirates, cod haulers off the populated coast. He found the men loud and unruly and their mode of transportation a macabre rocking cradle.

Give him a horse and some sturdy ground instead, and men who sat quietly around fires and spat tobacco. Give him eagles in a bright blue sky rather than these chattering, flying vermin that dropped shit on every cobblestone as he walked away from the early bustling docks and shrouded faux gilt of Madame Bettai's Pleasure Emporium.

The late dawn was a cool gray cloud, descended to eye level, a fine mirror to his mood and his hangover. If he were in a fog, being chased by barking shadows, it only made sense that the rest of the world was too. He headed up Pier Two Street, cursing its incline and the fact he had not noticed it very much when he was sober. Likely because he hadn't felt this drained, this heavy, and it hadn't seemed that steep when he'd had somewhere to go. Up and down from Madame Bettai's to the Seagull, which had an unfortunate name but damn good beer— he'd gone all night from one to the other with a couple cheery enlisted men from his battalion, breaking rules of protocol and completely unconcerned about it. They'd bought him rounds and he'd paid for their women. Come time in battle they'd feel all the more need to look out for him, when that wasn't always the guarantee between officers and their men. Not on the frontier.

Behind him there came some commotion, as a ship had arrived the night before from the northern region—or so the talk had propagated in the Gull. The sailors were still working to unload their trade, crates of who knew what. Whale blubber, bone for women's corsets, bloody fur—things that contributed to the rank odor and creak of the docks. Jarrett looked back and down the hill out of idle observation, easily distracted and remembering that somewhere, somewhen, Father Bari had spoken to him about the white North. But in his numbing state he couldn't recall details and gave up his curiosity to the fog.

The Mastiffe was the ship's name, emblazoned in yellow on the side of the dark hull. Again a small tug of familiarity, but nothing more. Dog breed, he thought, with thick recognition and wandering relevancy. Wolves of the sea, the battleships claimed themselves, though this whaler was no navy vessel. He'd had run-ins with wolves in his life, out in deep forests. Mostly they shied from men, but if the navy captains knew that, it would ruin the romantic image.

The Mastiffe's sails were rolled up, the mast spires standing black and stark against the murky sky. It looked like an old vessel, squeezed and cracked by Northern climes. No predators of the sea in port now; the battle groups were far out in the ocean, at war with Sairlander convoys. Instead the biggest aggression came from the gulls, giving ruckus, whirling above the roofs of ware-houses, pubs, and offices all crammed in a haphazard line along the shore. Jarrett held two fingers aloft at them, but it was more for his benefit than theirs, before turning about and aiming himself up the crest of the hill, one arduous step at a time.

His black frock coat flew undone but he grasped for the folds and pulled them tight around his body. A couple golden buttons were lost somehow. The morning mist chased goosebumps down the back of his neck, and an errant thought made him check his pocket for his cap. He found it there, so breathed easier. If he lost any part of his uniform, besides the buttons, his father would kill him.

On that thought his fingers wrapped around the pol-ished ivory handle of his gun, snug deep in its holster, and he exhaled cool mist and a sense of relief. He didn't remember strapping on the belt before he left Madame Bettai's, no surprise. The strumpet on the bed had been a welcome distraction. But there they all were: his gun, his cap, his ability to still walk; maybe he was minus a few buttons on his coat and a little bit of his integrity, but all in all he was in fair shape, just well enough to find his way home, sneak through the back door, and grab a bottle of whiskey to accelerate the morning. He could pass out after a final skirmish with some gat and hope for another go at it before his furlough ended. His father the general was a busy man, so the only one likely to notice his schedule was the head maid at his father's house, and Louna happened to be quite fond of him.

His feet knew the route even if his clouded mind jumped in retreat at the shadows. Despite himself he still carried vestiges of nightmares into the waking day, growling images that had chased him this early from bed and away from painted, pouting company. Some things one didn't want women to witness.

The going was long. He knew it was a fair hike to begin with when he was too lazy to look for a carriage, a bugbug, or even a random horse that he could "borrow" (though that would be only in sheer desperation). The morning was crisp enough, even at this time of year when the first warm winds of summer were hitting inland. The ocean still clung to the late winter and blew upon these shores. He missed the fort.

Rubbing at his nose, eyes to the cobbled street so he wouldn't trip over his own bootlaces, his shadow stretched long and blue by his side from the watery illumination still dripping from the gaslights along the curb. A few urchins leaned in crooked doorways, with hooded gazes and stacked newspapers at their feet. One or two asked him if he wanted the news, but he ignored them. More talk of frontier battles with the Pangani Nation, parliamentary games with the Patronael, moral decay and corrections calamaties? No, thank you.

He could be aware of the world outside of his frontier home without caring about it, a subtlety his father refused to acknowledge in him. Every furlough back to Nev Anyan seemed to drill this home, and thus his overnight excursions to the emporiums and the pubs. He fought enough on horseback, with saber and gun. Words held the greater potential for strife, and he tended to find more of it here in the civilized part of Ciracusa, in its greatest city, than in the field.

He did prefer Nev Anyan in the morning, though, in its yawning hours before the place became utterly congested by people, animals, and noise. He didn't aim for the commercial district anyway, so as the shopmen opened up their doors and the first signs of carriages and drays began to dot the secondary streets, he turned east, to where Pier Two Street gave way to Temple High Street in what must have been a poetic form of planning by the first citizens two hundred years ago. What better place to put the church district than at the top of the path that led to vice and villainy?

The world was certainly less busy the farther he got from the docks. The buildings stood more proportioned, the windows larger and protected by awnings that curved over the sidewalks like stiff eyelids. The streets broadened out to accommodate various modes of travel, as well as the surge of pedestrian traffic that filled the lines of throughways by high noon. He stumbled along, a solitary footman, between the temple tower's clanging call of the hours. A quick glance as he passed the vaulting portico told him he had thirty minutes to beat the next bell ringing, until the curlicued iron hand struck the sixth morning hour. The swept street was wide and clear and quiet. He shut his eyes for a moment to ease the throb behind them.

And opened them again to find a uniformed figure in his way, seemingly out of nowhere.

His hand twitched toward his gun but paused before any untoward action. It was only a young man—rosy complexioned, blinking. The boy looked to have been roused from a deep sleep, slapdashedly dressed but buttoned to the throat. He gave a misfired salute, nearly taking out his eye, and began to speak. Jarrett kept walking, broadsiding the flank of the temple and its incessant hill, forcing the soldier—likely one of his father's minions from the city's army barracks—to trail him in conversation.

"Captain Fawle, your father requests your presence at the house."

"That's where I'm going."

"Sir, *immediately.*"

The urgent tone warranted a closer look, so he gave it. "That's where I'm going, *immediately.*" It occurred to him belatedly that since the soldier had known precisely where to intercept him on his route back from Madame Bettai's, he wasn't fooling anyone with his late-night exploits. So this specific call to arms was for reading him the riot act. His step slowed considerably.

"Sir, he said to tell you that he doesn't care where you rut, this is business of some import."

The boy's tone was understandably nervous. He must have been compelled to use that precise sentence, and some part of Jarrett wasn't at all surprised. It was just like General Cillein Fawle to force this sweaty young soldier to deliver a line like that to a captain in Ciracusa's army. But he wasn't going to hit the messenger in lieu of hitting his father. He was a better leader of men than that, even in this state.

"Run ahead and tell him I'm on my way." He gestured farther up the street in the vague direction of his father's house.

"Yes, sir." The young soldier managed a straight salute this time and hurried off, mission accomplished, and all too eager to leave.

Jarrett sighed, fishing his cap from his pocket and plopping it onto his head. Despite himself he sped up his pace. At this rate, with his pounding skull and leaden feet, even at a hangover hurry he was going to be late. Breathing deep again in a more focused attempt to clear his head, he fussed at the flat collar of his coat to raise it. Though the sun was rising, it did nothing to burn away the cold.

His father's house had been standing since the monument to Ciracusa's first heroic general was erected in Upper Town Square nearly 170 years ago. When Jarrett was a boy, General Fawle had routinely told him that when the day was clear on a bright Mais-day afternoon and people were at the temples, one could stand on the east side of the square, at the old general's flank, look straight down Gold Court Street, and see the iron gates of their home. Jarrett had gotten the impression, even at a young age, that his father was trying to tell him that military greatness was the path of every Fawle man, despite the fact their ancestors had been pitchfork farmers back in Sairland.

Ironically, the elder Fawle had predicted well. Being the only member of the family besides General Fawle himself who had survived the wasting cough twenty years ago, Jarrett hadn't argued when military school at thirteen meant leaving this house and its iron gates for the better part of four years. Just standing in front of the gates, looking up at the red brick and black shutters, made him heave a sigh.

The neighborhood was quiet, not only because of the time of day. He'd long left behind the potential bustle of a wakening city and entered the straitlaced avenues and back alleys of the affluent citizenry, where a line of intricately wrought gates, trim lawns, and weekly washed cobblestones accompanied one's steps as closely as a shadow. Tall trees infiltrated the line of gaslights standing erect in regular intervals at the curb, their branches barely decorated after the long winter, casting dark arterial lines across the ground. Faintly, on some parallel street, he heard an early carriage roll along in echoes just beneath the sound of clopping horses' hooves. Some bank manager, perhaps, or an equally rich businessman giving an illicit missus a discreet ride out of the district and back to the adjacent slums.

Feeling a tongue of cool air tickle the back of his neck, as if the commotion one street over somehow pushed a reminder to his reluctant stance, Jarrett shouldered open the gate and stepped through. He took his time easing it shut once again, all of his movements careful and slow, if only to prolong the diatribe he was likely to face once he was inside.

That sidelong thought diverted his steps to the right flank of the house. He padded down the narrow alley between the red brick wall and the tan one of their neighbor, brushing his arm against manicured bushes until he faced the solarium's door and the wide glass pane that gave an unobscured line of sight into the gloomy innards of the mansion. He didn't see any ready movement in the long hall through the solarium's open doors, or figures of either the servants or the general passing from one room to another. If he could only sneak up to his bedchamber and splash himself with ice water, he would be alert enough to deal with one of General Fawle's lectures. There simply wasn't any other officer in Ciracusa's army—or navy, for that matter—who could make him feel like he was back in the junior academy despite his years fighting on the frontier. That the young soldier had implied the matter was one of "import" barely touched his mind; everything was something of import to the general if he deemed it, and he himself had felt the brunt of such important matters by way of loud reprimands, sometimes even in the company of other men.

He tugged open the door of the solarium and stepped inside as quietly as possible.

"Jarrett."

The voice wasn't particularly deep—his father didn't have the resonating baritone of some great orators or military leaders, but what he lacked in booming depth he made up for in precise, clear pronunciation. Every syllable, consonant, and vowel. The hard sound of Jarrett's final letter seemed to ricochet off the long wooden floors, the standing clock in the main hall, the curling bannister leading to the upper floors. He didn't try to be discreet as he let the door shut behind him with a clatter and walked through the solarium to the hall, straight to his father's study at the front of the house. The servants were nowhere in sight, which was his first clue that perhaps this truly wasn't about his late-night exploits after all. They tended to evacuate only when private matters were at hand, and shouts from the general were hardly private anymore.

"Come in here," General Fawle said, when Jarrett just approached the threshold of the study, cap in hand, coat open and loose now that he was inside. Still, he felt his breaths constrict and the pounding behind his eyes increase. Early morning light brightened the room, bending angles of gold across the wide mahogany desk behind which his father sat. The surface of the desk was predictably neat but oddly absent of the typical stack of papers, map rolls, and heavy tomes of history he was used to seeing when he visited. Instead, the main item was a creased and cracked leather-bound journal, shut and tied by a black string.

Jarrett moved across the red Marrakol rug until he was standing directly in front of his father and raised his gaze to the other man's gray eyes. His nerves pulled taut despite his fatigue, giving a contradictory jangle in his system that he knew well from those exhausted intervals between skirmishes in the field. Any minute now someone would sound an alarm and he would lose the luxury of weariness.

The alarm came through the stare of his father, sitting there with the sunlight behind him like he was a gleaming gargoyle atop a high temple roof. Even at this hour he was squarely turned out, not quite in full uniform but somehow still a perfect officer. The ironed gray shirt was buttoned to the collar, and the gentleman's black silk choker gave the appearance of a back so straight no blow could break it. Jarrett had no doubt even his father's tall boots beneath the desk shone in daylight. If the man stood he would be the perfect columnar silhouette of one of Ciracusa's most decorated generals, and not even his medium stature could undermine the effect.

Though Jarrett was the one standing, and loomed a full head taller if he and the general were shoulder to shoulder, he tended to feel small beneath such a gaze. But he managed a professional stance, right arm folded behind his waist, the other holding his cap securely to his left-side ribs. It was the best he could manage in a state of obvious dishabille.

His father didn't invite him to sit in one of the two leather seats facing the desk, and he was not so dim to take the liberty. The vague smell of oiled leather and polished steel seemed to emanate from the very walls, but that was just the way General Fawle maintained the books and swords and one ancient suit of armor displayed around the study. The scent contributed to Jarrett's latent nausea.

"Father Bari is dead," the general said, without any preamble.

Jarrett blinked. "Father Bari is dead?" he heard himself repeat, like a simpleton. "How?" No formalities, just the question.

Maybe the general was sensitive to the shock of the news, because he didn't reprimand. His hands folded on the old journal. "This is the priest's notebook...I've been reading through it all morning. He speaks of you in its pages, he speaks well of you..." The general trailed off as if this fact were unlikely or confusing.

Now Jarrett wanted to sit, and damn his father, he did anyway, lowering himself unceremoniously into one of the brass-studded leather seats. He rubbed a hand across his forehead. A nightmare had sprung to life in the day and seemed to thread the sleeping and waking images together. Sudden memories tumbled forth, descriptions from the priest of tall black ships and colorful sailors.

"How...he'd just sent me a letter a month or so ago saying he was going back North? But I didn't hear from him again, I just assumed..." It wasn't unusual for the old Father to drop off the edge of the earth, so to speak, as the man had held a passion for rough terrain, foreign environments, and much to Jarrett's confusion, the abo population. That was how they had met, ten years ago at Fort Sheare, and the man had been a kind soul to Jarrett from the first. It was how he treated the abos, no matter where he met them: desert, jungle, ice. The priest sought them all out and wrote his stories and his experiences in—gods, through his muddled mind he had not recognized the journal. But of course it was Father Bari's. His eyes pained him from the increasing sun, so he had to shut them for a moment. "Was it on the voyage, did the ship—?"

"No." The general paused and Jarrett looked up at him, squinting, wondering at the unusual hesitation.

"No, but...?"

"I think I ought to take you to the Hess."

Prison. Jarrett blinked, slowly this time. "Why?"

"There's someone...there's something you need to see."

"A criminal? Was he murdered? Was Bari murdered?" So his mind went immediately to the thought of violence. His frustration took hold, an easy emotion to slide into in the face of all the gray talk. Why would his father want to drag him to the House of Correction, why the dodged questions? He wanted the priest's journal and stared at it, but his father rose, tucking it under his arm.

"I'll have Louna send for a carriage."

The ride was interminably slow. Jarrett leaned his shoulder against the wall inside the carriage and peered around the edge of the curtain to the city rolling by, but he didn't see the details, just a wash of familiar shapes and colors. The rectangle of buildings and cobblestones and bobbing top hats bled into a morass of gray and black. The sun had fooled the city and now hid behind long clouds again. Perhaps it would rain. His father didn't say a word as they bumped their steady way along the most trafficked road in Nev Anyan—the Statue, born from the focal point of the city, a great marble figure of the country's founder, Taon Ciracusa, riding high on horseback atop Admiral Hill. Statue Road paralleled the River Brendt, so when Jarrett glanced to his father he saw the silver wavelets out the portside window, and across to the other side of it sat Va. Kore Prison. They weren't headed over the bridge, though, as the Hess bore only short-term offenders, or so said the policy. Jarrett was grateful, as he had heard stories about Va. Kore, tales of filth and murder that had reached even the brigands on the frontier. Why they were even going to the Hess was still a question, and he asked it once again.

"Why won't you explain this to me before we get there?" So he would know what to expect. The fact Father Bari was dead still hadn't quite hit the ends of his nerves. He just felt cold and too dry-eyed, and for the life of him he could not remove from his mind, even temporarily, his many random memories of the priest. They infiltrated the silence between himself and the general like ghost fingers, playing with his thoughts.

Just half a year ago he'd sat with Father Bari in his current post at Fort Girs, over a stew, and heard fond stories of the seal eaters of the North. Father Bari had given him a *sul,* what the Aniw of the Ice called a snow knife. He remembered asking with a laugh, *They have a knife for snow?* And Father Bari had replied, *They have many different kinds of snow.* The priest had tales, as exotic as anything from Marrakol or Cutarz. Even more exotic than magic-wrought myths from Sairland. Jarrett kept that *sul* in his footlocker when he wasn't on patrol or on a mission, beside his broken first compass and the odd keepsake from comrades past. "General," he said again.

"Be patient," his father said, looking out at the Brendt. "This is not something so easily explained in words."

The Hess. So named by the prisoners themselves, early on in its first tenure as the House of Correction. The low language and sometimes incomprehensible slang of the underworld population had infiltrated even the broad streets and upper-class visage of people like General Fawle, until all of Nev Anyan referred to the compound in Ironstack Fields as the Hess. Coal fires burned religiously, though walking into the Hess one would assume a flame had never been stoked there at all. Jarrett felt the pricking jaws of ice even through his buttoned coat and had to tug on his riding gloves immediately upon entering the outer building. The general strode ahead, a slim and hardly statuesque figure, but he held himself with the efficient purpose of a skinning blade. Soon the warden was leading them both through the warrens of the compound, past the offices and alarmingly crowded waiting area, down a narrow passage toward the holding cells.

The stench grew worse the closer they came to the

noise and darkness of the convict housing. As they passed barred door by barred door, Jarrett stopped trying to see past the shadows to the pressed faces peering out at him. He was tempted to ask the warden if these people were ever washed or fed, but it would be pointless, and their pace did not allow conversation or even idle questions. He faced ahead, watching his father's back, until they stopped at the end of the row of cells.

"We've got 'er chained," the man said over his shoulder at the general. He unlocked the cell door with a clanging iron key and pulled it open, then stepped aside immediately. The general looked back at Jarrett.

"Go on in," he ordered. It sounded like an order.

Her? was Jarrett's thought. He stepped forward with a dark glance at his father, and then at the warden, but the man only lowered his eyes and fiddled with his ring of keys.

Jarrett dodged the arc of the door, one hand on the gun at his belt, and faced a pair of stark blue eyes.

The large gray wolf shackled to the corner of the cell lowered its ears and snarled. But that wasn't enough to keep Jarrett's gaze fixed, as shocking as it was; he'd seen wolves aplenty on the frontier, though why it was here he didn't know. But his attention slid to the form of a girl lying in a heap at the animal's feet, face obscured by a mass of black hair. He assumed it was a girl from her small figure, but he wasn't certain. Fur clothing and pale gray animal skins covered her body, making a soft bulky armor through which his stare could not penetrate.

The wolf snapped its jaws toward him and he jumped. A hand landed on his shoulder, and he spun to find his father, calm as a Mais-day morning, watching the wolf. Far from afraid, the look in his eyes was one of fascination.

"This is what killed your Father Bari," the general said.

"That animal? Then why didn't you—" Shoot it.

"No," the general said. "The girl." He let Jarrett go and approached the growling wolf, crouching just out of range. The wolf stretched the chain as far as it could go from the stone wall of the cell. The iron clanked and rang as the animal paced, then attempted to charge in a rage, only to be pulled up short by its neck. Its claws scratched the rough stone floor, leaving white marks. The low snarls echoed around the empty cell and Jarrett twitched, almost forgetting himself enough to reach out and pull his father back from it.

But the general stared straight into the anger of the beast and smiled.

On the frontier, one didn't play with wolves. Though shy by nature, all it took was a prime male to anger and the results were often bloody, if not fatal. His father seemed mesmerized by the animal's ferocity, but Jarrett's heart gave a molasses thud in his ears. How was the girl asleep in this ruckus? How was she alive? *Was* she alive? She lay unmoving, as if she hadn't budged an inch from where she'd been cast. He approached her slowly, around by her head and farthest from the wolf, but the animal's warnings ratcheted up in frequency and lowered in pitch. The chains rattled as it tried to get at him. He gripped his holster tighter.

"It can't break free," the general said, in his calm tone. "Somehow the iron holds it."

Somehow? "This girl..."

"She's in some sort of trance."

Jarrett looked up at his father, had crouched by the prone figure without thinking. "A trance?" Repeating, again, like an idiot. But nothing of this excursion had clarified anything about Father Bari's death.

"She's a witch," the general said and rose to his feet. He held out the old priest's journal, as if he were handing over mission orders. "Take this, you'll need it. We'll go speak with Captain Mackenzi...it was on his ship Father Bari was murdered."

"General." He took the journal but didn't move, even as his father—now completely ignoring the enraged wolf—walked to the cell door. "General, *a witch*? There's no such thing, not even among the abos." As this girl clearly belonged to, though he didn't recognize the skins and fur. Perhaps a Hasky of the North? He had seen strange things in allied Pangani encampments in his time, but foolishness often followed a belief in the wild ways, a dependence on improbabilities instead of the hard truths of nature. People were too plain for witchery. People didn't need witchery for the acts they perpetrated on each other.

"Are you so certain in your beliefs?" his father said. "Do you think you know the abos so well?"

Qoyotariz. The name surged to the top of his mind, bringing with it the taste of iron at the back of his throat. His protests rang above the wolf's growls. "It's all smoke and magicianry!" Like the stage shows in the Roog district of Nev Anyan.

"Wars have been fought on smoke and magicianry," the general said. "But they no longer teach you these things in our academies."

*   *   *

Captain Mackenzi seemed to be a nervous individual. Jarrett stood just behind the general's shoulder and watched the diminutive navy man glance from left to right in the warden's office before taking the offered seat. General Fawle perched on the edge of the warden's desk and Jarrett shut the door, affording them some privacy in the borrowed space. There wasn't much to look at in the room. Utilitarian and rundown, and in a single glance he noticed water stains on the ceiling and holes in the corner floorboards. The desk rocked once, an inch down and up again as the general shifted his weight.

They'd been in the place for only half an hour and Jarrett wanted to leave. Even more so because of the book held under his arm, at moments seeming to burn through his coat for how much he wished to sit somewhere, open it up, and read it from page one. Father Bari's last words, his entire experience on the continent... yet where had his explorer's heart gotten him? His need to "help the abo," as he had put it long ago? They'd exchanged many words on that score, Jarrett who fought the savages from hill to valley. Bari had enjoyed a spirited debate on any subject.

Captain Mackenzi had watched him die. He had shed tears over it, or perhaps that was only his odd nervousness coming through in the sheen of his eyes. He glanced up at Jarrett and Jarrett stared back, wondering what exactly this man had seen.

General Fawle asked it.

"There was a girl in my brig," Mackenzi said. "Then that—dog. Wolf. Whatever it is... I swear it hadn't been there when we left those shores. It wasn't there below with her. My men said she was a witch. They said so." He passed a hand over his face as if to wipe away his own memories.

Ignoring the man's wild claims for now, Jarrett asked the more prosaic question. "Why was she in your brig?"

"She killed one of the army men." Mackenzi paused in his fidgeting to glance at the general. "On the land. He went to that Hasky encampment and she killed him."

"That little girl?"

"She's a witch." Mackenzi's eyes had the round appearance of someone who'd seen either devils or deities. "Her and that wolf! It tore out the priest's throat. It would've eaten him if my man Kuit hadn't been with him."

All the while, the general said nothing. Jarrett pursued the mad claim with some doggedness. The journal in his hands, the old leather, had begun to chill in the stone air, despite his grip on it. He felt it through his gloves somehow. "Why didn't you kill the animal?" He said it perhaps harsher than he meant, but what did it profit anyone to have that wolf alive now?

"Kuit shot it," Mackenzi said. "And it didn't bleed."

The silence was enough to hear faint clamor in some other part of the jail, voices rumbling and the echo of footsteps.

Jarrett blinked to ward off some inchoate memory. More dream. More nightmare that still left footprints from his sleep at the docks. He tasted mud and smoke on his lips and pushed at the back of his teeth with his tongue, looking at his father now with impatience. "This is why we're here?"

"It wouldn't leave the girl," Mackenzi insisted. "It wouldn't let anyone near her until we cornered it with flame and iron. That thing is a cursed animal. It's some sort of—"

Jarrett bit down to stop himself from calling the man a deluded dimwit. "General."

"Captain Mackenzi," his father said, as if he'd just awakened from a passing sleep. "Explain to Captain Fawle how the wolf got on your ship." He did not even address the incredible statements.

"I don't know, general."

Jarrett shook his head. "Forget whatever it is your men think they saw. Might not the animal have jumped aboard somehow, stowed away on one of your boats from the shore?"

"I said it hadn't been onboard." The sea captain's face stiffened like an effigy. "I said it can't be killed. Are you questioning my word, sir?"

"I'm questioning your perception, sir." *Never mind your sanity.* "Because otherwise how did it get there? And how can any animal not be killed?"

"That witch...it's hers somehow, I'm telling you. *It was behind the bars with her.* We anchored ashore here, Father Bari went down to fetch her with my man Kuit, and that *thing* jumped out at him. From *inside* the brig."

This was going to make a fine tale to tell his men. "Perhaps it had slipped between the bars after coming aboard," Jarrett said.

The general spoke up. "This can go on for quite some time. You see, it takes some convincing." He spoke to Mackenzi, cutting off what Jarrett knew to be protests brewing in Mackenzi's chest. The man was practically off his chair with emphasis. And yet somehow *he* was in the wrong for doubting this madness?

He said to his father, "General, the captain makes no sense."

"The captain makes perfect sense," the general said. "I want you to listen to Mackenzi."

Remnants of his hangover persisted at the back of his throat. Sour. Sickening. Jarrett shouted at them both. "A priest of the gods is dead! Yet you men conjure up this faerie story—"

"It's not a story."

"I want answers, Father. You dragged me here."

Mackenzi would not let it go. "I am telling the truth!"

"Shut your mouth," Jarrett said.

The general stood from the table and came toward him. Jarrett tried his royal best to put his weight into the floor, because he knew his father would seize his arm and attempt to force him from the room, as he often did in times past. Everything by force of arms if not force of will.

But the general only held his shoulders, looking up into his eyes. The general had to look up and often didn't like to do it, so this action gave Jarrett a start as sure as any bark or bellow. He gripped the journal tighter in doubt.

"Jarrett."

This voice was not his father's...at least not as it was married to the face that he knew. This man had cuffed him across the jaw for less in his time.

"Captain Fawle, it's imperative that you take heed of what Captain Mackenzi says and that you open your mind in a way to receive the reality of this situation."

The words struck Jarrett like a paper arrow. Nothing of

this situation felt real. In fact, as he stared at the general's gray eyes, he found it difficult to hold on to any thoughts. From the gray morning to the gray walls in this jail, he was in an utter fog. The headache began to pound again, but it didn't feel like the leftovers of too much drinking and too little sleep. It was confusion and unsteadiness pushing at the back of his forehead, his eyes, trying to force him to see something that simply wasn't there. To what end?

"Sir," Jarrett said.

"That girl in there," the general said. "That girl and her wolf. They are one and the same being."

"Sir?"

Over the general's shoulder, he saw Mackenzi shifting about in his seat. General Fawle's voice was too quiet to carry across the room—on purpose.

"If you took off your coat this instant and threw it to the floor, it would still be yours, would it not?"

"...yes?"

"Read Father Bari's journal. We need you to somehow put that coat back on the girl."

His headache spiked. *We*. "How—"

Now his father shook him. Hard. "Jarrett. You must do this before I let you return to the frontier. Do you understand me, boy? You will read that man's journal and you will understand what that girl is doing, and you will *fix it*. I want her awake and alive. I do not want to be dealing with that animal. Do you understand me? It cannot be killed, only done away with." The general released him and opened the door behind him. "Learn the difference and learn it quickly. We've not time to waste." He walked by and out the room.

Jarrett stared at Mackenzi and saw no clarity there at all. But he did see fear, its black slither making shivers across the other man's features. Fear and foreboding, and he reckoned the navy captain saw the same in him. Not let him return to the frontier? The general had never held that as a threat over his head, had in fact preferred to have him away, especially when he began to prove his mettle far from home. The general liked to win, and Jarrett won him battles. But what was this battle now?

He looked down at the worn journal in his hands and took a breath. Open his mind. So Father Bari had implored him too, once upon a time. About many things. Wolves that could not be killed? Witches from the great North? He walked back to Captain Mackenzi and sat where his father had, at the corner of the warden's tilting desk. His voice was measured this time, apologetic. Battle nerves made him look without wavering, made his thoughts for now focus like a spyglass. Despite himself his father's tone engendered a mental salute and a snap in his intentions. This was his duty, apparently, and he knew how to talk to men to gain their confidence if he needed it. Before he opened Father Bari's journal to read, he must glean what he could from the man who'd seen him last.

Mackenzi stared up at him with an open mouth, and Jarrett wondered if the captain had gone mad from too many weeks at sea. And if so, what then was the reason for his father's madness?

The murder had been brutal. The wolf had indeed torn out Father Bari's throat, leaving a broken body, a marred

figure according to Captain Mackenzi. Jarrett walked
from the office and the jail with the images cluttering his
mind, the journal held against his ribs with gloved hands.
It seemed to capture the cold and keep it in, bleeding onto
his fingertips.

He met his father with some small shock. The general
had waited for him and stood outside the iron gates of
the Hess with a swan-necked black pipe between his lips,
puffing away. The smoke was an old smell, as sharp as
burnt autumn leaves. It conjured tintype memories of
a forbidding study and curt dismissals at bedtime. The
general leaned against the carriage in an odd form of
repose and Jarrett stared at him, feeling the cold attach
to the skin of his own cheeks. It was a cloudy day once
more, no sun for relief, and a wind carried across the
Brendt to chase the late winter through the wool of his
coat. He must not have been inside the Hess for more than
an hour, yet his body bade him go to bed, bury himself
somewhere so he could awake to a new day.

"You knew Bari," General Fawle said, breathing out
the smoke. "You can decipher some of his notes. You
know the abos. I need you to know *that* abo." He jabbed
the mouth of the pipe toward the jail.

"She's a Hasky." Aniw, as they called themselves.
He knew that much, though the other word was the one
he'd heard in his own world. The one Bari had said was
wrong, even insulting.

"There are enough similarities," the general said. "For
our purposes, anyhow."

"And what purposes are those, sir?"

The general pulled at his pipe, saying around it: "We
will discuss that later."

Jarrett watched the blue smoke curl in the air, then looked off down the street. A policeman's harnessed black horse stood a dozen yards away, tail swishing. "The Father's funeral service, do you know when it is?"

"Teden-day."

Three days from now. Of course. If one had the luxury of time and the means to preserve the body, unlike battlefield deaths, three days from the day of death was proper in the ritual. He was not well acquainted with much of the doctrine, but that part he knew. Death was a soldier's sport. He nodded and moved to climb into their carriage.

His father caught his arm. "The sooner you do this for me, the sooner you'll return to your garrison. But until then you'll remain at my house, and you're to talk about this to no one. *No one.* Do you understand me?"

He wanted to shake off the touch, half inside the carriage as he was, wanted to sit and stare out the window without his father's confusing insistence clawing at his back. Demanding he give it heed.

But instead he only nodded again and waited to be released.

With the curtains drawn in his upstairs room, the shadows hung from ceiling to floorboards like robed priests bending over a ritual consecration. Just enough lines of light filtered through to add shapes, and Jarrett lay on his back staring at them. Dots through the lace could be eyes on the ceiling, an open mouth, some animal's maw with the fangs reaching to the corners. Reaching down to him.

As a child he used to make pictures out of random shadows, but lately the shadows had ceased to be so random. They followed him into daylight like bold thieves. They reached deep into his pockets and stole his hidden valuables. They came on four feet like wild specters, like silly tales from abo stickmen. They came on the hot breath of a demon sitting on his chest. The shadows made him sleepless and jumpy; the nervousness hadn't ceased after his encounter with Qoyotariz, only worsened. So Major Dirrick from his garrison post had sent him back here. "Take a break," he'd said. As if distance could cure what tracked him into his dreams.

He shut his eyes and pressed the heels of his hands against them. Without even looking, he sensed Father Bari's journal sitting on the writing table where he'd left it, cast in the false dusk of the room. The silence inside these walls held in the muffled breathing of nightmare sound. The air felt dead. He couldn't even hear the servants shuffling about in other parts of the house. Maybe they were outside, sitting for a moment with pipes and smoke. Maybe he was alone, or asleep, and his heartbeat was just another aspect of this persistent, confusing world that bled now into his waking life.

The journal sat like a weight behind him, tugging.

He opened his eyes and looked toward the desk. He couldn't ignore this morning no matter how hard he tried, any more than he could ignore what had driven him to this damn city in the first place. Avoidance did nothing but force another's hand, until *he* was forced. The corner of Father Bari's journal stuck out over the edge of the desk; the end of the string that bound it up hung limply

from its tie. It was a small bedroom and he only had to
stretch out his hand to seize the journal.

With a sigh he pulled himself to sit and grabbed the
book without looking. In hand and in his tired state it
felt heavy and warm, unlike how it had been in the Hess.
Was it possible for objects to breathe like living things,
to grow cold or retain heat like common bodies? His
thoughts wandered and he let them, going in circles, a
tiny mirror to the motion of his hand as he unwound the
journal's string from its button tabs. He turned the thick
cover, blinking to clear his eyes enough to squint at the
stain and ink on the paper.

A second stretch of an arm pushed the curtains open a
crack, just enough light so he could discern the handwrit-
ing. *Father Bari Konstanz.* The man's script was befitting
a priest, evenly slanted with just a bit of flair at the end
of each sentence. But understanding the words didn't
guarantee a knowledge of meaning. Or so the general
implied.

The first leaf of the journal was simply the priest's
name and a stamp of the Varana Ingen Order of the
Church: an image of Va. Ingen's footprint, ringed by iron.
Va. Ingen, the father patron of explorers and, perhaps not
surprisingly, orphaned children. Father Bari had always
talked about the children he'd met on his travels, and
how it was the children who made him believe in the
commonality of all peoples. So was the order's stance
as well, a new idea, to be sure, for a relatively new order
in the Church of the Seven Deities. Once Ciracusa had
been discovered, it became important to devote an entire
branch of the Church to expanding the tenets of the Seven
Gods and Goddesses to every new abo they met. An

idealistic order, Jarrett had always thought, and one he'd had little use for, just as any other part of religion. But discussions with Bari about the conflict of that idealism and the battles he knew on the frontier had never swayed the old man.

Jarrett ran his finger lightly over the imprint of Va. Ingen's symbol, then turned the page. A dense scrawl of black writing twined on the paper. When he flipped all the pages he saw scores of it, on both sides, broken only by the occasional drawing or smudge or what looked like tea stains. A subtle draft of jasmine wafted up to his nose as the pages fluttered between his fingers, then he stopped the flip as the first blank pages caught his eyes. The unwritten parts; they started two-thirds of the way in the journal. The end of Bari's writings, the end of his life.

Jarrett pushed the pages flat and turned them backward now, beginning at the end. He read.

He fought it page by page, like a horror he could not stop examining, but eventually he sought sleep. Images from Father Bari's detailed writing scattered in his head—ammunition powder that he tried not to light. Magical Hasky people who claimed their ancestors were dogs? Pangani tribes that could speak to the forest beasts? He knew similar tales in old children's books from Sairland that his mother had read to him and his sister before they'd died. Faerie stories. Yet Bari had chronicled his findings, even wrote out in detail the rituals these abos used, their incantations and dark objects, whatever madness he'd encountered after a sip or five from some hallucinogenic tea or herbal flower dust. That seemed the simplest explanation for the things the priest had experienced. One would see or believe anything after a good dose of alcohol or "demon medicine."

Yet Bari had been a man of the order. Surely this was not something the Church accepted, but discouraged in their priests?

He had no one to ask, at least not immediately. Sleep was a fine anodyne to the incoherent threat of Bari's beliefs. He slept until a loud knocking on his door roused him again. The journal lay flat open on his chest and he could tell, even drowsy, that the light had changed outside. Now pale slants hit the floorboards of his room, hours beyond what they had been when he'd passed out in slumber. The servant Louna's north isle voice spoke through the door.

"Cap'un Fawle, ye fadda is wantin' ye in his study, sa."

"All right," he croaked. He heard her footsteps pad away and managed to get himself to the washstand at the corner of the room. His father called, he must answer, as obedient as any table hound. The mirror above the stand gave back a poor image, an unconscious frown, some random recollection of his lack of choices here that manifested itself in an expression he wouldn't bother to hide once he went downstairs. What would be the point? The general wanted him on this mad task; he was compelled. He poured water from the porcelain jug into the basin and splashed his eyes.

As he left the room it was habit to straighten his collar and shirt, set his mind to a comfortable blankness that could keep his temper reined. More orders, what next, he

ought to ply some magicianry in the Roog? He made his
way down the stairs with unconcealed heavy footsteps;
he'd pointedly left the journal behind on the bed.

It read like a cursed book, something too strange and
vaguely evil. Perhaps it was his sleepy mind. In blazing
day, fully awake, he would not be so spooked. But the
hour bent toward dusk, the domain of spirits. How was he
supposed to make sense of dreams and fancy? He wanted
to be back on the frontier, in his familiar routines, where
things died if you shot them and men told stories only for
entertainment. He had a protest ready and waiting at the
top of his mind as he strode the last few steps to the study
door—and stopped.

Two men stood within the room. One was his father,
the other a Pangani tribesman.

Qoyotariz.

His mouth dried out in one breath. His hand darted to
his hip where his gun should have been, but of course it
wasn't there. Not in his father's house.

And it wasn't the Soreganee warrior. This abo's markings
spoke of another tribe.

The abo noticed the move; amber eyes tracked Jarrett's hand until he let it fall back to his side. For a second he thought he saw a copper gleam in that gaze, but
it died.

"This is Keeley," the general said, with a certain
amount of bland satisfaction. "He's a Whishishian tracker
for the army."

Of course he was. Jarrett recognized the black paint
around the eyes. Different tribes decorated themselves differently, and this one's attire may have been some odd amalgamation of tailored Ciracusan dress and yellow-hill-tribe

skins, but there was no mistaking the pointed bone earrings, like tiny tusks, pinched through the man's earlobes,
or the way the paint around his eyes made his features
look decidedly feline. He was shorter than both Jarrett
and the general, which was unusual for a Whishishian.
Even as tall as Jarrett was, he had encountered many
tribesmen who met him eye to eye. Perhaps this one was
still young. It was difficult to determine age in the abos
until they grew very old. He'd seen his fair share of young
warriors and aged stickmen, but they just didn't seem to
develop like Ciracusans...or Cutarzi, or Marrakola, or
any number of transplanted cultures that made up this
country.

After reading what he had in Father Bari's journal, he
wondered now if magic played a part in that.

Ridiculous.

The Whishishian seemed to recognize him too, if only
for his wrinkled uniform. The silence was loud.

"Jarrett," his father said, drawing his attention away
from the abo, though Jarrett still felt the amber eyes on
his face. His nerves stretched. "Keeley will help you with
Father Bari's journal and that girl."

It wasn't unusual to use Pangani trackers, of course.
He'd had his own back in Fort Girs. But he tended to be
resistant to ones he didn't know personally, because in
his experience they could prove wildly unreliable—to
the point of betrayal. His father, who had impressed upon
him that he could not speak of the girl in the Hess, now
trusted this hostile?

"I think I can manage Father Bari's journal on my
own, thank you."

"This is an order," General Fawle said. "You can be sure of Keeley, he's been my man for quite some years."

Indeed so? Then why had he never heard of it? Keeley wasn't a Whishishian name, and the only way Jarrett knew for any Pangani to gain a Ciracusan name was by grant. Someone had trusted or liked him enough to give him a country name, and he had, for his own reasons, accepted it. From the general?

He couldn't argue, only be on guard. And if he tried to converse with his father now, he knew where his temper would take him. Acquiescence and distance were his best options at the moment, common tactics when dealing with the general. "Very well. Then I have things to discuss with him, don't I?" He didn't wait for his father's dismissal and refused to act like he was pleased by the development. "Come with me," he said to Keeley, then turned about and left the room.

He didn't like putting his back to the abo, but he had to assume the man wouldn't attack him in the general's own house. Once in the hall, however, he paused and stood to the side, gesturing toward the solarium with a show of politeness. Of course it was hardly that, and the abo knew it. Keeley didn't break stride, only acknowledged the obvious change of position by a turn of the chin, then passed him to the end of the hall and through the door. Jarrett followed and shut it behind them once they were alone in the glass-walled room. Though there wasn't much sun, it still had the feel of being in the yard, blue bushes and tall maples standing just on the outside. Transparent shadows from the trees made finger lines across the two white chaises and the maroon-stained Marrakol table. The scent of potted lilacs in two corners of the room was a misleading calming aroma; there was nothing calm in this meeting. Jarrett remained standing and so did Keeley. Who still didn't speak but in no way gave off an appearance of obeisance.

It was always best to come at an angle with an abo. "Do you like my father?" He kept his tone neutral and was rewarded with a mild look of surprise. The Whishishian's head tilted a fraction but he said nothing. "Where are you staying in Nev Anyan?" Still nothing, and Jarrett wondered if this abo could even speak the language. So he asked it in the short-form trade tongue of the Nation, what the tribes used to communicate among themselves when they spoke different dialects. "Ykadama-m'Sarrishda-ye?" *Do you understand Sarrish?*

"I understand you," Keeley said, in that stilted abo accent. "But I don't want to answer those questions."

Jarrett studied the unblinking face, wondering if this was the man's idea of humor. Probably not. They could be a literal lot if they weren't well-schooled in "Boot" humor, as they liked to call Ciracusans. And just because Keeley worked for the army didn't mean he'd ever been invited to sit around a campfire and trade jests. Likely he'd been sent beneath a tree in the vicinity of the horses with a tin cup of coffee, far from common phrases and camaraderie.

"My father said you would help me."

"With the spiritwalker in the prison."

So he knew it all, it seemed. And would not respond to anything outside of those concerns. Jarrett pressed the back of his teeth with his tongue. "Spiritwalker. You mean witch."

Keeley shook his head once and now rounded the table to sit himself on the long chaise. As if he'd been here before. "No witch. She is what we call a spiritwalker. For my people—*janna*. For her people? I don't know what they call her."

"You've heard of her people?"

"Only what the generali told me. I didn't know people would live with such cold."

It was beginning to feel much like his benign interrogation of Captain Mackenzi. "And what did he tell you? Exactly?"

Keeley said, without any of Mackenzi's nervousness, "He told me that the girl and her Dog are separated and you must bring them together again."

This was the talk in the journal that had forced him to sleep, to seek an absence in oblivion. He walked to the door leading to outside and leaned there, staring through the glass at the tall plants and geometrically patterned stones that decorated the lawn. "The priest she killed... supposedly killed... was a friend of mine. He used to talk sometimes about these things, your people." He looked at Keeley with a smirk he could not contain. "Your people and your... *changing*."

"It's not a change. Not if her spirit walks the same trail as ours."

"I don't understand any of this rubbish. I saw a wolf in that jail cell, and a girl."

"Your father believes her spirit walks the same trail as ours. My people. Our *janna*."

Jarrett laughed and shook his head. "My father..." Is a stranger. Perhaps a lunatic. "Why are you helping?"

"Because the generali asked it of me."

Whishishian or no Whishishian—one of the few tribes in the Pangani Nation that held alliance with Ciracusa—Jarrett thought he sensed a round lie from this abo. He stared at the broad face and implacable gaze. "And you're going to help me? You're going to explain… how to *put away* that wolf?"

Keeley took an audible breath. "It is no wolf. It's her Dog. It's her Dog as my people also have Dogs. It is her ancestor."

Qoyotariz had called him a dog. He'd thought it merely an insult. He felt the smirk fade from his face and wiped a hand over his mouth.

"You understand," Keeley kept talking, "our spirit-walkers are kin to those who came first. They guide us."

"Shut up for a moment, gods be damned."

"What is the matter with you?"

His feet had moved to the farthest side of the solarium. Staring out he saw nothing but darkening shadows. "Nothing is the matter with me." He shot a glance at the abo. "You just speak madness."

The abo didn't blink. "Show me the Father's book."

The godsdamned book. Anger brought him focus. "Can you even read it? Do you read Sarrish?"

"I read. As you should read. You will have to know words. You will have to sing them to her Dog, to tame it. Only then will it be put away."

That phrase. Not killed, not leashed. This idea that his father had suggested, and that he had read in Father Bari's journal…putting away the animal like it was some sort of—coat indeed. Or a pocketwatch. "And where will it go? This…dog?" It had looked like a wolf to him, but this tribesman said different. Father Bari called it a

Dog in his notes. As if it were somehow domesticated. "This dog will just disappear?"

The abo shook his head and blinked once. For a fraction of a moment he seemed frightened. "No, it won't disappear. It will lie in wait like a hunter." And before Jarrett could muster a platoon of thought, Keeley beat him to it. "Do you like your father?"

So the abo had a sense of humor after all. Jarrett smiled, but he would mean it more if he proposed marriage to a Lower Roog whore. "Clever."

"You seem unwilling to work with him."

"And you don't. Unusual for an abo, isn't it? Even if your tribe is one of our allies."

Suspicion could gnaw like termites on a bit of bark. The silence held dust.

"My people have been your allies for many seasons." The abo paused. "And your prisoners."

"Are you a prisoner?"

"No more than you."

They could spar just as well with daggers. One could not let down one's guard, and the careful conversation recalled a night under rain, a face in his face, speaking in the trade tongue. *I mark your men by you.* These abos were fond of riddles.

He blinked and soldiered his words, straightening away from the glass. Not on the retreat, damn this savage. Abos were fast on their feet, but he hadn't quite met any that were this apparently young and this quick in wit when conversing in Sarrish.

"You're rather far from your tribe."

Now he met with silence.

"I know this because I've been among your people

out on the frontier. Yet here you are with a country name and the ear of a general. In our biggest city." Still nothing. The pieces were not difficult to fit now that he gave it thought, as this was a child's image. He'd seen the schools himself on vague visits as a boy. The general had marched him once or twice, before his mother had died. "You're one of those buckfoot students, aren't you?" Transplanted children, taken from their tribes and reared in Ciracusan schools. Not with Ciracusan children, though. The idea had been to tame them. Instead they had become merely trained, and like wild beasts, they'd found ways to disobey.

He'd heard stories when he was older of these children bloodily rebelling on their headmasters and headmistresses until the government had ceased the program countrywide. Ostensibly the children were to be returned to their tribes, but many of them had not been wanted once they'd been "tainted" by the Boot People, or simply hadn't made it back. Some had even chosen to stay in Ciracusan cities and towns, often as paupers or beggars. Even abo whores were not unheard-of and were considered exotic.

The news of such goings-on had always been like marbles rattling around in his mind, easily shot and discarded when more important matters took his attention. But now here sat a buckfoot child, grown to warrior width, in his father's house, no less. By Keeley's silence he suspected he'd hit the mark.

But then the abo spoke. "You don't know."

"What don't I know?"

"You don't know your father."

"And you do?" Yet what he truly thought was the abo

had not spoken a lie. His father had never been one to parent, only domineer, and he had ceased to expect anything more or less. If the world gave war, so could it give such a father, and sometimes there was no rhyme or reason to enlighten the conflict, at least not any that anyone remembered. Old resentments became the bold and only reason for battle, and he had never felt much else from the general. Or given much back.

The abo had fallen silent again. And he was tired of the pursuit. The day was darkening, and so was his mood. He left the Whishishian in the growing dusk.

In the rattling echoes of the end of a day when the servants shuffled from room to room latching windows and drawing curtains, Jarrett found himself in the kitchen, by glowing lamplight, nursing a cup of Marrakol mint tea and scattering cookie crumbs all over the table. Father Bari's journal sat spread-eagled in front of him, out of harm's way of the plate, but he wasn't reading. He listened. His father and Keeley were still at council in the study, and though the doors were drawn Jarrett could discern the low tone of voices and the creak of floorboards beneath pacing footsteps. Would the abo leave?

Eventually the study doors down the hall slid open, giving a whisper like the house was sighing. No more voices, but a patter of boots sounded like light thunder up and down the main hall. One pair grew closer to the kitchen, and Jarrett kept his back to the doorway, concentrating now on the priest's journal as if he had been at it all along. The other set of footsteps went up the stairs, and he thought perhaps he should take to carrying around his gun indoors if that was the abo behind him now.

But his father's voice said, "You're still awake."

So Keeley had flown to the upper level, and it made Jarrett think of his unlocked bedroom. "The company lately has made me reluctant to sleep." He glanced over his shoulder at the general. "At least with both eyes shut."

"Come, now." General Fawle walked around the table, eyed the crumbs upon the whorly surface, and set his hand along the edge. He looked down from his standing height because he could. Jarrett was tempted to rise and tower, but that would be too inciting, and he was tired among the dancing shadows.

"Is that abo staying the night?" His voice was sharp, he didn't hide it. Words worked where physicality dragged.

"He is welcome in my house, yes."

Now Jarrett leaned back, bracing a palm on his thigh and curling his fingers around the top of the journal. His father's face was plain, as if the warmth of the room did not penetrate. "Why do you trust him? Where did he *come from?*"

"I've known him since he was a child, Jarrett. He's been back and forth among his people until he was adult and came to work for me. And he's Whishishian."

They were one tribe in the Pangani Nation that had been more or less consistently amicable with Ciracusa, even back to the first landing by Sairland exiles two hundred years ago. However.

"You know the stories as well as I do, father. Buckfoot children can't be trusted, and adult abos only barely more. Why him?"

"You use Pangani trackers, do you not? How do you know they won't lead you into ambush?"

"Some of them are our allies. With conditions." Always with conditions. "Whishishian children revolted in those schools as well as any Soreganee." Raw enemies, the Soreganee, of both Ciracusa and many tribes of the Nation. Vicious, beady demons.

"Tragedies," his father said. "Those times were filled by tragedy."

And these times were not? With a war by sea against Sairland and one by land against four of the six Nation tribes? If these were not tragic times, then they certainly cast a black shade of desperation over Ciracusa. He stared at the general. Compassion was not one of the man's staple traits.

"I consider Keeley an advantage," the general said. "And I need his help in this task. I believe you need the help, and so you two must work together. For me and for Ciracusa."

They had visited this notion at an earlier hour. "Care to explain it now, sir?"

"Our resources are stretched." Now the general pulled back one of the oak-hewn chairs and sat himself. He didn't quite sigh, but his exhalation was one of restrained frustration. "You know this. We cannot continue to fight two wars on opposite fronts."

"The abo bands do continue to hassle our troops."

"And the Sairlanders." The man's voice was sharp. His gray gaze reflected the guttering flames around the kitchen. "They ebb and flow but always rise up like monster waves in the hopes of crashing upon our shores. We can't allow that to happen again."

He knew his history from the academy. The Settlers' War had been eleven years of sea and continental conflict, consuming every ragged tribe and barely established frontier town in Ciracusa's infant life. If it weren't for the allied tribes of the Whishishians and Morogo, and a hard-won military pact with Cutarz, they would have surely lost that war and likely been driven farther inland by their Sairland ancestors. Perhaps it was the fate of both men and countries to always war with their forefathers in some way. Though the general regarded him as someone between soldier and son, he often thought his father would have preferred the martial responsibility to any patriarchal obligation. Memories of the dead female half of their family only added to the distance. But such discussions did not rise between them. It was easier to talk of war.

"I believe," the general said, "that the answer lies in our knowledge of the abos. And the first step is understanding their demon ways."

"You're in earnest?"

It was the wrong tone. His father had tolerated his objections, both loud and implied, the entire day. Now he received a steady glare.

"I advise you to read some more on the history of your ancestors, Captain Fawle."

"I've read, sir. Sairlandish history is taught in the academy." His bristle by now was a habitual thing, poked and prodded by such conversation.

The general stood to lean over him and pressed a hand onto the dead priest's journal. "Then you will read what hasn't been taught."

*   *   *

On Teden-day it stormed. Spring's darker temperament emerged in earnest for Father Bari's funeral, and Jarrett sat at the front of the grim temple, listening to the fury of cloud tears pounding the stone and sapphire glass. It didn't always rain for death; he'd attended enough of these ceremonies to know that on occasion the sun knew no grief, like strangers who had no care for the deceased. On the battlefield, men sometimes fell beneath blazing light or rainbow-hued skies, and night and thunder played no part in the mourning.

Not so for the dead priest. Father Bari Konstanz warranted all the black regalia befitting a servant of the Seven Deities. The innards of this grand church were festooned by dour banners falling from high ceiling to cold floor and the reoccurring imagery of the Seven Branches—a cluster star that dotted the walls in translucent marble. The glowing ghost light of candle flame illuminated the purple shards of glass inset in the stone. Mosaic patterns stood high and blade-like at the front of the temple between monolithic sculpture, then descended along the flanks until all light disappeared at the back corners of this hollow house. If the display was meant to mimic the true nature of the afterlife, Jarrett resolutely hoped all the holy men were wrong.

He felt scrutinized beneath the seven towering images of the deities as three of them gazed with graven solemnity down upon their children. The watchful eyes of the benevolent Three Goddesses shone marble white, while the Four Gods stared toward the temple's main entrance, welcoming or warning. It was difficult to discern intent in the stone eyes, but perhaps that was the point.

Thunder buffeted the skin of the church, felt in echoes from the safe indoors. He was not alone, but the mourners were dispersing. Doors opened, letting in lightning flashes and the sound of pelting rain, before shutting again. Open and shut, bringing the scent of wet stone and persistent smoke. The High Priest of Nev Anyan had set Bari's enwrapped body afire in the burning yard. Bellowed purification rites as the rain shot down had managed to defy the wet just as surely as the thick leaping flames. Many of the mourners had stood beneath umbrellas; some of them had known Father Bari, and wept. Many had not but had come simply for the pageantry, out of some sense of morbid curiosity.

He hadn't brought any headcover and so sat bedraggled upon the pew, finally finding some peace and shelter after such a macabre open show. The rain had managed to flood most of his finer sentiments. Now he just humored the damp cold and remained in blank acceptance of the death. It was a well-traveled reaction in his soldiering, and he had walked sore miles in companionship with it.

Now he didn't want to go home where his father and Keeley waited. Neither of them had the decency to show their faces here, even when it was Bari's journal they were scouring for mad purposes. He was not a believer yet he had come, and he wondered if the kind old priest truly was in a place now that would confirm his lifelong faith.

Jarrett looked up at the tall deities, whose cowled heads scraped the carved, arched ceiling, and found no answer in their silent stares. Did they even know that the Haskies existed? Did *they* believe in the magical Dogs?

The High Priest would tell him that these old gods did not have to believe, they simply *knew*. If certainty was the domain of deities, then it was a rare arrogance to think one could understand them, or the world. So much of this world he didn't find certain at all, besides death. And yet the holy ones preached the possibility—while Father Bari had claimed belief in the abos and their witching ways.

"You were at the funeral," came a voice from behind him.

Jarrett turned around with some alarm, as he hadn't heard anyone approach, much less take a seat at his shoulders. But there a body sat—a priestess, by the drape of her gray robe. A young priestess with ascetic cropped hair and small blue eyes. Blue in the dusky cast of the stained glass around them. She was not familiar but seemed of racial kin to Father Bari—angular features and dark skin reflected the firelight dancing at the feet of the stone gods. Jarrett took his time releasing the hold he had on the side of his wet coat. He had not worn his gun, of course, but the reflex was one he couldn't stifle for ceremony.

"Yes." He said it plain. "I was there." This was no grand deduction, judging from his soaked attire.

"I knew Father Bari as well," the priestess said. Her hands weren't in sight, pushed into opposite sleeves. Perhaps against the chill of the temple. Perhaps in religious repose. "I'm Sister Oza. And you're Captain Jarrett Fawle?"

It was a question only in tone, not in knowledge. Jarrett didn't reply.

"You're quite suspicious, aren't you?" she continued.

"Not at all." He was. And he wasn't pious. "Father Bari was a singular man." They had that opinion in common, he assumed.

"Indeed he was. He was an expert on the primitive cultures our people have encountered. I suspect his only regret was he never made it off this continent. There are so many other places he could have explored."

"There are enough abos on this continent to occupy an army." Jarrett smiled at her, but he knew very well it was a shade insouciant.

She smiled back, but not with her eyes. "Spoken like a righteous military man." Now she rose to her feet. She was a tall woman. Even when Jarrett stood out of recalcitrant politeness, he didn't have far to look down to meet her eyes. "I shall leave you be, captain. But I'm certain we will speak again in the future."

"Perhaps not." He inclined his chin to her. If he had his way he would be back on the frontier by the end of the month.

"No." Her smile remained. Her teeth were very white, or perhaps it was the light. "I am certain. You see, I'm your garrison chaplain now. At Fort Girs. I've been appointed to the post. So I will see you there when next you ride." She bowed her chin right back at his surprised silence.

"We've a chaplain already, Sister. Father Timmis."

"Yes," Oza said. "But I am to take his place. So am I directed, and so I must go." Her smile remained unchecked but he wasn't fooled. The Church had more hidden motives than a cheating wife, and he would not get her to tell the tale. At least not now in her own territory. She stepped out of the pew. Her ritual obeisance to the Seven Deities bent low at the waist, her movements precise.

It was unusual, if not unheard-of, to place a priestess at an army post. But the Church had its odd ways and its strange followers. They spoke in great depth about the mysteries of the gods, but Jarrett had always found men to be the true mystery, if only because of the secrets they withheld. Whether she had indeed been a friend to the late Father, he would never know. But perhaps she would be useful.

He watched her stride down the center aisle of the temple, her back held straighter than any trooper on parade.

It was more than a little strange to walk into the Hess with a Whishishian tribesman at his heels. It was rare enough to see one at all in a city the size of Nev Anyan, and by the look on the warden's face, he had never seen an abo in the flesh. Jarrett blockaded the man's stare, questions, and possible objections with a terse tone and a quick order to lead them to the Aniw girl's jail cell. Because of his rank (and likely the remembrance of the general's earlier visit) he and Keeley were taken there without delay. Curiously, the Pangani tracker asked for the key to the animal's irons. Rather than question the man in front of the warden, Jarrett ordered it to be so and watched as the warden left, and Keeley pocketed the key, giving no explanation, not even in one of his "I don't wish to answer your question" moments that Jarrett had become all too familiar with in the past week.

He and Keeley had spent five days reading through Father Bari's journal. He couldn't say he was much more enlightened about all the magicianry, but he could now discern certain words in the Aniw language and parrot them back. To his ears these "words" sounded more like he was alternately chewing and choking on bark, but it was his best approximation. Bari had been such a meticulous notetaker that his visits with the Aniw were all closely detailed, including some sort of ceremony wherein the "Dogs" were let loose. Capitalizing the animal in his notes seemed to indicate these were the beasts that grew from the tribes' spiritwalkers... though "grow" was hardly an apt term. Keeley had tried explaining the idea to him but, curiously, his father's first image of casting a coat aside stuck to his mind. The Dogs weren't a skin, but they somehow belonged to the *ankago*. That was the word for spiritwalker in the Aniw language—the person, man or woman, in an Aniw tribe who could trace their ancestry back to some sort of godlike dog.

More than once Keeley had shown the slightest irritation at his disbelief in these things, and he found himself more than a little impatient trying to wrap his mouth around the foreign language, never mind the bizarre incantations used to "Call" the Dogs. He'd worked with Pangani tribesmen before and knew a few words and phrases in the various Nation languages, but the Aniw he'd never met, and neither, of course, had Keeley. Even if Bari had written the language phonetically, it was a mouthful. "This probably won't work," he'd told his father more than once in that week, as if the magic were even... possible, never mind probable. But all General Fawle had said was, "You're going to try anyway."

The threat was mild but still implicit.

Between himself and Keeley, and Father Bari's notes, they'd managed to put together what seemed to be the proper phrasing to control this girl's Dog, and so here they were back in the cell. The wolf—it still looked like a wolf to Jarrett, with the long muzzle, long legs, and tall hackles of a wild thing—let off a startling snarl as soon as they entered. The chain slid and rattled as the animal paced, and Jarrett wondered if it could snap. If this Dog was somehow powerful, or related to old gods, could it not break free? But Keeley had said that their gods weren't like Ciracusan gods and that iron somehow bound them.

I don't believe in gods, he'd told himself.

Trying to stay focused on the task at hand instead of getting into theological arguments had proved tiring. It was important, the Whishishian said, that he believe.

He could believe in the girl, insofar as he could see her still lying at the animal's feet, as unmoved as before. He didn't think she'd even turned over in the intervening days.

"She's not dead?" He looked at Keeley, who stood rather far from the Dog, by one of the walls. The Whishishian claimed his own people had their version of the *ankago,* and it was on that knowledge and Bari's experiences that they based their learning of these people. He'd tried questioning Mackenzi again, and a couple men in his crew, but most of their stories involved a kind of distant prejudice that he didn't find helpful. Besides, none of them had ever been invited into a Calling ceremony. The Aniw seemed to have trusted the priest; or they were, as Bari had written, "charmingly open, without guile, and willing to learn."

"She's not dead," Keeley said. "She waits." He crouched by the girl's form, avoiding the threatening wolf, and touched the mass of dark hair, slowly pushing it away from her face.

Jarrett moved forward to look down at her, trying to ignore the beast, whose anger in snarls and growls only increased. It strained against its iron collar. His nerves jumped but he willed his hands steady. "She's hardly more than a child."

There was a surprising line of tattoos on her face. Even though he'd read Father Bari's descriptions, seen his drawings, and knew that many of the young women were given tattoos when they were of childbearing age, it was something altogether different to see it. Soot-black dots stitched a contoured line from her temple, along the top of her cheek and across the bridge of her nose, to the other side of her face. Concentric circles capped each cheek and her chin, but beneath the exotic lines he saw a young face. Perhaps it was another deception like the ages of the abos he knew, but he didn't want to ask Keeley now... what difference did it make? He still had to do what he was ordered to do: quiet this beast and wake the girl. "I don't know how we're to hear anything above this..." The chains constantly slithered as the Dog paced.

"You must ignore it." Keeley glanced up at him. He looked nervous himself, and Jarrett began to wonder, now that they were minutes away from attempting this insanity, if there were things the Whishishian had not completely told him.

"I suppose, then, we ought to begin." He opened the journal to the marked page with the incantation scrawled in black.

"We will have to release the Dog from its shackles."

He stared at the man. And remembered the key. "It'll kill us!"

Keeley shook his head, but Jarrett didn't know what he was denying; it certainly wasn't the statement.

"You can't let that animal go."

"It can't return to her if it's not free. Begin the song." The abo took a breath and stepped toward the raging wolf. He remained just beyond its biting jaws, arms loose.

So they had to; *he* had to do this. Jarrett moved closer to the girl, palming his sidearm, then looked down again at her sleeping visage. It would have been sleep if it weren't so slack and lifeless. If she breathed he couldn't truly tell, buried as she was beneath the furs and skins. He tore his gaze away from the pattern of tattoos on her face and read the incantation silently to himself, one last time. He was going to garble the words despite hours of practice, probably breathe in the wrong place, stumble over the phrases that he had only a vague understanding of…He licked his lips and began to "sing."

It wasn't any kind of old tune from Sairland, no lullaby or winged echo like the baritone voices in the great musical halls of the city. The Aniw's idea of "song," the language in this Call, was a guttural growl interspersed by deep breaths and expelled grunts. Pointed words of respect and deference slid between the sounds, invoking the old gods. Cajoling them.

He felt more than a little silly in the task. It all sounded to his ears like a poor imitation of the Dog they were trying to harness. He barely heard himself over the growls of the animal and its pacing from one side of the cell to the other. He fixed his gaze on the journal, had to, in order to keep the flow of the words and the cadence of the Call, but the sudden shudder and stretch of the Dog drew his attention. He watched through a heavy beat of shock as the animal grew quiet, its blue gaze tilting up to him, looking through him.

Keeley stepped to the animal, pulling out the key, easing up to its blind side as it remained fixed on Jarrett. Rather than a cock of ears to indicate it was listening, the wolf watched him like a predator preparing to attack. He heard his own words begin to fade.

The Dog blinked and Keeley snapped: "Continue!"

He'd seen a show once, in the Roog, where a master hypnotist supposedly mesmerized a member of his audience by shining a light and dangling a pocketwatch in a steady rhythm. Perhaps this was a similar engagement. Once he picked up the song again, Jarrett felt the words falling out of his mouth in such a rhythm as that pocketwatch, but he wasn't sure who was mesmerized...himself or the Dog. Its hackles flattened, and for a stuttered moment the eyes seemed to shift and shape themselves into something more human. Rounder. Sadder.

It stepped toward the girl on soft pads, making no sound save for the quieter scrape of chains across the stone floor. Forcing himself not to fade, Jarrett watched as Keeley followed the animal and gently took hold of the lead chain closest to the iron collar and slipped in the key. His wrist turned and the lead fell slack, but rather than pull it off the thick fur neck of the Dog, the abo just stepped back toward the wall. The Dog advanced until its muzzle hovered over the girl's face.

The corners of Jarrett's sight began to darken. His

head felt light from the constant breaths he pulled in and shot out in song. His throat scratched raw, and his lips were becoming numb in his attempt to wrap them around these foreign words. If he choked now, would it set the Dog free of its spell? He stood barely aware of Keeley motionless in the shadows, or the worn leather against his fingertips as he held the journal as level as he could, glancing down even if he didn't really see the words now. He wasn't sure if he'd even kept the pattern of sounds. But the Dog continued to be engaged and it stared straight into the girl's sleeping face.

A long pink tongue flickered out and traced over the dark tattoo lines. All over. Not unlike any pet dog, gone to greet its master.

Not unlike Qoyotariz and that invasion upon his mouth.

Jarrett stumbled and the rhythm broke. The wolf's tail flicked and it raised its head, turning to stare at him again.

Don't move, he thought, words dying completely.

"Captain," Keeley hissed.

He'd faced down predators before, but always with a gun in his hand. Here it was at his hip, but something told him if he even reached for it the Dog would be on him. He stopped breathing, preparing for the leap that would bring the animal's jaws to his throat.

But with a start, the girl's lips parted and she heaved an audible breath. Her hand lifted and stroked over the beast's cheek, and it turned back to her. Though her eyes were shut her breathing continued, and the Dog gave a shake of its entire body, casting the open iron collar from around its neck. It clattered to the stone floor. The Dog lowered its muzzle again and licked her cheeks. Lips pulled back, revealing long fangs. It seemed ready to bite her, but as she continued to stroke its fur it crouched lower, growing still, and soon began to fade.

Like tendrils of fog or smoke, the edges of the animal's fur began to curl and disappear until whatever force controlling it just ate it up from the outside in, becoming gray filter through which Jarrett saw the shadows of the cell and the girl lying beneath its four legs, breathing it all in. She inhaled the wild smoke, absorbing it through her nose, her mouth, even what seemed to be her skin. The black of her tattoos.

The animal became as thin as air and then nothing at all.

Jarrett's hands shook.

He dropped the journal. It landed on the discarded iron collar, tossing up a hollow clang, and the Aniw girl opened her eyes.

THE HESS

The Dog. Sjenn felt the rage like a bite around her heart, pain in the struggle to beat and beat. Blood traced the edges of her teeth...or what had been her teeth. Blood of a priest. She tasted it at the back of her throat even still. She felt the declining pulse. The beat of it and of her own heart sat hot in her chest, flames of red that reached to the backs of her eyes. The sound and the insistent push forced them to open.

She lay on cold. She was still the Dog in her mind, and there stood a man above her with the frightened look of prey in his green eyes.

Though her limbs were heavy she launched for his throat. But in the disarray she hadn't seen the second man. He stood just out of her line of sight, in the shadows, and as the green-eyed one fought her off, the other grabbed her arm. So she turned on him just as the irons snapped around her wrists. He stumbled back, letting her go, and she tried to keep going, to get at him, both of the men now backed toward the wall.

She remembered the chain. It drew her up with a yank, bringing her to her knees in a way it never had with the Dog. The slap of her palms to the cold floor shoved her strangled cries to a choking halt. The blood taste was stale on her tongue. Long ago, like from caribou meat. Not from a murder.

She had murdered. The priest had taught her that word. She had killed a man.

She'd killed two men.

Her arms tucked inside the matted fur of her clothing. She bent over, forehead almost to the stone, and wept.

The Dog had residual memories, like tracks in the snow before the wind wiped them away. Men came in and out through the door, looking at her, standing over her. Kabliw men. They spoke in a manner she did not fully understand, and her Dog understood less. Threat came with the immediacy of starvation. Faces hovered that she didn't know, words formed that she'd never heard.

They talked to her, like the priest had talked to her. Like her father had talked to her in her dreams. And she watched their feet, scuffed black boots that paced from one side of the room to the other. Room, cell. Prison. This was the picture Father Bari had shown her, black lines cluttered together to make up an image of men and women weighed down by shadow. She could see no horizon. No land. No sky. Just the boots and their low shuffle across pitted stone. Little light seeped through the slats on the door. They brought food but she couldn't eat it, didn't know what it was. Kabliw food, cooked and mashed up like something regurgitated from the belly.

From deep in her chest, the Dog crouched. One song would release it again, but she was afraid. The boots were dark and stiff, not the fur flexibility of her own. They sounded hollow when they hit the ground.

A different man appeared in the sharp angles of the open door, backlit. She hadn't moved from her shackled position against the wall. He approached and crouched down. She saw his boots, then his gray pants leg, his hands clasped between his knees. When she looked up it was an older face than the two before, older gray eyes and a dark beard, the way Kabliw men grew them, as if they wished to cover up their expressions. He said, "My name is General Cillein Fawle."

She knew that meant he was a hunter of sorts. Like Captain Mackenzi. These men gave each other titles like they bore clothing upon their bodies, but it wasn't like an *ankago*. It had nothing to do with their ancestors.

"What is your name, child?"

Her mouth opened but she couldn't find air to talk. Instead she coughed. General Fawle picked up a tin cup from the floor and offered it. She saw water within, black from the inside of the cup. It wasn't the belly food, so she took the cup and sipped. It tasted like seaweed and iron and she almost gagged. But she drank it down and he asked again: "What is your name, child?"

"Sjennonirk." If the rest of his questions were like this, she could talk. Perhaps. If the corners of the prison didn't appeal to her so much. She had come to want the corners in the absence of open land. Her Dog wanted the corners so her back was protected. This man had blank eyes, even if his mouth smiled.

"Sa-yen...?"

"Sjennonirk." Kabliw mouths couldn't speak Aniw names or words very well. But she had no intention of teaching them. Not like she had with Father Bari. Where had that gotten her or her people? She drained the rest of the water, then put down the cup. It made a tinny sound on the stone. Her fingertips brushed the flat surface and it was as cold as ice.

"Sjennonirk." He said it right this time. "Do you want to go outside?"

Now she looked back up at him. Though the Dog wanted her back protected, they both yearned for the open air.

The ground hurt her feet and she walked slow. Every-thing here seemed nothing but angles, things that could bruise just by standing still: the prison walls, blackened brick, corners chipped away in places as if the very air somehow carved them away like the high winds did to snow dunes on the Land; the cobbled ground, some vol-untary beach of stones that these Kabliw chose to line the world with; and even the grass, when she drifted to it thinking it would be the cushion give of tundra, gave back nothing but pain at the soles of her feet. The earth here was as unforgiving as these Southerners.

Though this General Fawle matched her slow walk out of politeness, he led her away from the tall black gates, kept her within the borders and shadows of the prison. She knew so many Southern words now, and not just by looking in a book or taking a priest's word. On the other side of the gates was a road. Carriages. *Horses*. She stared from her distance, but the general wrapped his hand around her arm and guided her away, along a narrow path that just circled the main building. She was outside but she was not free. It was no different from standing on the top deck of the ship that had brought her here.

So she kept her gaze to the ground. His boots were loud; hers scuffed like a sick whisper, and she was so hungry even the Dog paced within her. Wanting blood.

The general said, "I'm sorry you've been in that cell for so long, but you see, we didn't know what to do with that wolf at first. Or... what do you call it? Your Dog?"

Hadn't Father Bari told her not to speak of her Dog? What of the trial? Their laws? But the priest wasn't here. It was just this man with his hand around her arm, and her hobbling steps. Her parka felt too heavy. The air here was damp, the sky a muddy gray. All the smells around her made her squint and avoid deep breaths, but she could feel this place already sinking beneath her skin. One blink and she could see the bear of her dreams, but even he was silent here. As was her father. Dead in the dream and dead when awake. He had died in that dream to bring her Dog forth. To kill.

"I want to go home," she told this man. Maybe he would realize that this was a mistake and she had meant no harm.

"I can't let you go home, Sjennonirk." He said her name with more confidence than he had in the prison. "We can't allow that after you've taken a man's life. Two men."

"But he had a gun. And a knife." She was tired. She had said this so many times to the priest, and the priest hadn't listened. She had more success speaking to the bears, or a walrus, or a whale.

The general paused their walk to turn her to face him. She had to look up, and he placed his hands on her shoulders now, like one would with a child. Perhaps he thought she was a child just because of her stature. He wasn't the tallest Kabliw she had ever seen, but he was still taller than her Aniw height. His hands felt broad.

"I will give you a choice, Sjennonirk. Or do your people say Sjenn? Father Bari called you Sjenn."

He didn't seem angry when he mentioned the priest. Maybe he didn't mind that he was dead. Sjenn nodded without speaking, and it seemed to be good enough, because he kept talking.

"I know this jail isn't a nice place for you. I have some power to get you out of it, but you'll have to do something for me."

The Dog, deep-seated in her human spirit, raised its eyes. She looked from the stiff buttons of the general's collar up into his eyes. "What?"

"I would like to know more about your Dog."

She blinked. This Kabliw believed in the *ankago?* "You know about my Dog. You controlled it." She was still unsure about that, did not understand how it had happened, who had done it. Were the two other men she had seen upon waking some sort of spiritwalkers? Yet they had not been Aniw. Though her memories of their faces and their voices were vague, she knew that they had not been Aniw. Father Bari had told her a little of the tribes that lived this far South, shown her the same dark lines that made up images of exaggerated faces, and those Southern tribes had frightened her when she was younger. They'd seemed ferocious. They were, Father Bari had said, always at war with his people. He had taught her the word *war* as well. So she knew *general* in that, and did not believe this man's words.

"We only read what the priest had written out, what he said it would take to make your Dog disappear. We weren't entirely sure it would work."

"It should not have worked," she said. "Only an *ankago* or kin of the *ankago* can control the Dog. Where is this *ankago*?" Were there more of her people in this city and she had never known? Had they been here so long she couldn't recognize them?

Something about her reply made the general smile.

"You can have all the answers to your questions if you agree to help me, Sjenn. If you help me, I will help you out of this prison. Isn't that a fair trade?"

When the whalers had come on their big boats they had talked of trade. Furs and fat for their metal and food. And then later on they had brought guns. She thought that was not a fair trade at all, and neither was this. What did he mean by help? Father Bari had said he wanted to help her, and he had brought her here.

"Don't you want out of that prison, Sjenn?"

"I want to go back to the Land."

"You may," he said. "In time."

She didn't believe that either. Yet what choice did she have? He still held her shoulders, and she looked back at the prison doors. The windows were black, just like the brick. Windows made of glass and iron and lead. There was so much she knew only from books, that she had to trust from pages and words that weren't her own. She thought of returning to that darkness, the dark like the drawings on those foreign pages, and the stink that accompanied anything from the South. She thought of going back to the box room that had somehow been worse than the belly of the ship that had carried her here. They'd chained her because they feared her Dog. And now this general, this man of war, wanted to know about the ways of the *ankago?* Because they had one among them?

She would never know anything from inside these walls. She could not return home if they sent her to trial. She would disappear here, and her family and her tribe would never see her again. Maybe it was these thoughts or the damp air that brought her more fully out from the spirit of her Dog. The Dog's voice was nothing but a low whine now at the pit of her stomach. Perhaps these Southern men had tamed it enough to make it retreat, but she was the only one who could hope to control it. Control it until it was time to let it go again.

She pulled her parka tighter around her body. Though she was used to the cold, she could not stand the lack of horizon. Instead there were buildings as far as she could see, past the gates and across the street. She wondered how long it would take to walk home if she started now. Twice as long as it had taken to come South? But she was unsure even how long that had been.

"Sjenn," the general said, giving her shoulders a light squeeze.

"I will help you." She looked up at his eyes. Those were the only things she recognized here. These Kabliw had eyes, even when half their faces were obscured. "I don't want to go back in there."

He smiled again. "Then you won't. Good girl." He let her go now and his gaze ranged over her head. She couldn't tell what he was looking at. "Good, good girl."

The carriage was very unlike a dogsled. It stood high off the ground so that the general had to grip her hand when she stepped up and into it. It rolled, not skidded across the rough stones, pulled by two horses. They were large animals that she barely glimpsed before being engulfed by the carriage, hemmed in on all sides. These Southerners liked being enclosed; meanwhile she tugged the small curtains to the side so she could push her face into the open air as it breezed by in their ride. But she got only a glimpse of the city too, before General Fawle drew her back again and shut the curtains, tying them together. "Nobody should see you," he said, and when she asked why, he didn't explain. So not all of her questions would be answered after all. She wondered if she could mark time, like Father Bari had shown her, until all of the general's words proved to be lies.

The ride was long and rough, with many stops and starts, and she only stared at her hands as they trundled through the streets. Every now and then she heard the big horses whuff, the sound loud enough to carry over the constant clapping of their hooves on the ground. She knew that men rode them and was glad that the general had not made her climb atop its back. It would be like trying to ride a caribou, and she couldn't think it would be possible, and surely it would be painful too.

Eventually the carriage stopped with a tilt and clatter, and she felt the driver clamber down from where he sat atop. Still wrapped in her furs, she clutched at them as the door jerked open and a waft of cool air floated in. It made her take a deep breath, realizing that her head felt stuffed by the tobacco scent of the general. He seemed equally eager to climb out and this time did not take her hand but let the coachman hold her elbow as she stepped down in front of a shoulder-high iron gate. These Kabliw loved their iron, as if they meant to keep out all of the world, even the spirits.

"Come, Sjenn," General Fawle said, motioning her forward toward the doors.

Father Bari's pictures hadn't prepared her for the grandiosity of the real thing. This house, not made of snow or wood, stood impossibly tall and cast long shadows straight over the street and even the trees, doubling the dark on the stone. Evening was falling, blanketing a murky blue glow along the roofs of the surrounding buildings, and Sjenn paused on the porch, staring up, wondering how many of these houses existed here, so many that you couldn't see land at all.

Before she could glance back over her shoulder at the carriage and the horses, General Fawle placed a hand to her back and gave a guiding push to direct her into the house. As a plump yellow-haired woman approached to greet the man, she realized that this was the general's own home. Why had he brought her here—was this her freedom? The careful glance from the other woman made Sjenn pause just inside the threshold. Glossy dark floors spread before her, long timbers like those that made up the ship, though these were smooth and shone so well she spied dark reflections of the furniture on its surface.

"Louna, get Sjenn situated upstairs. Draw her a bath."

Sjenn stared at the woman, ignoring the general's coaxing words. She wasn't afraid so much as suspicious, as this Kabliw stranger looked on her as one would an errant child. Sjenn walked where she directed, toward the stairs, more stairs than she had ever seen in her life. They led to secret chambers in this grand house, and she curled her fingers around the bannister, biting down. She would not be coddled or handed so readily from one Kabliw to another. Before this woman Louna could touch her to guide her like the general had, Sjenn climbed the steps ahead of her. She was exhausted, and the effort to reach the first landing before the stairs curved did not help, but she was determined.

On her way up she passed images of men and women and children, black and white, drawn and painted in such detail she had to look twice to be sure they weren't frozen spirits caught inside the frames. Some of the pictures were even more accurate than a drawing and looked all too real in their flat worlds. She would have stood and stared for longer but Louna was at her back. If she only stopped there could be tension. Being in this house seemed to make things uncomfortable—she sensed it behind her and from the nature of the air. She breathed it in as she reached the upper floor and stood at the end of a long hallway. More pictures separated the chaotic flower design of faded blue and yellow on the walls.

"This way, child," the woman said, tugging on Sjenn's elbow to guide her farther down the hall.

"I'm not a child."

Louna watched her out of the corners of her eyes and let her grip drop away. The Kabliw woman didn't say anything more, just opened the door...so many doors in this place, far more than even Father Bari had told her about…and led her inside yet another room. Why did Kabliw need so many rooms, so many doors, so many walls and bricks and clothes? Her people lived on the unprotected land, in snowhouses for the winter, in skin tents for the summer, and did not require these objects to survive. Where did these things come from?

Inside this new room she paused, feeling oddly large and cumbersome against the clean, unwrinkled lines of wall and furniture pushed neatly into edges and corners. Nothing seemed touched. It was as if the general had built his home, then left it empty. Who had been here last, if anyone at all?

"Right," the woman Louna said, waddling like a ptarmigan to a white tub in the corner. "Ye git y'self undressed while I warm up the water." The woman's narrow eyes looked at her up and down. "Best give me those…things." She waved at the fur clothing.

Sjenn pulled them tighter around her body. Undress in front of this Kabliw? No. They held a brief stare before Louna finally left, taking a large pitcher with her, and Sjenn padded to the single window and tugged the silken curtain aside to peer out.

She was high up. She caught only a glimpse of the street far below before stepping back, letting the curtain fall. The backs of her legs hit the side of the bed and she sat, sinking a little. It made the bed croak like some dying thing, and she shifted in alarm. More croaking. So she just stopped moving, staring down. The blue and red rug between her feet lay faded, aged by sunlight and footsteps. Every object, from mirror to doorknob to table clock, grabbed her attention in flits, but she didn't want to linger on any of them. These things would not make sense the longer she stared at them, any more than some words in the Kabliw language would ever be understood. Learned, perhaps, but not understood.

"Nothing," she heard herself murmur. Nothing in this Kabliw world was familiar. Her Dog was a restless sleeper and she shook, sitting on the strange high bed. She shook, but not from the cold.

They layered her in thin cloth that fell to her toes and let the air pass through and up her sleeves. Kabliw clothing that she couldn't protest, because Louna took away her furs, saying something about burning them. She could have fought, but she heard the heavy boot steps on the floor below and knew the general waited. This was part of the trade for her freedom. They would dress her like a Kabliw, comb out the knots in her hair, expect her to drown herself in the tepid water until her skin felt raw and exposed. She stood before the long mirror in the small room, Louna behind her smoothing the puffed shoulders of her dress, and saying she looked "much better."

She didn't like to look inside this mirror. The face staring back at her was some odd opposite. The clarity was alarming. No ripples, no taint of blue or shadow or reflection of cloud to mar her image. Instead, just the opposite. She noticed the way Louna avoided looking into her eyes for too long. Did the tattoos disturb her? This woman's face was as unmarked as that of a child or a man who was not an *ankago*.

The lampblack were lines she knew well from touch, from the way her Dog licked her face in that gesture of obeisance and acceptance, yet now even they seemed unfamiliar markings on the burnt brown of her skin, set against the pale blue and rose lines of this Kabliw dress. The form was wrong in its pattern and cut, in its lack of fur or soft skins. These weren't Aniw lines, or Aniw texture. She couldn't stop tugging at the sleeves and the ribbon cinching her waist. She plucked and writhed in the constriction all the way back down the steps, following after Louna. Barefoot on the smooth wood. She didn't make a dent, but the plump woman caused the planks to creak.

Old bones. That was the Kabliw world, full of old bones and echoes.

What heavy boot steps she'd heard from above now ceased the closer they grew to another room on this lower floor. Past ticking clocks and more hanging pictures, the house was so quiet she couldn't even hear past the walls to any commotion outside. The silence was loudest when she found herself inside a red room, the colors rich like blood and smoke, with curious shelves of books—more than she'd ever seen, even from Father Bari. The air was scented with gun oil, like the man she'd killed in the snowhouse. Her stomach twisted. General Fawle stood within, looking exactly the same save for the absence of his cap. Standing a bit apart were two other men.

Her Dog stretched in the pit of her heart. She knew these younger men. One was very tall, with eyes the color of the tundra spring or a Dog in rage. Eyes the same shape as the general's, so perhaps they were kin even though this one had a smoother face. No beard. The other man was not Kabliw. A Southerner of a different sort, like Father Bari had explained. "They're like your people, in a way." So he'd said, though she saw no cousin resemblance in this one's golden gaze.

"Sjenn," the general said. "This is my son, Captain Jarrett Fawle, and our friend Keeley of the Whishishian abo tribe."

She said nothing and neither did they. Only their eyes talked. She saw questions behind the son's face, but he didn't ask them for some reason. She looked back at the general.

"What do you want?" No need to hesitate, not now that she was here, standing in the Kabliw dress, her feet cold and sore on the hard wood.

All three men seemed a little surprised by her bluntness. They were the type to hide their intentions, perhaps. It was a Kabliw trait.

"My son." General Fawle gestured to the younger man, who looked at his father with nothing close to love and only a reluctant respect. "I would like you to teach him the ways of your Dog. The ways of your spiritwalkers. That is what you are."

It was not a question or even a request. She saw nothing but an iron insistence in the bearded man's stare.

"I cannot. He's not Aniw. He's no *ankago*."

"You can."

Was she dealing with a madman, some broken animal that could only be sent off to die? She didn't have the power to command this Kabliw. She'd already killed two men. And this one kept her from the prison. He could just as easily put her back, and despite the dress she wore, she knew it to be so. This was the biggest lie of all: he was not truly kind to her. All of his smiles dissolved into threat.

If she refused again, would he send her to a trial? So she said nothing.

"Father," Captain Jarrett Fawle said, and Sjenn watched as he turned from her to meet his father's eyes. "Why in the name of the gods do you think she can teach me anything about her people? And for what exactly?"

Because there were guns in the snow. But she didn't say that either. She didn't fully know, and the son did not speak to her.

And the father did not speak to the son. He only said again, "Sjenn, I want you to teach my son the ways of your spiritwalkers. I know it can be done. You must teach him your Dog."

"It can't be done." Once more. Once more looking into the shards of his eyes, hoping that he would see the impossibility in his own words. "I am of my father's people, my ancestors are not your ancestors. Your son will have no Dog." Could her words ever make sense to this man, even if she spoke his language?

"Jarrett's the one who put away your Dog, my dear. Didn't you say only a spiritwalker had that power?"

She looked again to the son. He seemed as surprised as she. All along the tribesman said nothing and he was the only one in that room who seemed staid in the midst of the conversation. Was this no shock to him?

"A spiritwalker or kin of a spiritwalker," she said. "I don't understand how your son did."

"You don't need to," the general said. "I only need you to teach him. You *will* teach him, however long it takes. You won't be returning to your people until you do this for me."

So this was the true trade. And it came to her as heavy as a whale-burdened ship.

*   *   *

Captain Jarrett took her outside. Just him, excusing them both from the general and the man Keeley, and the general did not stop them. Was she to begin this impossible task now, to teach this Kabliw to be an *ankago?* Through the long house, through doors made of glass, outside to the cool air and gray skies, and the towering giants she recognized as trees...at least here she could breathe. Though the grass felt sharp at the soles of her bare feet and she didn't dare walk on the rocks. She was cold but it was familiar, even in the damp. No walls on either side, she could stretch out her arms if she wanted.

The walls were just more distant here. Other houses, more trees. More fences. She saw other roofs made of black and gray, and far behind them a sliver of dirty yellow as the sun arched away. The edge of the earth didn't exist here. This Kabliw world stretched on forever, and every small shrub and peeking flower seemed only to be here on the good graces of these hard surfaces. This world would never melt, could bring no spring, but it wasn't like her Land. Sjenn crouched on the grass, dress pulled over her knees, and wrapped her arms around her legs. Down this low she could see more sky, it seemed.

Jarrett Fawle hovered near, casting shadow, walking to and fro until he just stopped beside her, looking down. The toe of his black boot poked a patch of dry grass nearby. She wondered if his feet could feel, or were they so choked up inside those leather tombs that he stood dead from the roots? His eyes were the greenish-gray transparency of blindness.

"I don't know why my father insists on this." He spoke

quiet and slow, perhaps for her, and there were curves to his words that sounded different from Father Bari and the men from the whaling ships. Perhaps his thoughts came at this measure too, steady and careful. Could he be careful? When she didn't reply he stepped once away, then seemed to catch himself and finally sat beside her, arms folded about his drawn-up knees. He was not a large man despite his height, but she watched him warily from the corners of her eyes. "I don't understand any of this, frankly. You, your magic. But he told me that you killed my friend."

There had been two. "Who was your friend?"

His voice sounded caught by nets. "Father Bari."

She pressed a brown blade of grass between her fingers and tugged until it uprooted. "He was my friend too." That was no lie. "I didn't want to kill him. But my father said. And the priest brought guns to my people."

"Your father said to kill Father Bari?"

Hadn't she said? "Yes."

"But why?"

"He brought these men and their guns to the Aniw." Now she looked him straight in the face, so his eyes couldn't hide. "Why do your people bring guns to the Land? At first you brought craft and things like iron and silver. You said you wanted sealskin and bear fur. To hunt the white whales."

"I don't know," he said, but he looked away. "Father Bari wouldn't want guns near your people. He never had."

"He came on the ship, and they came with guns. Your *army*. Father Bari is the *ankago* of your people, isn't he?"

"No..." His head tilted like a wolf's as he looked back at her. "Is that what he told you he was?"

"He said 'priest.' But he was first. Every tribe has an *ankago,* and the *ankago* speak between the tribes. It was my grandfather Sjennonirk that welcomed the first of your kind to Aniw shores. And it was Father Bari that welcomed him back."

"I see," the captain said, but she didn't know if he truly did. How could she be sure of what this man or his father or any of them saw? "Are you certain they were army guns?"

"Father Bari said the men were army. They wore clothing like you." She pointed to his black coat and yellow buttons.

His face seemed to frost over; his eyes become hard like water at the first touch of winter.

Had she spoken wrong? She pulled at more of the grass.

"How old are you?" he said. Not the question she expected.

Age in their years. "Your priest said I might be twenty-something."

"Don't you know? Don't you have birthdates?"

She shrugged.

"You look much younger. Suh-yenn."

He tried her name. She stared at him. "How old are you?"

"Twenty-nine."

"You look older."

This made him blink. She wondered if he would take offense, as she could never tell with these people. But instead he just said, "My father seems intent on keeping us on a hook."

She thought of char fish flailing at the end of a deep ice pole. "He thinks you have *ankago* power."

Captain Jarrett smirked, eyes rolling up to the darkening sky. "And what do you think? You're the snow witch."

These people could lie, but she could not. She wanted to put her head down and cry, but they wouldn't understand that either. Even the sky looked different from the bowels of the Kabliw earth. "You Called my Dog. My little spirit. She wouldn't listen if you had no power."

And that thought seemed to frighten them both. He looked away, and she looked at the ground.

They put her back in the room where she'd taken a bath. It was the box shape of a sled and smelled more strongly now of crushed flowers. Not the flowers of the springtime tundra, though, or the black berries she picked from the ground with her mother in the summer. The air here was old. The woman Louna or someone else had turned up the table lamps on either side of the bed. They gave light but very little scent, surrounded by a globe of glass. Sjenn sat at the edge of the deep mattress and stared at the pulled curtains. She could not climb down from this height to run away; she couldn't even conjure her Dog. Her body would remain here, locked in this room.

The doorknob would not turn.

She didn't know how long she sat there, watching the light wink at her on the wall, tickling the shadows at the corners of the room. Then a scratch came to the door and low bootsteps sounded from the other side of the floor's gap.

"Go away." She thought of the men in the ship, their laughter leaking from opposite walls.

"Sshh," came the voice. The door rattled lightly, like a wind had taken it, and then opened.

Captain Jarrett stepped in and shut it behind him.

She wished for her *sul,* or the teeth of her Dog. Instead all her fingers grasped was the quilt at the foot of the bed.

"It's all right," he murmured, moving to the window and peeking through the curtains. Night. "I can't get you out of here, but…"

"But?"

When he looked at her there were too many shadows on the side of the room where he stood. She could not see his eyes. "But I think you ought to see where Father Bari rests."

She wanted to say no, but this was not what her father had taught her. Even killing a caribou required the words. This was Kabliw ritual, and Captain Jarrett did not seem eager to leave until she agreed. And perhaps she should agree, as long as the Dog paced restless in her veins.

Sjenn looked down at her bare feet.

"You'll need shoes," he said.

The dress felt too thin for the night. She wanted her furs, for the warmth and the scent of home. But she wanted many things from home and none were in reach. If even her cousin Twyee were here, perhaps the world wouldn't seem so strange. But she wouldn't wish this place on her kin; better to think of her family free on the Land.

Guns in wooden crates. She could not find better

dreams even in her wishes. This Captain Fawle moved about the room, a reminder shadow of the men she'd seen on the snow.

He found her some "slippers" to wear in the small closet attached to the room, black velveteen things with a flat soft heel. They still managed to pinch her toes. She didn't ask where they had come from and he didn't seem willing to tell her, but they didn't look large enough to fit a woman Louna's size. Maybe there were other women in the house that she hadn't seen, a mother or sister or some girl that served this family. Other female faces looked out at her from the pictures on the wall, all barefaced and nearly bald for how strictly they pulled back the hair to their skulls. Yet she heard no other footsteps here but those of the male boots. Maybe these slippers belonged to a dead woman.

She almost opted to go barefoot, but he said their path to the priest's resting place was treacherous and she could not. When he went to the window and not to the door, she paused in the middle of the room. He pulled aside the curtain and threw open the window.

"Not out there," she said.

"He'll hear us if we go through the downstairs," the captain said, one leg already arched over the sill.

"No."

A feather breeze drifted in, caressing up her arms. She folded them against her body. He looked back at her, eyes narrowed, and it was then she spied the gun at his waist, below his jacket as his outstretched arm revealed it. The handle was bone white.

"Why not?" he said.

"It's high." Perhaps these Kabliw liked to pretend they

were birds, but she knew if they fell from such a height they would die all the same. They were not indestructible, despite their guns and their great ships.

"It's dark," was his answer. "Just don't look down. I'll hold on to you."

It was not said as an offer and his eyes were sharp. What kindness he'd seemed to have outside the house earlier must have died with the day. The Kabliw were changeable like the winds, and she was from tundra stock. The permanence of the ice.

Dogs did not like the tall places. But she forced herself forward, toward the dark.

He offered his hand and she didn't look down.

They didn't climb down anyway, but up. Away from her window stretched iron steps that he said were for "fire," though how a fire could just start here she didn't know. *Don't look down.* He crossed first to the narrow black platform, and it rattled a little beneath his weight. Could it hold them both? So he said. The windowsill stabbed sharp against the bottom of her left foot, through the slipper sole. Her right foot firmly planted on the brick ledge, and her right hand clasped to his coat arm, and she gripped the top of the window for balance. *Don't look down.* One step to be where he was, and she had to trust that he wouldn't let go.

"I feel sick."

"Step over, come on." He pulled. He was tall and strong and she couldn't fight. Her balance upended. The black world beneath her and glowing dots of light whirled at her feet, but then her feet hit the iron with a clang and he steadied her. Hard grip on her arm and her hands on the rail. "All right?" he said.

"No," she said but began to climb when he did. Her heart ran so strongly she could barely breathe, but on the rooftop, doubly high above this city, suddenly she saw the long horizon. Blanketed in black, but it was there, broken by the jagged roofs of other houses. When she looked up now there weren't as many corners to her vision. The tops of the buildings were like the floes she used to skip in the early spring, when a misstep meant a fall to the cold sea. "We walk?" She pointed across the roofs.

"Yes. It's faster, and he won't even know we're gone." Captain Jarrett didn't smile but he sounded lighter in the voice. The lilt of mischief.

She followed. They were wraiths scudding across the flat roofs like the loose top layers of new snow. The wind was a hard hand, and she had nothing but her dress. Across the lines of hair in her eyes she kept her stare on his narrow back, the way his coat flew open and the long scarf trailed behind him like the flags she'd seen on the masts of the whaling ships. He did not turn about. They made their way like this, skulking, hungry. She hadn't eaten since the jail.

Did he know where he was going? He didn't seem to deviate or falter, even in mere moonlight. The only other illumination came from the scatter of yellow gas lamps at their feet, in the trenches of the street level. They were above the world, yet every jut of roof and chimney was the unnatural angle of manmade horizon. She longed for rocks and piled drifts of snow. In the northerly parts of the Land there would still be snow in the spring, breaking apart only beneath a high, unchecked sun. Cloudless days. The feel of ivory shades over her eyes to protect against blindness. The bark of dogs eager to pull a sled. She wandered.

Her foot hit the pockmark of a disrepaired roof and she tumbled. Hands and knees slapped gravel, rubbed raw and stung. Jarrett Fawle seized her arm and dragged her body up. He'd turned around after all. But then he let her go.

"It's just down here. Watch your step."

She thought in desperate innovation that maybe she could survive this Southern city if she ran now. But once she climbed down another line of iron steps to the narrow alley below, the stink and slick feel of wet stone beneath her feet made the inclination die. She wouldn't know where to go. From her height she had seen no end to this place. It would take more than a day to break free, and even if she could see the northern way from the scatter of stars overhead, how long could she survive without food?

The ache in her belly grew deeper.

"You're shivering. I thought you people lived in the cold?"

She heard more challenge than interest in his tone. But he slipped his coat off and wrapped it around her shoulders. The weight surprised her, but she clutched the lapels, smelling the tobacco smoke embedded in the wool. Yet it felt good and warm and she held it close, looking up at him and the frown just discernible in the liquid light. He wrapped his scarf twice around his neck, as it had come loose in their trek, and headed out of the alley.

"Stay close. If you get lost..."

She would be lost without recovery. The lines in the cobbled streets weren't the familiar wind patterns on rolling snow. Perhaps even the moon was different here and she couldn't depend on it for direction. Looking up she saw the storied stars, giving tales and advice, but could their voices be depended upon here? Perhaps they spoke a different language as they looked down on the Kabliw world. Perhaps they couldn't be trusted either.

The loneliness penetrated this thick Southern coat. She watched the back of his white shirt. It was easy to follow at least, like the whip of a dog's tail.

He took her 'round the overhanging stomachs of squat buildings draped in night. Down narrow passages and behind brick walls she thought she heard the rumbles of angry voices, or the impatient twist and screech of doors opening and shut, like valves. Blood flow of the city, what was its name? Nev Anyan. And the people in their long dresses and tall hats were the sinew, lining muscle, connecting to the bones of their world, the empty echoes of places she could not see, only hear. One building looked much like another, more faceless than tractless land, a blur of gray and bumps and the stench of close living. She kept her head down so nobody saw her face, didn't want to know if they looked her way. She didn't want to see them either, pale figures, drifting feet, and occasionally an odd man squatting in the gutters blowing on a long pipe. Faces covered in hair, wrinkled, glinting eyes. Women with their bosoms open. Sjenn shrank away, the collar of the captain's coat pulled up along her cheeks to hide her tattoos.

Her Dog could skulk these streets, be swift around Jarrett Fawle's legs instead of her own stride fallen behind. He turned once more to usher her along, to direct her to a towering edifice that seemed to make the night even blacker below. Moonlight barely touched the base of this building. She looked up, neck straining, just as a clang and clatter belted overhead. She jumped and Captain Jarrett said, "It's only the bell tower."

It was loud. She covered her ears with her hands and the coat slipped off her shoulders. The captain caught it, held it over his arm, and tugged on her elbow.

"It'll stop in a minute."

It rang ten times and the world echoed. She shook off his touch but he seized her again, and she knew there would be no blocking it out. None of it. It was a church, but made of stone, not wood like the one room Father Bari and his brethren priests had built on the Land. She couldn't see how high this one went—it scraped the belly of the sky. Jarrett Fawle guided her up broad steps, through a pair of spread, elongated legs of one of their gods. He was carved into the face of the building, or maybe the building was birthed from his back and those of the other gods beside him. She remembered the Kabliw had seven of them, four males and three females, and there were seven doorways on this church. Seven ways to get to paradise. Seven ways to descend to darkness. Father Bari's old books had taught her and her people, and she had thought them fascinating tales.

But now his words were alive in this cold dominion, in the arches and columns bending above. Inside the church she felt swallowed, behind the ribcage of its power. She was in the heart, it seemed, and every flicker of candlelight reflected the beat of its pulse.

It was as quiet as death. Her slippers made no sound on the long roll of deep blue carpet that spread from the threshold toward a twin display of the seven monolithic gods. Outside and inside, they kept watch. The benches facing at an angle inward were empty. Rows of soldiers, they seemed, like the images of marching war she had been shown in books.

Jarrett Fawle did not let go of her arm. He walked her toward the gods and paused beneath their canted gaze. Three looked down toward her, the others held their stares across the long span of the church. They were ten times her height, and even with glass above her the moonlight didn't reach their stone toes. For details she depended on the firelight. She saw the rounded folds of their carved clothes; they were draped as Father Bari's had been.

A creak of wood sounded at their left and a priest emerged from behind a red velvet curtain. She caught a glimpse of a slowly shutting door before the drapery fell back in place. The priest walked toward them with long strides, but when he was close enough that she could see behind his cowl, the features were those of a dark-skinned woman. A woman or a young man, unsuited to any other life but that of a priest. It was difficult to tell through the fall of the loose robes. Sjenn stared and the woman stared back. Her blue eyes seemed to spark with fascination. She didn't look away like the servant Louna had.

Captain Jarrett and the woman seemed to know each other; she greeted him by name.

"This is the Aniw he spoke of?" the woman said. Her voice gave her away where the robes could not. And Jarrett Fawle said yes. Would they cast her into the darkness now for murdering their friend? If Captain Jarrett disobeyed his father by bringing her here, how much farther would he go? She wished for the woolen coat again, some kind of heavier protection than this flimsy dress allowed.

"I want to take her to see it," the captain said, and the woman priest nodded.

"Come." She walked by them both and led them across the front of the church, toward another velvet curtain. Secret rooms? So many rooms. Sjenn could not count them all, like she couldn't count the stones in the floor or the candlelights dotting the walls. Or the people in this city.

Behind the curtain and through an arched door they descended. Sconce light led the way. If she had just left the heart, this was surely the bowels, a resounding cavern of stone and damp that didn't creak like the ship but groaned in its own way, with echoes. Spirits? They had spirits, these Kabliw, or so Father Bari had claimed, though they were not like Aniw spirits despite what he'd said. They were not of the Dog, and if they were not of the Dog they weren't of the People either, had not been born from the Land and traveled great distances across the snow and tundra. These spirits seemed to linger in corners and avoid the light. Every flame they passed whipped a protest at their destination, so that she almost turned and ran back up the worn steps, up toward the feet of the gods and their blind, uncolored stares.

But Jarrett Fawle guided her back, a hand between her shoulders, and the woman priest stepped before her, sure in her booted footfalls like a thief. They brought her into a domed room, filled by holes, and in each hole lay a pile of human bones.

Sjenn stopped in the middle of the room, a waft of chill air crawling up from her ankles, over her knees and thighs. She twisted the sides of her dress and shook her head once. An entire room housing the dead? No wonder the Kabliw spirits lingered and could not, even by their priests, transform. They were trapped by stone. Gaping eyeholes stared at her at every turn; holes in every part of the wall from floor to ceiling, stopping only as wall met the curve overhead. Dead priests. All murdered?

"Come here," Captain Jarrett said and all but dragged her to the right, away from the living priest, toward a cavity that sat at her eye level. In it lay a clutter of bones— long, short, broken, black. The skull sat atop it, *sul*-sharp at the cheekbones. A couple of its teeth were missing. "This is Father Bari," the captain said. "This is what's left of him after his body was burned."

After she had killed him. She yanked her arm from the captain's grip but didn't attempt to run. He would catch her. He stood looming behind her shoulder, and her sight narrowed on the shadowed bones. Her Dog growled, and in the memory of her dream her father whispered an endearment. She should not be sorry. On the ship she hadn't been sorry, in the jail the Dog had not cared.

But her father hadn't been the one to kill this priest. And in the end, it had not been the Dog either. They were her memories, and this was all that was left of her deed. She was all that was left in this city, a spiritwalker trapped among trapped spirits.

Captain Jarrett took her back to his father's house the same way, silent and hard in his driven direction over the city roofs, as if he were trying to roust some bad thought with this headlong pitch through the night. She had to be quick to keep pace with him, and any time she lagged he rounded back and caught her arm. He gave her his coat again, she pushed her arms through the long sleeves so it would not fall off, but she didn't think it was a true act of kindness. "You can't get sick," he said. But she felt sick already. From the cluttered and clashing smells, the closed-in spaces filled by bodies. Long ago when the first priest and first fishers had come to Aniw shores, they had made some tribes sick. Father Bari said the Kabliw had tried to avoid that, they had inflicted themselves on the Southern abo tribes and had learned, but even with the trying it had happened.

Maybe here she would make the Kabliw sick. Or because she was a lone Aniw they would overpower her anyway without even trying. The coat she held around her body could bring the sickness to her. Wearing the Kabliw could be as bad as eating their food. Or standing before their remains. Could the bones of Father Bari curse her? Was he angry that she had killed him? Was that why Captain Jarrett took her to that place, so the face of the dead could look upon her and know her from beyond the middle light?

She received no replies. She couldn't ask the questions, not with his back to her and the street far, far below.

He let her descend first, just the way they had got out. Back inside she sat on the bed, felt grounded and oddly grateful now for the flowery scent and the warm light. He closed her window and the warmth began to seep in.

He held out his hand to her. For the coat.

His anger was a slow thing. She saw the way he had waited to take her to the church. His eyes held revenge like one held a child—close and protective. She would not be able to rip that child from his arms, so she removed the coat and passed it over. Without a word he took it and walked out.

The door clicked shut and she heard the lock turn.

Another dream, the black Dog. Her father's Dog. Her father was yet alive, resurrected from the jaws of the bear. The air was dead where she stood, the way it could never be on the Land. Soundless. Still. Her slippered feet scuffing on the top crust of ice made a brief sound, then fell into nothing. She wore the dress but felt no cold. The black Dog circled her again. It growled, flicked its ears back, paced with a hunter stride of muscle. She could not understand it this time, and her own Dog remained quiet.

Absent.

Her father spoke to her and she could not hear him.

She awoke on the floor and vaguely remembered climbing off the narrow bed to spread a blanket on the rug and lie down. The bed was too soft and it had made her coil and shift, until finally she found enough comfort on the floor to sleep. Barely. Daylight flung toward her face from around the edges of the half-pulled curtain and she rolled, sitting up to rub her eyes. She half expected to see dark jail walls or the bars of the ship prison as Father Bari peered in at her from the other side.

Another blink and she saw eyeholes, but then her vision cleared and it was just the pattern on the white vase, perched at the end of a small table across the room. This room. As she sat there she heard the traffic outside, even through the window glass. Carriages trundling, the distinctive clop of horses' hooves. Voices calling to each other. This city knew no silence, and what sound it gave was not the expected beat of nature. She crawled to the window and rose up to her knees to peer out. Still dizzy to look from such a height. It was a bright day, giving glare to the straight houses and tall dead lights on the sidewalks. The glow was gone with the darkness.

The door behind her swept open and Sjenn turned, feeling guilty to be looking out at the world for fear they would think her ready to escape. But it was only Louna, straddling the threshold with her wide stance. Her apron had gray dust smudges on the front.

"The general wan' ye for breakfust, chil'."

That meant food. The hunger had settled in the pit of her stomach and roused again at the attention. She pushed herself to her feet, blinked away a sudden rush of dark spots in her sight, and walked by the woman, unkempt. Her slippers shuffled on the stretch of floor down the hall. It was hard to lift her feet in this place. Though the dress was light, it hung with an uncomfortable weight.

The house looked different in broad daylight and so did the men at the table. She didn't see the abo man Keeley, but General Fawle and his son sat at one end of the long setting—plates, shining glasses that caught the light, silver knives and forks and spoons, and delicate-looking white cups. The fragrance from the food was almost overpowering, and she rubbed at her nose.

The Kabliw liked to eat on stiff chairs, and the general pointed her to the one across from the captain. The drapes were pulled back, but the curtains were thin enough to let in light, so that she squinted a little as she sat, moving around on the seat though it did no good. The back of the chair forced her to keep her shoulders wide. The bottoms of her slippers just scraped the rug beneath the table.

They were looking at her, but she looked at the food. The only thing that seemed edible were the biscuits, which she knew from Father Bari's visits, and the tea. Cooked ham, eggs, and brown toast all turned her stomach, and she kept her hands below the brush of cloth hanging off the table's edge.

The general spread some honey on his biscuit. His skin appeared pink, as if he'd either been out in the cold too long or the heat. Perhaps from a morning scrub. His dark hair lay slicked back, his white shirt collar perfectly tightened around his neck. "I'll be traveling to Lacamb today to speak to the Patronael." He addressed it as much to his son as to her. She didn't know these names and said nothing. "I expect you two to get to work. I want reports." This last was definitely to the younger Fawle, who sat pushing his mashed-up eggs around on his plate with a long fork.

Sjenn kept her hands to herself, staring at the food. It wouldn't leap to her plate on its own, but she couldn't make herself disturb her stillness with movement. How did this man expect her to teach his son the Dog? Yet he'd dismissed her protests the day before, as if he knew better.

"Are you listening to me?" the general said, and before she could look up to see if he were indeed speaking to her, Jarrett Fawle replied.

"Yes, sir."

She wondered why she was even sitting here at all. Why be in this elaborate house if they locked her in at night anyhow? Her eyes caught the shining edge of the knife near her plate.

"And how exactly is she supposed to teach me?" the captain said.

"Begin as you had—with the old priest's notes. Something more must be learned from him. Begin with your own history."

Nobody asked her and she did not volunteer. They thought it as simple as reading a book.

"And what if she can't teach me?" The younger Fawle asked it, the thought swimming at the back of her mind. They both spoke as if she weren't there.

"She will," the general said, cutting into his meat.

"You sent soldiers up north," the son said with a tone of suspicion. "With guns."

The general took a sip of his tea. "What of it?"

"What are you planning?"

"To protect these people." The elder Fawle's knife waved and flashed in Sjenn's direction. She did not want the attention from such a utensil and sat unmoving.

"From Sairland?"

"You forget how far they travel to attack us. It's only a matter of time before they leave their barbaric mark on this entire continent."

"Unless."

"Unless?"

The young captain looked once at her. "Your interest in magic is peculiar, Father."

"As I said, we can learn from these people." The

general no longer wished to speak to his son. He turned
to her. "Won't you eat?"

These men were not a family, despite resemblance
and rearing. They sat at this table like enemies too long
together. She was witness to some punishment that held
its crime somewhere in the blood.

"This isn't my food." She couldn't stop herself from
making a face.

"Yes, I know you people eat your meat uncooked, but
that's not how we do it here. That would be barbaric. If
you think you'll get sick from this, just eat the bread at
least. Hadn't you ever tried anything the missionaries or
the shipboard men brought to shore?"

"Not a lot." Her grandfather and father had, mostly.
She was hungry, though, so finally reached for one of
the biscuits on the pyramid pile. It flaked a little when
she set it on her plate. She watched the way the general
pasted on the honey and dipped her own knife in the
flat jar before her plate, copying. The taste was so sweet
it made her cough and she grabbed the glass of water
nearby. The liquid was transparent and cool as it rolled
across her tongue. Not like ice water, but it tasted some-
what clean.

They were both watching her with curiosity. She knew
that stare. She had found herself visiting it upon every
Kabliw that touched Aniw shores, early on.

The general picked up his teacup again and sipped.
"Keeley will remain here with you both."

"Why?" Captain Jarrett said, in the same tone he'd
used last night on her. Displeased. Resigned.

"Because I've asked him to. Because I want her
watched."

"I won't run," she said. "Where would I go?" On four feet she could make it, but what of her body?

"She won't go anywhere, and neither shall I," the captain said, but it wasn't the voice of obedience. It sounded more like accusation.

But the general just smiled. "I know."

Soon he left them at the table, and Sjenn heard the door open out front and the soft whuff of a horse. He was gone on his carriage with no word of when he would return. She hoped it would be a while. Captain Jarrett still poked at his food, and she had created a crumby mess all over her plate from the biscuits. She'd eaten five.

"You can take me to the ships," she said. "And let me go. Then you can go too."

"No, I can't," he said.

"Why not?"

"He's my father and my general. Besides, he'd find me and drag me back. And he's got that bloody abo on my tail, the gods know why."

Maybe the general knew his son was tempted to disobey. She was tempted.

Keeley walked into the dining room. Had he been lurking in the hall? "He believes that much of her magic and much of my people's are the same." He must have heard what the captain had said but he gave no evidence of it other than his words. Sjenn watched him as he took up a chair at the far end of the table and sat, his hands on his knees and his back straight. Had he also slept in this house, to come strolling in here with such ease? He looked exactly as she'd seen him the night before, half Kabliw and half abo, with the black paint around his eyes, not unlike her tattoos. But his weren't permanent.

"We're not the same," she told him.

"My people's *janna* also call the Dog," he said. "If that isn't common enough?"

But it wasn't the commonalities she feared. Differences bred misunderstanding.

"*My* people don't 'Call the Dog,'" Jarrett interrupted. "So the fact my father wants me to 'learn' and the fact he's got you to mind us is preposterous. If he won't let us go until his mad scheme's in play, then he won't let you go either, and you're going to sit there and tell me that you'll do whatever he says?" It was a flood of words, as if the absence of the general had broken down a wall. "I don't know a single abo that will do whatever a Ciracusan says in that blind fashion unless he's been completely enslaved or he's got something else in the works. Not even the allied tribes. And you're not quite like a slave, are you?"

Keeley walked this house without guard. Sjenn wondered if this man and the captain had met in one of their battles. They spoke as enemies.

"I'm no slave," the abo said. "But you seem to be."

"We all are," Sjenn said, when Captain Jarrett began to stand. "In this place." This was not like trying to temper hunters among her people. This captain wore his gun to the table. These kinds of men shed blood on each other. She wanted to push her chair back and leave the room.

The abo tribesman looked at her. "He said the words and trapped your Dog. Something is different in him."

They both looked at the captain. What was different?

"I'm going for a walk," Jarrett said and rounded the table toward the open doorway, out to the hall. Soon the front door opened and shut. With some force.

Sjenn clenched her hands together and hoped the abo

would get up and follow him. But he didn't. Instead he looked at her, leaning forward until his hands rested on the edge of the table.

"Please tell me about your people."

Father Bari had wanted to know about the Aniw too, and it had taken years before the betrayal came. She stared at this abo man and didn't answer. So he said that his people also shared some common Dog, some ancestry of a kind, but what did that mean? He still warred with these Kabliw. He still did as they told him to do, at least where it concerned a Kabliw with power. Why did he want to know about her people's power?

"Sjenn," he said, and it sounded the right way, even if she could tell from the pause and dip in his tone that the Kabliw speech, much less her language, was not his original tongue.

"Why are you with this man?" she said before he could ask her anything more.

"The generali?"

Of course the general.

"Long ago," he said, "he saved my life."

"When? What happened?" If Keeley had a tale to tell, she would listen as she would when the People came together.

"I was a very young boy," he said. "My tribe was attacked by the Soreganee. Their people and my people have always fought, even before the Boot People came. The generali saved me, and when I was put into the Boot People school, he saved me from there too and sent me back to my people. He has always helped me, and sometimes he asks for my help too."

She didn't think General Fawle could be kind without trickery, but she didn't say it. "Boot People?"

He gestured around to the house.

"Kabliw," she said.

"That's your name for them." He nodded once.

"They come from the boats," she said. Giving that much away couldn't be a threat. "Aniw." She pointed to herself. "We come from the Land."

"Have your people been to Nev Anyan before?"

"No." She saw what he was doing. Now the questions came again. She stood, brushing crumbs from the front of her dress. "I don't want to answer your questions."

"They're only questions, Sjenn."

On a second thought she scooped up a couple more of the biscuits and shoved them into the deep pockets at the sides of her skirt.

"They lead to guns," she said and left him there in the empty dining room.

She set the biscuits in the little wood-scented drawer beside her bed, hoping that if they forgot to give her food later on that she could eat this. So far her stomach wasn't unsteady, save for the dread. Captain Jarrett hadn't returned, but at least Keeley hadn't followed her to this room. The woman Louna was nowhere in sight, though she heard shuffling footsteps creeping along the floor in echoes from other parts of the house. She would dare to explore if it didn't mean being locked in again if she were discovered. The general hadn't said she could roam this house, and looking around the room at the clutter of furniture shapes and dusted drapery, she didn't think anything would be different elsewhere anyway. Going outside, even in the sunlight, would get her lost.

Going out in the dark had led her to a church. She thought of the eye sockets on Father Bari's skull. They still seemed to be looking at her when she shut her own eyes. His grin was gap-toothed. Gone were the dark skin and wide cheekbones, and any of his reassurances that he had the best interest of her people in his heart. If Captain Jarrett had a right to be angry at the priest's death, how much right did she have too? Here she was, in this general's house, prevented from returning home.

Unless she taught. Unless she did the impossible.

She didn't know where to start or where it would end. But eventually she heard a carriage roll up outside and below her window. Seconds later the door opened and shut from the lower level and she knew it was the captain. Boot steps sounded up the stairs. He had a long stride, one with purpose. She stared at the door. It was unlocked. Where had he gone, and was he going to take her to another church or to some other aspect of this city? Would it look different under the bright sun like the Land tended to be? She wasn't sure she wanted to see these buildings and these people without the cover of darkness or clouds.

Captain Jarrett's march went straight past her door. A few moments later another door down the hall opened and shut.

The Boot People were strange indeed.

The captain didn't come out of his room. Sjenn heard Louna and other female voices calling to him through his door, then mumbling among themselves as they drifted past her room. She kept her door shut and nobody talked to her, had seemed to forget she was there. She supposed as long as she wasn't running out of the house they didn't care. She was tempted and had to shut her eyes a few times to place herself somewhere open, if only in her mind. But they were just images, and the middle light continued to be distant. She could not conjure her Dog when her body would be so unguarded. So instead she mashed the heels of her hands against her eyes and breathed in deep.

After many heartbeats she ate another biscuit and stood by the door, looking at the doorknob. The general didn't return, and Keeley was nowhere to be heard. The sky darkened outside at a steady pace, pouring in violet light that she watched crawl across the floor toward her position by the bedroom door. Soon she wouldn't be able to see her way unless she lit the lamps. But they had left nothing for her to light them with.

She opened the door. There was one narrow window at the end of the hall by the top of the stairs, but Louna or one of the other women must have lit the lamp cones on the long wall. Sjenn picked her way down the hallway toward what she assumed was Captain Jarrett's room, right at the back corner of the house. It was where his bootsteps had seemed to disappear. Sense said that she ought to leave him alone, but how would she ever go home again if this man didn't help her? She couldn't count on the general. She couldn't trust either of them. But Jarrett Fawle was the one she had to teach. They shared a confusion at least.

She stared at the door, then leaned and put her ear against it. No sound. Bending down she saw no light through the gap between the door and the floor. Perhaps he was sleeping. But it had been a long time, from day to night, and the scurry of servants back and forth. They would not enter, out of fear or respect, or maybe this was something he had done before. And maybe the door was locked.

Sjenn knocked twice with the heel of her hand. "Captain Jarrett."

The creak of a body rolling over on a mattress filtered through the wood of the door. She pressed her palm to the flat surface. Knock again?

"Captain Jarrett, your father's women are worried." She squinted at the grain. "He wants reports." If they didn't somehow do something, maybe the general would become frustrated and throw her back in the prison. She would not go back there because this Kabliw captain couldn't rouse himself.

"Bugger them," came the reply, barely heard. It sounded thick.

She put her hand on the cool metal doorknob and turned. It opened.

He had the curtains drawn and nothing but shadows greeted her, some gray, some dusk, some black and impossible to discern one from another. If she were in her Dog she could move into that black with the vision of the middle light. But as it was she stood in the doorway, still holding to the knob, and peered toward the bed. Just enough illumination bent into the room so she could see where it was, at the right of the covered window. And on the bed lay Captain Jarrett, facedown, his boots hanging off the end of the mattress.

"Captain."

"I'm asleep," he said.

"You're not asleep." Why did he claim something so obviously a lie?

"I'm asleep."

He didn't tell her to go away. She ventured farther inside. The closer she got to the bed, the stronger the smell became. She knew that sharp, faintly sweet scent. Some kind of alcohol, maybe even a smoke drug too. She'd seen the Kabliw sailors on the shores when she'd sneaked in Dog form near their encampments. Kabliw in their makeshift cabins, with their raucous behavior, and all of the trash they left behind.

She got as far as a foot beside the bed before his hand shot out and caught the front of her dress, yanking her down toward him.

She yelped and tried to balance, but his hold was hard and her body smashed into the edge of the bed. Both her hands found the warm material of his frock coat—he still wore his coat as he lay abed—and shoved. He held on.

"Let go!" The thin material of the dress started to tear. She didn't shove again.

She wanted to open her mouth and Call the Dog. Its teeth would tear into this restraining arm.

The fist bunched in her dress opened out. Her resistance cast her to the floor, hard. She sprang up, anger recoiling, closed her own fist and knocked at where she saw the shadow edges of his shoulder.

His hand flung out again. From its fingers came the glint of steel. The blade sliced the air and she stepped back, stumbling once again to the floor.

"Get away from me, demon." His voice was a low murmur, not the bark of retaliation she expected. It made her freeze, leaning back on the hard floor, her heels digging into the worn rug that scratched the edges of her skin. The Dog inclination paused too. The captain's eyes were feral green and not entirely sober or sane. She saw them through the dim light. "Why've you come?"

The light behind her shoulder from the hallway blotted out. She looked up and around in time to see Keeley stride in, yellow skins and dark Kabliw jacket casting opposite light in the folds and creases—yellow lines on the black, and black on the yellow. He reached down and grabbed her up, even as she struggled with him too. It was enough of a fight that once she was on her feet he let her go but set behind his shoulder.

"You get out as well," the captain said, still brandishing the blade. It was longer than a *sul,* nearly the length of her forearm. A soldier's weapon.

"You're drunk," Keeley said.

"Thank you," the captain said. "I wasn't sure." His arm dipped. The knife clattered to the floor.

"When is his father coming back?" Sjenn asked the abo.

"I don't know. He didn't say, did he?"

"How far is this place he goes to?"

"Far," Captain Jarrett mumbled, dragging himself to sit up. His head lowered as his hands grasped the edges of the bed. Even in shadow Sjenn saw him sway a little in that movement, even sitting down. "It'll take him at least a day and a half to get there and the same to return. If he's going to see the Patronael, that alone can last for days."

"What's the Pat—" She eyed the dagger on the floor. "Patronael?"

"The Boot People chiefs," Keeley said.

"Well, that's as good a description as any," Jarrett said.

"What is a chief?"

They both looked at her.

"Leader," Keeley said. "Like your *ankago*. But without the—"

"My people don't have your demon magic," the captain said. "Now the both of you get out. I feel cursed already." He lurched to his feet, heading toward the corner of his room.

Sjenn moved out of the way. He ignored her and aimed for the mirror and washbasin set against the far wall. Before anybody could stop her she took one step and scooped up the dagger and ran from the bedroom.

"Sjenn!" Keeley called after her.

Perhaps this had been the reason that had drawn her to the captain's room in the first place. Now she had a weapon. Stolen, but so was she. This weapon wasn't her Dog but it would do. She ran into her room and shut the door behind her, leaning hard against it.

"She took my bloody Trant!" Even through the muffle of the wood she heard the captain's protest. Sounds traveled easily between these thin walls, knocking back and forth against the hard surfaces of the Kabliw world.

"You shouldn't have dropped it," came the reply from Keeley.

She thought about dragging the small chest of drawers over in front of the door. Footsteps stomped close before she could move, though, so she kept her back pressed to the door as the captain knocked, then rattled the knob.

"Where do you think you'll go with my Trant?" He

talked through the wood as if he were standing right behind her ear. His voice wasn't loud.

"I have nothing," she said back. "The general took my furs, your priest took me from the Land. I have nothing!"

She expected a shout, another bang from the other side. More footsteps as Keeley maybe joined him and both of them tried to thrust the door open on her.

But instead only the captain's voice sounded again. "That's not my fault. But that is my blade and I want it back."

She held the leather-bound hilt and looked down at it. In the glow of moonlight she could just discern round engravings on the long metal sheen. They meant nothing to her, were not words she could read, if they were even words. They looked like decoration.

"Open the door," Captain Jarrett said. He didn't sound drunk at all now.

"No," she said.

They could wonder. They could beat this door down if they wanted, and even if she knew she would somehow have to return this stolen thing to the man, for now at least she could pretend she had some power over this possession. For just a little while she could think she had control.

Sleep was restless and on the floor again, right in front of the door. They didn't break it down, force their way in, and strip her of the weapon. But as daylight began to crawl across the dusty boards at her feet, touching the edge of one discarded slipper, she knew they also would not let it go. Any more than they would let her go. Her back ached from the curled position sitting up against the door all night. It was just dawn, weak light, changing from deep purple to the pink haze of new flesh. Newborn skin being cast over the bone antlers of this world. Could this city shed its sparring horns long enough to let her pass? Dog thoughts wandered through her mind. She could almost smell the caribou in the warm air. It was too warm, but her mouth felt dry. She hadn't eaten a thing all day yesterday but the biscuits and some water. When the doorknob turned again above her head, she hadn't the strength to push back.

The arch of the door moved her aside by small force. She crawled a little out of the way. The blade slid from the pillow of her lap to the floor beside her and she reached to pick it up. But swift steps inside jarred her thigh and Keeley knelt beside her, his hand clamping around the hilt of the blade.

"You don't need this," he said.

What did he know? This was his world far more than it would ever be hers. But she released the dagger.

"Where is he?" She was surprised the captain hadn't come to fetch his blade himself.

"Asleep. Passed out." The Whishishian paused. "Dreaming."

She stared into the gold eyes. So the Kabliw dreamed. "I'm hungry," she said.

"You should eat."

"Not this food." She drew back from him as he still knelt there, and pulled her knees up beneath her dress. "Will he be mad?"

"The captain is often mad," Keeley said. "Or so his father says."

"How can you tolerate them? How can you live here? I want to go home."

She would have liked to have heard his honest answers, but perhaps he had lived too long among the Kabliw. His Boot People. He didn't answer at all. Even so, she thought that was better than a lie.

After Keeley left with the blade, Louna brought warm water for her bath. The fat woman even brought food, most of which she couldn't eat. There were more biscuits and some fruit: an apple and a pear. She knew these things from the ship. There was a thin soup with a flavor she didn't know, but it was good enough to drink. The ham and eggs she left alone, as well as the cheese. She didn't like how it smelled. She ate before she had her bath, and Louna brought a new dress too, a dark one that sat looser and felt heavier. It itched and Sjenn took it off immediately and put the other back on, even if it was worn from her wearing. The day got warmer as she sat on the bed, her legs pulled up, waiting for the reason she was here in the first place. The captain had to come in at some point. They both knew the inevitable.

When he did, knocking only once, he strode straight to the window and threw it open. She thought he wanted to take another walk through the iron stairs, but he said something about needing the breeze and just left the glass open. A small wind made the curtains billow, and it felt good as it reached her on the bed.

Curiously, he said, "You look better."

His hair floated away at the edges, as if drawn to something in the air, and there were shadows beneath his eyes. He wore no jacket, just a plain gray shirt, one half untucked from his trousers.

"You look bad," she said.

"The abo returned my Trant," he said with a frown. "You take it again and I'll hurt you. Understand me?"

"Grab me again," she said, "and I'll take it again."

"You're the one who entered my room."

"You're the one I have to teach. If we don't go about it your father will hurt *me,* not you. I *won't* go back to that jail."

This was a dogfight. She'd seen them around the sleds, sometimes angry with each other. Circling. Snapping. Her own Dog coiled in her chest, but it had been a long time since she Called. Since she felt it truly answer her. In her dreams it was silent. And the middle light was a distant land. Like the Aniw shores. Her father had fallen silent in her last sleep, and this morning she had no patience for the Kabliw. The desperation of the ship still grabbed her in this daylight.

"You can be very good with Sarrish," Captain Jarrett said.

"Your priest was a good teacher."

It was a fact, but she suspected how he heard it. A reminder. The skull and bones. Let him remember whom she had killed if that would keep him at bay. Let him feel even a little fear, a little hesitation as he stared at the tattoos on her face.

"How are you going to teach me? You said it was impossible."

This was the bigger risk. She had to trust him.

"I need my Dog."

"What does that mean?" He still hadn't moved from the window. The gap of space between them was far enough neither of them could easily touch, even to stretch.

"I need to Call it. And you need to let me. And when I am finished you need to Call it back." She thought suddenly of her cousin Twyee, her guardian. Ice fishing. Wrestling the dogs. Jumping the ice and laughing.

Captain Jarrett was speaking and she hadn't heard.

"I have to see you from the middle light," she said, overriding his words. What he thought didn't matter now. "I have to see you with those eyes. And you will trust that I won't kill you, that my Dog will not."

It was a shallow victory to see the doubt on his face. She didn't need his blade to make him afraid.

She thought this desire to scare him was enough to make her own spirit ashamed. But all the same she didn't take it back. She needed only to remember both the iron bars on the ship and the stone room his father had trapped her in. She needed only to remember, even vaguely, the way her Dog had raged.

Despite what war sat between Captain Jarrett and the abo man, the captain called in Keeley for the ritual song. They both were afraid of her Dog; they had seen it in full fur, guarding her body even shackled by chains. They were wise to fear it, and she told them that so long as they made no threat toward her body once she was separated, she could control her Dog in the middle light, at least enough so it wouldn't kill them. She was rested, fed, and alert. Not like how it had been on the ship or the prison.

They didn't understand what the middle light was, but this wasn't the time to explain. If she couldn't see the captain from her Dog's eyes, then there would be no progress as the general wished it.

Both men looked unsure, but she turned away from them and lay down on the bed.

"Stand by the door," Jarrett Fawle ordered the abo, and without argument Keeley went.

"Put your knife away," she said, staring at the blade now in the captain's hand.

"If the animal attacks me—"

"She will attack you if she sees the knife." She tried to steady her breaths, the Call already winding through her mind. It would be a home, going back to the middle light, reaching out to touch the power of the dark light so it could guide her. Even if it left her body exposed. She wanted to go. "My Dog urged me to kill that man Stoan for the gun in his hand. Put it away."

The captain obeyed. She pressed her shoulders back to the bed and took a deep breath. Lying down was easiest, even if she felt at a small disadvantage with the two strange men not very far from her, standing with weapons somewhere in their clothes. She couldn't see Keeley's, but she assumed he had one if the general allowed him to carry one in this house. She had nothing but the dark light and the strength of her Call, but they both could be strong persuasions in any Kabliw argument or threat.

She stared up at the ceiling away from them. Sunlight cut the rough surface above her into triangles. Sun or moon, her Dog would roam. All it needed was the middle light.

Sjenn began to sing. The liquid she'd drunk that

morning and the warmth of the bathwater had soothed her throat. Her Call was steady. Her eyes fluttered shut, and from deep in her chest the animal stretched, coaxed by the dark light and her words.

The Dog was waiting. And she was impatient.

Men. She smells them before she sees them, two tall figures across this small space. Nervous, their sweat evaporates in the air, but not before she catches the scent. They are the same men from before, in the jail, but she doesn't have her anger here. The body of her Sjenn lies beneath her; she stands above it, solid, and the body is solid in its familiar outlines. It stretches like a foundation and she feels it to be home. Still calling to her in echoes that her sensitive ears can hear. Though the mouth doesn't move and the face is serene even to her eyes, the song still travels through the length of her bones, along every muscle to stroke every sinew. The lines on the opposite face are brightest to her, glowing like the sun. She knows sun, even in the middle light.

She turns her own face to look at the men and they become motionless. Not even breath. So they can see her. Standing still, she can be seen.

She leaps off the bed and shakes out her fur. They step back, and this allows her to dip her nose and sniff along the floor. New scents. Wood she knows. Wood like this comes with the hands of man. Cut, pounded, shaved, glossed. It doesn't interest her after a while and she looks up again. The men are gray like winter dusk, and everywhere the real light touches seems to shimmer like rays along the sea waves of her home. Silver and gold and violet shade all angles of this room. This is the world wherein she can breathe.

Her lips pull back, tongue snaking out, and the air is cool to taste, though warmer than she's used to. She's traveled. Her body, her Sjenn, has traveled far.

She walks around the edges of this room. It's much different from the other one, which had been dark and cold. Where the chains had been. Here she is free. At the window, the source of the air, she sets her paws on the sill and peers out. All seems too bright, trails of motion leaving imprints along the vista. Her gaze maps it out. There are hundreds of lines, more than she's ever seen before. Ears prick forward. The Land doesn't speak here, but there are different echoes.

"Is it going to jump?" A voice behind her.

She sets down from the window and turns, tail swishing once as the man closest to her—the one whose voice she knows from a different place—takes another step backward.

"It heard you," says the shorter man. But she ignores that one.

The tall one has golden eyes in her sight, even if some vague human memory recalls the clear green of them. In the middle light, through her sight, he has gold eyes and a darkness around his edges. His companion is solid like ice, though warm liquid streams and swirls within the confines of his form. Familiar to her, like most of the People. Her People. But the tall one is a trapped outline, as if someone has marked his spirit with the lampblack *ankago* symbols. It sews him up far tighter than a tattoo. He cannot be released as he is. Curious man.

She paces closer.

He steps back until his shoulders almost hit the dead flat form of the wall behind him.

Strange man, to be so stitched together. *Unravel him.* She growls at him to hear him speak again. But the sound seems to make him quieter.

So she leaps at him, knocking him back on the chest with her paws. He cries out and falls, they both crash down, and when the other man takes a step she turns and snaps at him until he backs off.

The one beneath her paws reaches for the weapon in his coat. She can see it through the material, the hard outline that is not of the Land or any animal. Her jaws clamp around his wrist before he can withdraw it, but not hard enough to tear him up. She only wants to hear him speak.

"My gods! Keeley!"

Her claws dig into the wood floor as he struggles. He grabs at the fur at her flank, but she twists away, teeth and jaws locked. Snarling. Will he not speak?

"Get it off me! Shoot it!"

"Bullets do no good. Stop moving!"

His sleeve tears against her fangs. Skin scrapes. Men are salty. He stops moving.

She growls again, but through the sound she can hear his harsh breaths. Her ears twitch back, close to her skull. She looks him in the eyes.

There is a Brother deep within him. She can see him move behind his human gaze, a scared little thing that does not know that he is even bound. It's in the tone of the man's voice, the scent of his fear. Somewhere behind the simple outlines of his spirit, his *little* spirit wanders around in circles. It paces the same puppy pathways, but it possesses the light of power. It senses the middle light. Like any Dog, it senses its own boundaries, where man fades away and animal breaks free.

She lets him go, tongue lapping out to flicker across her nose and teeth. Strange to find a kin in this place, but somewhere in her long memory, back through the age of ancestors, she is not surprised. Once there had been no such things as men. Once she'd had no need of them at all.

She looks to the window again, where the sounds pick up now that she pays attention. Unfamiliar animal scents tickle at the back of her tongue and the inside of her nostrils, even touching the points of her short whiskers.

"What do you want?" he asks her. He still lies on the floor like a subservient pup.

Infant god, does he not know what he can be?

She has no interest in teaching him. He isn't of her kin or her kind.

In two strides she runs toward the window and jumps out.

Her paws touch grass below with small impact, as neither air nor heights restrict her. She wants the ground, and the middle light delivers it to her. This is her world and it has no boundaries. One more leap takes her over the iron gate, and the street here spreads before her with empty wonder.

Eventually she finds people and the filth of their existence, far more than any Aniw camp, more even than the sailors who touched and cluttered the shores of the Land. Through the din she wanders, beneath the legs of the tall stinking creatures that are as faded light as her puppy kin. The puppy kin she sees too, skulking in the shadows of brick structures that are as opposite to the snowhouses as she can imagine in the generations of memories flowing in her mind. Her Sjenn knew the horses and the scent now becomes permanent, affixed to the image of these long-legged things with nervous demeanor and streaming tails. They don't like her. Some rear at her passing and the men around them curse. She knows curses, but they don't know to curse *her*.

Farther she roams, slipping through the middle light so that she is mere shadow to the eyes of the unseeing. Movement makes her a flutter to the gaze of man and she is swift, slipping along the rough walls, beneath tables in bustling markets, past the pigs groveling for tossed bits of vegetables and fruits in the wet, fuming gutters. Iron carriage wheels rumble by, gigantic omnibuses with people sitting atop like *hokis* of the tundra, their heads bobbing up and down with the motion of their going. She hunted *hokis* back on the Land and avoided the bears like she does these buses. The wind of their passing scrapes the end of her tail as she dodges them, unfrightened.

They can't touch her. She is curious and free.

A pack of little brothers and sisters hide from her in the alley, beneath cords of draped clothing spanning one building to the next. This area of the city holds the scent of blood and waste deep in its crevices, between brick and mortar, flowing through the drainage tunnels beneath her paws, rumbling from the depths of the basements and fire hearths. Even in the broad daylight there is darkness here in the way the men and women walk briskly from place to place, or in the way some of them don't move at all. Those lean in doorways with the slow movement of disrepair or uncaring, spitting out tendrils of smoke into the choked, warm air. They don't look at her, she's just another shadow at the corners of their eyes. The gas lamps are a dead gray, as yet unlit.

She spies a couple of the puppy kin nosing beneath damp, torn newspaper at the mouth of the alley. When they see her they dart back deeper into violet shadow. They don't even snarl at her, don't think to contest her presence in their territory. But the little brothers and sisters never did understand the true nature of territory. That is why they commingle with men without demand.

Still, she pads toward them, crossing the cobbled street, much emptier here than from where she first came, as if most in the city avoid the boundaries around these four wide corners.

The puppy kin scatter to opposite ends of the alley as soon as she enters in. They can always see her, just as the dogs of the Land and unlike the two-legged inhabitants of either North or South. Dogs are simpler, sometimes sweeter spirits that can be easier to please and more quickly driven off than others of her own kind. These Southern dogs are unkempt; one has spots along his back, dun colored. The other is a black, long-legged male with a blaze of white on his chest. She sees ribs and scents old blood. He stares at her, quiet, then barks once.

It's been a long time since she's been among even the distant cousins of her ancestors. They are strangers, but then, she is a stranger here too.

She walks closer, twice their size in full fur, and to

them, curiously absent of familiar scent. The middle light bathes her in the cold and prickly ice smell of her home. They're confused, but some rituals are the same. The black one stands his ground and she noses his side, nuzzling along the short fur toward his tail. Soon the second spotted dog joins in, and after a few moments, a couple more that lurk at the back of the alley creep forward, willing to share. To know. They are awed by her.

In the empty space where her People should be, she finds some solace in these gentle few.

It's simply a matter of remembering—where the place is that she had left so many hours ago as this world marks time. As the gas lamps along the streets cast their milk-white light to the cobbles, she lopes her way back to the house with the solid instinctive ability of any Aniw. It is in their blood. All she needs are the landmarks of scent and the familiar signs of the middle light, telling her that she has been here before. Her own passing affects the middle light, makes it shift and glow in memory of her presence, and so she tracks her own paws back to where her Sjenn's body lies bound.

She cannot pass through the iron gate, so must jump above it, but the red bricks of this house are no barrier, just as sea ice and tundra hills are nothing but terrain, neither obstruction nor enemy. In the middle light all are impassive.

Walking forward, she passes through the door like smoke, and with swift steps she casts herself up the stairs and down the hall. The door stands open to the room wherein the human body waits. She runs in and jumps up to the bed to sit, tail curled around her hindquarters, and the two men in the room give a great start. One sits at the small desk by the window. The other sits on the end of the bed—the tall one, whose little spirit coils and retreats as she appears near him. He presses a hand to his chest as if it pains him, and then to the side of his head.

She turns away from him and looks down at the body. It's untouched. Dipping low, she nuzzles the side of Sjenn's face, bringing the scent of the city with her. But of course her Aniw doesn't move. She looks toward the man at the desk, tail thumping once on the bed, ears canted forward.

"It might want to return," he says to the other. To the pale frightened one.

"How can you tell?"

"It waits. Maybe you should begin the Call."

He rises from the bed, away from her. Rubbing the wrist she had seized. "I'll get the Father's journal."

After he leaves, footsteps fading down the hall, the other man regards her with eyes deep gold in the middle light. Almost the same color as the tall one, though they are much different in form. He flows faster when he stands, the running rivers that make up his body cycling like wind-whipped snowdrifts from the center of his chest. No little spirit within him, but he has, in moments, the calm colors of the People she has come to love.

"Where did you go?" He moves closer, slowly.

She licks her fangs, yawning.

"Where did you go, great spirit?" His voice is quiet. Close enough now to reach out, his fingers trace a soft line down the back of her neck.

She tilts her head, then snaps at his hand, but not to bite. Just to warn. Just to see the way he pulls back, cautioned and humbled.

She yawns again. He strokes between her ears and this time she lets him. He is careful, and she watches his free hand and how it holds still by his side. Empty. Soon the touches begin to draw her eyes shut. The world of men pulls at her, though between blinks she still feels the gray and violet haze of the middle light. But there are some gifts to being close to men. She discovered this long ago.

When the tall one returns he stops in the doorway. The blunt silence of shock creeps out from his stance.

"You're mad," he says.

The man ceases his strokes and steps away.

She growls a bit at the tall one. She's seen madness and this isn't it. But she has no language for the memory that they will understand, or that she would want to tell them.

Sjenn waits for her. She knows in this calm that it's time, and as the Kabliw man opens up his leather-bound book she stands upon the bed, over the body of her Aniw descendent. There is no reason to fight as yet, no explanation she has to give for her wandering the city. Perhaps Sjenn will remember, perhaps not in detail. When the tall man begins to Call, his little spirit adds its voice to the words.

It's a voice older than where she's wandered, older even than the Land that she remembers, as if she can simply go back there in a blink. Perhaps one day. The voice is sweet to her. It is one of her own.

Just like this body is one of her own, from ages as

the ice moves. She has ties to this body, and she looks down upon it. The circles and lines upon its face invite her to kiss. To taste the salt skin. And when she does, the middle light converges upon her, engulfs her, entering through her fur and her own skin. Her eyes, nose, and jaws.

And then it slowly, gently, pulls her apart.

It was a soft awakening, the way her Dog slipped back to curl inside her like the little spirit it was, nestling against her own. She drew a deep breath, seeing the ceiling once again. The angle of the light had changed. The lamps were lit and the shadows had emerged. Shadows with long edges and patterns unlike any she'd seen on the Land. For a few moments she simply breathed and blinked at the ceiling before she became aware that Captain Jarrett and Keeley were both still in the room.

She saw the captain first as he stood by the foot of the bed, the priest's journal in his hands, a wild look in his eyes. Despite the shape of the Trant dagger pressed into the side of his frock coat, she was no longer afraid of him in any way. Something simpler traced his Kabliw edges. She wanted to reach out for a quick heartbeat and see if she could touch this new strangeness, but Keeley spoke.

"You ran off. Where did you go?"

Her mind and gaze flitted to the window. Yes, she remembered that.

"Out there. Out to your city." She pushed herself up to one hand. "Water, please."

The abo fetched it for her from the jug on the desk. She held the glass in both hands and sipped.

"What did you see?" Captain Jarrett asked, the more important question.

It drew her attention and she stopped drinking. It was in his voice, she knew now. She remembered that like a childhood recollection. It wasn't entirely clear, and there was more emotion behind it than solid images. He was a frightened little thing that had a voice he didn't yet know how to fully use. So had her father called her when she was a small girl, barely able to hold a *sul*. "I've seen the puppy god," he'd said with a smile. And she'd known then that she would someday be her tribe's *ankago*.

This Kabliw man was not of her people, though. How did he hold a Dog at all?

"What did you see?" he repeated with more urgency.

"You," she said. "I saw you and your Dog."

He shook his head. Keeley stared at him.

"My sight is pure in the middle light," she said.

"What is the middle light?"

"It's the world in which my Dog exists. It's the world of the spiritwalkers, the world of my ancestors."

"I'm not of your people," Jarrett Fawle said and gestered to the abo. "*He's* closer to your people somehow than I would ever be. So that's impossible."

"Are you certain," Keeley said, "that your father was faithful to your mother?"

Even awake her sight doubled slightly, tendrils from the middle light that would fade the longer her Dog slept. So she saw the blood lines trace between both men and reached to grab the captain as he made for the abo man in threat.

Her fingers clawed the back of his coat, pulling him up short. His arm knocked her back.

"Be still!" she shouted.

It alarmed them both so much it stopped them—Captain Jarrett from his attack and Keeley from his stance of defense, one hand inside his jacket.

"I meant it only as a question," the abo said, calm.

"I know who my mother is," Jarrett said. "So shut your savage mouth."

"I saw what I saw," Sjenn murmured, then louder when the men continued to stare at each other. "I can teach you."

The captain kept shaking his head. "No."

"It's what your father wants."

"It's not what I want," he said.

"I can teach you," she said. And stopped herself.

"But?" Keeley said. And she wondered again what stake he had in any of this; was his interest just loyalty to a man who seemed to have his own selfish concerns?

"But," she said, "I don't know that my Dog will."

She remained on the bed after they left, but her sleep was restless. Captain Jarrett insisted she was somehow wrong, that there would be no "training," and nothing she nor Keeley said convinced him. Maybe he'd change his mind once the general returned. Keeley believed her. She remembered his soft hand on the back of her neck, when she was in the middle light. She wanted to ask him about his people and what their *ankago* did for his tribe. He called them *janna*. Were they somehow cousins to the Aniw? How could they possess a Dog as well?

But he left her alone after Captain Jarrett disappeared to somewhere else in the house, and all around fell silent save for the distant noise on the street outside her open window, the echoes of the horses and women's light footsteps. Heels on cobblestones. Though it hadn't been her skin and body out among the city streets, she decided to take another bath. With the water warm she didn't think she'd get sick, and Louna and one of the other servant girls were willing to help. They protested her return to the same dress, but she pulled it on anyway. It felt a little more familiar now, though it was a skin she would prefer to exchange for the soft rub of the seal's.

Beneath the covers with the lamp down low, she told herself that tomorrow she had a focus. Despite what the general might want, she now knew there were *ankago* in the South. Tribal and Kabliw. Even if her own Dog felt disinterested, the thought of these strangers possessing the same power made her sleep uncomfortable.

The white bear emerged again in her dreams, and her father was nowhere in sight. Instead, on the icy shores of her home lay the long boxes of guns she'd first seen weeks ago. What were those soldiers doing now, with her so long away? Not even Father Bari had had an answer. Her family had wept when she was taken away, but against men with guns they could do nothing.

The bear remembered. In her dream it paced along the rocky water's edge and nudged the boxes until they upended. On the horizon countless more ships floated

on the sea, their tall dark sails making spearpoint silhouettes. Waiting.

For three days Captain Jarrett avoided her. He left in the
mornings and returned at night, once drunk, the other
two times sober but quiet and absent. Keeley lurked about
the house, doing what exactly Sjenn didn't know and
could not pin him down long enough to ask. Now that
she was curious about his tribe he seemed disinterested
in being near her. Perhaps he was afraid, despite the
willingness to respect her Dog. Perhaps he followed the
captain in the other man's wanderings. She herself moved
from the dining room to her bedroom to the "solarium"
(as Louna called it), and often out to the backyard to
take in the air and see more than four walls. The walls
made it hard to breathe sometimes unless she shut her
eyes.

The days had warmed considerably since her release
from the jail, and it tired her early in the evenings when
the first traces of moon began to overpower the sun. Venture into the city she could not, though she sat in the front
sitting room looking out at all the many carriages and
people flowing past in the day. When Louna drifted in to
bring her a simple white tea, she asked the woman why
the tall men and women in their dark coats seemed to be
going in circles.

"Circles, child?"

No matter how many times she told Louna that she
wasn't a child, the plump woman continued to call her so.
So she had stopped saying it.

"They go down the walk." Sjenn pointed out the

window. "Then they disappear around the corner and come back around."

Louna seemed perplexed. "Ay, they do not. Why would anyone think t'do such a ting?"

Sjenn turned from her and stared out the window. "These are all different people?"

"Of course?" Louna said. Though her voice tilted upward, there was no question in her look when Sjenn glanced at her. Just amusement.

Sjenn looked back out again. This Kabliw city was larger than she could imagine. In the darkness of her rooftop trek it had been difficult to see how far they had gone. There had been so many turns and angles. But now this new knowledge, coupled with the shadows of what her Dog had seen, made her heart contract. She almost saw it in her hand, the way she looked into the guts and pink things of a seal she'd just slaughtered. This was her bare heart in her hand, and it struggled to be heard.

It seemed impossible that it could be heard in the clatter and bang of this world. Did every one of these Kabliw have a gun—man, woman, and child alike? Would they all eventually come to Aniw shores?

The deception of the day's sun sank beyond her remembered horizon. There was no tundra here, not among these dirty buildings and likely not beyond them either, on their outer borders. Every way stood blocked.

The fourth night Captain Jarrett came to her door because she was pacing. He had locked her in again, as he had every night, and as soon as it opened she shoved by him and down the hall.

"Sjenn!"

She ran down the stairs and out the front door. She knew he would chase her but it couldn't be helped. Outside. The night closed in as sure as the walls, and she shut her eyes, clutching the iron bars of the gate. She tried to think of herself out somewhere open, where turning your head didn't mean you'd meet a wall. But every breath pulled in the scents of this city, the dirt and dead things wafting in from over the tops of buildings and through the heavy doors. It didn't matter that these streets were clean. The wind carried it all, like it could on the Land when nothing obstructed it.

"Where do you think you're going?" His voice approached behind.

She kept her eyes closed. "I don't want your world."

"Well, you're stuck with it."

"I can't breathe here!" She let go of the gate and turned around, pressing her back to it, to feel the cool lines through the dress. Not quite like lying on the ice, but better than too much heat, the sticky pull of the dress when the day was at its height.

"Why can't you breathe? Just slow yourself down." He stood more than an arm's length away, white-shirted under the gaslights, untucked as usual. He seemed not to care when the general was still away. He was unshaven and untrustworthy, and these were the first words he'd spoken to her in four days.

"Your world is a box." She gestured up to the house. "You live in boxes with lids. You keep yourselves in. This isn't my world!"

"I can't help that. You're here now."

Her heart ran, but it had nowhere to go.

"Come back inside," he said. She noticed his eyes flicker to the shadows and the pools of lights, as if he expected a wolf to leap out at any moment. Or perhaps he feared other people.

"No," she said.

"Sjenn, you must come back inside. You can't run away, you'd get lost."

"I'm lost here." She hadn't really thought to run off when she had the desperate need for air. But now she turned about again and peered through the bars to the slant of buildings across the street. Quiet street, blank windows. It was late. "Out there I would be lost and free."

"They'd kill you within the week. You'd go somewhere that you weren't supposed to and they would kill you. Not every Kabliw would feed and clothe you. As much of a bastard as my father is, he did that much at least."

"He won't let me go home."

"Well," the captain said. "He won't let me either."

She heard his footsteps approach. He wore slippers too, not his normal boots. They barely made a shuffle and scuff on the grass behind her. Then he stood next to her by the gate, enough of a distance away that she could not claw at him.

She was too tired right now to strike out, even if she'd wanted to do that. But he was mild. He had no dagger. His clothes were loose.

"Isn't this your house? Where your father lives?"

"After a fashion." He took a deeper breath and looked across the street where she had been staring. "But I haven't really lived here for years and years. My home's out there." His chin nodded up.

"Where?"

"Out beyond the city. Far, far beyond this putrefied city."

"I don't know that word."

"The dead city," he said.

"But you're Kabliw."

"Not all Kabliw like it in Nev Anyan. Or Lacamb. Or Terrez and Sairvil and Nev Junyu…"

All names she didn't know.

"Those are cities in Ciracusa," he said. "Nev Anyan is the biggest, but there are other, smaller ones. Ciracusa is…all of this. And out there. Where I call home there are no cities, per se. There's just land."

She looked at him closer. He still stared outward. "I come from the Land. Is there snow in your land?"

"Sometimes. But I doubt it's anything like your kind of snow." Now he met her eyes, peering down at her with that narrowed gaze as if he couldn't quite pinpoint her stare. "Father Bari had said that you have different types of snow. Is this true?"

"Yes. There isn't one type of weather, so there isn't just one type of snow. Some snow builds houses, others just fall. They fall differently depending on the wind. They feel different."

It was more than she'd wanted to say, but talking of home made her think of it and it made the breathing easier. She thought of her mother sewing up mittens and Bernikka making faces when Uncle snored too loud. She thought of Twyee's laugh.

"He really loved your people, you know," the captain said. "Bari truly did."

Though she didn't want to hear that, she knew it to be true.

"He liked to tell stories of this place," she said, instead of agreeing outright. "He showed me a map once, but I didn't understand it. I don't remember everything he said. But sometimes the things he said scared me and my father, and my grandfather. Sometimes we didn't want him around but we invited him into our great snowhouse anyway. Because he was always kind to us and liked to hear our stories too."

"That was his way."

"I'm sorry he's dead sometimes." Sometimes she wasn't, and it was hard to admit. "But my Dog..."

Captain Jarrett looked away again at the mention of the Dog. And she became fully aware of the iron gate once more and how far from home she truly was—as far as he claimed he was from his too. But perhaps it was a false empathy. He could still turn around and see the faces of his own people.

"I really can't understand any of this, you know," he said, just quiet enough for his voice to reach her and no farther. "Your magic."

"It's not magic."

"Then what is it? Religion?"

"No." If she had to teach so she could go home, she had to try to make him believe. "We call it the dark light. It's just the truth of my people. It's the power of our Land. My ancestors were great spirits, and long ago they mingled with the Aniw. They loved us and we loved them. And from their spirits come the *ankago*. The little spirits were the first of this world, and they will live forever through the *ankago*. They are my ancestors."

"But they're wolves. Dogs."

"No." She didn't know if he would ever understand, but there sat that little spirit in his own form, somehow, and it was too caged. "They appear as dogs. And dogs have always been a great help and companion to my people. But they are not dogs. That's just their form, like your form is this." She gestured to his body. "And mine is this." She tapped her own chest. "Why is one stranger than the other? This world is full of different forms, from your horses to your cats and birds. Like my bears and whales and walrus. You have gods that are in your form as well. Why that form and no other?"

He was silent, thinking. His gaze unfocused. "I don't know," he said finally. "I'm not a very religious person. I used to get in arguments..." He didn't finish it. "My father told me to read the history of my people. From before we landed here on Ciracusa. He said it would help me understand you better." He shrugged a little as if this point was still undecided. "We came from a land across the ocean, you know. My ancestors. Did Father Bari ever speak of Sairland?"

The name seemed familiar, but only vaguely so. "He told me your people were at war with them. He told me once that the world was far larger than the tundra." She hadn't truly believed him until now, here among the Kabliw and their city.

"It is. My ancestors are just one of many types of people. Long ago they drove out their own and we landed here on Ciracusa. Back when this country had no name but what the abos called it." He took a breath. "I was taught that the people left because they disagreed with their king, they refused to go to war for him. But in these other readings..." He rubbed his eyes.

"What?" The disturbance in his expression confused her.

He looked down at her, one of his hands curling around the iron gate. "Some say it was because Sairland had a separation of belief. Some believed in old gods, and others believed in the Seven Deities. And so they wouldn't fight for the old gods and were driven out. But there aren't many books that give details of this, or of much that occurred before Taon Ciracusa founded this country. I would likely have to return to Sairland to discover more."

"What do you believe?" If he didn't agree with the teachings of his own people, then what was his truth?

"I don't know," he said. "And now maybe I know even less."

"You should believe in your little spirit," she said. "You should believe in your Dog."

His breath was audible then, and drawn out. "And if I don't? You say you see something in me that I don't see or believe. Then what?"

"Then your father might be angry. He might put me back in the jail. Would you let him?" She stood here talking to him as one would with a friend, though she knew better. He only wished to understand something, and if he didn't, he might not care beyond that. His moods were unpredictable, the shadows in his eyes grew darker each day.

"I mightn't be able to stop him, in all truth," he said.

What was all truth? She wanted to ask. But she didn't think he would know, even if she heard the truth in that statement. No matter what she did, there might be no good tomorrow from it.

"What do you think your father wants? Why does he want you to know your Dog?"

Captain Jarrett was silent for so long she thought he hadn't heard her. His stare remained on the street across from them, through the iron bars. "Knowing my father, he probably thinks it will give us some sort of advantage. He only ever thinks about the war. The abos and Sairland…" He pressed the heel of one hand against his forehead, as if trying to block out a sun pain. "You should've seen his face when he saw your Dog in the Hess…" The words stopped, his hand dropped. Sjenn waited but he said nothing more.

"You took me on the roofs," she said.

"Yes," he said.

She pointed out to the darkness between the pools of lamplight. "Let me take you on the streets."

"But you don't know this city."

She looked up at him. "My Dog does now."

She needed to show him, for him to be unafraid of her Dog. If he learned that, then he would be unafraid of his own. But the suggestion alone to travel out to the city at night made him dubious. Back up in her room, with the priest's book in his hands for when she needed her little spirit to return, he paced instead of standing still. A distraction. It was going to be a battle every day and every night, and the longer they battled, the longer this war. Then the general would return and be angry that he had not yet won what he wanted.

Fear drove them both, it seemed, but in different directions.

"I will try to teach you," she said, though her little spirit curled and murmured at the idea. Too soft for her to feel intention, quiet as her father in her dreams had been quiet for days. But in the middle light at least there came some clarity. Some freedom.

Captain Jarrett looked at her with eyes that sought escape. So at least they had that much in common.

❧ THE DOG

Jarrett didn't know if there existed an image more frightful than that of the animal as it emerged from the girl. It spooked him, plain and simple, where midnight storytelling and long shadows had always failed. The fact the smoke creature was formless at first, then coalesced and solidified, was something out of childhood nightmare: ghosts that comrades claimed to see on old battlegrounds, or tales he remembered the other boys in the academy recounting to scare each other when they were all supposed to be asleep. Restless spirits, angry souls. Even the Church itself had stories in the Septangent Codices, and if one were to believe in the Seven Deities, they walked the earth as well, half in it, half outside of it.

Sjenn called that realm the "middle light." Was this what the Church meant? Yet they claimed the Aniw and the abo tribes were demon believers.

He didn't know what to believe as he watched that

wolf—Dog—shake itself while it stood on the bed, as if casting off water droplets. It had bitten him and his wrist was still bruised. He knew better now and kept his blade hidden. The Dog hopped off the bed and walked around the room, just as it had the first time. Sjenn lay like a dead body on the bed. Keeley, whom Jarrett had summoned into the room again before Calling the Dog forth, walked closer to the Aniw and looked down at her.

"A shell," he murmured.

"What?" Jarrett said, tracking the Dog with sight.

"We are this without our spirits." He pointed to Sjenn.

"Father Bari wrote that they believe they have two." His words came strained. The Dog pulled half of his attention. "This thing and…the one we are all supposed to have." Though it was difficult to remember everything the old priest had recorded, especially as he'd read it all rather quickly in disbelief, trickles of words surfaced the longer he found himself in this madness.

Madness. That was one word Bari had never used in his notes.

"The spirit sleeps when the little spirit roams," Keeley said. "So it is with our *janna* too."

Jarrett didn't reply. The nature of the soul was something constantly debated among the religions, old and new. The Church claimed no commonality among the people, anywhere, but rather a superiority. Father Bari had said different.

And yet they were different. The Aniw, this abo.

You shine like the moon.

He was different. He shoved his sleeve over his mouth as the Dog paused and looked up at him.

"Captain?" Keeley said, to his silence.

"Be quiet."

But the Dog seemed unconcerned that Keeley was near the girl. Trying to understand its behavior after only a couple encounters proved fruitless, as it now loped toward him, gaze fixed. The blue eyes of the creature were striking. So unlike Sjenn's, whose gaze was a simple, open brown. His stomach gave a faint, painful lurch. It traveled up the middle of his chest until he had to force a deep breath to try to assuage it. Fear, probably. Unsteadiness. He felt them both like two creatures chewing upon his bones.

"She said she wanted to take me out there for some reason." He gestured to the window.

"Then you should go," Keeley said. "I'll sit here with her."

That was, after all, his job. So the general had said. To watch over her. Was this what he had meant all along?

There was still much that his father had not told him. He'd seemed so convinced that it was possible for Sjenn to teach him this Dog, these beliefs, and that it would somehow impact the war. And now *she* was even convinced of it, though her purpose for wanting him to learn surely was different from the general's.

But he would not know anything standing there.

"You should go," Keeley said again as the Dog turned and headed for the door. This time. Not out the window, thank the gods. It had jumped and survived. He wouldn't be so fortunate. "But be careful," the abo added. A tad unnecessary.

"If I don't come back," Jarrett said, "tell my father good riddance."

*　　*　　*

Following the Dog was more difficult than he'd antici-pated. It seemed to *want* to lose him once they were in the open street. More than once as it—she?—disappeared between the pale glow of gaslights, he had to pause to make sure she had kept a straight course and not darted off through the dark when he was looking someplace else. Silvery and quick, the Dog moved among the night deni-zens of Nev Anyan as if this were as much her domain as it was for the dippers and the crushers. He was glad he wasn't dressed in any particular fanciness, as it would cause less suspicion in these parts. He wasn't certain this Dog would come to his aid if he were attacked, or if a strolling couple policemen decided he was suspicious and decided to harass.

She traveled through the rear end of the Roog, past bird-fluffed ladies in voluminous skirts and their dark-clad gentleman companions, toward the haphaz-ard layers of the slums. Why there? he wanted to ask, but the Dog didn't wait. Strangely, nobody else cast an eye to the animal as it dodged legs and carriage wheels, or the occasional wooden walking stick, even when an animal that size and color was never before seen in Nev Anyan.

Was he the only one to see her, then? The flick of the thick tail and the white paws appeared to flash as they hit the puddles of light along the cobbled curbs. The streets grew more narrow and dark and ominously quiet as they skated the southern point of the Lancank district. It wasn't all in all very far from his father's house, but that fact was largely ignored by the middle class. It was far enough to be out of sight, ragged banner buttresses aside. Not even the police trolled here with any regularity, and Jarrett, a captain in Ciracusa's army all the same, hesitated before diving into the shadows.

"Dog," he hissed as the animal forged ahead at an easy lope. He could turn about and go back the way he'd come. He wasn't yet in any area that would get him lost, and if he were to get lost, standing at any street corner in Lancank was not the place to do it. Maybe the Dog couldn't be killed, according to Mackenzi, but he was a different sort.

He stopped, hearing glass break from somewhere in the tallest rookery. He only saw uneven outlines in the night, as the gaslight didn't diffuse high enough to touch the upper floors of the crammed buildings and their many boarded-up facades. Even the moon didn't seem to want to venture here, as its light would probably be rebuffed by those who thrived in shadow. Jarrett backed up a step, looking at the eyehole windows, seeing nothing behind them.

The Dog had disappeared.

There existed reports that the wasting cough still held sway in some nooks of the slums where even doctors didn't dare venture, much less any municipal responsibility. Stepping foot in one enclosed room could be a death sentence, and that he would not risk.

He wanted to turn around and head back, at an unashamed clip, since shouts from some domestic fight began to leak through the thick clutter of walls and warrens. As if in response to this disturbance, others began to yell back, low speech, barely discernible as they began to layer in anger. He headed toward the Roog; though not exactly a safe district either, it was always well lit and carried traffic well into the night as people spilled from chantaparlors and velvet gambling houses. The noise grew at his back, so much so that he barely heard the barking.

Still walking fast, he looked over his shoulder. The Dog was coming toward him, followed by four others—what looked like strays. Were they going to attack him? He had his blade beneath his coat and his pistol, but he remembered Sjenn's caution that brandishing a weapon was a sure way to make the Dog aggressive. He held his hands free, a little nervously, and eyed the strays. They carried disease too, and a couple of them were rather large. One in particular was a sleek black with long legs and amber eyes. Feral.

He found himself standing still as the dogs swirled around him. They didn't invade, which surprised him, but merely sniffed and brushed against him. The Dog stood a couple yards away, her eyes a glinting sapphire in the lamplight.

He could *feel* the difference between them now. Beyond the intelligence he saw behind the Dog's eyes, these strays were tentative and oddly subservient. They nosed at the backs of his hands in a way he didn't think Sjenn's Dog ever would. He stood still until they seemed to have had enough and wandered off again, dispersing back into the shadows. The black one was the last to go but disappeared the quickest, blending right into the night.

When he looked for the Dog, he didn't see her at first. A silver blur appeared in his periphery just before the animal jumped at his right side, knocking him to the ground. She sank her teeth into his shoulder.

It wasn't much of a fight, or even a struggle. The bite seared through his flesh, drew blood immediately. The Dog bounded away. He rolled, left hand clutching the wound. The pain branded him and he spat curses that fell into the empty air.

The black dog noses at his face. It's daytime already, did he pass out? The streets are empty, silent, and high above the sky sits a cloudless blue. Taking a breath sounds too loud in his ears, the stone beneath his cheek too cold. He shivers and tries to roll over. His shoulder aches and he remembers the bite.

Why is the city so silent? He can't even hear echoes.

He tries to set his hand on the ground to push himself up, but his balance is off.

No hands, only paws.

This startlement makes levering a trial, but lever he does, onto four legs. Shaking. And even standing, the black dog is at eye level to him, staring at him with curiosity.

The instinct to yell overshadows all other intentions. He tries, but what comes out is an animal howl. Then the black dog spreads his stance and barks repeatedly, angry and fanged. The only recourse is to run, but his legs don't move. Why can't he move? His howl descends to a confused puppy mewl.

The black dog launches at his throat.

*   *   *

Amber eyes. For a second he thought it was the dog come to attack him again, or some shadow semblance of Qoyotariz. His heart trundled in his chest over the rocky terrain of panic, but in a blink his sight manifested Keeley leaning over him. Saying something. But Jarrett didn't hear him; the stabbing pain in his shoulder was a loud distraction to his senses. He lay on his back, limbs drifting, it seemed, away from his body. He wanted to raise his hand. He saw the motion of his fingers across his sight, a couple heartbeats later than he thought he should. Fingers, not claws.

"It bit me," he mumbled.

Where was the sky? He only saw darkness interspersed by round halos of light behind Keeley's shoulders.

"I know," the abo said. "Hold still."

"I was a dog…"

"You were what?"

But he didn't reply. The lights died one by one, like somebody snuffed them out to leave only the scent of smoke behind.

Night still wrapped around him when he awoke again. Or was it the next night? Motionless in his own bed with a cool breeze that made the curtains drift—he barely felt it, tucked beneath blankets. Louna stood by his wash-stand wringing out a cloth.

"'Ey, Cap'un Jarrett, sa."

"Did I sleep the entire day?"

"Nah," she said, coming closer, drying her hands on the front of her apron. "It's still the same evening. Be dawn soon, though." She glanced at the window. He had

moonlight and his desk lamp to make out her features.
They were tight with worry.

"What happened? I...I was out there..." He didn't
think he ought to mention the business with the dogs. Or
the Dog.

"You just rest, cap'un." She pressed a warm hand to
his forehead.

"I don't want to rest, I want to know what bloody happened." He caught her wrist, but not too hard. None of
this was her fault. "Please." A strong scent of herbs and
dried blood swirled around his head like a drunken haze.
He felt drunk, but without the accompanying pleasure
buzz. "Where's that abo and the girl?"

"Oh, I don't like them 'ere, Cap'un Jarrett." Her frown
deepened as she sat on the edge of his bed, much like
she'd done when he was a boy and had taken fever. Her
fingers rubbed at his sleeve without her thinking, as if
the motion would soothe her as much as it might him.
But he wasn't soothed at all. "They're in the girl's room
with the door shut. And there's an animal...but that abo
demon says not to trouble it. Me an' the girls don't know
what to do."

And he didn't know what to tell her. She couldn't kick
them out. He couldn't even kick them out. "How did I
get here?"

"Ye don't rememba? Is a bad business, cap'un..."

"What happened?" He almost didn't want to know,
but better she told him than the others. Her voice at least
was familiar when his mind felt too cluttered already by
strange doings and stranger threat.

"The abo went out to find ye. He said ye were gone a
long time. Then he was gone a long time, but came back

and ye were bleedin'. He wouldn't let me help, 'stead he used his demon medicine on ye. It's stunk up the whole house. He said if I troubled your bandage he'd be angry."

"If it heals me, then..." He'd used Whishishian medicine before, out in the field, and it did tend to work for bleeding injuries. He reached up to touch the pad of cloth at his shoulder. It was bound and held there by strips of more material wrapped around his armpit. With a small groan he pulled himself to sit up. "Hand me my shirt, please. And a glass of water." His throat felt sore, but it hadn't been bitten. His hand drifted up to feel the tender skin there, to be sure. The black dog. Which dog had attacked him? Which had been real?

He did not like this business of questioning reality. So now he would go to the abo himself. And he would shoot that Dog to prove the absence of dreams.

It sat at the foot of the girl's bed and didn't even raise its eyes when he shuffled into the room, one hand holding his shirt together as his entire right arm felt too sore to move, to even be pushed into a sleeve. Keeley kept vigil by the window on a single wooden chair. Jarrett shut the door behind him with a solid click, staring first at the calm animal and then at the abo, who appeared less calm. That was at least a backward comfort. Pain and discomfort ought to be shared; he was generous with his misery.

"Thank you for this." He pointed to his shoulder. "Now I'm going to kill that Dog."

"You know it won't—"

"I don't know anything!" Shouting or not, let the animal attack him again. His gun formed a solid, cool shape at the back of his waist. "All I know is I was out there and then it came at me for no reason. Then you...how did you find me anyway?"

"I tracked you."

This wasn't an open plain or even a dense forest. Tracking someone in a city was an impossible task. Unless one were a dog.

"I mean," Keeley said, standing and taking a step toward him as if to emphasize his proximity, "I followed you. Her Dog returned without you, and I asked it to lead me back to you. Eventually it did, at least in the general direction. I guessed the rest. You lay on the stone and you were bleeding, so I brought you back. She is still asleep." He looked at Sjenn. "So you must wake her."

He needed to sit. He crossed the floor to the chair Keeley had vacated and plopped down.

"I don't feel like doing a damn thing that concerns that cursed beast. Or her."

"When you were delirious, you said that you were a dog."

He blinked, as if that would help him see past the shadows in the room. Or to make sense of what he'd just heard.

"I was delirious."

"She says you have—"

"I don't care what she says." Yet it was the same night, and he remembered awakening in some sort of day. But it must have been a dream. A hallucination. This magic talk had taken its toll on his mind, and injured he had wandered.

The abo had no good news at all.

"Your servant brought me a message from your father. He returns three days from now."

Since he couldn't avoid it, he said the words to make the Dog disappear, and as it faded once again and Sjenn took a breath, he was only too happy to see it go. Stifled nightmares that dissipated with the dawn were still heralded with some gladness in their departing, and so he felt steadier at the absence.

But he wanted to pitch the journal across the room, all of Father Bari's notes and this thing that he'd been relegated to…he didn't know what to call it, but it had a hint of slavery in the scent. The beck and call of this need that wasn't his own.

He thought of disappearing, of packing up his gear and heading back out to the frontier. What would his father do, follow? Throw him in prison for disobeying an order he would bet wasn't logged in the army records anywhere?

He sat at the foot of the girl's bed as she recovered, taking minutes, and told the abo to leave.

Maybe there held enough anger in his voice that indicated he would brook no argument. Keeley walked out without a word. Jarrett hoped he would go to sleep and that would be it for contending with more than one demon believer for the night.

He sat there and waited, saying nothing. Eventually the girl spoke.

"What happened to your shoulder?"

"You don't remember?" He wondered if lies followed

her intentions. He knew the abo lied. Even if these Aniw seemed to be more honest a people, perhaps she had learned in her few days here, or on the long voyage from her land. Perhaps she suspected he hadn't come back to her room unarmed.

"I..." She rubbed a hand over her eyes.

He stared at her tattoos. Three times now he'd watched the Dog disappear from his parroted words and, it seemed, these unintelligble markings on her skin. They were enough to obscure true expression. Perhaps they hid more than that as well.

"Your Dog," he said. "You. You attacked me."

Her hand lowered and she blinked at him. After a moment she struggled to sit up, reaching for the glass of water Keeley had set on her nightstand at some point during the last few hours. Solicitous Keeley. That was another matter entirely, and Jarrett pushed it to the back of his mind so he could deal with the one in front of him.

He waited for her to drink, find her voice, figure out a lie if she had to, and stared at her eyes. No tattoos covered those, though they were close. He could still see the shift and blink of her eyes.

"I taste blood," she said.

"It's mine."

"Did you dream?"

That wasn't the question he expected. His shoulder gave a spike of pain as if he'd moved too suddenly. "Nightmare."

She looked down.

"Here," he said, to seize her attention, and pointed to his own eyes. "Look here. I trusted you in that mad suggestion to go out there. With your beast. And you led me straight to the rookeries, where your Dog attacked me. Hey." Her gaze had started to drift. He snapped his fingers below her nose. "Why did you attack me?"

Her wandering wits seemed to still hold sway. It took her long moments to answer. "My little spirit has her own will sometimes. Maybe she wanted to shock you into..." And she left her thoughts again.

He had no patience, not with pain working its own dire magic. "If there is some way to kill your Dog, I'll find it. Do you hear me? I am *finished* with this." He got to his feet.

"You can't kill her."

He was at the door in two strides and put his hand on the knob, giving it a turn and a yank. The rage was a simmering thing at the pit of his chest. It felt like an animal's regard before it chose to attack. He didn't seek to abate it. Instead he wanted to encourage it.

Her voice followed him, stronger by the word. "You can't kill her. And if she so chose, you couldn't see her either."

"Then perhaps I'll kill you." He looked back at her. "That would kill it, wouldn't it?"

She didn't answer.

"Wouldn't it?" He pushed, to hear it from her.

She looked rather small sitting in that bed, in clothes that clearly didn't belong to her. But she'd said she wasn't a child and whatever magic she possessed was no child's plaything. None of this was child's play.

"Yes," she said. Her gaze was defiant too. No capitulation there.

So neither would he capitulate. He walked out and

turned the lock with the key his father had left him. Wild things should be imprisoned or shot when they encroached on his territory—that inclination had nothing to do with a Dog.

He had three days to wait, perhaps even less. Knowing his father, the man might show up a day early. Jarrett found a bottle of whiskey from the dining room cupboards and tethered himself on his bed with the intention to get a full bout of drunk. He had a stiff arm and a bleeding wound despite the staunch of herbal pack that Keeley had administered. This pain would not go away, and he didn't think it had any true cure. It traveled from the bite, through his neck, and curtailed behind his eyes in a steady thrum. If he had to feel like he had the worst hangover in his life, he planned to chase it with a real one. If he were lucky it would make him pass out and he wouldn't dream.

When he was halfway through the bottle, Keeley appeared in his doorway and asked after the girl.

Jarrett lifted the pistol from where he kept it on the bed beside his leg and pointed it at the abo.

"I have the key, and she's not going anywhere. You, on the other hand . . . you can bugger off. And while you're at it, you can report that to my father as well."

"You are brash," the abo said.

"How well you know me."

"Can you listen?"

He sipped at the bottle but didn't swallow much. The lingering warrior made him wonder, and though his defenses were high, he sat and stared at the abo's boldness, in this house that didn't belong to anyone but a Fawle.

The watery pathways of his mind slipped a little over the edges.

"Good gods."

"Captain," the abo said. "Listen to me."

"Good gods. My father said he's known you since you were a child." His stare searched. The abo was short for a Whishishian. His amber eyes had a curious angle to them, and though they were on opposite sides of every aspect of life, the more he looked, the more he saw some glimpses of common scenery. The general paid much attention and offered some hedging trust to Keeley, and it was beginning to make a sickening sort of sense. "Get out of my fucking sight."

"Captain, you must listen. You should not let this woman teach you her Dog."

"Of course I shouldn't!" The grip on his bottle felt slippery against his palm. "Nor should you even be here!" He laughed, falling back against the pile of pillows at the headboard. "You...my father...gods, no wonder he ran off the frontier and put himself in this stinking city."

"What are you talking about?" the abo said.

It amused him beyond reason. He felt far away from reason. He had a secret now, though it was glaring. He could spill it, but that would mean acknowledging it beyond these fettered jibes. And he was not drunk enough for the full barrage of this conversation. "You shouldn't trust him, dear Keeley. He's not so generous with his family. Not without cost."

"If you hate him so, why do you follow his orders?"

So sat the question. He could wander a long time in

the mire of it. But he'd long established shortcuts over such treacherous terrain. "Love has no place in war, Sir Buckfoot." He laughed again.

Keeley's dislike pulsed in a wave at him from where the man stood in the doorway. Even drunk, though, he could hold a weapon, had in fact been in brawls and come out better than his opponents. A soldier's skill.

"There is a reason the Dog only follows the *janna* line," the abo said.

"Because your people were indis—indiscrim—" This was no word capable of forming out of his sauced mouth. "Didn't care who they bedded?"

If their positions were reversed, he had no doubt he'd be shot by now. But that was the case with all abos since the beginning of Ciracusa as a country. He yawned.

"I don't do this for you," Keeley said. "But your nightmares are no random thing. They will only grow worse."

The tone of it set him square on the path to sobriety. Damn the bastard. "What do you know about my nightmares? What do you know about my father's plans?"

"I won't make talk with you on this while you're drunk. You'll think it just a story and brush it off when you're alert."

"Don't tell me what I will and won't do!"

The abo stared at him for only a second more, then walked right out.

If he'd had strength or will enough in his arm he would've pitched the whiskey bottle after the man, but the door shut too suddenly for that. Without a target he decided not to waste his drink. Let the savages do what they would. He listened for commotion elsewhere in the house; perhaps the abo would ransack the place in their mutual frustration. The thought alone made him cackle, even when all that returned to him was silence.

He sought coffee in the kitchen, in the dawn hours when the cold crept along the floorboards and awakened only the mice. All the house groaned asleep as he sat at the table, letting scent and steam wash over his aching eyes. Drunkenness had not waylaid the nightmare barks, and as if to rub it all in, Keeley appeared again, dressed like a Ciracusan save for the bone tusks in his ears. The clothes were wrinkled, the long black hair in some disarray. Jarrett squinted at him from the table, elbows on the top and both hands in the sides of his hair. "Is that one of my bloody shirts?"

"I found it in the room."

The room, of course. The spare room unoccupied by the Aniw. They were a menagerie of guests.

Keeley sat at the table uninvited. "Are you sober now?"

"No."

"You need to listen. I've been reading the priest's book."

He raised his chin and looked around. He couldn't remember where he'd left the damn thing.

"It was in Sjenn's room," the abo supplied. "I took your key when you passed out. You can't let her teach you the Dog."

He stared at the other man.

"I will give you the key, it's upstairs. But now you must listen."

"I'm listening. You say nothing I haven't heard

already. What do you think would happen to all of us if
we refused the general? Hm?"

"There is madness in what he does."

"You see this only now?"

"No." The abo leaned toward him, stretched out a
hand, and placed it palm down on the table near to his
arm. "The Dog breeds through the *janna* line because
without the *janna* blood, the little spirit devours the other
spirit. Do you understand? It must be the same for Sjenn's
people."

"Then it's a good thing I have no little spirit. I'm neither abo nor Aniw."

"You are different. You are something your priest did
not write about. It may be impossible to properly teach
you. Even in his notes he marked differences between the
Nation tribes and her people. Some tribes need no Call to
control the little spirit. You—"

"Then what am I?" Perhaps he was still drunk enough
to ask such a thing right into the abo's earnest face, to ask
about the thing that had followed him from the frontier.
The coffee taste turned acrid at the back of his throat. He
remembered copper eyes and blood-red beads stitched
into skin. Acid churned in his stomach.

"You have a Dog," Keeley said, like he was delivering
news of death. "Sjenn says you have a Dog, and the *janna*
are never wrong about such things. But your father might
be the only one who knows what you are."

The third day came and he heard no carriage, no horse's
harness. No word. He packed his bedroll and his saddle
sack, hoisted both over his good shoulder, and clumped

his way down the steps. Louna was just emerging from the kitchen and started in surprise.

"Cap'n Jarrett, where ye goin'?"

"Home." He handed her the key to the girl's room, even if she had one already in order to feed the Aniw, but he certainly didn't need it now. He stared for a pointed second into the familiar old eyes. "Don't let her out."

"But your father..." The servant woman, out of anyone else in the house, knew the rift between them, what had been there even before his mother and younger sister had died. He had never learned the reason for that, and it didn't matter when the conclusion was disdain. "Stay, boy. Sober up before you—"

"I'm sober. It took being drunk to realize that I truly don't need to be here." And he truly had no desire to gain answers to his questions. Not if the source was his father, who dangled insanity before his eyes like a hungry fisherman. And he was somehow both bait and fish.

"Your career, boy."

Because they both knew that it wouldn't be beyond the general to throw his own son into the stockade.

"My furlough's been up. If he sent word to my post superiors, it wasn't to tell them that I've been holed up in this bloody house minding an Aniw woman and her cursed magic. I'll take my chances on the frontier." He leaned to kiss her cheek. "Don't fret. Now I'd better go to the stables and retrieve my horse. If that abo gives you grief, shoot him in the foot."

He felt lighter at this decision, at the ability to move and the thought of being back among his men. Those were familiar grounds, and even if his father chased him all the way to his post, he knew he could count on his troop in such an instance. Even if it were a danger to them. They had survived too many skirmishes and pitched battles to desert each other so readily. The general, on the other hand, had never fought alongside him. As a son he felt even less obligation to be loyal than he did as a soldier. Those were the bare facts of the matter, what endowed all the proper lines and carefully displayed memories in this house. Such was the confidence in this thought, with the light of day and an absence of parent to blaze the trail. He might as well act on it once he could.

He turned from Louna's worried expression and pulled open the door.

And there sat the sight of his father as he climbed down from the carriage. It had rolled up at the end of the short walk from the porch, and he hadn't heard it in the cascade of his own thoughts. Instinct almost made him shut the door again before the general looked up, but no such fortune befell him. General Cillein Fawle saw him standing in the arch of the doorway, supplies at his back. This was the dress of a man on his way forward.

"Desertion?" the general said, having to pitch his voice louder considering the distance.

"Duties," Jarrett said, through his teeth. What could he do? He waited on the threshold as the general approached, straitlaced as usual in stiff uniform, slowly tugging off his gloves. He could have been walking from his room soon after dressing for how unwrinkled he appeared from the journey.

"Your duties I thought I'd made clear," the general said, pausing as he passed Jarrett on the threshold. His voice remained low. "Get inside now." And he kept on, greeting Louna without breaking tone.

The carriage was right there. He could walk out, climb in, and order the driver to gallop. Of course he could. But it would be nothing but the futile struggle of an insect caught in a spider's web. His timing in this affair was one window short of a leap to safety.

Biting on the inside of his cheek, he turned back into the house and shut the door behind him. Louna reached for the burdens on his back without a word and he handed them over. Still, his movements were heavy as he followed his father into the study.

"Where's the girl?" General Fawle said, standing behind his desk.

"In her room."

"Louna!"

The woman appeared in the doorway. "Yes, sa?"

"Gather Keeley and the girl. And make it quick."

"Yes, sa."

Jarrett listened as the heavy footsteps scurried off. The general continued to stare at him.

"Where did you think you were going, captain?"

"I think that must be a rhetorical question." His gaze dropped to the sidearm at the general's waist, because he would not be surprised if he found himself shot. But he managed to return the stare to his father's eyes and trusted in his height to add impact to the attitude. He saw the man about to erupt like a prodded beehive and threw it in. "I don't believe this Aniw magicianry will do a bit of good against the Nation, much less against Sairlander boats and their bloody soldiers. I don't believe this is anything but some mad scheme cooked up by desperate generals and clouded statesmen." The general began to speak, but he didn't honestly hear a word. He just raised his voice. "Have you even seen what she does? That wolf attacked me!"

"It's not up to—"

"Not to mention, I absolutely refuse to work with that damned Whishishian. I don't care where you got him." The pause was palpable. "Or with whom."

The words fell into a cavernous silence. It was a righteous risk with the gun barrel straight before his eyes. Or perhaps that was just his father's glare. The general seemed unable to grasp the proper words, a feat in and of itself that Jarrett seized as an extant victory in this ongoing war.

"*You are an insolent child,*" the general said finally, and for all the words or ammunition that could be flung, Jarrett accepted those. They were not unheard in his past.

More might have volleyed forth, as the general's mouth was just warming up to move, but off to his left in the doorway Louna cleared her throat, bobbed her head, then picked up her skirts and retreated. In her place stood the Aniw girl and the Whishishian tribesman. Jarrett walked to the bookshelf so he would not be forced to stand beside them in the following fracas.

But the hurricane died as soon as it had swept in. The general said to the girl, "Well?"

If ever there was a time for the Aniw to learn how to lie, it would be now. Jarrett looked at her as she stood there, wan despite the natural dusk of her skin and the pattern of dark tattoos across her cheeks. *Lie,* he willed, as if his thoughts alone could push the words from her mouth. Lie so the general had nothing to hope on, whatever his hopes, no matter the outcome. Jarrett had made up his mind already that even in failure he would at least be free of this, that girl, her Dog, and the clatter of new disturbing things that trod through his thoughts. He yet remembered his dream and the black dog. He wished to kill it and the past few days. He wished to burn the priest's journal and the beginning of this all.

But Sjenn said in a flat tone: "There is a Dog." Her eyes found his. "But it's bound."

The general's voice held a certain urgency. "Can you release it? Can you teach him to control it as you control yours?"

"I don't know."

He was a witness to continuing insanity. He wondered if it was as infectious as the wasting cough.

The girl just kept on speaking. "There is no total control over the Dog. My ancestors would never be so absolute in their giving. Sometimes their thoughts are not my thoughts. And he is not Aniw."

"But can you try?" the general said. "Can it be done in some manner?"

"I won't agree," Jarrett said.

"You'll do as I say," the general said, "or you'll spend the remainder of your days in Gordorin with the rest of the traitors and deserters. That is, if I don't have you shot."

The man hadn't even the courtesy to look him in the face as those words were delivered. Jarrett couldn't stop himself. "You mean you wouldn't do it yourself, Father?"

"Do not push me."

This was the familial love of his youth, grown to an adult despising. He never remembered where and how it had begun, but there was not a single memory that entailed a lick of affection from this man. His more tender family had died years ago, and since then he had only a military leader to answer to on all fronts of acquaintance.

The general looked back at the Aniw. "What do you have to do to him to train him?"

"It would help if he were cooperative," she said, the first wise thing he'd heard all day.

"He's not. What must you do?"

Jarrett sat in one of the study's leather seats, since it elicited no difference in this conversation that he was standing there at all. The clawing at his gut made the back of his throat taste sour, as if some beast in his belly were blowing rancid smoke up through his insides.

"He would have no Dog if it can't be released," Sjenn said. "So I must be able to release it, or there is nothing to control. It will remain a puppy form and it will cry out to deaf ears as it's been doing his whole life."

"You sentence me to death anyway," he said to the general. "And for what?"

The man pulled his gaze from the Aniw and the silent abo, and looked at him.

"For the *war,* you ignorant boy."

"And how exactly is my becoming an abo for the good of the war, Father?"

The general faced away from Keeley and so did not see how the Whishishian straightened up with a breath, as if he had something to say. Naturally he said nothing at all, but the general had plenty, and Jarrett put on a face of mild encouragement, finding some distant humor in the guise. Humor sometimes was all a situation provided when all other emotion fled like frightened grannies.

"The more you understand an enemy's advantages," the general stated, "the better to conquer them. Call it

magic, let them call it their *Dog*"—he spat the word—
"what does it matter what it's called or even if it's
believed if it exists regardless? You can believe it now.
I've believed it for a long time. I've tracked the way these
abos have harangued our army for years. I have learned
a few things, and you'd do well to shut your mouth and
follow my orders."

All humor slid from his face, he felt it; he found no
ready repudiation of these words. They conjured Qoyotariz amid the fog of memory, as if the raging abo were
some dark secret he was too ashamed to let into the light.
I mark your men by you, the Soreganee had said.

As if he possessed some other light, some other spirit,
that demon eyes could spy from a moonlit mile.

Sjenn said the only way to release his Dog with any
control was through tattooing his face in the manner of
her own. He heard the words and rose to his feet again,
because even madness had its limits. The shouts were
many, the tension high. His father hollered him down.
And for the first true time in his life with what was left
of his family, he was sorely tempted to pull his pistol and
murder in cold blood. Commit patricide, no less, in a way
that would surely send him to straight disfavor with the
gods, even if he didn't believe in them. Such an act could
perhaps summon a divine retribution regardless of belief.
He had thoughts on that track, as stubbornly constructed
as the rails darting out from the cities toward the frontier
he might never see again.

Devil magic. He wondered if his father had mentioned
this all to the pious Patronael in his journey south.

"You put those markings on my skin," he said, "and you will lose me the respect of my captaincy. They will think it belonging to one of the tribes." He pointed to Keeley, who remained wisely silent throughout the uneasy proceedings.

"If this is the only way to conjure that animal, then it will be done. There are no other current candidates." The general's eyes grazed over the Whishishian but did not linger. Instead he said to Sjenn, "Tell me what you need. Immediately."

It needed pain and no alcohol, and a strong abo to hold him down. The Aniw woman wielded a fine needle and lampblack ink she gained from burning foul oil. Jarrett found himself on his bed with nowhere to go and nothing to say. The Aniw said all *ankago* and women of her people endured it like they would childbirth, and the discomfort was a little thing. He had a bite on his shoulder and had been shot five times in his life. But the consistent pricks upon his cheeks made him delirious with grief. He was losing something here, or perhaps a few things. Pride was only one of them.

All through the process the Aniw girl sang, and it was a dark song to his ears, riding on the shoulders of his blood.

It took some tight days to recover from the fare, with cool pats on his sensitive, swollen skin and a watchful eye for any signs of fever. Or so the Aniw said. Louna's eyes alone as she gazed upon him told him enough even before a mirror was cast in his way. He stared into the little round reflection, sitting up in bed and holding the silver handle, and could not even rouse the tears. Which may have been just as well. The salt would have stung.

He was not as intricately adorned as Sjenn, but it was far more than he'd ever thought he'd have in his lifetime. He was no friend to the Nation, with any tribe, to the point of sharing more than an idle pipe and braid of leather. Yet now upon the lines of his cheekbones embedded these petal swirls, with smoky fingers poking at the brown hair at his temples. If he blurred his vision he appeared to have a couple vast black eyes. The skin around the disgrace showed pink from the abuse. If ever he resented an act more than what had been perpetrated upon him because of his father, he could not readily recall it.

He hated. The pain in his distant shoulder could no longer compare.

'Round the dinner table, two nights from his forced tattooing, the general informed all and sundry that he was sending them back to the frontier. Keeley was present; Jarrett was not, at least not in mind. He sat there with his knife and fork, and a hardy steak that Louna had prepared just to his liking. She felt some compassion for him, the only one in this odd cabal. If the Aniw felt anything besides a wasted desperation, she didn't show it. He barely glanced at her. She still didn't eat much of the meals, and it had begun to show. But he wasn't alertly there to say much else and took the general's news without a nod.

"There have been more raids on the border towns

these past few weeks," his father said, as if this was
something unknown.

"That's what happens in war," Jarrett roused himself
to say, because his resentment knew no true silence, it
seemed. "Send him out to speak to his people, why don't
you?" He pointed his fork at the abo. "Or better yet, put
her and her Dog out there. Since it can't be killed."

"You're needed," his father said. "And your superiors
have begun to inquire after you. I thought this would
please you."

"I am very pleased," he said.

"You are a captain in the Ciracusan army and you
obeyed my order. That's all your men need to know. I
hear tell they respect you a great deal. Should you explain
to them what minimal requirements I had for you, they
would accept it."

"You mean I can't relay the tale of an animal that
comes and goes out of the thin blue air?"

The general didn't choose to reply to that, as it was
obvious what the answer would be.

"So what should I tell them exactly, Father? As you've
told me to do this and that without equivocation, provide
for me the appropriate words so that I may parrot back
to your satisfaction." Sarcasm, like a butter knife, was a
blunt instrument. But he could bludgeon well with such a
tool until he'd worked up a proper sweat.

"There have been army men before you," the general
said, "who sported the tribal mark."

"My lack of affection for the tribes as a whole has been
a harried tale among my men. I fight them, after all."

"We have allies."

Jarrett stared across the table at Keeley. "So it seems."

"I want you to learn control," the general said, and he did not mean control of temper or vice. The man thought this Dog a weapon of some sort, an abo weapon more elusive and more deadly than a poisoned arrow. And if the abos had it, so should General Fawle's army. Or at the very least his son, the experiment in it all. The thought alone seemed to shore up the heat of pain beneath the Aniw marks on his skin. He considered his butter knife and the amount of muscled force it might require for him to plunge it through thick flesh.

The general was still speaking, oblivious to all but his belfry scheme. "You're to take Keeley out with you as your new abo tracker, and Sjenn, so she may continue your training in the Dog. Make something up about a bonding between you two, if you wish, and let imagination take the rest. Or do as I say and frankly tell them you are on my orders." Nobody questioned General Fawle, he believed. "The men are simple and, as I said, loyal."

"They aren't stupid, however."

"You have attitude when you wish it, Jarrett. You can convince."

The low threshold of his surprise was a marvel even to him. Cart these two unknowns back to his garrison? After he had been absent for longer than his recognized furlough? There would be tales, all right. They would go well into the night in the enlisted barracks. Perhaps this was the real reason they were returning. If he disappeared off the face of the earth, it would be more difficult to explain than the tribal marks.

"You leave on the morrow," General Fawle said, to drive the nail into the torture plank. "All three of you."

"I shall remember to wear my hat," he said. For what protection it would offer on the ride.

The general had enough clout to book them passage on the new railroad, heading east, but he insisted they go where the least amount of people would notice. That meant on horseback, one apiece, and it was up to Jarrett to lead. It was nothing new—he had arrived in Nev Anyan on horseback, opting out of the clanking beast that began to cut its way through much of the growing congested coast. Fingers of iron bent toward the frontier in a similar fashion, hammered and laid down upon the ground by roving groups of navvies. The gangs linked the outlying parishes and towns with as much rowdiness as productivity. Jarrett didn't mind avoiding that commotion, his two unwelcome companions notwithstanding. He would have preferred it alone as well. He was most comfortable on horseback, bent to nobody's schedule but his own, and in the open air.

His horse, at least, he could trust, and he was happily reunited with the animal at the army stables situated by the northern end of the River Brendt. His mount was a sharp-tempered and battle-scarred blonde mare named One Hoof—for the fact it took only one of her hooves to fell a man when she kicked. Her temperament suited him, and he loved to lavish affection on her by way of apples and sugar cubes when he found himself on a hard ride without company. Unfortunately, for this ride he had company and the general to see him off, when he would have much preferred the man not be the last person to offer any words of wisdom before the trek, as he was wont to do. But the general was invested in the venture and so he appeared, like a bad omen.

Add to it, Keeley was granted a tall black gelding and sat astride it like the warrior he was, despite what mild actions he'd shown to date and this odd affinity with the general. But Jarrett wasn't set to disabuse him of his blindness, because it served him well enough if the abo couldn't see. *He* had eyes and he planned on watching Keeley closely through the ride.

They could make swift work of the terrain if it weren't for the Aniw girl, who seemed more than a little frightened at the prospect of getting up into the saddle.

Louna had at least provided for the girl some basic brown trousers, a rough-stitched blue shirt, and a colorful shawl often worn by the Whishishians and well-favored even in town. This way she would not be limited by dress and would draw the least attention. With a dappled kerchief 'round her neck and a necessary hat sitting pertly on her dark hair, she was about the size of a half-grown boy. At idle glance she could pass, and the general seemed satisfied.

"You'll have to mount," Jarrett told Sjenn, already atop his mare with one leg curled around the saddlehorn in rest.

A young corporal held the bridle of the skittish younger mare as Sjenn attempted to climb on, assisted by a wooden box, as she was a diminutive figure next to the animal. But her horse wouldn't settle and Jarrett wondered, without any present inclination to say it aloud, if the horse could sense the Dog in her.

"She won't bite," he said instead and let the interpretation fall as it may. Of course he meant the horse, but perhaps he should have been calming the horse with such talk about the Aniw.

After some trial and restless steps from One Hoof and Keeley's mount, Sjenn finally landed square in the saddle for what must have been the first time in her life. She tottered there a little before the corporal, straight-faced at the sight, went from stirrup to stirrup to fit her booted feet. All through it the general watched and said nothing, but the end result seemed to satisfy.

"Yours will follow mine," Jarrett told the girl. "Just hold the reins—corporal, show her—and make sure its head is pointed toward my mare's arse. Keep a stride between them, lean forward when we hit a climb, and back when we descend. Keeley will bring up the rear to make sure you don't bolt. If she throws you, try to land in a roll and out of the way of her hooves. All right, then." He slid his own feet into the familiar stirrups now and rose a little in the saddle before resettling. Out of the formal uniform so as to be better incognito on the journey, the worn and welcome leathers on his body felt more at home ahorse than any of his time back in his father's house, clad in cotton shirts. He could even forget about the details on his face, at least as long as he removed himself from any mirrors and other reflective surfaces.

He walked One Hoof by the general and took advantage of his lofty height. The iron-shod hooves made an impressive clatter on the cobblestones, a volley of ammunition fire. He rested one gloved hand on the holster at his waist. "Hopefully you won't be seeing me again," he said by way of farewell.

"I will," the general said, with common stoicism. "Don't fail me in this test, Jarrett. I will see all of you again."

Unfortunate accidents on the road would not be tolerated, he meant. Jarrett wanted to scoff at the concept of the test, but the general had more than enough resources to hunt him down should he see it fit, and it was wise not to challenge the prospect that far. As much as he wanted to and as much as he had even now. He was leaving; he could take what he'd escaped with and run.

So he faced ahead and spurred his mount forward toward the guarded gates of the army compound. He did not look back, even to see if the others followed. He knew already that they would.

He didn't say a word as they rode out of the city. He reckoned the Aniw and the abo kept their chins to their chests in order to avoid suspicious glances, as they were in a place so crowded in daytime. They had one mounted soldier as an escort to make the passing quick, as one would have to be bold folk in this civilized quarter to intercept an army officer. Once or twice he looked over his shoulder and sure enough, the girl was still astride her horse and Keeley behind her, as combination in dress as any buck boy with the ear of a Ciracusan general. His skins and his coat marked him well used by the army, and for this he received a wide vacant circle around his ride.

Soon enough they hit the dwindling outskirts of the main population and lost their uniformed guard, and by the late hour of the afternoon they were on open trail with little obstruction of carts, single mounts, or poor foot traffic. The weather was a cousin claim to what swept through Nev Anyan on any given day. Here, with less audience in stone and wooden walls, the wind and glare from the diamond sun fell to glory along their path. Jarrett squinted and pulled his hat lower and more securely on his head. Spring may have already warmed the cobbled streets of the city, but it was no forward charge with the way a long winter could be, and he felt it here now. The air held bite and the grass lay yellow from its dead slumber months.

Traveling single file afforded him the privacy of no conversation. Not that he would've said two words to them even if they rode abreast. They broke for a brief meal of coffee and bread, he and Keeley dipping into their saddle stores for dried beef rolls, and the Aniw girl mashed on a biscuit and drank her water from a skin. All of her supplies had been provided by the general, thus they were army issue. She was conspicuous up close but nondescript from afar, though anyone with half an eye could see she was not comfortable upon the horse. She was probably in pain, despite his affording her time here and there to stretch her legs, yet she didn't complain. He was glad of it, because he didn't think he had a twinge of patience for a whine. He was a brisk rider, and any grace he gave was so she wouldn't faint off her mount and cause more delay. The sooner he got back to his troop, the happier he would be.

They continued on this vow of silence until the sun began to curve away and more soft colors birthed in the sky. The landscape for this first day lay mainly unchanged as hill after yellow hill greeted them, with some birch and pine forestry off in the distance here and there. White and gray board homesteads, their chimneys puffing to the sky, could be seen as well, but Jarrett kept their angle well away. With the dying sun came a new cold, and he fished his woolen scarf from his saddlebags and wrapped it twice around his neck.

"We'll stop at dark," he called back to his line of followers, the first words spoken since their leaving Nev Anyan. They didn't reply, but he knew they'd heard. There was nothing else but the birds to compete with his voice.

By nightfall he led them off the beaten trail, such as it was in this vast country, and found a sparse bit of shelter beside a needled pine and its friends. It was welcome enough to light a fire against the descending chill and find some peace for the sleeping hours, where occasional traffic of man or animal would not likely obstruct their stay. Neither would abos disturb, as this land was long claimed by Ciracusa, its indigenous population either relocated or extinct.

Jarrett tethered his horse to a low branch, hobbled her, and left the other two to take care of their own and Keeley to assist the Aniw. He unsaddled One Hoof to give her some rest, left her to graze, then set about to feeding himself by the cooking flames. It was a regular meal of biscuits and coffee and a couple resistant pieces of hard tack that he softened up in the hot drink. He carried enough essentials to get him to Fort Girs plus a day, just in case, and all through the meal continued the stubborn silence that brought him amiable patience where conversation would likely blast it all away.

The abo ate with his rear firmly planted on his liberated

saddle and blanket, and watched the night. Above head an owl hooted, a comforting thing to Jarrett, though he saw the Hasky girl look up with some surprise.

"Bird," he said. And now that the silence was broken and his belly filled, he asked out of idle interest: "Do you have birds where you are?"

"Yes," she said. "Many."

"Owls?"

Her head tilted, and from that single motion he thought the answer was no, or she didn't understand the word. He would offer the hope that maybe on their ride she would see an owl but clamped his teeth on that. It smelled too much like an offer of friendship, and his skin still ached from the tattoos. It took only a slight brush of his sleeve over his face to make the reminder a scraping blatancy, and for the resentment to rise again like a death stink. Nothing could hide against that. Even the commonality of their forced position in his father's task didn't engender a sympathy.

The abo was another thing entirely.

"So," he said toward the gold-eyed Whishishian, his mind less on pleasant talk and more on pure information. "Back when my father blurted his ridiculous intentions, in his study, you looked like you had thoughts of your own. Do share with your riding companions. We have fire and food, now we need a fetching story."

The abo said, "I have no stories."

"Come, now." Jarrett smiled. He spied the Aniw staring at him from the corners of his eyes. "I don't know an abo that isn't fond of telling stories. Something about your ancestors, a battle, some great old demigod and its trickster ways?" Now he didn't smile, and Keeley caught it. "You do know what my father wants, don't you. More than he's said."

The Whishishian tossed the dregs of his coffee into the fire. The hiss and pop from the flames shot up between them. "Your father wants power, Jarrett Fawle. Just like the rest of you."

A little clatter and clang sounded around their small camp as Jarrett rinsed out his tin cup and plate with what water was in his canteen (he knew a river upcoming on the morrow so he could refill), then set it all aside so he could shake out his blanket and settle down for the night. Their conversation had died as abruptly as he'd instigated it, and short of holding a pistol to the abo's head he knew he'd get no farther. So sleep.

"We ride at first light," he said and rolled his back to them. His gun he kept by his hand, and his rifle closer. Steel bedmates served to discourage mutinies, or at least he hoped so with these two. He planned to doze with one ear open.

It didn't take movement toward his person to accomplish what they did. He became aware of a calling voice from the distant din of his own muddled dreams and could not make out the meaning. Sleep, even in its surface best, held him down enough until it was too late. He opened his eyes just in time to catch sight of the Aniw woman kneeling some short distance away, Calling out in that grunt and gasping breathsong that was now known to him. Calling her Dog. Or was she?

His hand closed around his pistol, but much too late. The rest of his body felt heavy, like nightmare, and before he could blink twice the Whishishian fell upon him, seizing his weapons and drawing them out of reach.

His face felt on fire. The tattoos seared a memorable pattern to his brain. Somewhere deep inside him, where none but guts and fear resided, a little creature pawed at his heart, putting a stop to it.

The stars commingled overhead, then faded to moonlight.

The ground is graveyard deep, and he feels himself much too close to the falling flame. Any second now someone will toss the light in and up he'd go, up to meet the stars and the winged god sent to escort him to the next life. Perhaps Father Bari would meet him there, an equal spirit with a body long burned.

Except in his mad dash around the field he stumbles upon his body, a shock, his slack sleeping body on its blanket, with open eyes and parted lips.

His cry is a puppy mewl. Touching that silent figure means putting down a limb he doesn't realize he possesses in his confused flurry. He looks up, perhaps for that guidance, and sees only statues. Pillars of low light, they seem, walking toward him. Flowing like smoke trapped in a glass bottle. One glows more than the other. The night carries a scent of pipe tobacco and hangs in murky gray sheets overhead. He doesn't remember it being so before, but everywhere looks different. The grass is a roll of shadow and diamond light, the horizon an indigo line stretching farther than his sight. He stands transfixed by the deep violets and stunning golds, and the bruised melting colors of the trees, so much so he forgets about his body and the two pillars edging closer.

One of them speaks. The voice is one he knows from the womb, or farther back. Back when many such voices peopled his memory, in argument and in love. Back when blood mattered to decide the fate of how far he would go and who with, one paw in front of the other. The voice tugs at him as if it has him around the nose, forcing his head to turn and look up.

The brighter figure gestures and he tracks the ends of the fingers. He almost leaps up to bite them. But the song is adamant and he remembers his silent body. There it lies, a dark, motionless thing, but familiar like a bed one fumbles for in the night. He takes low drunken steps to the still form. The face entices him, what pale visage he sees from the touching moonlight. The marks upon the illuminated surface of skin seem to speak, though they use no voice. Instead the language is one of gesture and need. Reawaken from this sleepwalk. It isn't good to let the body lie so unprotected.

He dips his head and licks the starry dark swirls on the pale cheekbones. What was silent begins to sing again, or perhaps it's just his ears pricking forward, catching the sound once more. Heartbeats make a clatter in his mind, twin bells ringing, calling him to nocturnal prayer. Wake up, they ring. Cold bleeds through his warmth, and as he looks up at the tall people in their smoky garb, the light begins to rip apart.

He follows soon after, into the dark, like a suicidal widow after her fresh dead man.

*　*　*

One cough woke him. The cool point of a pistol bit into his cheek. On the other end of it was the abo man, and beside him stood the Hasky. Brown eyes on the same sheen of face. They wore twin sober expressions, no longer silent as the ride. Jarrett clawed at the soft ground beside him, a heavy weight still presiding in his chest and his bitten shoulder revisiting the pain of the initial incident. Breath expelled with labor like a plowing in the noonday sun. The dawn stretched low behind the abo's shoulders, casting new crimson light on the yawning day.

"You watch yourself with us, Captain Fawle," Keeley said. "Or this girl here will Call you out."

"Get that," he said, "away from my face." But his voice sounded weak and carried no striking note. Keeley took his time retreating, but the Aniw girl still stood near. Jarrett pushed himself to sit, swallowing to move his dry mouth to moist. His throat felt stiff; any word forthcoming would only be the tinny squeak of air squeezing by a shut door. He rubbed his neck. "So," he said. The light came hard against his eyes, making him squint. Yet it wasn't even a true morning. He shivered.

"I saw your Dog," the Aniw said.

"Shut your mouth," he said. His guns were nowhere in sight. His glare found the abo to make a pointed invitation. "Seems you had some dire conversation in my sleep. And this was your conclusion?"

"It suits us," Keeley said. "You don't threaten her and you don't threaten me."

"To the flames with the lot of you." His heart set up a sprint in his chest.

"I saw your Dog," the Aniw said. "It's different. But it listens to the mark of my people on your skin. It listens to the Call at least. I wasn't sure that it would."

"Just get away from me!" He couldn't stand yet but he lashed out at her to make her step back. Abo and Aniw both watched him as he sat pulling breaths. He wasn't going to indulge this crazy talk, though it took long moments to shove the shadows aside. With slow frustration he hauled himself to his boot feet, then immediately leaned over, hands braced on knees. The world rotated in an attempt to fling him from its spin. He stayed afoot until it mostly passed, then pushed himself toward his horse. He had to move. At least with movement he didn't dwell.

"We're leaving."

The morning ran like molasses as their quick camp became yet another ghost in the middle of a field. Once in the saddle and feeling more sturdy, he clomped his way to Keeley's mount. "I want my guns back."

"No, sir," the abo said. "Not until we get to Fort Girs."

"I'm a captain in Ciracusa's army. You give me my guns."

But the abo was a stubborn man, and as their gazes met, Jarrett knew him to be a killer also. Such as most men tended to be this far from civilization. It didn't even take a caravan mile to get here. Trees, open sky, and other phalanxes of nature seemed to bring out the wildness in any plain soul. He could argue until nightfall and get no farther than a spitting distance to his weapons.

If this was his father's intention at all, he would not be surprised.

"I am a soldier with a long memory," he said.

Keeley nodded. "And I am Whishishian."

The conflict, to be sure, was inbred.

Two against one were not the best odds, but he had fought before in his life with less. Still, they had magic on their side. The longer they rode, the more that violet night seemed like a dream whose tendrils could quickly be blown away. Another dream, another nightmare. He collected them now like keepsakes found after a burning rite.

The sun sat high, his hat sat low, and they rode endless silent tracts without a word between them. Not even the abo and the Aniw spoke to each other, though Jarrett wondered if in some way they didn't need to. Who knew what naked anger they shared beneath their skins? Perhaps it was a buck trait he wasn't privy to and would never understand. A mutual dislike of Boot People things might require no long breath or riddled words. As he knew the way to Fort Girs, he had to lead. They remained at his back with his guns.

He didn't call for rest at the appropriate times. If this was their threat, then he needn't accommodate them but rode hard, as though with intention to relieve a starving company. Once or twice looking over his shoulder he saw the Aniw girl with an ill expression. It was a petty revenge but he took it. The sooner he returned to his post and to his men, the better off he would be, and whatever these people wanted to concoct to tell his father they could.

After a brief rest and relief in the mangled brush, they set off again. Another two days and they would be at Fort Girs. Each blade of grass seemed to slow him down,

for how desperate he wished to be back. Back to the
place that had been sanity in the midst of an insanity he
understood—the long days broken up by patrols and protection of travelers or mail. Once in a while his regiment
went to battle against still bitter and rootless abos who
roamed the landscape they held on to with a vengeance.
And it *was* vengeance against Ciracusan expansion. But
such was a routine and a reality he embraced. He let himself sink into musings of familiarity, but it was impossible
to forget or forgo the demons at his back. Worse still
when the Aniw rode up to meet his trot.

"You can't deny it," she said, as if they'd carried a
conversation all this time.

He kept his gaze ranging ahead, far across the mottled
grass, with woods at the edges of his sight. There was no
trail here, not the way he led them in order to avoid other
travelers. There was only the direction of his memory
with the guiding gaze of the sun. "I did well not knowing
about it for twenty-nine years."

She shifted around in her seat as if there were ants in
her saddle. "Your Dog did not behave like any I've seen.
It's a pup...your ancestor. Which isn't unheard-of, but
there is something different in him."

"I'm not Aniw."

She frowned. "I know."

"Your magic won't protect you. Your...dark light.
Whatever it is you call it. You sleep as sure as I do. Both
you and Keeley."

"Yes," she said. "But even if you threaten us, you'll
still have your Dog and you'll still have to learn it."

His nature tended to rebel against cold inevitabilities
delivered in such a tone. "I don't have to learn anything.

Even Keeley has cautioned me against your magicianry, and I don't care what my father says. He can't force you from miles away. You can make anything up and tell him, he won't know."

"He'll know. What if he asks you to use the form and you don't know how? I don't know what Keeley wants, but what if the general's plans are nothing you or I can stop?" All proper questions, but he didn't offer enlightenment. She kept on. "What if there is a real danger in your not learning to harness your little spirit? There is always danger in the gifts from the spirits, for we are only people, we weren't born from the dark light like they were."

These possibilities sat unanswered between them. If she didn't know, then he could hardly offer options. But her troubled tone of voice slid beneath his dismissive thoughts.

She carried on. "What if the general doesn't believe me, if I lie for you? What do you think would happen to me?"

"Not my concern."

"He doesn't seem to be a man that would let things go. Why do you fight against what will come to you anyway?"

Because it was in his blood? Because nobody liked to be forced? Because he didn't understand what and why and how?

"Because I don't owe you my acquiescence," he said instead.

And so ended his intent on this speaking thing, this silent listening. He spurred his horse ahead at a hard and defiant gallop.

*   *   *

They were a trio of oddities in the early afternoon riding up to the wide, encircling wall of Fort Girs, which had gifted the same name to the town that had been built up around and below it. One had to travel through the thick outskirts of raw greenery and uneven dwarven home-steads to get to the pimpled hill, atop which sat the stone walls, batteries, and blockhouses of the military fort. The black cannons faced the wide adjacent river, from which much trade flowed, and farther in the distance sparkled the Sister Lakes. Jarrett had the environment laid out in his mind before he even fully got there, so anxious he was to get within the walls of his home, look down on the town from his watchful height, and recall saner times. Before the Aniw witch.

But first they took a cloppity journey through streets and around lots that held much in common with the town's bigger sibling Nev Anyan, which was now a full week's ride away. Though the founders of both cities were different, the plan and intentions were nearly the same. Fort Girs was the birth canal through which their nation was born, just as much as Nev Anyan was the seed. With the army garrison protecting this acred plot, they could see attacking abos from miles around, on both land and water, and greedily guarded the necessary avenues of their commerce. Such trade and goodwill came by the northerly settlements and others up and down river, bearing pelts, boatloads of exotic foods, mined elements from neighboring towns, and other worthy freight— what couldn't be brought overland or was simply easier shipped by waterway.

If Keeley was familiar with the town he didn't show it, when Jarrett checked to his side where the abo rode. As for the Aniw, she seemed just as destitute here as in Nev Anyan. Her back slouched, her head curved down, perhaps conscious still of the tattoos on her face. Jarrett was conscious of his and kept his kerchief pulled up, bandit-like. But he'd changed into his uniform outside the town walls, and so their way lay largely unobstructed, save for the regular detours created by the day traffic of peddlers, wheeled transportation, animals, and various raggedy people. They weren't anywhere near the strait-laced streets of the town's affluent. A military officer rid-ing with what appeared to be two abo scouts, even in the big market, was not entirely a foreign sight. The horses climbed higher up the slant of street.

The main gate of the fort proper stood guarded and tall, reinforced dark timber from the spreading trees and impos-ing spikes of iron to keep the bold abos at bay. He loathed the moment when he would have to reveal his marked-up face. The guards at the gate, looking a little desultory in the high sun, took his furlough papers and glanced over them before giving him a hail through, patting One Hoof's rump. Of course they recognized him, kerchief or no, and while it might have been strange for him to be so covered up, not to mention late returning, they didn't much question it even in looks. It wasn't their place.

Now surrounded by many black-coated army men flow-ing around the edges of the parade ground with horses and crates, or marching back and forth on drill, Jarrett felt the silence befall his forced companions. He promptly but-tressed One Hoof against Keeley's mount and held out his hand. "My weapons." Surely the man saw that there would be no point in holding on to them, when Jarrett could easily order some passing corporal to restrain both Whishishian and Aniw. They were completely outgunned in the center of this garrison, and Jarrett felt himself breathe more clearly now than through the entire ride.

Keeley pulled out the army rifle from his saddle holster and handed it over, and once Jarrett had that in hand, the abo passed over the pistol as well.

"Thank you," Jarrett said, not a stranger to wry words, then motioned to the two hostlers that approached to see to the horses. "One of you, go fetch Lieutenant Ven Dy." He dismounted, pistol now holstered and rifle in the crook of his arm, and handed over the reins before he unstrapped his bedroll and supply pack from the saddle. By then the lieutenant was on approach, a tall, gangly figure who never managed a straight cap no matter how hard he tried.

"Captain Fawle, it's good to see you back." The man's dark eyes traversed the terrain of the two abos, then back to Jarrett's face. "What's the kerchief, sir?"

"I want you to escort these two...my companions... to secure quarters." Meaning he wanted a couple guards on them both and four stone walls to keep them in. "Where is Major Dirrick?"

"In his quarters, I think, sir," Ven Dy replied, blinking at the briskness.

He had no need to labor over long discussion, and now that he was back in the bustle and business of the fort, he certainly didn't feel any impulse to fall back on the fear of frightening magics and his father's threats. Both the abo man and the Aniw girl were not pleased with the new development, judging by their cautious expressions, but

developed interaction they received, the kind that made
Jarrett unencumbered for the first time in weeks. If he
could only refuse to look in any mirrors so as not to be
reminded of the dire marks. The thought of it alone warranted a hard look in the girl's direction, then he simply
walked off, supplies and weapons in hand. His breath
came back too warm behind the mask of the paisley cloth
but he didn't remove it, arms full, as he made his way to
the officers' barracks.

The short row of rooms was unremarkable and in need
of paste repair. He didn't dawdle in his own compart-
ment—just long enough to dump his gear on the narrow
bed and pat his sidearm before striding two doors down
to knock on the major's. No reply came back at him, and
he called through for his superior. Still no reply, which
only meant the lieutenant's information had been either
wrong or out of date. The familiar face of Sergeant Malocklin passed by, puffing on a pipe, and Jarrett asked him
the same question he'd asked Ven Dy.

"I saw the major at the quartermaster's," the big man
replied.

And so his trek continued, along the little lines of
hill that made up the rear traverse, toward the long stone
buildings of store and supplies. Spring had barely touched
this height as well, and there must have been a recent cold
rain despite the round sun now; the ground lay top-layer
muddy and quickly covered the edges of his riding boots.
He went to the main double doors of the food storage
building and peered into the filtered dark.

Sure enough, Major Dirrick cut an officer's blade-like
figure in the murk, broad-shouldered and finely trimmed
on every uniformed edge. A couple jacketless enlisted

men, and the chief in charge of keeping the regiments fed, loitered nearby. Jarrett felt a little silly in his bandit's cloth, but he could not unmask in front of these random few.

"Major," he said, keeping himself to shadow just to the right of the entrance where the door blocked some light. "Captain Fawle returning from Nev Anyan, sir. May I have a word?"

"Of course, captain." The major excused himself from the men and their inspection of the stores, and drew closer. "Why in the gods' names are you wearing that nonsense over your face? You look like a backcountry brigand." The man was never one for long sentences and bandied pleasantries.

Jarrett tugged down the bottom of the mask just enough to reveal the top end of his unwanted tattoos, what showed at the height of his cheeks. "Sir, my father didn't send word?" he said, into the major's astonished couple blinks.

"Of that?" A finger pointed at his eyes.

"Can we talk in your room, sir?"

"Indeed we may."

Though he received some odd looks cast his way for his screened appearance, tongues would wag in private and not to his face. He was glad when their brisk stride brought them swiftly to the major's barracks and the man had discretion enough to shut the door behind them.

"Now remove that thing," he ordered.

Jarrett untied the bandanna and held it at his side, twisting the ends between his fingers.

The major's pale hazel eyes bore into his skin, and they were almost as painful as the needle used by the Aniw. "Take off your cap."

There would be no concealment at all. Slowly he pulled off the article, pushed a damp lock of hair from the corner of his right eye, and stared straight at the man—because he would not be cowed and concede his father the victory of his fleeing dignity.

"What happened to you? I thought you went on furlough, not captured by some damn abos." It was said in a tone of morbid but insistent fascination.

"Not quite, sir. But I brought back with me a Whishishian scout at the orders of the general." He didn't have to state which general. All of the army knew who was his kin.

"Report," Major Dirrick said.

"General Fawle's got me on orders, sir, which I'm not at liberty to really discuss. I imagine he'll forward some formal word."

"Infiltration?" The major was rightfully confused, as a few tattoos upon the face didn't make him automatically accepted by any tribe. "I don't recognize your markings, soldier. But you say you can't discuss it."

"I can't." He tried in some manner to keep the resentment from his tone, but perhaps the other man's shrewd dark regard saw it anyway.

"What about your regular duties here?"

"I don't think they'll be too affected. Other than I'm made to utilize the Whishishian." Some things about that abo he could certainly not reveal, so his tone trundled on in what he hoped was resignation. "Keeley's his name and he's apparently rather good. We could use him on patrol since I assume we're still in need of a Whishishian tracker." After the last one had perished by the hand of Qoyotariz's warriors. If Keeley perished just the same, who was he to obstruct fate? "Speaking of which, I'd like to get out to the field as soon as possible." Away from the town below or the stares of his comrades. Where he preferred to be—out there with a wide view of every dusk and dawn.

"We have other stores of scouts," the major said.

Indeed they had, ones that were tried and tested, and one or two that spent time in the fort among the men. Buck people who wore boots and rode horses even better than some experienced cavalrymen.

"This one comes recommended by General Fawle." He almost offered the prospect of sitting the abo in the army stockade until the general demanded he be let out, not just for overnight security. But then what of the Aniw woman? Put her there too, indefinitely? Who knew what letters General Fawle might send to the garrison commander, and should they contradict Jarrett's official disobedience he could find himself brought up on charges at the very least. It wouldn't pay to push too hard against the general's pride, and he had shot every verbal cannonball at the man before he'd left. Absence could brew a deep discontent. His feet felt heavy upon the ground. "There's a girl as well."

The major's gaze was long. "A girl."

"Yes, sir, she comes with the Whishishian. I've got a guard on them both, but…she's part of the general's orders."

Major Dirrick didn't move for a few moments, as though his own boots were stone blocks weighted to the earth, but eventually he ran his palm down the lower part of his stubbled face and walked to the small dirty window of his quarters to stare out. "This is a strange business,

Captain Fawle. But your father is one of our army's great generals. We must trust his judgment."

He could say nothing else but an agreement.

"You went to this willingly?" Major Dirrick asked then, gesturing to his face. It was the one question Jarrett had hoped the man would avoid. Dirrick was a reasonable leader, respected by every man in the fort for his skill and sense of fairness. That he sometimes took a personal interest in his soldiers was not unique to his life. Jarrett had served under him for three years now.

He found it difficult to lie to this man. But lie he would, or the implications would leave a larger crater of questions that he simply could not afford. "Yes," he said.

The major stared at him, first in his eyes and then around them at the swirls and shards of black marks. "Gods, man," he said, in a quieter tone. A more sympathetic one.

The simple exclamation created a curious stone in Jarrett's throat. He could not dislodge it, and so spoke around it in a hoarse acknowledgment. "You recall Father Bari of the Varana Ingen Order?"

"I do."

"He is lately dead," Jarrett said.

Dirrick was not a slow man. He was silent in his contemplation of this fact and their new visitors to the fort. Of course the major also knew the nature of Bari's exploring feet and of all the tribes he had encountered. "How did he die?"

"Animal attack," Jarrett replied. It was the truth, the simplest form of it. The wildernesses in which they lived made the statement an unsurprising one.

"Then one day soon we'll raise a glass to the priest and the trees."

"Indeed we will." But not now. His business had been dispensed, and it was probably best to retreat, where explanations could find no root. "By your leave, sir, I'd like to corner some food in the officers' mess. It's been a long ride."

"Of course," Dirrick said. He was not a martinet. "You're dismissed."

Jarrett saluted and the answer came in kind.

Being on good terms with the garrison cook afforded him the occasional mischief meal or under-the-table treat, and so it was he managed some solitary time at the back of the mess with a plate of beans, bread, and beef, and a warm mug of chicory to wash it all down. The main meal of the day had passed, but he was afforded this extra before tattoo and took it gladly. Cook had been startled by his appearance but wisely said nothing, though the word around the ovens come breakfast tomorrow would likely be a rapid exchange. Soon the entire fort would know and walking the parade grounds might become a chore. The sooner he got out to the field, the better.

He leaned over his plate and prodded the gravied bread as though it might spring up and bite him at any moment.

"Captain Fawle."

Lieutenant Ven Dy loped through the door, avoiding long benches and longer tables to gain on Jarrett's position by one of the walls. Jarrett watched him with some forbidding, as not even the lieutenant's crooked cap hid his straight stare. He supposed he ought to get used to it.

"May I sit, sir?" Ven Dy pointed to the bench on the other side of his current table.

"As you please."

The man slung his long legs over the rampart of flat wood and settled in, folding his hands loosely on the table, though one errant finger sneaked out to prod at a rough whorl in the oak.

"Something on your mind?" Jarrett asked. Perhaps he should be a little nice, as he was bound to get questions from those he lived closely with, but he just wasn't in the mood. His food had cooled quickly and now tasted rather lumpy and raw at the back of his throat. He picked at it anyway so Ven Dy didn't see how thoroughly he'd lost his appetite.

"Well . . ." the man hedged. He tried not to point but his finger waved a little in the air. "That. The men will ask and I don't know what to tell them. You've gone abo!"

"I haven't gone abo, don't be a complete dolt." His clear irritation made Ven Dy lean back, and he knew he shouldn't be taking out anything on a man he trusted with his life. He drew a deep breath, rubbed at his still healing shoulder where it ached, and then touched the tender skin of his cheeks. The swelling had disappeared at least, so he wasn't as deformed. Quite suddenly he wanted sleep. "It's there to stay, whatever the case. Upon my father's orders."

The lieutenant's lips parted. "Why would General Fawle do that to you?"

Because he's a bastard. That, of course, was the kernel reply. Instead Jarrett just repeated, "Orders."

The silence was incomplete. Outside men talked,

horses moved their hooves over the occasional narrow line of stone between buildings. A dog barked. The routine of the fort and the familiar smells seeped in, yet he felt like a moon man fallen to the earth—out of place beneath his friend's scrutiny and the permanent alienness engraved upon his face.

"Convey to the men that nothing at all of me has changed otherwise," he said finally, looking Ven Dy in the eyes.

"Yes, sir," the lieutenant replied, though if he was convinced was another story. One that Jarrett didn't think had a ready ending—in either of their minds.

The food settled in him like pixie dust, pulling him toward a fanciful sleep. He made his way from the mess toward the officers' barracks, head down and striding intention aimed at deep oblivion, at least for a few hours.

But that desired time got waylaid by a body that shored up by his side, sudden and dark like an eclipse. He looked up to find the blue eyes and black visage of the priestess Oza. The sight gave him a start, as he'd long forgotten the woman had claimed to be assigned to his post. It seemed she hadn't lied.

"You," he said, by way of greeting. He was too tired for formalities. Or the presence of religion.

"Hello, captain." Her chin inclined. Her hands were pushed up into opposite sleeves, and her back sat very straight in the carriage of her walk. She had not far to look to meet his gaze or rebuff his frown with a tiny smile. "You look different."

Her lack of surprise at his sudden tattoos made him narrow his stare. "Is that all you've got to say about it?"

"Should I say more?"

"People tend to have questions." Unless, of course, they already knew the answers. They came upon his door and he stopped without opening it.

"I've come to give you this, Captain Fawle." Her hand emerged from its long sleeve and she offered him a small stone carving of the Seven Branches, which were tied to a leather loop. A twin to the one that hung from her own neck. The charm held the silhouette of a spiky star. "I noticed you don't wear the ward."

He didn't take the piece of pious jewelry, though it dangled prettily in the sun. The color shone pearlescent. "I find they don't protect against bullets and therefore hold little value for a man in my profession."

Her hand lowered slowly and the smile disappeared. "You are quite adamant in your disbelief. You know, even warriors have need of faith. *Especially* warriors."

"I've never seen faith keep a dying man alive."

"Then perhaps you've not looked hard enough." She raised the Seven Branches again. "This could protect you against the animal."

The animal. He stared at her and took a step. He leaned over her from this close proximity.

"What do you know of that?"

She didn't waver. "As I said. Father Bari and I were friends." Her hand bobbed. "Take the ward, captain. And should you feel it in your nature to return the favor, I would like to peruse the late priest's journal."

"I'm sure." He didn't take the necklace. And he didn't confirm whether he had the journal in his possession, though her guess had been correct. Either way, he would not bare his secrets in the face of this sister's mystery. He didn't forget it was religion that had gotten him into this madness in the first place. Gods and their demons, it didn't matter from which tribe, his own or some Aniw's. Their servants all seemed to have their own agendas.

He turned his back to the priestess and got himself indoors. Though the Church professed to be one largely lacking in violent intent, he felt her sharp reproach in his wake.

Sleep comes four-footed once more, only dream, for he hears no Aniw Call. He roams as a dog, but this time it isn't in Nev Anyan. The shadows and lavender moonlight descend on the fort to knit a ghostly atmosphere, fitting for the stories he heard from his men on winter nights before taps, or when they were in the field, those few moments before they rolled over and tried to forget they were in the open, subject to wolves and spirits. Flights of fancy, he maintained, in the blazing day where sense intruded on squirrelly thoughts. That sense rides low now, in the dream, as he pads around the still parade grounds, over by the wall, and up against the gun batteries.

Sjenn's Dog is nowhere in sight, not like before. No violet and gold outline of the Aniw girl in either two- or four-legged form. The Whishishian is nowhere either, and that makes him happier. His step increases to a trot around the grounds, spying the booted feet of fellow soldiers on guard and the occasional tiny flare as one or two of them light up their tobacco rollies.

He rounds the corner of the quartermaster's store and bumps straightway into the lean black dog from Nev Anyan's streets.

It turns and runs.

He chases it, four pale paws on the earth, swifter than he's ever run before in his life.

It takes him around the corner of the stores, across the open patch of ground near the well, and straight toward the spiked poles of the stockade, behind which sits a cobbled stone structure built to resist unruly attempts to escape. Doubly protected to keep the riffraff out and unofficial persons from slipping in, the building tended to remain empty unless some ballsy men disobeyed orders. Sometimes they captured deserters or abos and tossed them in. As far as he knows, the place is empty save for Keeley and Sjenn, unless some misbegotten fools ended up in there while he was in Nev Anyan.

Why this place? The black dog doesn't reply and he isn't even sure he asked it aloud. The animal disappears behind the western wall of the stockade.

He follows along the length of the wall, pausing now and again to paw the ground. Soon the door manifests itself…it seems to just appear, as if his attention alone gave existence to its lines. It stands barred, a subtle sort of offense, and from the other side of the log wall the black dog barks. It wants him over there. But how did *it* get there?

He looks up. The sky is a blur of blue with only a smatter of distinct stars. The spikes of the stockade pierce each little diamond light.

The black dog barks again. He reaches to touch the wall, the odd pads of his front paws resting against rough bark. This is dream, after all. Some dreams he walks on water, in others he flies. Here he is a dog with man-thoughts and no out-loud language. But in a dream does he have to speak? He hears no song either, no Call. Only the black dog. He pushes against the wall.

He finds himself standing on the other side, facing amber eyes. The dog nudges him in the cheek with its muzzle, then takes off again toward the stone building. Small square holes work as the only windows, barred. He stops below one and, with the same silent thought, imagines himself inside the cell.

And then he's standing there, facing the Hasky girl. She sits against the corner with her knees drawn up and her head bowed. But as he steps closer, she looks up. Though little light penetrates the dark in here, her tattoos seem luminescent around the edges. That gold light.

Her mouth opens.

The black dog is nowhere in sight. He turns all the way around but they are alone here. No abo either.

"I didn't Call you," she says.

He faces her again.

"I didn't Call you." Her voice rises. "You would not Call yourself. How have you come, little spirit? Why have you left the captain's body?"

The alarm in her tone raises his meager hackles. Ears lie back, and he bares his teeth at her. Her face changes, becoming less woman and more demon. Some kind of demon, distorted and gray. He backs up to the opposite corner, but her flaring tattoos mesmerize him. Her eyes bleed out the dark and shine unnatural blue. Though her body doesn't move, her face seems to draw closer, elongating, reaching for him.

"Get back to your body!" she screams.

And he awakes against the wall. Inside his quarters.

His body had bruises. He didn't remember climbing back into bed, or even really being out of it, but his chest and temple hurt like he'd been thrown against the wall. A vile awakening, and the sun was no great splendor upon his face either. That Hasky had done it to him, her and the abo. Their threats somehow transcended even common sense, knowing they were imprisoned for as long as he saw fit. He could see it fit for quite some time if this was their nightly entertainment.

He propelled himself out his quarters, forgetting boots, jacket, wearing nothing but his trousers that he'd fallen asleep in and a shirt that had seen better ironed days. He made a straight course to the stockade, ordered the guard to open up, and soon stood outside the cell door. It was a flash of resemblance to the first time he'd seen her, except there was no dreaded Dog. She sat in the corner with her arms wrapped about her knees. She stared up at him as he peered in at her, as if she expected him.

So he ordered that door open too and stepped in, waving off the guard. "What did you do to me?"

"Nothing," she said.

"I have these…dreams. You're doing something to my sleep."

"They aren't dreams. Not last night. And I did nothing. Do you remember?" Her eyes were uncommonly steady on his face. "I don't understand how you walked the middle light when I didn't Call."

He saw past her dark eyes, saw blue instead. A shiver

made a spider crawl up his spine, and he folded his arms against his body. It was much cooler in this stone damp than outside, where the air could travel and the sun touch. And she seemed tightly wound. Or perhaps that was his own standing coil.

"I saw you in the middle light." Her hand moved, tracing the air like it was a solid thing. "Your yellow Dog."

"My what?"

"Your Dog. It has yellow fur. Short fur. And pointed ears like this." Her palms perched on either side of her head.

Golden paws.

"Long tail," she said.

"Stop."

"It's happening. Why won't you accept it?" She frowned. "But I don't know *why*."

He didn't know why he was here. He didn't know what to believe. And Keeley's words rang loud, suddenly, in the chamber of his mind. *Don't let her teach you the Dog.*

"Please let me out of this prison," she said.

He blinked his thoughts back from the nighttime smell of grass and the flickering dots of tiny fires. Soldiers smoking as they stood the guard.

Her gray face and open mouth reached to him from the narrow column of her neck.

"No," he said. "Not yet."

And he left her in there, just as he'd found her.

Sister Oza was a determined soul and found him in the stables in the early afternoon as he took some form of leisure and distraction in the grooming of his horse. He hadn't been issued orders as yet. Considering the conspiracy around his tattoos, Major Dirrick had not placed him on a regular rotation of duty. He hoped for a field mission at some close date and any reason at all not to revisit the Aniw. He still had to decide what to do with Keeley but found his thoughts bent away from the abo at every slight wind of consideration. In the motion of his brush upon One Hoof's golden flank, he decided to float with that mental breeze on its own idle course. He was still muddle-headed from the nightmare and willing to be blank.

But the priestess interrupted and her tone was pointed. "Captain Fawle. Should I expect you at chapel later on today?"

She stood across from him on the other side of his mount, and he wondered if all religious followers were this hard of hearing.

"I refused your charm, so now you offer me chapel?"

"If you don't wear the faith, then you may still find some solace in the sitting."

"Not if your benches are as unforgiving as I remember."

"Oh, so you have seen the inside of your garrison's church?"

"Against my will." Not counting his troubled ramblings at poor displaced Father Timmis that night, funerals were held there and he had lost men. This sister made him pause his attention to One Hoof, but he resumed giving vigorous strokes on the twitching shoulder. But the priestess didn't leave and he stopped once more, resting his arms over his horse's back. "Tell me something, then, Sister Oza."

"Ask." Her face was amiable if persistent in its presence.

"Why are you here?"

"Do you mean in the spiritual sense?"

This woman had wit. He allowed a small smile, though his gaze was hard. "No. Why are you here at my fort?"

He half expected a studied dodge, but instead her shoulders seemed to straighten and she looked him in the eyes.

"We hold some interest in Father Bari's work. And in your father's."

This was going to be a shell game. He would reveal only one word at a time, and so would she, and so they'd chase each other's meaning for the duration of the play. "And what work is that?"

"You have no great affection for the general, Captain Fawle. Let's not pretend to be ignorant."

He had never before met such a forward follower of the Church. "What order do you represent, Sister Oza?" Something told him it was not Varana Ingen. She didn't seem to be attuned to the father patron of explorers.

Her blue-eyed gaze roamed around the open stables. That one breaking of stares seemed to allow the flies to make sound once more, and the day to trickle in through the rumble and sharp calls of the fort activity outside. "It's an order befitting this martial environment, Captain Fawle."

He didn't know why that came to his ears on the smooth timbre of threat. But it did.

"And so your interest in all things army?"

"Your father plays with powers he should not entertain at all."

"So you and your Church disagree with his battle methods." It was a well-honored tradition in religion to encourage spies. He was not much surprised now that she knew even a fragment of his father's dark deeds.

"Do you agree?"

"I would prefer all deities to stay out of the affairs of men. They seem to ignore us when we're in distress, so why interfere for the sake of plundering our souls?"

"Try," she said, "not to let your jaded religiosity get in the way of what's good for this country and what's good for our people. Alliance with the abos has always been precarious, but aligning with their spirits is foolhardy."

"And what of Father Bari? He believed in the abo spirits. He loved the abos."

"He didn't condone breeding with them."

He stared at her bold face and her bolder words.

"You are not your father's first attempt to infuse some magic in the Fawle line. You think him so careless to impregnate a Whishishian squaw to get a son by her, then seek out this son because he *cares?*" Her face was not quite mocking, but it held some satisfaction at her pointed revelations. "He thought it would be easier inherited that way, since the abos come from creation with their magic. But he was looking in the wrong place, and here you are, a surprising new avenue."

It was a good thing his horse stood between them, for the protection it offered this woman of the gods. No starry ward could have stopped his fist from flying if One Hoof had not been situated in such a convenient place. "It seems nothing much surprises you and your Church, however. So this is all idle talk with no point but prurience. Get on with it or get out of my sight."

Her answering smile was strained at the corners. "The Church will stop your father, Captain Fawle. It would be good of you to align with the gods you know, rather than with the spirits you don't."

She patted the flank of his horse and moved off. Soon she disappeared around the far stable wall, her footsteps fading into nothing.

It was not much later that Major Dirrick found him setting One Hoof back in her stall so she could chomp a little on the feed hay stacked there.

"You might want to reverse that beast right back out," the major said, and Jarrett looked at him with a slow smile, his hand on the horse's rump. This was a good distraction to his dreary, heavy thoughts.

"And why's that?"

"Because your painted-up face needs to see the countryside awhile." The major knew he was eager, and it reflected in his grin. "Come on, Fawle. You're too savage wild for these civilized walls."

It wasn't for pure recreation that they took the jaunt. Major Dirrick said he wanted a routine patrol of the outlying steads, though the latest reports claimed there had not been any Soreganee activity for a couple days. It was their responsibility to watch out for the intrepid few who laid down stakes away from the fort—farmers and miners and many other working folk—and so out they trotted, himself and the major and a couple other cavalrymen trailing behind them, out of earshot of casual conversation. They didn't expect to meet with the enemy, but they went fully armed nonetheless. One could never be too sure. For

Jarrett it felt like a spring picnic, and he contentedly sat astride One Hoof, patting her gamely on the neck as they walked the fallowed trail.

"Beautiful day," Major Dirrick said, a simple confirmation of the long white clouds and blue sky. The air even transported a light breeze, making the sun a welcome warmth instead of an intrusion.

Jarrett raised in his stirrups to stretch, then settled back. Though the sister's words still rankled, he found some respite with a welcome comrade. "Indeed. I could find a patch of green field and lie out until nightfall, if it weren't for our duties and my strict superiors."

The major laughed. "You are a lazy sot."

"Not in the rain."

Their good humor rested well between them and the horses. Dirrick rode a dappled gray gelding that often reflected the major's even temperament. Both were calm figures in the thick of battle, and Jarrett had been grateful for both in his past, among the unpredictable press of a pitched fight. By habit his gaze telescoped ahead, watching the almost verdant trees and low humps of hills, over which would be their first stop. After a few quiet moments he felt the stare on his cheek and turned to look at the major, some distant gloom now signaling on his happy horizon.

He looked away again. The empty landscape was a better vista than his friend's wondering stare. "You needn't gawk."

"I'm sorry, Fawle." The man sounded it at least. "I just don't know what could have possessed the general."

"A choice turn of phrase. Do you think me much changed?" He was looking for a flat-out "no" and wasn't ashamed to admit it.

But the major was never one to linger on lies. "I don't see how you couldn't be. You were far away and for some time." In Nev Anyan.

"You sent me there."

"You were struggling here."

Those long-ago nightmares seemed now like flights of girly fancy compared to the reality he now lived. Even the prospect of Qoyotariz sounded more manageable than this. "Well, then, I'm grateful."

Dirrick never did address his sarcasm. He read behind it easily enough. "Do you feel I contributed to this invasion upon your skin?"

Jarrett heaved a sigh. The bright day now lay shadowed by the talk, and there would be no break in the clouds. He resented the sun right now for its pale face and heat, as if the world deserved this cheer. "Don't worry. I fully blame my father for this abomination to my person."

"Did he *explain?*"

Dirrick was not a man to be merely satisfied with "orders." Not for long. But the general had warned him about the route of this information, and truth to tell, he wasn't eager to expound. He was drawn into this madness and was now perhaps mad by association. Practical men had limits for such things, and they were far from the army's seat of power.

"My father doesn't explain, he issues ultimatums. I'm a captain in his army, and that's the beginning and the end of it." He moved on. "What do you think of this new holy woman in our midst?"

It was a large enough newness to push even the question of his tattoos at bay.

"I think it odd the Church thought so promptly to replace Father Timmis. The men were fond of him."

He looked at Dirrick. "They were. And she is not so warm of personality or comely of face to lure them back again."

The major raised an eyebrow and adjusted his cap. His faintly freckled nose wrinkled just a little. "I haven't spoken to her past a basic good day." His religious inclinations were as much duty as anything, and more intellectual than spiritual. Jarrett understood the fascination in the history, at least where it concerned his friend's quick mind. "You've already formed opinion?"

"She's taken a peculiar interest in my comings and goings."

Now Dirrick looked at him, a long regard. "Why?"

"Perhaps my soul is in jeopardy."

"That's hardly a singular concern."

"She claims to have been a friend of Father Bari. And something tells me she is not unfamiliar with our choice of weaponry." He touched his holstered sidearm. "Do you know of any order within the Church that condones an armed priestess?"

The look of surprise was unhidden in his superior. "The Varana Drethe Order was disbanded a hundred years ago. You know the tales, don't you?"

"Vaguely." He had slept through much of his religion classes. "Perhaps I'm imagining things."

"They were a militant order born out of conflict with the uncivilized Sairlanders—long before our ancestors landed upon these shores. The romantic stories about their feats of faith and derring-do make the ladies swoon, but in my study it seems to me that they were far more ranging than that. Troopers, in their way, though at the time they dealt their brutality with blades."

His father's ancient suit of armor, of course. "But they were found to be too unruly for the preference of peace the Church pushed forward," he finished, recalling that much. "Are we so sure? Is history that well written?" After his own encouraged research into the annals of Ciracusan origins, he wasn't so convinced. Sister Oza's lecturing only raised more questions and brewed a paternal anger.

"There were no reports of women in the order," Dirrick mused. "That would seem a little strange."

He could not say it aloud, but strangeness was the one companion he found to be relentlessly reliable as of late. He let the topic go, and soon enough they were upon the first few homes on the other side of the hills. A distant farmer plowed his field behind a hulking ox, and a woman beat a mat with the end of her broom, creating clouds of dust to billow out from her wooden porch. It was a domestic sight and just as foreign to him as any thought of the Aniw girl back in the fort.

He could only stare upon the scene and wonder.

The next morning before drill, Colonel Ponne called Jarrett into his office, which lay in a neat center of a cluster of stone administrative buildings: the mail depot, the strategic room and library, and the fort hospital. Jarrett appeared in uniform, as neatly turned out as he could manage with a still aching shoulder and the residual shame of the tattoos on his face. The colonel was a diminutive, solidly built man, and rather round-faced, but he had that booming baritone voice that men like General Fawle couldn't muster on any given parade day. He stood behind his desk with his hands behind his back, as uncreased as a brand-new roll of spun Cutarzi cotton.

"Look here, Captain Fawle," he said, as if that simple address were some kind of urgent order. He tapped a sheet of yellow paper that lay flat on his desk. "These are orders from your father, yeah? They say that the two abos you brought in with you should be allowed to venture out on field missions if you require their assistance. What do you know about this, hmm?"

"Only what I told Major Dirrick, as well, sir." After a fashion, they were all in the same cursed boat. "I've orders, too, and that is to cooperate with them. They're part of some plan that the general doesn't feel the need to fully explain at this point." He lightly considered blurting his father's scheme, but it was unlikely anyone would believe him, and even if they did it was no guarantee they would side with reason. Though he knew his garrison commander as well as any officer, unreliable situations made expected action often unpredictable.

Ponne regarded him with a shrewd, bushy-browed mien. "Hm." Two moments passed. "And so you don't trust them?"

On this he couldn't lie. "Not entirely. I wouldn't give them guns and turn my back on them, but that being said, they've got reason not to cross us."

"That reason being?"

"Keeley, the Whishishian, appears to be the general's man for some time." Jarrett knew how little of his life would remain if he said much else on the matter. "The Aniw girl, well…she's far from home and she's made a deal with my father. She has to help or she won't go back."

"An Aniw girl?"

So the general hadn't explained that far. He didn't feel one bit saddened by his accidental slip. But to many people of the South, an abo was an abo, no matter the environment.

"She's from the Far North, sir."

"I see." Something in Ponne's expression turned contemplative, as if he were regarding some rare manuscript and desired to decipher the hand. He took an audible breath through his nose. "What about the men?"

Soldiers talked, it was an inevitability.

"My men..." This was the unsteady part. "I don't want it to affect my men. I'm assuming if they know I'm under orders it's a little better to take, and it's not because I've gone abo."

"You haven't, have you."

"No, sir."

The colonel "hmm"ed again, then took the seat behind his small desk. "Well...I say use them if you must. But, Captain Fawle, if they jeopardize our patrols here or endanger the men in any way, you feel free to shoot them, yeah?" He folded his hands on the paper sheet of orders and speared Jarrett with a somber look. "You feel free to shoot them dead."

He didn't think his father would have taken a liking to the colonel's point of view, but Ponne didn't command a garrison this large without his fair share of brutal rule. If need be he would sacrifice a lot for the safety of his men, and that was the type of leader Jarrett willingly served. This was his safe haven away from the general's dangerous fancies, even if *safe* was hardly the term for a life so close to the wilderness of the frontier. Whenever people tried to say that they were "safe enough" in the town below the fort, going about their regular way in trade and commerce, he would remind them of the skirmishes at trees' edge or the cannons pointed at the Sister Lakes. Danger was never too far and it was often on the move.

He didn't bother to talk to the Whishishian until Major Dirrick came to him again one late morning. It was a week since he'd returned to the fort, and he'd found some routine in dealing with One Hoof, presently watering his horse. The major told him Colonel Ponne required a company to venture out of Fort Girs and squash an incursion of abos that were terrorizing the outlying homesteads. Perhaps it was a little selfishly backward, but he was glad to hear of the news. Associations were strained with his men every time he walked into a room or across the grounds and they spied the marks upon his face. They were uniformly polite but clearly didn't know what to say, so they stared. It made for uncomfortable passage through the most menial of hours, and his one foray out beyond the town had whetted his appetite for more.

Now with the prospect of a skirmish ahead, he and the men could focus their attentions to a common discomfort, a common enemy, and they could see for themselves that they had nothing to fear from him just because of a few tattoos.

Even if he feared himself every time he laid his head to the pillow at night. Dreaming was an unsteady affair, and the thought of dogs—and Dogs—trotted through his mind in the most unconscious moments. Dogs bled to the forefront of his awareness like he'd laid a swatch of fresh cotton upon a gaping wound. Soon the darkness came with a threat of red and he was only too happy to waylay sleep for the good of a mission.

Which didn't help his waking worries. He tried not to think of the prospect of remeeting Qoyotariz, should the beady warleader see it fit to lead his band into the trajectory of some army bullets. He longed to kill the abo, but he didn't forget the bastard had him marked.

With that on his mind and evening oncoming, he took it upon himself to confront what was still there and visit the two abos in the stockade. He opened the door to Keeley first off. The man stood by the small barred window, looking out, and didn't even turn when Jarrett occupied the threshold.

"You're a good tracker?"

Now the Whishishian faced him, though he remained by the opposite wall. His resentment at this cage came at Jarrett on sturdy wings, so hard that he felt the flutter of it against his face.

"I am," the abo said.

"Then I'll do you a favor, though you hardly deserve it. We're to go against some rampant Soreganee tomorrow night. If you prove yourself reliable, I might find reason to offer more steady freedoms in this fort."

If he expected thanks he knew he'd wait a while. Keeley offered nothing but silence.

"Does this suit you?"

"I go where the captain pleases."

"I would be pleased to see you turned out with the field cattle, but I have my orders. My father wants you here to 'assist' me, or what have you, and so here we are."

The man stepped swift toward him but stopped short of touching as Jarrett's hand landed on his gun. The guard was just down the hall and they both knew it. Even in the shadowy light of the cell the abo's amber eyes were sharp and clear.

"Has that girl been teaching you the Dog?"

This same refrain. Jarrett didn't blink. "I would tell you things if you told me things, Keeley."

All abos were inbred to be wary of deals. "What things?"

"Have you never been curious as to why my father looks after you? You see he's not prone to grand generosity."

"I accept the generali for my own reasons."

"Which are."

"He sees it fit to treat me well. I would be a fool to turn away the wealth and power of a Ciracusan general."

Jarrett could almost believe the abo believed his own words. "I had hoped for something more than greed and vanity to drive your loyalty, dear Keeley."

He got no reply, in word or look.

"Does that Aniw girl frighten you?"

"Yes," Keeley said, without bashful hesitation. "As she should frighten you."

"As a wolf she is dangerous." Though he wasn't completely convinced of that encapsulation. There were broader considerations to the Hasky witch. She had Called his Dog on the trail . . . and that thought died where it lay. "You say you don't want her to teach me, but then you say you're loyal to my father. And *he* does want her to teach me. Your conflicting desires make for unsteady trust."

"Will you report that to the generali?"

"I have very little inclination to report anything to him, but I will make this very clear." He bridged that short gap between them and stared down at the shorter man. "You step out of line with me in any way, in fort or field, and I will cut you down."

Doubt did not whisk in their way at all. His words were driven home.

He had no obligation to love his dear father, and if that thought had never grown to full before, it was in bloom right now. The marks upon his face had fed and watered the sprig of it, and the life of this abo contributed to its health.

His true family had died long ago, and he had no need for any misbegotten kin.

The Aniw girl provided a more temperate conversation. She sat upon the floor of her cell, her back to the wall, and seemed unmoved by his announcement that he was heading out on the morrow. An empty tin tray and cup lay by her feet, so at least he knew she was feeding herself. Her head didn't rise, though, and her body seemed small, curled up into itself like a toppled-over spider. Her arms wrapped tightly around drawn-up knees, and her hair fell forward in rough black length.

"You know that Whishishian says you shouldn't teach me. That I should have nothing to do with your Dog."

"So you said," she murmured. "You don't want to know anyway, so it suits all but me."

She was pitiful, but he didn't find pity in his repertoire of current emotions. He had not forgotten the way she'd ambushed him with her magic on the trail. He had not forgotten the way her Dog had led him to be bitten, and attacked him itself.

"It may be fine that I shouldn't teach you," she continued. "No good can come from a Kabliw with this knowledge. And you..." Now her eyes tilted upward, surrounded by black and not all from shadow. "You and your little spirit will roam." Her breath pulled in, her voice grew rougher. "You and your little spirit will roam, and you'll be lost."

He couldn't move, pinioned by her stare. The words held the tone of a curse, or perhaps it was her dark regard. The matted hair in her face made wild angles on her cheeks, but not enough to obscure the swirling tattoos.

He thought her face would protrude toward him, like it had in his dream of the yellow Dog. The place she had said was no dream, but memory in the middle light. He blinked it away and noticed the ragged trim of her fingernails, how black they were beneath, as if she'd been scratching at the stone.

His feet slid backward before he knew he was doing it. Getting away from her, though she hadn't moved an inch.

"Be careful," she said. And for a moment he thought connection brought their gazes together. "Be careful of your Dog." It sounded sincere, but then she looked away, up toward the bars and the dying light.

He did not know what to do with her, and it made his limbs hang long.

"We'll talk when I return," he offered, the only expression of compassion he could muster, that he knew he wouldn't regret.

It brought her stare around to him once more. Her voice was flat and he thought he saw a glint of blue in her eyes. "If you won't release me, then get out."

It took no repeated tellings. He locked her back in again and quit the building, making fast work out of the distance between the stockade and his barracks. Inside, he retrieved Father Bari's journal from where he'd cast it in his locker and shoved it deep beneath his bed, where dust and mites could take it for all he cared.

He only wanted it out of his sight.

By the next evening, once through a basic day that he well appreciated for its lack of threat, he led the company from the fort. They were not a garrison at full strength—who was, nowadays?—so his infantry constituted fifty-five men on foot, carrying knapsacks and guns, and his cavalry a mere thirty. Recruitment was low in the army, and there was no helping it short of press gangs, as conscription in the Settlers' War had cut a straight and bloody course to unwieldy dissension in the ranks. Still, they managed. It took only a small number sometimes to raid an abo warcamp. Jarrett had long since learned that formal engagements often led to swift deaths when one was dealing with trickier opponents. They had been dropped upon from the trees at some point in his past battles, which had quickly dismembered any sort of ranking and order in the melee that ensued. Not again, he'd sworn.

The major had asked if he was going to utilize the general's abos, as the fort had begun to name them. This seemed to draw a muted respect for the buck people (they

didn't distinguish between Whishishian and Aniw, not
being familiar with the latter), as his father had a reputa-
tion and a long list of medals to make the average trooper
salute in his sleep if he should only dream of the elder
Fawle. The reason he gave Major Dirrick for his choice
sounded plausible and right: as they were going out on a
possible offensive raid against the local abos of the Nation
and he didn't think it an unfortunate possibility if Keeley
should get shot or killed in the action, he volunteered
the man to assist the company in tracking the dissident
Soreganee. Whishishian and Soreganee were ancestral
enemies, and so Jarrett reckoned the man could share the
task as well as his inborn skills. Dirrick agreed.

The Aniw, of course, he chose to leave behind, as a
woman in the company who had never before seen battle
or marched to one would only be a hindrance, and Jarrett
had intention to make this a quick, dirty work. Nobody
knew of her Dog or the threat it could be to enemies,
and he kept it that way. They filed from the town proper
just as the gaslights were glowing up, the officers' sabers
reflecting glints of pale light as they passed beneath the
halos.

They were a serious tribe themselves. The nighttime
sobriety cast a certain dire mentality over the whole
endeavor. It wasn't like he and the men had never been in
the field at night, or had never headed toward what could
be a fast and fatal end. But they skulked the shadows in
their dark clothing, with wakeful steps, eventually all
beneath moonlight when the walled town receded behind
them. The world turned what could be an eager launch
of forward activity into something full of calm contemplation of what was to come. Alert and quiet, it was the

way he preferred a march at night. Singing, whistling, or idle chatter were swiftly ordered down, and so they were a company of regimented spirits bent on a violent haunting.

They made their way for a couple hours. Jarrett rode at the head of the column with Lieutenant Ven Dy on his left and Major Dirrick on his right. The major left the command of the abo to him as Keeley was General Fawle's advice, and in a way Jarrett suspected his friend wanted him to lead this party, to reinforce the trust the men should have in him. He didn't disagree.

Behind in the march were staunch Sergeant Malocklin and the ragged lines of men he depended on, both ahorse and on foot. Strides ahead and making no sound in the grass was Keeley, within range of Jarrett's rifle and putting himself to good work for the safety and mission of the company. So far he had no complaints about the abo and had made it clear that should a complaint arise he was a very sturdy shot, even in the dark. The Whishishian had quite gotten the message.

In the failing light, whenever the abo looked back at Jarrett or circled back to update them about the chore, the upper half of his face was completely obscured by black, appearing as though he had no top to his head at all. Perhaps that was the intention of the black paint all along, in addition to being as fierce as it looked even in daylight.

"We are coming up to one of the ranchers whose home was attacked," Jarrett informed Keeley when the man walked along One Hoof's slowly bobbing head, listening for his orders. "There's a chance the Soreganee bastards haven't completely fled the area and may be hiding out in the trees. If you see any indication I want you to investigate, find placements, numbers, and any possibility of artillery on their part and come back to report immediately. We'll be waiting by that cluster." He pointed to a shadowy stand of trees trailing a broken-down fenceline long abandoned by settlers who had decided to uproot and move on. As many did when abo raids became too bothersome and the army solutions too belated.

"I'll return," the Whishishian said, as somber as if he were truly a part of the troop.

"Keeley," Jarrett said, before the abo walked off, out of his rifle range and out of sight. But he didn't need to verbally warn beyond that. The abo stared up at him, silent for the moment it took for that simple address to implicate itself in all pointed meaning, then took off in a silent dart. Jarrett turned to Ven Dy and rested his hand on the hilt of his saber, as it sat tucked into the saddle scabbard at his left side. "Inform the men we remain here. Quietly. They're to maintain night silence until ordered otherwise."

"Yes, captain."

The salute came prompt and precise, and Jarrett left him to it, exchanging a glance first with the major before turning his gaze out toward where Keeley had gone. Nothing stood in sight now but gloom and moonlight.

Should a man squint into the dark toward their company situated in the shadowed side of the stand of trees, he would likely and hopefully capture an unclear image of shapes that could be anything from bushes or rocks, to overturned barrows left out to weather. They didn't tether the horses in case they needed to ride far and fast, but held them by the bridles. Jarrett occasionally patted One Hoof's withers, but he didn't idle himself with minute concerns, even as he listened here and there to the quiet sounds the men made just in sitting or standing about, scratching at errant itches when insects traveled through. The majority of his attention remained outward-focused, and in half of an hour he recognized a certain shape forming out of the night, coming toward their temporary encampment. It was a sole figure with a familiar pony gait, scuffing the mottled grass and parting the air without a sound.

Keeley was a little breathless when he approached Jarrett, as if he'd been chasing rabbits. One Hoof tossed her head up in an abrupt acknowledgment or warning, and the abo laid a slow hand on the horse's nose, calming her with a peculiar stroke. Perhaps the abo had some kin with animals, but One Hoof was Jarrett's warhorse, and he was a little pleased when the mare rejected the soothing claim and dug her namesake hoof into the grass by the abo's feet.

Keeley didn't linger on the affront but delivered the news at Jarrett's look. "There are Soreganee." He turned his shoulder to point back to the way he had come. "Deep into the trees of that forest." He stopped himself.

Jarrett stared. "Yes? Numbers? Formations—" He dared not ask outright if Qoyotariz was among the warband.

"They have a family. I assume the rancher and his kin. They are Boot People. A man, a woman, and two children."

Major Dirrick breathed out. "Are they alive?"

It was not unheard-of for prisoners to be kept, even

barely, for either slave sale among some of the Nation tribes or for other nefarious and sometimes recreational purposes. Sometimes they were simply adopted and reared as tribal property, some warped exchange of life for life. Jarrett had seen the results of all methods in his time, and a cast-iron stomach would find it a battle to withstand the sight even once. Such things fueled the soldier in him.

"They're alive," Keeley said. "But in some peril. They are in the center of the camp."

Jarrett nodded. This was usually the place of prisoners, as they would be difficult to rescue in any melee and very easy targets should the warband decide to rid themselves of the enemy bulk. "Numbers?"

"I counted thirty-one warriors."

Definitely a raiding party, then, that was either too stupid to escape the area or was planning a morning attack on some neighboring steads. A mile from here, if he were not mistaken in his memory of numerous patrols and mapping expeditions, there lay a small group of similar families—immigrants newly imported from Ioen Aidra. They had started to influx this part of the country like the first trickles of a flood rain. Perhaps they found the climate similar to their oceanic isle, but in his experience they barely spoke Sarrish, making it difficult to communicate. If the rancher and his family were of similar stock, it would make the attack and rescue even more confusing.

The full report was no improvement. As any tribal raiding party, they were well equipped with tools of their trade: bows and arrows, blades of various killing edges, and some Boot manufacturing by way of rifles and pistols. The tribes were rarely so affronted by foreign faces to turn down an advantage in modern warfare, and some of his own people were not so patriotic to deny the swaps. It made fighting complicated and often bloodier than it ought to have been. Nation warriors were effective bloodletters equally on horseback or roughened footsoles, and dressing them in any sort of steel only made them deadlier. Luckily this particular set didn't seem to have much of a cavalry, but then again, the Soreganee weren't a plains people and they were locked up among the greenery. Still, his riders were adept and it made routing easier, should the enemy decide to break from the treeline.

He and Major Dirrick rounded the officers and delivered the tale. Together they devised a sound plan of attack and in short order they all filed out, leading their separate prongs. Now came the test of both Keeley's scouting and his own reluctant willingness to trust. He knew already his men had mettle.

The stealthy beast was not their inspiration, not with as many troops and horses as they were numbered. Some held back in the event of fleeing enemy, and the rest pushed forward. They were the splitting arrows from a dozen different bows, and their aim flew true.

The crash and fury of their first break through the trees startled the Soreganee raiding party. Abos were not slow off the mark, their warriors even less so. Soon the clatter and scramble of limbs and long hair wove a deadly thread through the tangle of forest and oncoming men. Jarrett picked his targets and scurried the life from a few. "The prisoners!" he bellowed, as a reminder to the charge. It was his goal, and he plowed straight for the center of the rowdy camp. Sparks from the tribal cooking fires flew as iron-shod hooves stamped through with deadly intent. Dirt kicked and flame threw. Blood soon spilled, dousing the dark earth, but it was not a sight to linger over either for enemy or comrade. One Hoof knew how to use her natural gifts, and Jarrett held tight to the reins as his mount reared, only to come crashing down upon the chest of a young warrior.

Battle time was a curious phenomenon that he could never readily explain, if explaining was a means to true understanding. Through the blur and haze of violent action he often found himself at the center of a shadowed diorama. Some figures remained so still that shooting them down became a children's art of easy pickings and flying feathers, yet he knew that there was no such thing as stillness in these games. His thoughts weren't calm, but they weren't a riot either. Instead they seemed to move with the steady steps of death on a march. He had little control, and yet control was granted. Perhaps because the outcome, of which he had no clue, would be upon him whether he held on or let go.

In the midst of the play of light and dark, the clash of voices and shouts of frenzy, he spied the huddled family crouched on a collapsed canvas tent. Their father was dead at their feet, some leather-bound Soreganee blade protruding from his chest. In the scatter of bodies and shaking of branches, the rancher's kin were soon forgotten. Smoke from expended rifles made the vision a murky tableau. Jarrett's nostrils burned, his throat pinched tight. Yet his gaze remained fixed, and every recent pain and injury became a memory far forgotten in the din.

He urged One Hoof about with one hand at the reins and a nudge of his knees, pistol firm in his right hand, spewing heat and sore apology. He bore through the dispersal of running men, his horse a strong encouragement against obstruction with the thunder of her stride and the impact of her bites should anything fleshy get in her way. Jarrett made to call out to the new widow, for a path had been cleared for her to take her children to some relative safety until his company could settle the night once and for all.

But he had forgotten about the foreign tattoos on his face. She looked up at him with a dead recognition. Only abos and wild men made such markings on their visage. He was a stranger upon a horse and he had the warrior skin. He knew why she hesitated to run for safety, but the minute had fled for such realizations to effect. He could not move fast enough.

From her skirts came a lifted gun, discarded perhaps by a fallen enemy body. She aimed it true and the bullet launched forth.

He would have felt the puncture if not for the animal. It came from his blind side and leaped in front of the shot. One Hoof reared, as surprised as he, and if it weren't for his instinctive skill to remain in the saddle he surely would have found himself making hard acquaintance with the ground. As it was, the screaming of his mount and the silent curses in his own mind focused his body to rearrange and guide, urging the startled horse to all fours and reasserting a sure hand on the reins once again.

Before him was the gray and white wolf. The Dog. It had taken a bullet and it did not bleed.

The sudden appearance of the creature seemed to knock the sight into the widow. As the two children wailed and cried, the woman sank to her knees as if all life below her waist had fled. The Dog turned and looked up at Jarrett, its blue eyes giving a spirit gleam to outshine any pure silver in a blade.

His wounded shoulder from days ago seemed to come alive once again, newly bitten. The chaos of the night collapsed. His steady march at the behest of unknown forces retreated at the presence of this animal, who walked the bloodied ground with its ears back and its hackles raised. Lips receded in a threatening snarl. It crossed Jarrett's mind to try to kill it, some manmade reason pushing forward in his thoughts. Now that he could think. Perhaps the woman had misfired. Perhaps the creature's hide was thick and blood not so easily seen in the shadows.

Perhaps it read his mind. It turned in midstride and jumped straight upon him, knocking him right off the saddle.

He runs. He thinks he runs from the Dog, but in glancing to his right he sees it match him stride for stride. And height to height.

His four paws hit the ground with a lighter impact than he's heard all night. He runs as if running is his only remembrance, this headlong flight so close to the earth. Instinct makes him avoid the brambles, the obstacles of fallen trees and thorny bushes. They stir up rotten leaves left over from winter, newly uncovered by long-melted snow. He scents spring come recent on the breeze and the sun beginning to rise at his flank. He scents *her,* wildberries and musk and a curious chill, as though the snow and ice never quite left her bones. She draws closer to his shoulder and grazes it with her teeth.

He veers away and shoots over a decrepit log. Some broad trunk seems to move right in his way. It makes him skid, hindquarters digging deep as he plows a short distance to a rough and final end. The Dog jumps upon him again, casts him to his back, and the muscled beats of snapping fangs chase the silence to retreat. He catches a ruff of fur in his mouth and hangs on, but she's bigger, stronger, and her broad paws give a shove and a scrape. He lets go and she backs up, four steps with a lowered head. He rolls and springs up, his tail to the wall of trunk that brought him up short in the first place. Panting breaths from them both fill his alert ears.

He shakes. Moving one paw leads to an unsteady lurch. His whine sounds like a reluctant hinge that needs tightening or an easy grease. Some door trying to shut. Someone stands inside a room, just out of sight behind the door. He blinks and wavers in yet another step.

Man. Man in the room.

Disjointed memories war for attention with the growing details of a dawning forest. Dappled golden light and deep violet shade. The Dog stands silent and motionless before him. They watch each other for a time, with a time that knows no limits.

Yellow one.

He stares at the blue eyes. They are equally fixed on him.

They both scent the intruder before they hear him on the fallen leaves.

Coyote. Eyes of copper, dun-colored pelt, muzzle low and ears back. He stands an in-between size with dark hackles raised. For a second the recollection of blood-red beading makes a ghostly pattern below the copper eyes, but that fades as his snarl echoes in the glade.

Moon, he seems to say.

The blue-eyed Dog charges him.

The light chases and commingles around their sparring forms, through the whip of tails and snap of jaws. He backs to the tree, chin bobbing low, some faint recognition of this aggressive intruder making his muscles coil for flight—until the coyote breaks free and darts straight to him.

He runs in the opposite direction, but the crashing weight against his side propels him to the ground. Muzzle to muzzle, the coyote bites him. Paws flail against dirt, body twists, the female Dog leaps in among the battle until the gunshot casts a quick and sudden stillness to the fight.

"Captain Fawle!"

A man emerges from the shadows to stop cold in his tracks. Bone talons through his ears and bone woven into his hair make small music. His body is a column of shifting smoke. Now all of them and the man form an uneasy square of mutual regard. The man carries a rifle.

He recognizes it. So does the other Dog, for she growls, and the coyote steps closer to the man, a bleeding gash upon his cheek from the gray Dog's bite. The weapon is a bright fixed shape against the more vibrant, moving form of the man. They all see it. Some whispering thought tells him that he knows what it's like to hold it in bare hands. To set the stock against his shoulder. To press the trigger and watch flare and smoke bloom out. To see it kill. It makes some part of him quake, and the other mad. Such things are enemies of nature, too soon flinging spirits from their body houses.

Perhaps the man senses it too. He slowly lays the rifle on the ground, then straightens up, his hands open at his sides.

Fight. The other Dog glances at him, then rounds her body to stand between the man and the coyote. He quickly moves to her side before the coyote turns on him again, and in a burst of weary irritation, muzzle burning from the bite, he barks three times at the copper-eyed Dog and bares his fangs. The bigger creature beside him echoes with a low snarl.

The moment drips slow before the coyote backs up, looking first at the bigger Dog, then at him. The man gets no regard, and then the coyote turns and disappears in the brush.

"Come," the man says. With some urgency. "Both of you."

The gray Dog goes first, with confidence. She grazes her muscled flank against the man's leg and trots toward the direction of retreat before pausing to look back at them. The man turns also after sweeping the rifle back into his hand, muzzle down. Man and Dog begin to walk away.

He paces on four paws to the spot where the rifle had lain. Sniff. Blood scent. Iron and polished wood. The thing would've been useless to him, his claws would only scrape the wooden stock and long iron, and he could not have moved it without a gamely push. The ghost of it left a depression in the ground.

In the distance a coyote howls, and he runs now to follow lingering footprints. They lead all the way back to the carnage.

*   *   *

He sees his human body first and more men around it,
looking lost. The man who found them speaks in a quiet
voice to a tall man among the crowd. There are other
bodies on the ground as well, less displayed in poses of
respect. Instead they're cast in ungainly heaps, flowing red
and dim in the middle. The sun grows higher and begins to
cook the earth. The stench makes him quake. The startled
exclamations of the men make him stop in his tracks.

"Don't shoot—!" one cries. Perhaps the same man
with the rifle and bones in his hair.

Not all the killing things are trapped in steady hands.
Bullets tear through the invisible fabric.

He yelps and casts himself forward, the instinct for
refuge. He parts through the standing bodies of men,
toward his own body as it lies stretched upon the ground.
He mauls the motionless form with scratches and bites.

With claws and fangs he shreds himself to disappear.
To safety.

The wakening was hard and intermittent. They'd thrown
him, long-limbed and human ungainly, over the back of
his mare. He came to in fits and starts with the abo walking beside, telling him it was all right. What his definition
of *it* was, Jarrett didn't know, but he had too thudding a
heart and heavy a head to argue. He passed out frequently
from either the jaunt, the pains along his body that he
couldn't quite remember getting, or all the blood rushing
to his brain from his upended position. He couldn't stop
it or right himself, he had no strength.

It was a long ride in dirty country, and the day grew hot.

The blue eyes startled him, so closely they hovered. His hand came up to shove it away—dark face, pointed stare. But something caught his wrist, and a quiet voice infiltrated his muffled fear.

"Captain Fawle. You must tell me where you put Father Bari's journal. You must stop this madness in its tracks, do you hear me?"

"Go away." He had no strength. His sight was full of shadow and some lingering lavender hue, as if all the world were in permanent twilight. Even with his eyes shut he thought he saw the darkness move, and the scent of this woman near him made him angry. He thought he caught some whiff of steel beneath her robes. His fingertips brushed the loose thick cloth of her sleeve. "Get out."

It was a futile mewl, no matter how much he clawed at her arm, at her face. She shoved him away, then finally stood.

"You and that girl are abominations."

The words floated free, disembodied from any sound meaning. What care had he for these dire judgments? He wanted only the open air.

The bed was no great comfort. They'd laid him there on his back without a fixed pillow, still in his uniform with the field and filth attached, boots too. A guard stood outside; he saw the coated shoulder at the edge of the tiny window where just enough daylight fell in to crush the shadows on the edges of the room.

He sweated. Summer bashed a hole in the cooling spring and let in all its fury. This weather could not be predicted of late. His head throbbed from it, or other things too difficult to remember. He lifted a hand to rub his chest and stared at it for a moment, thinking it strange in shape and color. Was it even his? A curious distance filed away from his awareness like marching soldiers bent on a far-flung mission. This hand looked and felt like it would never be truly attached again. Waving it about brought no real circulation, only a small stir in the dead air.

He managed to roll and cast his feet off the bed. Somehow his legs moved, as if they had single minds of their own and knew that the next logical motion was to stand. Once standing they were bound and determined to keep him upright, but his dizzy brains had another idea and he stumbled from the height, making it as far as the stick chair against the wall, a mere two feet away. He sat for respite, leggy intentions notwithstanding. This would do for the time being to let his heart settle and his breaths catch up. This was not all from the skirmish, he was sure, and yet he didn't care to think of much else. He'd had enough battles and did not need to recall the details of the show. Echoes still wandered around in his innards, banging on the walls of his nerves.

His clothes grew like a sticky second skin over his born layer. He felt mauled and held the seat edges to keep himself afloat in consciousness.

The longer he sat, the clearer his thoughts became. He leaned his elbows on his knees and pushed his face in his palms, deep breathing. If this was all he could manage right now, perhaps if he pressed hard enough he could shove out the thoughts that made no sense. Maybe it had been all a dream, the blurred state of heightened violence that allowed one to do the things one did with guns and knives. He'd seen men go mad on the field, only to retreat to more common senses once the pandemonium had died. He hadn't suffered from this himself, but lately...

They were hollow words that had no meaning. In his mired mental state he didn't hear the steps outside until they banged upon his threshold and the door was halfway to fully open. There stood Colonel Ponne and Major Dirrick, and a sea of curious faces bobbing and angling behind from other near parts of the fort. They peered in like he was some rare species caught behind a cage.

"Shut the door," the colonel ordered, and so Dirrick obeyed. But the window was still bare, uncurtained, and now the foggy faces pushed to gain some sight from the other side of the grimy glass. "Captain Fawle." The colonel's voice was loud. "Captain Fawle, look here."

He looked, but he found the man's distressed expression to be an odd mélange of lines and perspiring soft colors of pink and white transparency. The combination stank. It all fascinated him so that he completely missed what the man said. Major Dirrick hovered near, and his body held a wary attitude of concern, his hands hooked inside his belt and a constant frown upon his lips. Jarrett blinked at him.

"Is he dimwitted now?" Colonel Ponne said to Dirrick.

Major Dirrick approached and leaned down like he was about to talk to a child. Jarrett forced his mouth to cooperate by licking his lips and straightening back in the creaky old chair. His back hurt. He rubbed his chest again where the low burning feeling seemed ready to erupt.

"I'm here." Of course he would be. Where else? "I'm all right."

"You are not all right," Major Dirrick said, in an odd low tone. As if there were spies in the corners. "Do you remember what happened?"

Was this a trick question? If he said yes, would he be accountable? If he said no, would they see him as the liar?

"It's not my fault," he settled on, because that was the truth and hopefully held off the blame. "You see my face, don't you?" He stared up at Dirrick, ignoring for now the blur of uniform behind the major's shoulder. "He did that to me."

"Who did, that abo?"

"No. No, no. My *father.*" He felt naked and shifted around in the seat before pushing off from it, some stoked anger giving rise to a fire in his limbs. He shoved himself to his wooden footlocker and sank down on his knees in front of it.

"What are you doing?" Dirrick said, but still in that tone of caution.

The room was a tense wire, and the fear traveled along it with a chiming clang.

"Getting my gun. Where are my weapons?"

"He can't do that," Colonel Ponne murmured.

"We removed them," the major said.

It occurred to Jarrett that they weren't precisely talking to him. He shoved his hands into the various personal items in the locker, but he didn't have to search far to discover that they spoke the truth. His extra pistol, his second, older Trant knife...they'd taken even the ancient arrowhead he'd found at Fort Sheare years ago.

"Where are my godsdamned weapons?"

"Why do you need them now?" the major said.

What a ridiculous question. "I'm going to kill—" The mission. The Soreganee warriors. Qoyotariz. The coyote. A shiver staked claim in his limbs and did not free him for some minutes. "What happened?" And it was as if that one late inquiry brought the curious distance into the slamming forefront. Colors darkened, then brightened again before his eyes, like one of his superiors had drawn an imaginary blind over his window only to pull it back again. "Please," he heard himself say, to nobody. His hands curved around the top of the locker and melded there unmoving.

"Captain," Dirrick said. He took a step closer.

Jarrett saw the gun at his hip, in its brown holster. He moved abruptly to his bed and sank onto it. His heart pawed at the inside of his ribs. "Don't—" He held his palm up to stay the other man's approach, head tilted down. He saw a gray pants leg. If he just arched his gaze up a little more he could see the colonel. "Your pistol. I don't know what's happening to me. Give me a minute. Just...step away."

"Could the abo explain this?" The colonel's voice was a restrained disgust. Though what he was repelled by seemed a little more uncertain.

"It's not him." Jarrett shook his head. "This isn't his demon magic. The girl…"

"The girl is in a state in her cell. With that animal the Whishishian brought back."

He remembered. Which jail cell it didn't matter. He remembered the Dog's blue eyes and the way it had bitten his shoulder. He remembered the bite on his muzzle from the coyote. The ache of both remained, dull even so. He dared not lift a hand to his face to feel it.

"I need to see her. The wolf." They would think it a wolf. "I need to see the wolf and the Whishishian." He looked up, and they were staring at him as if he'd requested to touch the moon. "Trust me." They did not. "These are the general's orders," he said with more steel conviction. He didn't blink when he looked at them, and some part of his sense of courtesy knew that no captain spoke to his superiors this way, and yet they didn't reprimand him for it. They both stood in his cramped quarters like those tableaus of battle, moving in a different manner if they moved at all, while his gaze bore through like bullets at a couple easy quail.

"There was a dog," Major Dirrick finally said, "and then it leaped on you and was no more."

This was the thing they'd come to say, that he sat there thinking should never be said, silently to himself much less aloud in a room full of other ears.

"The men all saw it," Dirrick continued. The nail, it seemed, would be driven in. "Then you struggled and gasped and came alive, when we'd thought you dead. You lay on the ground and wouldn't move or breathe, so we thought you dead."

And he'd come back to life. That alone would have

been reason to fear or want to shoot, but the fact of the Dog made matters even less believable. One could accept miracles, as the Church had special privileges for those ideas, but this demon magic had no place in civilized society, among civilized men of war. This was how they thought of themselves. He scented the need to shoot or step away battling in these two. The same conflicting need collided in him and the knowledge that they could, in fact, kill him.

Their guns were like ringing bells, calling for his attention. To notice them so he could be rid of the threat somehow.

"These tribal marks," he said, even if he had little hope of them understanding, since he did not, "do more than sit on my skin as decoration. Or so the girl had told me." So he had seen.

"The general dabbles?" Colonel Ponne said, in the loudest voice he'd yet utilized in the room.

"I don't know what the general does. All I know is he is doing it to me." His soiled and rumpled blankets that he'd lain on with all the dirt of his fighting were an apt distraction to the filth he felt through the spoken words.

"He is who he is," Colonel Ponne stated.

Nobody denied it. They all knew his history—the battles won, his ruthless command. And there seemed little else to do about it.

"I need to see Keeley and that wolf," Jarrett insisted. "Where are they?"

"In the stockade," Major Dirrick said. *Where perhaps you need to be.*

Though it hadn't been said aloud, he looked into the major's hazel eyes and could practically read it there.

Clearly they didn't know what else to say to him, and perhaps this meeting was meant to help them decide what to do with him. He barely knew what to do with himself, but he fought against all unexplainable inclinations and forced his mind to think of practical things.

"What of the rancher's family?" Dead, most likely.

"We have the children. The father and the mother perished."

War made orphans more readily than it did heroes.

"They said they have an aunt and uncle in Ulila," the major continued. "So we've sent word."

"Good," Jarrett murmured.

"It was a fortunate encounter for those children," Dirrick pointed out. He looked at Colonel Ponne. "Captain Fawle did lead a good mission. There's little left of that band of Soreganee."

"Hmmm," Ponne said, still staring straight at him.

Jarrett took a deep breath. "Can I see the abo now?"

Nobody was comfortable. Nobody knew what was truly going on. Maybe they could all convince themselves it was a dream and every day that persisted on this could be another night of sleepwalking. He was willing to indulge in the possibility, but one look at their faces told him they likely would not.

"As we said," the colonel said. "They're in the stockade. You may go see the abo warrior, but be careful."

There was no other way to be with an abo. Jarrett stood and had enough presence of mind to nod at both the colonel and Major Dirrick. "I'd like to change clothes first..." He didn't really need to despite his less than clean state, since he felt no need to primp for the Whishishian, but he wanted a few moments of respite from the examinations.

They still regarded him as if something were going to spring from his head and attack them. He supposed, all things considered, it was not outside the realm.

With a terse reply and a last watchful glance, Colonel Ponne opened the door and stepped out. Warm air wafted in that immediately set the stuffy room to breathing again, and Jarrett began to unbutton his collar. Major Dirrick lingered, slower as he drifted to the door and placed a hand on the wooden knob.

"I don't know what's going on," he admitted in a low voice, "but it's some kind of godsforsaken thing. Isn't it?"

He didn't use the curse in the throwaway manner of most people, and Jarrett didn't hear it like that. If what his men and Major Dirrick had witnessed had been godsforsaken, then that could only mean that he was too. He'd never before been much of a believer in the Seven Deities, yet it was a strange irony to find oneself missing a belief when the opposite demanded acknowledgment. Could it be possible to be cast out of divine favor if one had no experience with it in the first place?

He saw no point in dwelling on theological questions, so he didn't answer. The major, his friend and a sometime stranger now, slipped out the door. The men still hovered outside until the colonel barked at them to get back to work.

It was an odd loss, this new sight. He'd become something to be scared of among his own people—a thing to stare at but not approach.

He couldn't think of that now, even as these small actions propelled him to more foreign association with the abo and the witch girl. He stripped off his soiled clothes and slipped on the other of his two uniforms. His body was sore, he saw bruises and scratches on his skin before covering it with clothing: his cotton shirt and trousers, no uniform frock. His boots felt heavy as he opened the door and stepped out into the bright sun.

Men walked the grounds, about their various tasks of hauling water from the well or guiding the horses around the grand parade. The sounds of drill spread across the groomed grass and bounced off the buildings. He crossed it all with his gaze down, hoping his hair hid most of his face, and suffered the silent stares that followed in his wake and started up ahead of him. It was a regular wave of scrutiny along both flanks and at every angle as he tried to lope with casual direction toward the obvious stockade.

The looks lingered there too, all the way inside and finally to the abo's cell, where Keeley sat below the barred window with the Dog beside him. Jarrett didn't want to ask that the door be shut, because he wasn't sure if he could count on the men to open it up again when he asked. But it was either this or he let the entire fort hear what he had to say to the Whishishian. Not that his voice could travel to all corners of the stone and wood walls, but it just had to go as far as a soldier's ears. Everyone knew that idle men gossiped just as much as idle old hags.

The abo seemed unsurprised to see him, which was fortunate, so they didn't fight and encourage speculation. Jarrett shut the door behind him, heard the guard outside turn the lock, and faced the young warrior with a keen eye to the Dog sitting near. She was docile or...at least quiet, paws flat, her long, full tail curled against her left hindquarters. It thumped once when he entered, her stare unblinking. One ear twitched forward.

"They let you come," Keeley said.

"They're afraid," he admitted. He took a step closer and the Dog raised her chin.

"They ought to be," the abo said. He didn't move at all. "They saw your Dog. They didn't know it was you and one shot at you. You jumped back into your body." Despite the steady voice there was a tightness about the man's eyes evident even in the dim light. "It's not the same as the Aniw girl. Or my people."

"Just shut up for one minute," Jarrett snapped, rubbing a hand along this forehead. His other hand stretched out, palm down. "Just...shut up." He strode to the small window and peered through the bars. Some of the men lingering near gazed in his direction.

The silence buzzed with unknown critters. The air stifled him and he tugged at his collar, even if he hadn't buttoned it all the way to his throat.

He was surprised at the sound of Keeley's voice, for it was gentle. And even more surprised at the nature of his question.

"Are you well?"

It did not placate him. Instead he looked at the abo with some irritation. "No, I'm not *well*. None of this is *well*. In fact it's pretty bloody sick, what's happening to me." The words revolted from his throat like he was filled by disease, and the only way to be cured was through his acid tongue. He pulled in an unsteady breath.

"This war breeds madness," Keeley said, in the same quiet tone.

It was a phrase well used among fighting men. Jarrett had always thought himself mostly immune, even in the thick of extended battles and fallen comrades. But lately it had not been so. The piled-upon years of violence grew a thick and unforgiving insulation to good dreams. Or so he'd thought. The bad had been kept in and the pleasant driven out. Until it had driven him all the way to a city on the coast and a father on the edge of some clandestine discovery. Now he didn't know what to make of it, or if anything could be made of it. Sense didn't seem to be easily fashioned and had no plans that he could engineer.

"I am sorry," the abo said.

Jarrett didn't know what to make of that either. "For what?"

"I will help you if I can," Keeley said, instead of answering. "As I did in that battle."

"Why would you want to help me?"

Now there was no mistaking the palpable sadness in the abo's amber stare. "Are we not brothers?"

And so it was cast down between them, like a gauntlet. He found his legs shook like they were stilts he hadn't yet mastered. He put a hand to the window bars and the warm iron seemed to anchor his stance.

He had no reply to that. The abo looked down at the silent Dog, who seemed all too relaxed in the state of this human distress.

Jarrett glared back out the window and said, "Where is Sjenn?"

He didn't mean the Dog. From his left side Keeley said, "Her body waits in the cell next to mine."

"She could be waiting with it." Walls did not keep

this creature in. Neither did human sinew tie it down.
It went where it pleased until compelled by the Call.
He understood something of it now, in the glimpses of
memory and unsettled feeling of being in the forest,
or under white gaslight. The will to roam was a large
one, but his nervous senses shivered at the thought.
He was too young, perhaps. He remembered what it
was to stand on four paws, and the image was a hard
one, like certain atrocities of battle. But there was no
denying it now that he saw it in the faces of every man
around him. They had shared the tension now. They had
shed blood.

Keeley said, "She could wait there. But she waits
here." A pause. "Will you guide back her little spirit?"

Because her way required a Call.

Jarrett shut his eyes. He gave a start when he felt a wet
nose nudge the back of his hand. He looked down and
saw the curious, intelligent eyes of the wolf staring up
at him. But the demeanor was nothing but Dog. She was
unafraid of him.

Something he could not fathom propelled his fingers
to touch along the powerful broad forehead of the animal
and course back through the short gray fur between her
ears. She gave a natural resistance but not to push away,
only encourage. Not unlike any domestic dog that wanted
to be stroked. Her muzzle brushed with insistance against
his hip. It was so strong a touch it almost set him off his
feet.

"One day attacking, another day affectionate," Keeley
said.

Because she was wild and owed no constancy to man.
Jarrett ran his hand back along her ruff but she moved

then, as if she'd had enough, and paced to the cell door before looking back at him.

It took no thinking, his steps trailed after her. He called out for the guard.

She beckoned and he followed.

FORT GIRS

More walls. Before Sjenn even opened her eyes she knew they stood around her with the hard silence of disapproving demigods. She shared some commonality with the structure now, she felt it in the layers of her skin and deep beneath where her little spirit resided. She'd walked through them in the middle light and been free on the land.

She blinked up at the shadowed ceiling of this Kabliw cell and recalled the rolling ground beneath her feet and the scent of foreign earth in her nostrils. Her little spirit had run a long time to catch up with Captain Jarrett, following the tracks of their beasts and their boots, and the residual color they left in their wake. A large passage of men always left something behind, and it had taken no extra senses to find her way through strange terrain, to the clatter and clang and acrid scents of battle. The guns had been plenty. She heard them still.

Now she heard voices from outside, the constant murmur of an occupied land. This fort was the future, she feared. Large blocks of Kabliw staking claim wherever they went. She'd seen it now in two separate places, and seen the violence up close.

Guns in crates sat upon her Land. Their great ships traveled great distances, like their horses did, to transport their claims across the earth, and now the tundra. She didn't think even ice could hold them back. Not if swelling seas could not.

"Sjenn."

The voice. It had a softer tone. It had Called her back. His hand had touched her back and her little spirit had not bitten him.

They'd tussled in the forest. It had felt like natural play among the towering trees. She'd wanted to run in joy, she remembered, and despite the clog of green, it had not been like these walls.

The other, third Dog she did not know, but it had seemed to know the captain's yellow Dog.

She pulled herself to sit and there he stood, Captain Jarrett and his yellow Dog. She saw it now that she'd *seen* it...and him. Even though his little spirit made no solid shape in the waking world. She knew the shape of the yellow Dog regardless and felt the faint outline of its body, crouched deep in the captain's chest. She didn't know what roused it without a Call, and that ignorance drove her despite herself. How could it be? Yet her sight in the middle light had been bright indeed, and her Dog and his had run in the forest. The man was just as nervous as his animal had been. He stood a bit aways.

She didn't even have to ask. He said to her first, "Would you like to walk outside?" As if the walls suffocated him as well.

Sjenn pulled herself to her feet. Her height was far short to his, but with the small distance between them she did not have to look up. Their gazes leveled. "Yes," she said.

His steps were slower than she remembered and it took no effort to match them. The sun was bright like a tundra spring sky, but there was no soft snow to reflect the light. She still squinted, though, and wished for shade. The warmth in the air filled her mouth and brought the thirst. They passed a well and he took her to it, some residual manners still left in him. A far cry from his treatment at the general's house, or his short visits in this fort. He brought the bucket up and scooped out a ladle of the clear liquid for her and she drank. It went too soon and he dropped the bucket back and they walked on. She would have preferred to sit under one of the trees near the corners of the fort, but the captain insisted on a walking circuit around the edges, following the high stone walls. Out in the open at least.

Even out in the open these Kabliw had an urge to build walls. They kept so much out it was no wonder they battled. No man liked to be ostracized. They lived by willing punishment upon each other, then wondered why they could not get along.

At least she could breathe and the air was fresh. Not even the strong scent of these marching bodies infiltrated too hard. So many men. So many of them in their dark uniforms under the scorching sun. Their shouts of commands echoed across the open field and bounced from wall to wall before they were released up into the blue

sky. Birds soared high above but too far for her to see
what kind. Perhaps one was an owl, like Captain Jarret
had said. But she could not hear its call. She thought of
the white owls of her Land.

Though the whole fort rang with activity, they walked
in silence for a time. His tattoos had healed completely.
The only redness now was in his eyes and the scratches
on his face.

Finally she said, "Where is Father Bari's book?"

He seemed startled by the question itself, not the
sound of her voice suddenly between them. He looked
down at her. "Back in my quarters."

"You Called without it."

He blinked. "Yes."

Some things, it seemed, became fast revelations.

He said, "I remembered the words."

"You know the Call," she said. "Though you don't
require it yourself. At least... not from me or any other
with *ankago* blood."

"So it would seem."

His Dog had been strange, like a language she could
barely understand. "Maybe," she said with care, "it's
because you are not Aniw. But you have Aniw markings
on your skin. Maybe your little spirit is confused. It is not
a simple thing to teach a little spirit."

He seemed somehow amused by the statement. "Is it
not?"

Her eyes narrowed. The Kabliw were as changeable
as the spirit lights in the late autumn skies. Always shifting in their expressions without prediction. Dangerous
to mock. "If Keeley's people can also have the *ankago*
power, perhaps yours do too."

"In faerie stories."

"Among my people, stories spring from truth. We can only tell what we've experienced, and even in the retelling it is something we know is true. Because our ancestors knew it to be true. The *ankago* have told stories since the Dogs first came to us."

"And when was that?"

She could not discern from his tone if he were truly asking, or asking to humor her.

"Father Bari must have written it," she said. The ground was beginning to hurt the soles of her feet, even through the shoes the woman Louna had given her. Her ankles ached too. These men and their intentions, even the land they lived upon, tended to hurt.

"He did..." the captain said. "He wrote a lot of fanciful things."

She bit the inside of her cheek and stopped walking. "Yes. They are as fanciful as your Dog."

He kept on in his stride for a few more steps, then turned to her.

"You're a stubborn, foolish man," she said and did not care that all around her were equally stubborn and likely foolish men. She had saved this one's life and yet his ritual was to mock. He couldn't seem to retain what it was to be the little spirit. He couldn't seem to revere it at all.

"I've been called that before," he said.

"By wise men."

"By my father."

"He is a wise man, though you hate him." She said it into his face and the dark lines of his new tattoos. They were oddly striking against his lighter skin. She had never before seen such markings on Kabliw, not so close to the eyes, where one glimpsed some vestiges of the little spirit. At least in this Kabliw. It didn't exist in any others that she'd ever met. She stared. "Your father knew of your Dog even if you did not," she said, to provoke him more or wipe that vacant humor from his lips.

"So it would seem."

"Yet you stand there and deny. Those are the actions of a foolish man. Would you deny the sky up above?" She gestured toward the thin clouds and their blue backdrop. "Or the land on which you walk?"

"I don't deny this thing," he said. "I just don't wish to accept it yet."

"And perhaps that's why you cannot control it."

He watched her and said not a word.

"You can't control it," she said. "It's clear to me now. Out you leaped in your battle, and in you jumped when your own people scared you. You bounce in and out like a hare with no direction. All legs and no direction in your run."

She said it with some harshness but he didn't blink. "My father wanted you to teach me. Are you saying you can now?"

"You're not Aniw. I don't know your dark light."

"You know more than anyone else, unless we went and kidnapped one of Keeley's *janna*."

"Did you know that other Dog?"

He looked away. "No."

"Why do you always lie?"

There began the infant crawl of desperation across his face. "If you can't help me, then I'm lost, aren't I? There's nobody else."

It was dangerous to feel compassion for men like him. "It is why I'm here, far from home. To help you."

She could hate these men, if not their land. Perhaps he understood. He seemed to hate his father but respect the general's rank.

"Teach me, then," he said, and for a Kabliw second there was an unmasking in his eyes. "Teach me so I don't do it again in front of my men."

She had noticed the stares during their stroll. Though the other men worked and went about their day, there was a pall of silence in their near vicinity as if someone had died and now walked among them. It was the respect and fear one gave to spirits. It was not the love and regard one gave an *ankago* of his tribe.

"If you are willing," she said. "And they will learn as well. You are power to them now."

His breaths drew ragged and he stepped closer. "I didn't ask for this. Where does it end? Isn't it possible to be rid of it?"

His little spirit. She said, remembering, "Only if you were to die." Once he'd cast that threat upon her. "Somewhere in your Kabliw blood, your people too followed the ways of the *ankago*."

He shook his head, but his denial did not change the truth when he heard it. She saw it working behind his eyes like a rising light. "That coyote, that other Dog..."

"You've met him before."

His eyes watered and he nodded, mute. The scratches on his face reminded her of the strange Dog's bite.

"He is another Kabliw?" Nothing now surprised her.

"No." Captain Jarrett sniffed and scraped a swift hand across his eyes. "No, he's from the tribe we fought. The Soreganee. I met him once in a skirmish before I went to Nev Anyan. He'd said...he'd told me then that he marked my men by me. He tracked my men by me. I hadn't known what he meant…"

But the guilt had settled deep. It was in every line of his face, especially in the sun-drenched webs at the corners of his eyes.

"He saw your little spirit. His Dog may see things even different from mine, as you are different from mine. My people depend on the *ankago* and the Dog. We track the caribou over every terrain. We beware against the great bear. It's the gift of our ancestors to the survival of the people. All *ankago* know each other in the middle light." She had traveled far to find this commonality, and yet it was not a reunion of glad tidings. The coyote had fought her with malice, and its eyes knew no respect.

The captain was scared of it. "The warrior Qoyotariz… he is not an abo one can reason with." Like Keeley was.

"Sometimes," Sjenn said, "the Dog must kill."

It was the thing that had brought her here to this Kabliw world. It was the anger that had proven to be shallow soil in their conversation, anger that now seemed distant on the Land, unmarked even by the stones of memory. The captain now understood what it felt to be threatened, where the only recourse was attack.

The Dog did not mourn human death.

Back in the cell she dozed. Her stint around the fort, in that high sun, sent her straight to restless slumber until the sounds of the door opening roused her once again. Through the haze of sleep and half-opened eyes she spied a robed figure venturing in. She gave a start of shock and pushed herself up to one hand. Father Bari had come to enact revenge.

But then the priest drew closer, holding another plate of food with a cup balanced to one side, and Sjenn saw a full face, not the bone hollow of a death's head. This was a woman dressed in holy garb, and her smile was white. She looked familiar and Sjenn struggled to remember the face . . . from days and days ago. In a different place. In a church so large it echoed and the gods grew tall like the sky and stood made of stone.

Sjenn didn't reach for the plate, so the blue-eyed woman set it on the floor.

"Hello," she said. "My name is Sister Oza. You are Sjennonirk?"

All the Kabliw world knew her name, it seemed. And she did not trust the teeth in this face.

"I knew the late Father," the woman continued. "We are of the same Church."

She looked toward the door. Had they allowed this person in to kill her? Revenge could come in many guises.

"I'm not going to hurt you. But I would like to help you."

She had heard that offer before. Her mouth was dry, so she leaned and plucked the cup from the plate and sipped the cool water within.

"You can free me from this jail?" That was the only sort of help that mattered at the moment.

"I can try," Sister Oza said. "I don't think you belong here."

"I don't."

The priestess crouched down, her legs hidden beneath long folds of gray robe. Her hands disappeared up the sleeves. She had very short hair, like some of these men.

"You know it's not right that there is any sort of mixing of your...magic...with the people of this country."

Sjenn stared at the dark-skinned woman over the rim of her cup. "He won't send me home unless I help him. Do you know General Fawle?"

Father Bari had known Captain Jarrett. Perhaps all of these Kabliw somehow had association.

"Oh, yes," Sister Oza said, with a pull to her lips that might have been a smile. But Sjenn wasn't sure, not when it contradicted the eyes. "We know the general very well indeed."

"He believes in the dark light."

"So do we," the Sister said. "Though many have forgotten, our people have a touching acquaintance with it. It's why the captain can do what you do. But it cannot be allowed."

She set the cup on the floor. "Why not?" Were they so afraid? Was that such an ingrained Kabliw trait, that they built forts and banned *ankago* light?

Sister Oza straightened to her feet now. The shadows fell over half her form, half of her face. "We did not leave one land of demons to come to another and be consumed." Then her tone changed and her teeth flashed once again. "I will free you, Sjennonirk. And this wrong will be no more."

That night she dreamed of battle. It was another Kabliw word, like *iron* and *gun*. Even their words were hard, and they seemed to have many names for the same violence. *Battle, war, fight. Skirmish. Attack. Bloodshed.* Different but related, like the many types of snow, but not nearly as pure or benign. Not even a blizzard could destroy as thoroughly as a battle, nor did it leave such red fury upon the land in its wake. Such was the Kabliw concentration, their common terrain. These Southern people who built great ships and yet could not embark on an exploring peace. Their war stretched from ocean to inland, and according to Captain Jarrett it had been going on for years.

It was her Dog who entered the fray, and though she had never before seen such wreckage among men, it had some recollection in its memory, far, far away. The Dogs had fought among themselves once, before their relationship with the Aniw. Long ago, when the caribou were not hunted by anything but bears and wolves, the Dogs had fought and split off into packs. And from those packs came the *ankago,* born among the different tribes of the Aniw. Born from the marriage of man and Dog, when the First Female had lain with Ankagok of the Tjerinnen tribe. Every tribe had a First Female story of how the spiritwalkers had come to be.

This would be Captain Jarrett's first lesson.

She dreamed she told him in the midst of battle, once his little spirit leaped from his body and ran away with her. Battle was no place for a pup. She had gone there searching, knowing he was heading to a probable end. Some mother instinct, maybe, or a puzzle that compelled her. She did not walk in the middle light now, it was only a dream, but it was as clear as a present-making memory. As the experience itself.

They had run, and bit, and in the jail cell next door he had seemed to remember. His hand had tasted of salt when she'd licked it and had felt like respect upon her head. This man could be soft beneath his hard layers and harder words. She'd seen his true face, and it had been afraid.

In her dream the pup grew into a strong golden Dog, sleek fur and long muzzle. His ears stood tall and open and his tail held a delicate curve. When he ran he made no sound. He was the open land of these grassy hills and soft dark soil, just as sure as she was the tundra ice.

And in her dream she looked behind them in their run and saw a black Dog far off on a hill. Her father watched.

In the morning Captain Jarrett liberated both her and Keeley from the dark cells and took them on a brief jaunt to the "officers' mess," as he called it. It was a place of eating, and they cooked their food here too. She smelled the smoke and heat of it before they got in the door, and then the overpowering scent of bacon grease and dark coffee swallowed her whole. These were the remembered smells of Kabliw sailors and Kabliw camps. They stank up the Land with it in obvious dominance.

The men here stared, and all motions upon their plates stopped completely. She stood close to Keeley. They were both weaponless. She noticed now even Captain Jarrett was, though he wore his uniform in full unlike the day before. Without any sort of overt acknowledgment, he led them without hesitation to a long table by the far wall and sat himself upon one of the equally long, scored-up

benches. What could she and the Whishishian do? They
sat as well.

It seemed to break a spell, and the quieter sounds of
eating picked up again. Subdued, but there. The captain
coiled his hands together for a moment before straightening up, unhooking his fingers.

"Right. Well you'd best stay here, they won't want
you by the food. Just don't move. I'll be back with something." His green gaze flickered to her. "Something edible
for you." He stood again and made his way through the
tabled ranks of men toward the back where the cooks
stood, dishing food and drink from tall blackened pots
and beaten metal jugs.

The smell began to seep too far into her body. She
leaned her arms upon the table.

"Are you unwell?" Keeley asked.

"I can't stand the stench," she said. "And this heat."

"It's not so bad today. There is a breeze at least." They
kept the door open to this building.

She barely noticed or felt the touch of air. Perhaps she
was the only one in this state. "It's warm for me."

He didn't say anything, only nodded. She looked
at him to distract herself. He wore no full black paint,
though the stain of it was still upon his skin as though it
would never wash off. Perhaps it never would. His dark
gold eyes were alert, probably because of their location.
He was a blatant enemy in a camp full of opposite allies.
He was the general's man, but maybe that was easy to
forget in this clime. Just a few days ago they had fought
other abos. How well did these Kabliw distinguish the
tribes? From Captain Jarrett's behavior, the line was fine
indeed.

Keeley seemed desirous to look around the wide room, at the watchful faces, but didn't want to look too closely. His arms stayed upon the table, his hands in plain sight, and his hair fell forward. Sjenn watched his gaze dart and then settle finally upon her for a few longer moments. But the presence of these soldiers drew his attention in a constant glance.

"Would they attack us?" she said.

"I don't think so. If they wanted to, they wouldn't hesitate."

"Captain Jarrett says his men are uncomfortable even with *him*."

Keeley nodded. They both understood why. It was the same discomfort they felt sitting here among all the Kabliw faces.

"He's nearly one of us now," the Whishishian said. Something in his tone seemed part distaste and part regret.

Captain Jarrett was not one of them in any way that would give him peace, Sjenn thought.

She didn't think she should mention the visit from the priest lady, though something about that white smile cast her ill at ease. Even more than with the company she now kept. But Sister Oza had said she would help Sjenn leave this fort. If that were so, then she could not tell Captain Jarrett, or even Keeley, who claimed solitude in his thoughts and reasons for his actions. So she held to her silence too, and waited.

"Has he been to see you often?" she asked the Whishishian.

"Not often. But some."

She wondered at the sad tone and thought it must be

their imprisonment. She might have asked after it, but Captain Jarrett came back to them through the tables of the men. The others fell silent as he passed, then picked up speaking again in huddled, quiet tones. The captain's face was mask-like in its restraint. He held a metal tray with three plates of food on it and three coffee mugs. He set it in the middle of the table and sat across once again from her and Keeley.

"Here," he said. "Eat up, you won't get another for a few hours at least."

She stared at the fried beans, bacon, and potatoes. Kabliw food. There was bread too, and she went for that first.

"You can't exist solely on bread," the captain said.

"Your meat makes me sick," she said, dipping the heel of the brown slice into her coffee before eating. It had a barely tolerable taste of smoke, but it was enough.

"Eat a potato at least."

She didn't make a move toward it, even though he prodded it with the prongs of his fork.

"You're no good if you're weak," he said, with the sort of care she'd come to expect from him. "And you've lost weight."

She knew that she had. Clothes were heavy, even this Kabliw cloth. Even in the heat she missed the touch of her sealskins. Would her family even recognize her if they saw her in this garb? She wondered if she would ever touch sealskin again, or embrace her mother. She wondered if she would ever again have need to wear her snow clothes. In the waking hours she felt spare like a fishing hook that could catch no fish.

"I would eat fish. You have water close by."

"There will be fish for dinner. Should I tell them not to cook yours?"

So he was learning. "Please, yes."

His gaze moved to Keeley and then back to her face. "You are a strange people."

"We are a gathering of strange," Keeley said.

Captain Jarrett stabbed the meat on his plate. "That is the gods' cursed truth."

"Have you kept the Father's journal safe?" Keeley asked.

The captain paused in his attack on his food. "Why do you ask?"

"It may have answers to the questions of your—"

"Not here," said Captain Jarrett. His eyes moved over their shoulders and his frown etched deep. "Keep such talk to the stockade and nowhere else."

He had duties, the captain said, and it clearly didn't entail letting a couple tribespeople loose in the fort. He took them back to the stockade and seemed almost apologetic for having to lock them up separately. "Colonel's orders," he said. His manner had been agitated the entire time in the mess hall, but Sjenn didn't blame him. His own people mocked him silently, darkly, and the punishment was felt as it would be for anyone. She'd seen similiar behavior in her own tribe when a hunter or a woman cast off on their own or disrupted their fellows. It was the surest way to influence bad behavior into something good, but she was not sure it worked the same way among the Kabliw.

"When will the lessons begin?" she asked him,

standing again in the cool darkness of the cell. At least it was a little protected here from beneath that sun.

"I don't know. We'd have to find somewhere private and I don't know..." His gaze drifted behind his shoulder. Down the hall they heard the guard belch. "I would like to take you outside the town, but they won't accept that. Even if I said it was on my father's orders."

Of course they wouldn't.

"I'll talk to Major Dirrick," he said, but he didn't seem hopeful. His eyes held shadows beneath them, sucking the light from the green color.

He left her there in the jail with few other words. She had no visitors. The sun arched away, giving little light into the darkness now. Sounds were distant as the day progressed and men went about their business of war. Marching, she heard, and shouts of order. Horses walked around, led by their masters, washed down and fed and exercised. They kept a care of these large animals like the Aniw did with their sled dogs, so at least there was some form of respect in them about something. Cousin dogs barked but she could not call them. It would not be something she could do here without perhaps angering the guard.

She stood at the little window and looked out for hours. The horses were not so scary from this distance and neither were the men. The guard left her alone, and from next door she heard no sound from Keeley. But Keeley tended not to make much sound.

Sometime toward dusk, when she tired from standing and curled up on the straw-covered floor once more, there came footsteps outside. They were heavier than Captain Jarrett's. Perhaps the guard to give her food?

She sat up to greet him. The door opened and a vaguely familiar man stepped in. He was tall, but not as tall as Captain Jarrett, and had a sparse brown beard. But there was nothing weary or bloodshot about him like she had noticed with the other man. He let the door shut behind him, left the guard outside, and stood there for a moment just gazing at her.

It reminded her of Captain Mackenzi's stare but it was not quite as nervous. Or nervous at all. He had the bearing of a man who did not find fear in much.

He removed his cap and smoothed a hand back over his short hair. "My name is Major Kaje Dirrick," he said.

So he was polite too. But he wore a gun like most of these Kabliw.

She pulled herself to her feet, rumpled in her days-old Kabliw clothes that were better suited for a man than for a woman. They held no form to them upon her body and the edges had begun to fray. She was smudged from head to toe, for they had not compelled a bath all this time, unlike at the general's house.

"Sjennonirk," she said, placing a hand on her breast.

His mouth opened slightly as if he wanted to repeat it but decided against it. "I see," he said instead. "Of the Hasky?"

"I am Aniw."

"Ah, yes. Of course." He moved closer. She didn't back up, and he stopped after two steps, veering a little to the right to look around the cell as if he'd never before seen it. Perhaps he hadn't. He didn't seem the kind of man that would have to stay in here for any length of time. She knew that was another form of Kabliw punishment when the kind of ostracism she'd seen in the mess hall did not work. "You've come here on General Fawle's orders," he said.

These were things he knew. She didn't say anything.

"And that Whishishian? Him too?"

Perhaps he wanted to hear an answer. So she said, "Yes."

"And you bring demon magic."

This was the question. She said, "No."

"What do you call it, then?" His stare found its way from the stone blocks back to her eyes, and they were of a different status from the captain's. There was an honest interest in his gaze that she had not seen so early in Captain Jarrett.

"We call it the dark light. It has nothing to do with your demons."

"Do your people not have demons?"

His questions came like the pounding in a drum dance. They were dancing here, and he had not wasted any time about it.

"Do your people have demons?" she asked.

"Some say we do."

"My people don't argue. We know our spiritual forefathers. They teach us to fear only the things worth fearing."

"And demons aren't worth fearing."

She wondered at this Kabliw fixation on the idea of magic and some class of evil they thought it held. "Only demons that are real," she said.

"I saw Captain Jarrett come alive when a little dog jumped onto him. What do you call that?"

"That is his Dog."

"His dog?"

"He is not a demon, though your people look at him

like he is. He is what our people call an *ankago*. He is a spiritwalker."

Major Dirrick showed no surprise, only a thoughtful cant of his chin. "What does that mean?"

"His ancestor was a Dog."

The man laughed. But it wasn't one of mocking. Surprise shored the edges of the sound, but just as quickly as the reaction poured forth, it died. "Somehow that doesn't seem too far-fetched."

"They aren't dogs as you think of them. They aren't those." She pointed out the window. "The dog is just the shape. I've told Captain Jarrett about them, why don't you ask him?"

"I prefer to come to the source. The men say you are also a dog. They're afraid."

"The Kabliw seem to fear what they cannot conquer."

He took a step closer to her. The light was fading, and he seemed insistent to perceive her face. She still didn't move back and she saw his eyes take note of it.

"There is no going back for him, is there?" he asked.

"Going back where?"

"To the man he was before he went to see his father."

"I don't know that man, so I can't answer."

"Do you know this one?" he said.

This Major Dirrick was not like Captain Mackenzi. He was even much different from Father Bari. He didn't pretend to be kind in his questions, only efficient. And he was not intimidated by asking, much less by the answers she gave. Yet he hadn't the cold distance and superior attitude of General Fawle, or the disdain of Fawle's son. He was a rare Kabliw.

"I know this one a little," she said. "But he is complicated and stubborn."

The corner of the major's mouth curled faintly. "So
you do." That hint of humor faded fast. "I wish for you
to help him, Sjennonirk." He had waited to say her name
aloud, but he said it with accuracy.

"I said that I would, if he's willing. If I know how to
help him." She hoped she would not regret it. "But I don't
know if I can. He is different."

"You would help on the general's orders?"

Confronted so bluntly, she felt the answer before she
said it. "I would regardless. I am *ankago* too. I know what
it's like to walk the middle light. In the middle light he's
lost, so I must help him." If she refused to guide him, who
knew what his Dog would do? She didn't know his yellow
Dog, but he knew even less. If it ran rampant, not one of
these men would be safe. But she didn't say that to Major
Dirrick. Though he was calm in the discussion, he still
wore a gun. "I need to teach him," she said. "But it can't
be among these men."

The major looked at her, assessing. "There aren't any
free patches in this fort that could not be walked up on."

"So Captain Jarrett said. He suggested outside of the
town."

The man fell silent for a minute.

"That might be more than a little impossible, unless you
had a guard. But then that wouldn't be private either."

"You may guard?" Out of all the men here he seemed
able to accept the truth. Perhaps he would be equally
accepting in the face of the Dog. He had seen it once
already without a need to shoot, and he was speaking to
her out of interest in the captain.

"I may," he said.

"If you truly want to help," she said, "then you will."

His tone was thoughtful, as if he'd learned something new. "You are a simple people, aren't you?"

Sometimes she did not understand these Kabliw at all. "Is not the world a simple matter?"

"Not here."

"Then you are lost too," she said.

He placed his cap back on his head. "Perhaps we are," he said. "Perhaps we are indeed."

Her night was fitful and hemmed in, and she did not dream. Not even her father visited her. He had not spoken to her in a long while, not even in the middle light, and the white bear was silent too. If even her threat animal didn't deign to visit, to warn her of what was to come, how, then, could she be guided? Was she now so far from home that they could no longer reach her even in the middle light?

She wondered if Captain Jarrett roamed when his people went to sleep. His Dog didn't visit her. It was an unpredictable thing. The bugle call when night fell was a lonely, wailing sound, a long note so unlike the staccato heartbeat of the drum. It sounded like a manmade howl. It followed her well into sleep and awoke her the next morning with a different, furious birdcall. Perhaps it was that noise that staved away Aleqa's little spirit and managed to frighten even the great bear.

The morning passed without Kabliw commentary. Her food was delivered by the guard, on the familiar beaten plate, and it was not anything she could readily eat. Once again she picked at the bread and downed the coffee, and ate one of their apples. It all had begun to work an agitation in her as well. Captain Jarrett's distracted movements from the day before seemed to have bled onto her. But at least the nausea was absent, as this day seemed cooler than the last, though the sun shone broad.

As her night had been intermittent, she attempted to sleep in the day. It didn't truly work and by midafternoon she was pacing. When Captain Jarrett came to take her and Keeley to dinner, she all but shoved by him out the door, but the guard was there and already considered her a witch or demon conjurer. She didn't get far, and the captain slipped a hand around her arm to guide her first to Keeley's cell, and once together he acted as an escort to both of them until they stood outside of the stockade.

"I know," he said, staring at their harried appearance. "But the colonel insists you remain somewhere secure."

"This fort isn't secure?" she said.

"Not enough for you. At least..."

Her Dog.

"I'm hungry," Keeley said, and that put a stop to the other unspoken complaint. They had air now. They could get food.

Again at the table they seemed to encourage an uncommon quiet. The captain shifted around in his seat as he tore his bread apart, eating it without any expression of delight or acknowledgment.

"What have you been doing?" Sjenn asked him. While they'd been kept in the prison.

"Fatigue. Drill."

These words had little use to her. So she bit a small portion of the small boiled potato. It had a tangy, unpleasant taste and she drank more coffee.

"I spoke to Major Dirrick," she said. "He promised to help." She wondered where Sister Oza was all this time, and what of that offer to free her? Would she even take it now, now that she had promised to help this man?

So many words and even more intentions. If someone opened the door and displayed the Land in front of her, she would be hard-pressed to delay, even for this lost Kabliw. What, then, of her *ankago* spirit? Her Dog seemed to accept the captain's little spirit, seemed curious about him now. But sometimes the Dog had a fickle nature and easily forgot her own interest. Back on the Land, back among her people, it could be easy to forget this place.

Save for the guns on the shore. And this mad general.

"I want to get out of here," Captain Jarrett said. His eyes blinked rapidly, moist.

"Yes," Keeley said. As if it were an obvious thing.

It was one thing they all had in common.

"And go where?" she asked. Where would he fit in now?

"I don't mean escape." The captain leaned back, hands upon the table, playing with his fork. "I mean, I need to do more than walk around this fort and—" His voice lowered. "Contend with the troops."

"Can't you ask Major Dirrick?" She remembered how the man had seemed honestly concerned for the captain's welfare. There were connections here among these Kabliw that she did not see, and yet all the time she was allowed out here she saw only the way Captain

Jarrett walked the grass like a lone wolf. Even when she'd followed him to the battle he had ridden ahead of his column and not spoken much. Her Dog ears had heard barely any voice, and there had been something silent and withdrawn about him. Perhaps this was what was required to lead men, though the *ankago* were never so distant from their people. Perhaps it truly was the marks upon his face that separated him from what he knew. This would agitate her too.

"I've spoken to him. Those children we rescued from the Soreganee..."

She had forgotten about the children. This made her frown. The longer she was isolated, it seemed, the easier it was to forget her *ankago* spirit. Perhaps this was why her father didn't speak to her. The frustration tugged on her insides.

The captain still spoke. "Their aunt and uncle can't make the trip to Fort Girs, and their town is a day's ride away. We're to send an escort with the children. I mean..." He leaned forward again. "I want to escort them instead of packing them into a stagecoach and waving them off. They can get attacked again along the way. They've lost both their parents, for gods' sake."

He sounded like he had given this argument before, and recently.

"Won't the major allow it?" Keeley said.

"He's not sure. He doesn't know if I ought."

"Why not?" she said. But she thought she knew. So the captain didn't answer and they sat there in swift silence.

"I am better off out there." Captain Jarrett's chin gestured up, directing their gazes out the door of the mess hall. Out the gates of the fort. "I can't stand one more day or week in here. Treated like some godsdamned pariah." His tone was low and not a little resentful.

"You might need to get used to it," Keeley said.

The captain's look was long. "Can't you people ever lie?"

The fort dogs howled. She lay in her cell shivering, as the night had brought an uncommon chill and not even these Kabliw clothes could protect her from it. She was too long in this South; it had infiltrated her bones, and now any small cold made her curl up. She couldn't sleep and the dogs called. Maybe they spoke only to the moon, or maybe some other need drove them. She stood and walked to the tiny window, tiptoeing to peer out.

The lock behind her clattered and fell away. She turned to see two silhouettes in the doorframe, one behind the other.

"Come on," Captain Jarrett said. "Dirrick and I will take you out."

She hardly believed it. They could be apparitions and perhaps she dreamed. But as she moved closer she saw the nervous expression stamped upon the captain's face. No spirit would fear like that.

"Are we not allowed?" She hesitated now. They might not get shot if they were found outside the gates, but her presence was a different matter.

"We're allowed," the major said from behind Captain Jarrett's shoulder. "By me. But we must be quiet and quick."

The three of them hurried bundled against the chill

and slipped like wraiths from the stockade. The guard didn't stop them, and she guessed the major's rank was a strong enough convincing. They took horses, Major Dirrick's gray and Captain Jarrett's gold, and she sat behind the captain, holding to his coat as they trotted past the gate guards and the men returned salutes. They weren't questioned, and even with torchlight she didn't properly see the faces of the soldiers who let them through. Perhaps they wondered, but they would wonder in silence.

The town of Fort Girs looked different at night, like Nev Anyan had. What worn columns and sagging walls stood in the unforgiving sun now seemed staunch and solid in the glancing dark. Moon white made the shadows strong and the bleached-out colors an almost pretty tint. Blues and dark violets and the pale yellow of the gas lamps cast the world in a false middle light, but she liked the blur of details all the same. This image would do. The streets were quiet save for small stray animals and the occasional blown paper fluttering at the horses' feet. Their gait was easy.

Out from the edges of the sleeping population they rode, encountering only a few who didn't look much in their way. Perhaps it was the straight saddle the army men took, or perhaps the strangers caught a gleam of silver gun in the belts of the riders. She just gripped the black shoulders of the captain and kept her head lowered, her feet dangling on either side of the horse, far above the path.

She had seen the night landscape only as her Dog, but with human eyes it still encouraged an inclination to run. It was vast and forever and empty if she didn't look back at the town and its walls. She wanted to slide off and start walking, stepping on the softer soil, no stone in sight. She wanted to sink her feet into the earth and hope that in her walk she would somehow hit northern ice.

But that was impossible. She kept her seat and let the men urge the horses over the faintly illuminated grass. Far off to her right shimmered the edges of one of the lakes. Hills and trees in the opposite direction created black mounds that blended with the night's horizon, making a solid line against the bend of stars. She looked up. The faint sparkling bowled above her here like it did on the Land, unobstructed by firelight or the tall arc of buildings. She took a deep breath.

"This seems like a good spot?" Major Dirrick reined in his mount by a dwarven copse. They had wandered off the trail and now stood more among the wild bushes and a trickle of maple trees.

"Well enough, I suppose," the captain said and glanced over his shoulder at her. Without waiting for a reply, he swung his leg over the neck of the horse and jumped down to his feet. It was not far to go for his height, but for her, now alone on the animal, it seemed a giant leap. She gripped at the saddle in case the horse decided to dart ahead, but then Captain Jarrett seized the reins and the horse dropped its face to the grass.

She wasn't sure how to get down without falling, but Major Dirrick saved her from the task and walked up, leading his horse, and offered a hand. She grabbed it, and his shoulder, and pulled her leg over the horse's back in a much more ungainly motion than the captain had managed. The landing on her feet shook her ankles and the major held on.

"All right?"

"Yes. Thank you." She bunched her fists into the sides of her Kabliw trousers.

Major Dirrick went to Captain Jarrett's horse and offered to take its bridle in hand. "I don't know what you had in mind, but...I can stay out of your way." He walked the horses to a nearby tree and began to tie them to it.

Captain Jarrett looked at her, and she at him. The light was poor, and as they didn't suggest they spark a fire she didn't offer the option. Perhaps they didn't want one that could draw eyes, if eyes had followed them or could see them from the trail.

The captain glanced over at his friend, then faced her, his arms folded to his chest. "I don't know about this."

"Neither do I." She stepped closer. He was nervous, and so his Dog must have been doubly so. "Yours is not controlled the way my little spirit is...so I'm afraid to Call him out as I did once before."

"Then what are we doing here?" His tone snapped like the wind.

This was going to be a battle, just not one with guns. She sighed. "When you wandered to my cell a few nights ago, what had you seen? What drew you there?"

He glanced at Major Dirrick, but the man was occupied with the horses. "There was a black dog. I'd seen it in Nev Anyan when you...when your Dog had taken me to the rookeries. But it can't be that dog, can it?"

They were both trying to make sense of his ability. "If you see another animal in the middle light that isn't a Dog, and it isn't in your waking world, then it is your threat animal."

"Threat animal."

"What Father Bari once called an omen. Or har..." She struggled to remember the word. "Har..."

"Harbinger? I think he'd written about that."

"Yes. Sometimes it shows you things. Other times it will guide you. It's not always clear. But you learn to understand over time."

He rubbed his palms across his face. "Will it ever hurt me?"

"They have their own will." She remembered the white bear's attack on the ship. "They will do what they must to help you. Or stop you. Sometimes it isn't kind. They aren't a part of your little spirit, but they come from the dark light."

She half expected an argument, but he stood motionless, accepting. Perhaps the dead priest had written about this too.

They had far to go and only so much time in the night.

"You must sleep. And I may meet you in the dream. From the dream perhaps you'll join my Dog in the middle light, and we will see what we can see."

The insects plied a strong song to divert their rest. Sitting in the grass Sjenn watched the shadowed form of Captain Jarrett as he lay a small stone's throw apart. Farther still sat Major Dirrick with the horses, and sleep did not bend toward them like the moonlight. Though the captain was quiet she heard his breathing, and it was not the pattern of a body reaching for dream.

She considered the possibility that she was being

foolish. How could she truly teach this Kabliw when she didn't understand his Dog? Could a man be taught language if he had never spoken a word, or even been around those who conversed? Perhaps. Over years, patiently, in a lifetime. But General Fawle wouldn't wait a lifetime. She didn't think he would wait even a season.

Sitting on the quiet land, with a growing nighttime chill, she gazed up at the stars and pretended they looked down upon this Kabliw world in the same way they did upon the Aniw. But did these celestial Aniw spirits wink their eyelids at her when she was among the Kabliw? Did they wink at the Kabliw as well? How could they, if the Kabliw didn't believe and called them by different names? The stars could have many different names, and be many different spirits, Father Bari had said. But she didn't think so. How could Aniw spirits in the stars find favor in the Kabliw, when the Kabliw didn't think they were Aniw spirits in the first place?

She had not understood Father Bari's claim that some people from his land would not believe her little spirit. She had not understood the resistance to the truth, and yet she had faced it for many days now. Because the Kabliw had different truths. If the Kabliw were as right as she was right, who, then, belonged to the spirits in the sky? Who, then, did the stars look down upon? Where did the Aniw spirits go if they could not go to the sky that the Kabliw had claimed?

She heard the horses whuff. These tall creatures moved with the speed of sailing ships, it seemed. Would the Kabliw and their gods claim even the night sky from her people, like they seemed to claim the Land with their guns?

Outside, beneath this broad canopy, she missed her home with the sharpness of a *sul*. But fallen snow was more forgiving a terrain than this task she'd been set. If she couldn't help Captain Jarrett, she knew that the fort's stockade would be the least of her troubles. She looked at the captain now and found him sitting up, like a prodded corpse, and his features were as black as the night.

"I can't," he said.

"Listen," Major Dirrick said, a hollow voice from the dark, and Sjenn heard in that moment how the insects had quieted.

The grass seemed to exhale toward her and she turned to her right, in the direction of the breeze.

The men saw it two heartbeats after, and both of them drew their guns, Captain Jarrett now on his feet to face the tall robed figure in their midst.

"Put those away," Sister Oza said. "I'm not here to fight."

Both men didn't move. Their silver guns aimed, throwing moonrays. Sjenn rose slowly and some instinct made her move toward Captain Jarrett, away from the priestess.

"Why are you here?" the captain said, with no tone of friendliness in the timbre of his voice. "And I'd like a full answer this time."

"Your father would win this war against Sairland and the abos by any means necessary," the woman said. "The Church doesn't condone this way and I know neither do you. Any of you. You, captain." She took a step closer and looked at both men. "Nor you, major. And certainly not this poor Hasky girl."

"The Church," Major Dirrick said, "also claims to be a peaceful force, yet something tells me you're not of any benign order, are you?"

"She's not," Captain Jarrett said.

"Even the gods require a sword arm on occasion," Sister Oza said. "But it doesn't mean we wield it without care. Sometimes the sword must be sheathed. Other times it must be on guard."

"You people never speak plain," Captain Jarrett muttered.

Sjenn thought she understood this woman. Sometimes the Dog was more helper than hunter in the tribes. Other times it bared its fangs. But Sjenn didn't think even a priestess could be trusted, especially one that skulked in the night. Sister Oza was no *ankago,* and even as kindly a priest as Father Bari had led the Kabliw to her shores, and that had led her to be captured and flung here like a piece of loose slate in a blizzard wind.

"The general uses people," Sister Oza continued. "Captain Fawle, you know this to be true. He used the Church's servants for his own knowledge and ultimately his own gain. It's your father that has set his sights on the Far North." Her blue gaze made knitting glances toward Sjenn, and Sjenn found herself tangled in them. "It's General Fawle who wishes to stake claim in the tundra and sends a vanguard of weapons and soldiers to that land. He wants their magic knowledge like he yearns for it among these abo. He thinks it will help him win against the tribes and against Sairland. But not every order is willing to be the stooge of the military or these wars. Father Bari's unwitting role in it is an example to us all."

She lost what else the priestess said, in the deep echo of those words. Her people. The little spirit, curled up in her chest, gave a stretch of awakening. But it could not run here. It couldn't be freed here so long as her body was anchored to this dark earth and these Southern boundaries.

She thought of Keeley and his disparate tribe.

"You would have us disobey my father?" Captain Jarrett said, his hand flexing restlessly on his gun. "If you know him like you say you do, you know that he wouldn't allow us to live after that. Certainly not this girl."

"Do you not accept casualties in war, Captain Fawle?"

"I hear that question a lot from people who aren't at risk."

Sister Oza's voice deepened. Her hands were hidden up her sleeves and Sjenn stared at them, not at the woman's eyes. "Do the noble thing, Captain Fawle," she said.

"I am not from noble stock. We Fawles tend toward a self-serving nature."

"I think you must go," Major Dirrick said. "Priestess. I think you must return to the fort, pack your things, and ride away."

"You know I can't do that. I'm on orders as surely as this captain here. And not even your colonel can supersede them."

The people of the stone gods may not have had *ankago* power, but Sjenn was beginning to see that they had power nonetheless. This woman was not afraid. There was no scent of that around her at all, only a staunch confidence and a certain relentless fervor. She didn't smile here in the dark. Her business came with the shadows and moonlight.

"Then," Major Dirrick said, "I suggest you leave us and keep your distance."

"And tell Colonel Ponne where I found you?"

The insects still remained silent. Even the horses were motionless. This woman carried no gun, but her threat came steel-tipped.

"Don't," Sjenn said.

"Sjennonirk," the priestess said, "I'm trying to help you. You know this to be madness."

Perhaps these men held a stronger threat, but her Dog instinct did not like the scent this priestess gave. Sjenn said nothing, and that may have been answer enough. She didn't want this woman's help after all. She didn't want to communicate anymore with servants of foreign gods, especially ones who hid their hands and offered smiles.

"Get on," Captain Fawle said, "before I mistake you for a wolf in this deceiving dark." In the quiet of their cabal, his gun made a loud click.

"Very well, but the Seven Deities will watch." Sister Oza stepped back, once and once again. "They will watch you, Captain Fawle." Then she retreated without another word, blending easily with the night.

"I won't be sleeping at all now," Captain Jarrett said. He didn't holster his weapon.

"No," Major Dirrick said and moved finally to unhitch the horses. He handed over the reins of the captain's yellow mount. "Let's leave this place."

Sjenn rode back behind the captain again, gripping his jacket. Neither of them said a word, though the question hung like a slab of meat before them—a dead, heavy question, stripped of skin and life. She did not know what to do with the captain's Dog now.

She did not know where it would lead them, or where her own Dog would go in this expanding terrain.

Though the captain may not have slept the rest of that night, she fell into it back in her cell and found herself dreaming. Back on the ice floes with the white bear and her father's Dog, white and black on a landscape of cold quietness. All color seemed bleached from her sight and she was a woman in their midst, vulnerable and Kabliw-clad.

"Why haven't you come to me before?" she asked the black Dog. "Please tell me what I can do."

He paced around her, ears back. "Kill the priestess."

"Aleqa, no." The sadness at such a suggestion made her irreparably tired, even in dream. She had killed Father Bari at his behest, had killed that Kabliw Stoan because of her Dog's instinct, and it had brought her to this land.

He growled now like he had then, her father, and the great bear yawned with a show of fangs.

"She wants to stop this, Aleqa. How can she be a threat if she wants to stop the general?"

"Some things cannot be stopped." The black Dog snapped at her fingers and she pulled her hands up to her chest. "Some things are meant to be. The people and their ancestors are meant to be. Kill the priestess."

"I can't!"

Her voice fell into the dead air, fell into nothing, and nothing was all that came back to her.

*   *   *

Captain Jarrett did not visit her in the day. Nobody did, except the guard who allowed her time alone at the communal baths to finally cleanse herself and had the decency to stand with his back to her. Afterward she was fed and she ate (in her cell), and she hoped the captain's Dog had not roamed.

He may have been feeling in a generous mood. Before sundown he brought them out again from their cells, her and Keeley, when the bugle horn sounded (it did incessantly throughout the day at regular times) and men began to hurry to and fro from their final work for a small segment of relaxation before retreat. If the Kabliw normally tended to lead their lives by regimented hours, it was even more so among the army men. Captain Jarrett explained this to them while he presented them each with a brown leather ball to kick on the far end of the field, near to the stockade gate but enough away that it did not loom above them.

They would play, he said. And though the shadows had grown thick in the pockets of his eyes, his smile held the small mischief of a child.

He devised a game of kicking the ball around and between two sticks shoved into the earth. It was no real competition, but it held a similarity to the sport she'd played with her cousins on the sea ice, with a bloated walrus head and a typical joy of sending objects far off to be chased. For the short duration they were able to feel less like prisoners, so much so that some of the other men began to gather around, then asked to join in. It took no demon magic to play with a ball and she was, after all, the only woman in the fort that was not a forbidding priestess. Perhaps they decided to put aside fears to see her run about, even in her oversized clothes and loose trousers. Or perhaps they just regarded her as a young boy, considering her smaller size, and a brother to harass.

She thought where language and strangeness set up barriers, the common need to play tended to tear them down. She remembered her fascination as a child with the first Kabliw she'd ever seen, some of those young sailors off the great ships; or the pictures Father Bari had shown her of odd ritual and remarkable faces so different from her own. But some things had been familiar, like his explanation of what Kabliw children liked to do in school, what games they found fun, how they liked to sing. Some things were very similar to her own rearing, her own people.

In the short hours before night fell she ran between these stern Kabliw men and some of them laughed at her quickness. Even Captain Jarrett smiled and seemed to cast off some of his agitation, his distraction. Keeley joined in, forgetting for the moment perhaps that he was the only Whishishian tribesman in the midst of Kabliw cannons and fortifications. Would they ever be so trusting as now, gunless and willing to kick a ball? Inevitably teams formed, a loose request arranged with little delay. The rivalry was light. In the end her team won and a couple of the men patted her shoulder before Captain Jarrett intervened, out of breath from the activity and claiming sourness at the victory. He'd been heading the opposing team.

It wasn't until the men dispersed that she noticed Major

Dirrick standing at the edges, willing to be drowned in the shadow of the stockade gate. He called Captain Jarrett over and Sjenn found herself drifting to Keeley's side. It was as if with the breakup of the game all fun was forgotten and what men remained in small groups talking looked over now with a certain somberness that belied the smiles she'd seen just moments before. A couple of them brushed their hands at their sides as if expecting to find a gun—as if expecting they'd need one. She and Keeley stood alone and waited for the captain, and none of the men approached. At least they seemed to acknowledge that the captain had charge over her and Keeley and would not force a command.

"This would help him, I think," Keeley said. His concern for the captain had seemed to grow with the weeks. "Not hurt him."

He didn't mean in any way physical, and Sjenn nodded once. "Maybe that was his idea all along." He had to have understood his men in some way to lead them as well as he claimed he did.

"It helped us," Keeley said.

She watched the men disappear at another bugle call. "For a time."

The moon was a contrast light to the dark descending now. She looked up at the stars barely visible in the waning blue and did not want to go back into the cell.

"Some things about this land are beautiful."

The Whishishian didn't speak for a few moments. "Maybe only if you look up and not in the direction of any Ciracusan settlements."

Though his tone wasn't bitter, it wasn't quite accepting.

Her gaze dropped from the deep blue sky to the dark amber of his eyes.

"You said the general saved your life."

"Yes," he said.

She peered up at him. No, he didn't speak plenty, but she did not think he had ever lied to her. And regardless of General Fawle's orders, he had taken his task of watching over her—and the captain—maybe more seriously than a basic order required.

"Do you miss your people?" she asked.

He didn't hesitate. "Yes. Don't you?"

"Very much. But as I'm here, I will find beauty in the sky. If there is anything in common that we have with these people, it's the sky."

"Does it look the same from where you are?"

"Mm." She stared up again, arching her neck back as far as it would go without tilting her off her feet. "The stars are a little different and I wonder what they think and if they are Aniw thoughts. The colors share some commonality...but I think the Northern sky is prettier."

"Maybe one day I will see it too."

"Does the sky look the same from where your people are?" she asked. He never spoke much about his people, and she wondered how long ago it had been since he'd seen them.

"It does not," he said in a flat tone.

That surprised her. "What does it look like?" She asked it before she thought that maybe she should not.

"It tells the future for the Whishishian, and the past."

"And this isn't good?"

"The future we see is full of Ciracusans."

That was, it seemed, its own answer. She looked down

at the ground. In the creeping night the green grass was now black and blue, as though bruised by the feet that had trod upon it all day.

"I don't want that future for the Aniw," she said.

"You might not have a choice," Keeley said, and it was then she knew for certain that he had never lied to her.

Major Dirrick walked back to them with Captain Jarrett and in some prearranged signal seemed to send the captain off with Keeley while he guided her aside in a slower walk back to the stockade.

"You enjoyed yourself on the field," he said.

"I like the open. I don't like it in there." She pointed to the high walls and the visible stone through the open gate.

"So Captain Fawle explained. He also proposed he take you and the abo along on his escort duty."

"The children?" So that was what they'd been discussing.

"Yes, the children that you helped save. I don't claim to understand all that he told me about you, or even why you don't somehow magic yourself away from this place or kill all of us for what we do to you, but I saw what I saw in that forest, with Fawle and his...Dog. And I am not the sort of man to explain away my own vision. I'm not a daft old codger who needs to doubt his own wits."

"You needn't doubt," she said and looked at him as he stopped just inside the stockade gates. Keeley and the captain had already gone ahead and disappeared inside. "Your wits saw true."

"Yes, unfortunately." He had a softer humor than the

captain, but it was not unaware. "So I think I can convince the colonel to let you go, and it would be best if you were all away from that priestess, I think." He sighed. "The morale of the men has also been inconsistent since the captain's arrival. They don't know what to think of you, or him, most of the time, and that last mission certainly didn't help."

"Will they follow him now?"

"They would give him a chance. He's always been a good leader to them and a good companion. Not all officers can carry that off, but I think he's learned a thing or two from his father."

"I don't think General Fawle is the sort of man to play kickball with his men?" She stated it as a question, because what did she truly know. But from her brief bouts of interaction with the elder Fawle he had not seemed the open-armed type.

"No, he would not. Precisely."

She understood.

"You must watch him, Sjennonirk. In whatever way you can. If he should... with that animal..."

"I'll do what I can, but it's sometimes in his sleep that his little spirit emerges. In startlement and in sleep."

"Then we ought to pray for an uneventful ride."

"You can pray to your gods," she said. "I will depend on my Dog."

He nodded once and that ghosting smile slipped to his features again. She thought him not that much older than the captain, beneath the stubble of beard. Or perhaps his wider eyes and the faded sun spots across his nose reminded her of little boys.

"I'll walk you in." He had a certain gentlemanly air

the kind that Father Bari had talked about that was the ideal of the Southern man.

Though she had no great desire to be locked up again, he made the venture at least tolerable step by step. Even the guard disappeared upon seeing the major and stood at a discreet distance down the corridor. He had been one of the men on the field with the ball, and she believed he had even been on her team.

"Why do you fight?" she asked Major Dirrick as he opened up the door to her cell and stood on the threshold while she walked in.

"In general?" he said.

"Why do you fight the abos?" She thought of Keeley, who said his tribe was not at war with the Kabliw, but he did not seem all too pleased by the current relations regardless. She half expected some sort of condescending explanation, but the major didn't speak for a long minute.

"I suppose, right now, it's because they fight us."

"Why do they fight you?"

"Because they'd rather we didn't exist here. They say they were here first, though I don't see how that matters anymore. It's been too long for that sort of thing to matter."

She wondered how anything could be dismissed. "But shouldn't you leave them alone?"

"We weren't always at war, at least not with all of them. Just as we aren't now. But too much blood has been shed for there to be a quick peace." His tone was patient like Father Bari's had been. But the priest's perspective had been different. He had not been a hunter or any sort of fighting man.

"If you weren't always at war, then why can't you stop?"

In the moonlight she saw his teeth appear. The smile wasn't happy. "You ask simple questions that have complicated answers."

"Why must they be complicated?"

"If this is your way of getting me to delay shutting this door…" But he was teasing.

"My people have never been at war. Not even with your people."

"We can hope it remains that way."

The shadows sat heavy in her chest. "I saw gun boxes on my shores before they took me away."

"For hunting caribou perhaps," he said. "Who knows if the priestess was telling the truth or how much she truly knows. She has her own agenda." His tone was not one meant to convince. Or to reassure. It was merely distrustful.

"Do you know," she said, with dread, "if your people plan to go to war with the Aniw?"

She thought of the bodies in the forest and the clatter and the din. The blood had been so much it had soaked into the earth and still left pools.

He stared at her, then slowly shook his head. "I don't know that. That isn't a decision someone like me would make."

"Who would make it?"

She knew the answer before he said it. "Someone like General Fawle."

She sat down in the cell against the wall, below the small window that let in her only light. After a moment the major shut the door. He bade her a good night through it, his voice muffled and maybe a little apologetic.

But she didn't want his sorry. She wanted out.

Perhaps it was foolish to Call, this night before these people bade her accompany an army captain out to the field. To escort children, they said, through possibly hostile territory. The words were as complicated as anything else about the Kabliw, where a straight course and a simple task never remained that way. They directed their days by bugle call and a cycling consistency of similar chores, day in and day out, broken only by the prospect of violence in other areas or recreation in the town below. Maybe they created the trouble with the tribes here. Maybe it wasn't truly about who had been first on the land, but who wanted to be the last. They built their cities to last, full of such embedded stone and settled people. They grew roots made of iron and fruits made of bullets, and set up impenetrable forests for their people to grow taller, towering over what the land provided in pines and birches.

She could not understand this way. She would think she knew some aspect of the Kabliw but some other thing would present itself in confusion. Perhaps there was no knowing them, any more than perhaps Captain Jarrett could know his Dog.

She Called her Dog forth, in as quiet a song as she could muster with the guard sitting down the hall and the fort fallen to a community repose.

*   *   *

Once her little spirit forms out of the dark, she gives a great stretch of limbs, looking up toward the moon as it hangs outside the tiny window. A leap through the walls marks a foray to freedom. She doesn't fear for her body here as she did in Nev Anyan, that big city that went on like the sea, stretching as far as sight allowed. Here she can return to her body and Captain Jarrett will guide her back like he did so many times already.

She goes looking for him, creeping along the edges of buildings and in the deeper shadows of the grounds. It doesn't take long to find him. Slipping from room to room in the row of officers' quarters, she feels him sleeping. She knows him for his restless spirit, the way the dark lines around him now shift and run like a flowing stream. A little unstable, as if one would dip in a paw and be carried away to the dreams that swirl silently in his mind. His back faces her as he lies curled on his bunk, the blanket pulled to his chest even in this warmth. She came through the door, unbarred, worked herself like the grains and whorls of the wood until it released her on the other side.

She props her paws on the edge of the bed, a heavy weight, then bounds up onto him. The width is narrow. He startles himself awake with a cry, pushing at her flank.

"Not you." His voice is thick from sleep.

But tonight she wants to roam. She licks at his face, over the shadows of the tattoos. He shoves her harder and rolls, trying to get away from her, so she hops off the bed and his body and sits beside it instead. She is not in a hurry.

She sits there for hours, watching him sleep.

*   *   *

Patience coaxes him out. Perhaps he feels her sitting there, or perhaps this is his routine now. Together they slip from the walls, over the cobbles and the grass, and like moonlight they cut through the shadows and the battlements. Out of the fort and down into the town. The people down below from the cannons and the block-houses also sleep, without the restless guard that patrols the heights. They sleep peacefully, and they depend on more than moonlight and hanging lamps.

Here on the straight streets, to illuminate all things manmade, the gaslights grow tall and narrow and iron black. Their light shines golden in her sight and does not discourage her. He lopes along beside her, an equally golden thing with a happy mien in the way his tongue lolls out. His ears angle, alert, and his tail splays out behind him in a confident curve. It's less frightening than being alone, and he hadn't shocked himself out to the middle light. She feels no need to tussle now.

They have the freedom of this people town and they run it the entire night.

When she awoke from the Call the next morning, Captain Jarrett no longer stood across the cell. He'd done it from a sitting position, near to her side where her Dog must have lain, waiting for him to come after their hours in the open. He had managed to draw his own Dog back into his body without a Call and seemed pleased that he could. It must have been more gentle than the other times. Perhaps he was learning by some instinct that she could never teach him, some Kabliw skill inborn in his kind—whatever kind he was, separate even from his father. To Call her back he brought and needed no book from the priest now, but he offered a cup of water. She took it gladly.

"Today we ride," he said. There was an excited gleam in his eyes.

She found it easy, that early day, to smile at him. Though she would not have minded talking about what he had seen or remembered while in the Dog form, he didn't seem interested in discussing the night. Instead he had the guard take her to the baths once again and left her there to later meet for the mission.

They convened at the stables, where the horses waited, seven of them. She recognized the one she'd ridden before from Nev Anyan, saddled and supplied already, with a young corporal much like the last one holding the bridle. Captain Jarrett was there already, along with a man he referred to as Lieutenant Ven Dy, and two other men who yawned in the bending light and scratched their stubbled faces. Keeley was there as well, already mounted. It was going to be a fast party and they all were armed, even the Whishishian. He had proven himself trustworthy, it seemed, at least for a task such as this.

Her nerves pulled taut as she managed to climb on the back of the horse and shifted around on the uncomfortable saddle with a small hold on the reins. Perhaps the animal sensed her unease, because it paced a little before Keeley reached out and grabbed the reins, of which she seemed to have no control. It was as if she'd forgotten the quick lesson the captain had taught her on the ride from Nev Anyan. It wasn't natural to sit atop this beast, but the more she thought it, the more twitchy the horse became.

"Steady," the abo said, with a gentler look in his eyes. He held on to both his horse and hers until her animal settled, then let her take the rawhide reins again.

The captain said something to another man standing by the head of his pale horse and held out his hand. The man placed a second set of reins in them and Captain Jarrett tied them around his saddlehorn.

"Who is this horse for?" she asked him, curious enough to dare the small commotion of the fort with her voice.

"The children," the captain replied. He barely glanced over her but instead looked around at the faces of his small patrol. "Ready up." His horse seemed eager and took a couple steps forward without any provocation from his hand or legs.

Major Dirrick emerged from one of the longer buildings, squinting in the light as he approached their party. "May the gods speed your way there and back again," he bade the captain.

"And if not them, our dependable mounts." Captain Jarrett grinned and saluted with some humor. The major shook his head and slapped the mare's rump. As soon as she started off at a comfortable trot, the others fell in line. Keeley next, then herself, and the two other men behind with the lieutenant trailing last.

Sjenn looked over her shoulder, holding to the saddle with one hand, and saw the major watching them from his spot. He had done this for them. He had made the fort gates open to allow her passage through to the wide land, only this time it wasn't beneath the cover of night.

She didn't know what the ritual was among the Kabliw, but luckily he did. He took off his cap and waved it once.

She wanted to wave back but spied Sister Oza standing at some distance behind Major Dirrick, on the parade grounds. Her stare made Sjenn turn back in her saddle, to face forward and be glad that they were leaving this place behind, if even for a time.

They collected the children from an orphanage in the city—a place where young ones without family were kept, an idea she did not really understand. Why didn't some other family take them in? With all the seemingly endless Kabliw in this place, why would children end up all in one house, with only a few adults to mind them and no family but each other? Now was not the time to ask with the children in their company, but she was not surprised at their wan faces and quiet natures. After losing their parents they had found no comfort in a relative's arms, nor perhaps even in the embrace of a kind adult. Instead they clung to each other atop the saddle of their single horse, two small figures, perhaps hardly nine and ten years as the Kabliw counted time—a boy and a girl. Captain Jarrett ordered Ven Dy to mind the children close and soon they set off once again, this time to the borders of the town of Fort Girs.

It looked different in the day, as all things did, all of its lines and dirt made sharper by the unequivocal light. Sjenn sat quietly getting used to the gait of her horse once again, warm but not uncomfortably so in the shirt and wrapped blanket around her shoulders that she tied below her chin where the thin rope had been stitched for just that purpose. It was a similar day to the one they'd had coming from Nev Anyan. "Good riding weather," she heard one of the men say behind her.

She found herself gazing at Captain Jarrett's back; it was directly in front of her as Keeley rode a little to the side in their loose and long column of seven horses. The black coat cinched high on the back of his waist gave a narrow and straight T form to his torso, capped by the ends of his hair along his collar as it poked from beneath the ever-present military hat. He kept one hand at the hilt of his rifle as it sat snug in the sheath at the side of his saddle. He didn't turn around immediately but kept ranging his gaze from left to right at the tall buildings and routine hubbub of the day beginning, until perhaps he felt her gaze and twisted around.

He must have sensed her in some odd way. He didn't cast a distracted look at any of the others or the traffic of the street but pinned her with an open stare that did not break in a blink. Then he turned 'round again and urged his horse to move a little faster. He wanted away from the congestion of carts and drays, the noise and smell of the multitude of bodies passing to and fro, and Sjenn could not blame him. All of the horses moved with his, following each other and ultimately their leader, as their military pack cut a swift line through the civilian horde, out toward the town wall, the limit before they reached clear land.

They turned a different direction from the one the company had gone on for the Soreganee attack. She recognized the arc, riding away from what Captain Jarrett called the Sister Lakes. Ulila was even more inland, it seemed, and their pace was brisk with few exchanged words. The children didn't fuss or say much of anything, not even a grunt or a yawn. They just held to each other, the boy behind the girl holding the reins of the horse like a little one born to it. He probably was. Sjenn watched in some wonder at their quiet confidence. Or maybe it was a numb determination.

There was no true pleasure in the ride, despite the sunny day and the constant call of birds. They were safe-guarding children across country known for its raiding history. This was the reason, Captain Jarrett said, that he didn't want to leave the tiny lives in the hands of stage-coaches and a shotgun. Not for these children.

She wondered in the drive of their canter if Major Dirrick had asked this spying deed of her for more than just a caring interest in the captain. Fawle's moods were not predictable, and what kindness he'd shown her the day before seemed leeched from his intentions now. It took them a few hours out, as the sun arched above, for Captain Jarrett to seem a little easier in his surroundings, though nothing of his demeanor—watching his back—indicated a relaxation of any real kind. It was more that he fell into a rhythm, as all the men seemed to, even if their gazes continued to slant out and over the rolling land, grazing upon the clumps of trees that dotted an area to the left or right of them. So much sun seemed to bake the grass to a more golden sheen than tundra green and blue, and she found the color enticing to the eye. It complemented the pale blue sky on the horizon and the deeper emeralds of the pines they passed.

Deep breaths were a demand in a place like this, and she took them often.

Captain Jarrett had said it was a day's ride there and a day's ride back. She could not count the hours like he did with his pocketwatch, but she knew from looking at the path of the sun that time passed at a crawl, it passed and carried on, and they grew closer to their destination and more away from any form of civilization. The Kabliw lived in clusters for this same purpose—because it tended to be dangerous to settle in the in-between.

Should trouble arise she wasn't sure what she would do. Cast her Dog into the fray? She would be able to do more defense that way, as she had in the Soreganee camp, but that left the trouble of her sleeping body in the open. Perhaps Keeley thought the same thing, for he lagged his horse a little so she could ride up side by side.

"I don't see anything," he said, "But we are gaining on the part of the land where it might hit. I'm going to ride ahead for the captain and see. If something happens, Sjenn, you must take your horse away and hide. Take the children if you can."

"And what of you men?"

"We have guns."

"I have my Dog."

"I can't fight if I must protect the body of that Dog."

She understood his meaning. He was not her cousin Twyee, and even if the general had told him to be her protector, out here he would be more effective with the other men. But this reality didn't make the idea of running any more savory.

For more hours they rode until the light began to fade once again. Keeley ranged ahead many times and circled

back, and always with the negative shake of his head.
This seemed to agitate Captain Jarrett more than relieve
him, yet Sjenn thought the less they saw of Soreganee
presence, the better. She had no desire to witness, much
less participate in, another fight, in Dog form or not, and
that crazed coyote was best kept at a stranger distance.
But Jarrett maintained that anything too quiet set him
on edge.

Another Kabliw trait, she thought. This inability to
accept calm good fortune.

But despite his almost roaring need to engage in
conflict, they arrived in the small town of Ulila safe and
sound, and the children were reunited with a grateful aunt
and a crutch-ridden uncle. Both were more elderly than
the parents had been but seemed plump with affection.
Sjenn watched with a certain quiet satisfaction that at
least the little ones would have a place to grow and flour-
ish, even in the bare land surrounding this outcrop town.
They seemed not much different from children she knew
from the tribes, though they dressed different and looked
different. Perhaps that was because all children shared
the same needs, no matter their country or their land. She
thought that it must be so.

The town itself was a far cry from Nev Anyan or Fort
Girs. It consisted of one main road made of flattened dirt
and two lines of major buildings on either flank offering
food, stores, livery services, and a hotel and saloon. Keeley pointed them all out to her, and a few more that looked
important in their frontage but seemed to house a meager
cluster of rooms compared to the buildings of the bigger
cities. But it had a quiet tone to it, this place, with people
who didn't seem eager to go anywhere in a set amount of

time. A couple of the men grumbled that they would've liked to have stayed longer, at least overnight. What was the hurry?

But Captain Jarrett didn't want to linger, not with his face in a town semi-regularly beset by abo raids. Even the constable in the place looked uncomfortable when the captain explained their presence there, and so any thought of lingering for relaxation went out of the plan. The people already gave Keeley sidelong looks for the brief stay they had, and any longer might have made them less grateful for the return of a couple children and more remembering of what had orphaned them in the first place. Anger, Keeley said, tended to blur the lines of reason, and some places were touchier than others.

They would sleep on the land, and personally Sjenn preferred that, for the Kabliw had looked at her strangely as well, and despite the size of the big cities she had seen, she felt more exposed in that littler place. Perhaps because when there was so much to look at people tended to look at nothing. But in a limited space there were only limited things upon which to cast your gaze, and the first flocks were always the oddest.

So they refreshed as much as they could in the town, men and horses both, and by total nightfall they found a grove on the outskirts of the town, off the trail, beside a narrow stream and shallow embankment so their horses could drink and they could refill their canteens. She had become a little used to the routine by then, in the quiet of the ride that all in all was not so completely different from when her tribe struck out a dog team on a hunting expedition. You took care of the dogs first before you took care of yourself, and then settled in for your own food and an opportunity to soothe aches and stretch muscles. On the early morrow Captain Jarrett said they'd be on the backward route to Fort Girs.

Lieutenant Ven Dy built up a fire inside a ring of stones and they cooked a little of the salted fish they'd carried with them and softened the hard bread in the grease. Coffee was poured and bedrolls unfurled. She found herself in a companionable silence between Keeley and Captain Jarrett, with the Kabliw riders making up the other side of the circle around which they sat, keeping warm in the open night air. One of the men didn't remain, however, but stood watch in the shadows, facing out. He held his rifle in his arms.

The night dozed on. They didn't talk much, and not about anything more than idle wonderings of animal habits and the virtues of some rich tobacco. She listened but didn't say anything, and curled up first, perhaps the least used to the motion of the company. She saved her body the trouble of movement by stretching out beneath her blanket. She'd gone on hunting parties before, naturally, in her own tribe when they needed the Dog for protection. This felt a little like that and her sleep came quick.

The shot woke her up, then the shouts. She barely blinked her eyes open before a hand closed around her arm and dragged her from her blanket. It was Keeley. His gold-colored eyes glinted in the moonlight. It was still night and the fire had died.

"What's—"

But she saw it before he could tell her. The pale yellow

flash of a creature bounding upon one of the other men. Beside him ran the coyote, only slightly larger but louder in his growls.

"Gods cursed!" the trooper cried, then another shot punctured the air. Pistols set off in a cacophony of injury.

"Sjenn, come quickly!" Keeley hauled her to a crouch.

"The captain—!"

"He is the Dog," the abo hissed. "That coyote—they are both mad. He's already killed one of his own soldiers."

She barely saw anything in the murky dark, but the body that had been a little ways beside her was motionless—Captain Jarrett. Another form lay on the other side of the dead fire, and that wasn't moving either. His soldier.

"I have to help him."

"They'll turn on us next!" The Dogs or the remaining men he did not clarify. His pull came sharp and hurt her arm. She stumbled against his side.

"I said I would help him! The town—"

It sat so near and helpless, its simple starry glow of scattered window candles a beacon to anything in the middle light.

What had provoked the Dog, the coyote's threat? She could not make out who was whom in the lack of light, but the pale snarling thing was easy enough to discern and the Soreganee Dog even more so. Captain Jarrett's Dog was rabid on his own men, and she kept tugging the other way, to get back to him, even as Keeley hauled her in the opposite direction.

"We're not staying around." His voice was hard. He nearly threw her at the horses, who were jerky from the noise and the presence of wild things. With brisk movements the Whishishian unhobbled and untethered them from their low branches and lifted her onto the saddle—shoved her, more like, until her foot caught in the stirrup and she pulled herself aboard. Her horse took off before she was fully seated and she grabbed at the reins to keep herself on.

"Keeley!"

He rode up swift beside her and took the flinging reins from her desperate grip, giving guidance and pace to their flight.

Soon the sound of the thundering hooves drowned out the crack of the pistol fire. They ran from it, toward the deeper night, where sunrise would be long in coming.

Eventually they slowed, and it was a shock to her that the world had fallen silent once again in slumber. She found herself crying. Tears wet her cheeks, whether from the breakneck dash into the wind or the sudden tight hold around some indistinct weight in the middle of her chest. Keeley didn't speak but kept turning in his saddle to look behind them. Finally, after long minutes of panting stride, he said, "I don't think they'll notice until too late. That we left. There was too much going on. Hopefully they won't track us."

Her heart still hadn't slowed despite their easier gait. The horses made softer sounds, seemingly oblivious to the action.

"What would make him do that?" the Whishishian asked. To kill his own men.

"I don't know," she said. "The other Dog perhaps. What did you see?" Because she hadn't seen much.

"I was on watch," he said. "Standing away with my back to the camp. I heard a yell and turned around. The captain's Dog was on one of the men and the other Dog helped him." His voice was as straightforward as his gaze. "When they finished with the trooper they went to the other, and that's when the shots started. I don't know which one of the men they killed, but the other men were quick upon the Dogs."

"They can't be killed. They won't be able to kill either of the Dogs. He will kill them all." She remembered the man Stoan, in the sometimes vague way of the Dog's recollection.

She remembered Father Bari and the blood at the back of her tongue.

She looked away from Keeley, at nothing. Her hands shook even as she held the reins.

"He must have been threatened," she said to the dark.

"Or he's mad."

"He is *not* mad."

"How do you know?" For some reason his tone hardened, as if she had somehow insulted him. "Sjenn, there have been others before the captain."

She blinked and looked at him through the murk. They had a little moon, but it was not enough to make out clear features or anything of expression. "Before the captain?"

"Yes. There have been others before the captain, other Boot People, who have tried the ways of the spiritwalkers. Of my tribe and of others. All, I think, have failed."

"I don't understand." The pressure in her chest seemed to travel to her mind. Pushing at the backs of her eyes.

"General Fawle has done this before, Sjenn. What he did to you. He's taken *janna* from the Nation and forced them to teach some Ciracusans their arts. It is a vile and unnatural thing that he does. He steals our *janna*. We have lost many Elders, our people. Whishishian, Soreganee...Pite and Morogo. So many tribes, we've become a people with dying wisdom. Our wise men and wise women are disappearing."

"*Why?*" It was the only word to express her horror at the thought.

"For his war against Sairland, for his war against us," Keeley said, and she remembered Sister Oza's words. She remembered it like one remembered the dead. The inevitability of truth made it difficult to swallow. Keeley still spoke: "For all their talk of our 'demon magic,' Sjenn, they want it badly enough to steal it." The pain was as equal to the disgust in his voice. "But it comes with a cost. They have all gone mad from it."

Her mind flooded with words. She sat there for some time as they trickled over her.

"But you." She finally found her voice. "You are his man."

"I am my people's eyes," he said. "Because the general thinks he has me by the collar. That's how I discovered the true nature of these Boot People." He rode a little in silence, then, "Your ways are different from the Nation. I think, in some ways, even more potent. Perhaps this is what the generali covets so much in your people."

She shut her eyes. Even her deep breaths were only stark reminders of how far she was from home. The air stifled now and tasted too green. The tears began again and there was no running breeze to wipe them away. She didn't care. Let them fall. They could fall until the morning and she would still be hollow. Like bone without the marrow.

"Captain Jarrett didn't know."

"No," Keeley said. His voice was just as bone deep and lacked some strength. He was sorry for the captain; that much was plain now. "I don't believe he does."

"We went running in the middle light last night."

She felt Keeley turn to look at her.

"We were running and it was free. He was not this way."

"And he is not Aniw. There is madness in these people, and the ways of our spiritwalkers only encourage it. Yet the generali continues."

"He's young." She looked back at the Whishishian. "Captain Jarrett is young and he has the Dog. It's there, it's my kin. It's your people's kin. He has something of our people's ways in him, somehow. That coyote, that Soreganee warrior knows it too. We shouldn't have left him, Keeley."

"You said yourself he can't be killed. Just as your Dog can't be killed. How would you have stopped him before his men or that other Dog killed us?"

"I would have Called my Dog."

"And then I would have had two bodies to protect and too many enemy still to watch for. While you somehow tried to coax him down."

She didn't like his warrior logic. Her heart said to help and she had ignored it. This was not the *ankago* way. She had killed two men herself, and that hadn't been her way either. Though Captain Jarrett was a soldier, this was not the way this needed to end.

"We can't go back," Keeley said as if he knew her thoughts.

"Then where will we go?"

"Not back to the fort," he said. "Not to Nev Anyan. We'll go to where my people live." His voice sounded steadier with every word. "We will go to my people in the hills."

"I want to see the town," she said.

"What town?"

"The one we abandoned to the wild Dogs." They had delivered children there. The people, though Kabliw, had seemed a gentler sort than those from the cities or the fort. Though Keeley now rode as guide as well as protector of her body when her Dog roamed free, this she would not equivocate. "We must go back to the Boot People town and help them if we can. This is the Aniw way."

Perhaps it was the way of his people too. He nodded once and turned their horses in a new direction, one that faced into the growing light.

The sun gave no cheery welcome on the sight they rode into. Instead the blazing white and heat of the grown day fell upon a red and roughened destruction. Bodies spilled from doorways as if dragged from the protective innards of the buildings, broken or ripped apart. Men, women, even the children. Sjenn pressed her hands to her mouth against the smell and this urge to upend the contents of her belly, while Keeley held her reins and their horses walked, agitated, through the scene. Blood stained the dirt street and wooden walkways, tracked through by animal pawprints. The certain quiet didn't break in sound or movement, only what they provided through hooves on ground and what wind dared to sweep the upper roofs.

She thought she recognized the boy and girl they had brought here the day before, but the forms sprawled so unnatural, faces ripped from their skulls, that she could not be sure. If it was them they had been hauled the length of the town from their aunt and uncle's home. Lines on the loose dirt, overrun by bloody trail, spoke of such rabid carousing. Dead people were cast willy-nilly all over, as if some great hand had scooped up Ulila and shaken it whole until the contents of life fell out and now lay squashed beneath the foundation. She had never seen such killing, not even when a hungry bear once attacked an Aniw camp. Not even in the forest when Captain Jarrett's company fought the enemy abos.

This was animal rage, combined with some human hatred for how thoroughly it had descended on these people.

"I don't think anyone is alive," Keeley said, a quiet raw voice. He held his drawn gun, his eyes darting on every point, as bloodshot as her own felt.

"The Dogs have gone too," she said. Or they would have leaped upon them.

Without discussion they rode out to the small camp they'd made on the outskirts, when their company had been whole. No bodies but the dead lay there; the captain was gone, his soldiers all reminiscent of the townspeople.

Sjenn pulled the reins from Keeley's steadying grip

and urged her horse away at a trot. The tears rose and fell without a jag of warning. She didn't know where she went, but the horse veered away from the death, by instinct, and that route was the one she wanted. Eventually the Whishishian joined her and they made a swift gallop over the calm terrain. The day grasped no idea of the massacre it had witnessed and mourned none of the fallen in its bright hail along their path. Once they slowed their gait again, she wiped at her face with her sleeve.

"We should find him," she said. "You can track him."

"I saw two sets of footprints leave that camp," he said, and there was no light tone in any of his words. "One booted, one bare."

The Soreganee warrior walked with the captain. His was a Dog she did not know either. This world felt more strange with each passing moment.

"I won't go alone into a Soreganee warcamp," Keeley said. "We should still ride on to my people in the hills. The generali will dispatch a search party for us, and we can't let ourselves be found."

She had forgotten about the general. She imagined the man in his high carriage rolling in a straight pitch across this land to make some sense of the dead town and his missing son. She wondered if he would even care. The priestess of the Church had been right—this was a madness no one should know.

Would that she could take this horse and ride all the way back to the tundra. The fatigue at the thought weighed her shoulders down.

"What of my home?" she said, though she knew the Whishishian had no answer. "My home," she said.

Keeley urged his mount to a faster trot, and hers picked up to follow after. She had little choice as this tall beast dictated her future path. As the captain's mad Dog had dictated her freedom now. But it was not the freedom of the tundra. Not yet.

Her home, she knew, slipped farther away.

THE SOREGANEE

How far they walked Jarrett didn't know. Qoyota-riz held the end of the rope that bound his hands together, and the abo was a relentless marcher though he was barefoot and clad in buckskin. The nightmare had become daylight, all he saw in every step. His mouth felt filled by blood even when canteen water flowed down his throat. All he tasted was the blood and beneath it the tang of raw flesh. Soon all the sunlit shadows and night-time moonrays shaped themselves into people, small and large, male and female, people all following his track, resting when he was forced to rest, walking where he was forced to walk. The dead became his company. The tall abo was his brother now in the dealing of this death. Qoyotariz was his guide.

He memorized the straight fall of black hair that hung around the abo's bare shoulders. He recalled the sharp copper eyes when they lay down on the grass for two hours of rest, his arms tied to a tree. He marked the embedded

ed beads at the corners of the warleader's eyes, hard
ears that resembled more and more a second set of eyes.
They didn't weep either. The abo talked to him, but he
barely heard and didn't understand. Fragments of words.
Sometimes the abo grabbed his face, explored as if curious all the Aniw markings upon his skin, fingers rough
and breaths close. He feared a kiss like the first one he'd
received from this man, but even that was a distant thing.
It was difficult to fear anything at all.

He'd slaughtered people and he couldn't be stopped.

After day and night and a cycle of repeating they
approached with bold steps upon the Soreganee warcamp, hidden deep in a birch forest. Warriors of all markings, feathers, and swagger emerged from the bone-white
brigade of trees, came up to greet their leader while the
women hung back by the skin tents and stared. Qoyotariz
said something in his own people's language, moving
Jarrett ahead of him with a firm grip on his shoulder
as they cut their way through the curious crowd. When
the touches grew too rigorous in their progress, the abo
shouted at his people and waved briskly in the air with
his battle blade. That made all interlopers back away.

Soon they stood before a tall tent made of deerskin,
its smooth sides painted with what looked like blood and
stitched around its circumference with beads of all sizes
and colors. The abo yanked aside the entrance flap and
shoved Jarrett in.

He fell upon his knees, wrists still bound, and
attempted to roll enough to get himself to the shadows,
across the half a dozen fox pelts that lay spread on the

floor. For a moment the abo's tall form blocked the light from outside, and then darkness fell completely as Qoyotariz crouched within and let the tent flap fall shut.

Hands raked over his body, tugging at clothes, stripping him of his last defense. In the dark there was nothing but his panicked breathing, vigilant against rebellion. The abo used the blade with expert efficiency and soon he was naked, absent even of boots, made newborn against the taut wall of the tent.

The air smelled of animal fur and skinned meat, deep smoke and crushed field. He flinched and began to shake as through the darkness he felt the abo's smooth face scrape near, a doglike nuzzle to his cheek. It lasted only a moment before the other man leaned away, shoved Jarrett's head down to the furs, then yanked the tent open again and slipped out. He took the torn soldier clothes with him.

He'd been scented now. They'd shed blood together and the deeds they'd done on those people washed out every other brotherly camaraderie he'd established with kinder kin. Every mark upon his face and bruise on his body encouraged a wild remembrance—he'd been as free as a man beholden to no one and no god. The surge it caused in his chest battled with the regret. Against the lack of light he had nothing but the sight of Dog memory and knew this power to be true—no doubt, no denial. The abo's streak of vengeance had sliced a decisive line down all wayward thoughts of faerie stories and far past history stricken from the country's letters. Magic did indeed exist and it held no favor for the human soul, it was no god or goddess upon whose feet he could beg for mercy.

In that middle light he'd run with Qoyotariz, urged by

fear and the eyes of a spirit much older than his own—
perhaps more mad than his own. The abo's red stare had
known no doubt either, only lust and aggression and the
confidence of victory as they'd ravaged that Boot People
town. They were every warrior's basic traits, if they were
to survive.

So it was now, as he curled upon the fox pelts. It
was survival left to him, like some long-dead ancestor's
unwanted gift.

Sometime in the night Qoyotariz returned and prodded
him awake with the point of a foot. He curled away from
it, knees up and elbows in, and tried to find some sense
in the dim light bleeding from the open flap. They had a
fire lit outside among their tents, and the glow brought
just enough shadow and discernment that he saw the
abo's copper eyes and beady skin lean closer to his own.
A curious expression.

Then the face retreated and a bundle of buckskin
clothing hit his body. Without a word more the warrior
left him again, alone.

He could do nothing but drape himself in the abo
wear, leggings that were soft enough to have been worn
by some other man, and a vest of the same texture.
They were dark tan in the little light, and they held
the scent of the earth and the animal that had been
stripped from it.

He curled once again on the fox pelts, creature to dead
creature, and marked the hours by the savage voices outside. To his ears some words sounded like argument. He
waited for an attack that never came.

*   *   *

Instead Qoyotariz returned, when the gaping hunger in his belly gnawed at nerve-endings. But the abo brought no nourishment, only grasped Jarrett at the back of his neck, pulling him to sit. Then the abo knelt across from him.

"Seya'ye," he said.

Jarrett didn't understand that word, so said nothing.

"Seya'ye." The abo slapped the side of his head.

He lacked strength and nearly fell all the way over, but the man grabbed him again.

"Seya'ye!"

"I don't understand, you damn—"

The cuff sent him sideways. His bound hands gave no balance, but the grip at the back of his neck held him in place.

"Qoyotariz," the abo said, pointing to his own eyes, to the blood-red beads stitched into his skin. Then he slapped Jarrett again and pointed to his nose. "Seya'ye."

"That's not my name."

Another slap. His bound hands fled upward in reflex, knocking the abo below his chin. The retaliatory slug to his chest winded him and he lay gasping on the pelts.

"Your name," the abo said in Sarrish. "You are no Boot anymore." The man grabbed his bare foot and gave it a yank. "No Boot anymore."

He held himself from kicking and just breathed. The rank scent of the fox fur made his eyes tear.

"Seya'ye," Qoyotariz said and pointed out of the tent, toward the night. Pointed up. "Moon Brother."

You shine like the moon.

The abo had found him on the trail, outside of Ulila. As he'd found him those weeks ago on patrol.

He knew why now. He knew this Dog for what it was—a curse upon him and all of his association.

He didn't feel the tears fall until the abo was close again and swiped his fingers across the salt wet. Then he licked the tips of his fingers, watching without pity. But that suited Jarrett; he didn't want pity. Pity was for those dead people in the town, not for the memory of his Dog and how eager it had become, running rampant through the street, through flesh and bone and blood. All it had taken was a bite from the coyote, this abo's Dog, some encouraged anger he hardly knew he held.

But he held it now, close to his chest. It beat next to his heart and curled in protective repose with the little spirit inside. It lay in wait and looked up at this abo, who fell to fascination on his face, tracing the Aniw lines with curious caresses.

"Seya'ye," Qoyotariz said. "I will rear your Dog."

It was what his father had wanted all along, wasn't it? The errant thought brought a sudden jar of laughter from the pit of his chest. The general had looked in the wrong place from the beginning. Sjenn was no true teacher, not for this stifled magic, this nightmare confusion of his world. She was too gentle a spirit, too calm a voice. She would not look into the slaughter he'd caused and forgive it. Who would? Not Keeley, some half-brother bastard and enemy of this tribe. Not his men or Major Dirrick or his father. Not that pious priestess and her violent judgment. Only this mad abo understood. Only this warrior who didn't recoil at his laughter or his tears, who had followed him like one did a fixed star in the midst of being lost.

"Qoyotariz," Jarrett said, when his laughter bled into new tears. And the abo let him be, sitting back on bare heels, and merely watched as he struggled to kneel before him and held out his bound hands. "Seya'ye," he said, into the dark copper stare. "I'm asking you, Qoyotariz. You fucking bastard." He no longer knew the difference between his laughter and his tears. The root of both was some heavy dark he had carried for many miles and now barely felt. "Release me." His hands shook, but not from fear. From insistence. "Qoyotariz. By all the bloody gods, *release me*."

The abo stared at him for a stone moment and no gods willed or blocked the Soreganee war leader from pulling his blade from the sheath around his hips. He sliced up and through the rope, freeing Jarrett's hands. And as soon as they were free the abo grasped them in one of his own, the blade pointed down.

"You run and I will hunt you," Qoyotariz said, in a quieter tone. The grip hurt. "Seya'ye."

Jarrett didn't pull away, only repeated the name. He said it twice, and then a third time until the abo smiled. There was no running. And there were no gods at all between them in that tent.

The abo brought him out of the shelter, in moonlight, and gave him rabbit meat and river water in a battered stolen army cup. All the others of the tribe, men and women, warriors and witches as they appeared, watched from silent circles as he stood beside the warleader in Soreganee buckskin, Aniw tattoos on his face. The glade held silence among the tents and the popping of the fire. Qoyotariz said something in his language and gestured to Jarrett. In the middle of the abo words came the word "general."

He held his breath. Was it possible this savage knew who was his kin?

The shadowed faces stared up at them. One young warrior at the edge of the fire said something with a sharp movement of an arm. Qoyotariz shouted at him and no more protests beat the air. Fear lay heavyladen with the burden of acquiescence. They were all beneath the will of this warrior, and the gleaming copper of the spirit in his eyes.

The early light struck a path through the night gloom and they set out ahorse. Such was the trust that seemed embedded in him now, though Jarrett knew the threat was no light matter. Qoyotariz had hunted him three times before and would hunt him now. The thought ran like a rodent over the planks of his mind, and disappeared. He would not run. That dead town was all the reason, and this forced ride beside the abo was the only glimpse of justice those souls had left to them. As their party passed tall trees and the spreading branches that marked the age of this land, he thought of rope and a frontier solution to his crimes.

But Qoyotariz rode beside him on a spotted red horse and told him in broken Sarrish that they were going to meet his father, that his father had come east on the iron trail and they would make talk with the general before three faces of the moon.

The shock was dull but potent even in its bluntness. All the world came blanketed on such muffled feeling and he did not try to cast it off. But he did question the idea of a meeting. The abo waved off the words and would not turn from the task. They were a warband, he and Jarrett and twelve warriors, weapons of spears and blades at the ready, skins in full painted regalia. They also held guns. He had none. He had thought in the dawn that they were going to battle. So soon against his father...As their horses' steps disturbed the grass he found a dribble of mirth in his mouth and let it out with a laugh. Qoyotariz looked his way but he said nothing. This dark humor was his to keep.

They rode all the way to Fort Girs. He saw the walls looming in the distance, and the Sister Lakes coursing a shining line on the horizon. The sight was brilliant to the point of drawing water from the wells of his eyes. But they did not approach the town gates, would not be let in except beneath capture, and that was not the abo's plan.

Qoyotariz sent no emissary, no message on smoke or bird. Instead they just sat on their horses and waited. Jarrett stared at the tall twitching ears of his black mount, or glanced aside at the beaded warrior, whose straight gaze remained fixed on the fort ahead.

Soon through the sunlight rode a posse of army men. They clomped forth from the gates of the town and made a direct path through the grass and scrub toward them. Close enough and Jarrett recognized all fifteen faces. Major Dirrick sat ahorse at the general's right side, his cap pulled low, his mouth a tight line. They all were armed and had likely spied the waiting abos through a magnifying scope. Qoyotariz hadn't needed to announce himself with words.

These former comrades would have seen him, bare-headed and buckskinned, the only pale face in a pack of painted ones.

The general was a colorless uniformed body of authority, unintimidated. Perhaps curious. His horse stood directly opposite Jarrett's, and so their gazes had nowhere to go but at each other. He saw nothing behind his father's gray appraisal, but rarely had he seen much of anything his entire life. He gave nothing back, for nothing was what stood between them. Even memories seemed too framed and faded to be anything but forgotten, some decoration that could not stand the test of time.

"You take our wisewoman," Qoyotariz said to General Fawle, without greeting or deference. His voice rang as clear and as strong as a temple bell in the open air. "Your son is mine now."

"You are a bold fiend," the general said, with a slow look to the abo. His mount scraped a hoof into the ground and Jarrett thought of his blonde mare, a regret that hit him like an arrow when no lit thought of dead comrades managed to penetrate. "You come here and think we can't shoot you? You think I can't retrieve my son right now?"

The words traveled with the velocity of bullets, but the abo seemed armored beyond the expectations of mortality.

Men all around them shifted with discontent.

"You are not here to die," Qoyotariz said to his father. "I am not here to kill. Take your son now and there will be death."

Death was a soldier's sport, but they were not here to play. It was never play, he knew, not when rules were so readily disregarded. Not when Dogs ran rampant on the field.

Jarrett felt the steady regard of Major Dirrick on his face, the man's questions on the edge of sound, stifled before they tipped over to his ears. He didn't meet the stare, only looked at his father, who refused to look at him now, so set was he on the immediate enemy. But then that attention slid when Qoyotariz reached across the gap of space between his horse and Jarrett's and spread a hand at the back of his neck. The fingers were rough and warm, and struck five lines up into his hair. They held on.

"Seya'ye," the warrior said. "Tell him."

The sound of his own voice seemed contradictory to sense. "I won't go back."

It was a final defiance in a war that wasn't kind to surrender. The rage at the repudiation boiled deep and stinking in the general, some hidden sulfur preparing to shoot forth in his direction.

"You did this," he kept on, with the abo's touch along his neck, wringing the words from him when the past days had been filled by fearful silence. But fear here held a spurring note, and it rang between him and this man who claimed some ownership of his blood. But there was other blood now. He had shed bodies of it and saw well enough that everyone on this field knew it. "You sowed this in me, Father. So now you will reap it."

The spring breeze kicked a gentle path across his face but he wrenched from it and the abo's touch. He seized the ropes of his horse's bridle and turned toward the backtrail. Qoyotariz didn't stop him. Major Dirrick said his name but one kick to the animal's flanks took him in plunge and thunder far from the tension of these men.

Under threat of the Soreganee warriors, his father let him go.

The country was a false freedom spread in contrast color across his sight. The gold and blue hues could almost be the middle light. He could ride a long time in exploration of it, spied upon by no one and held to nothing. But this wasn't a practical claim in his thoughts. He knew the coyote would be close behind him, and hard upon that the fear of the army and his father's focused enmity.

And this reality settled, finally, like a winter cold all across his skin.

ACKNOWLEDGMENTS

Thank-yous to a few hardy souls: my agent, Shawna Mc-Carthy, for patience, prompt good advice, and encouragement. My editors Devi Pillai and DongWon Song, both of whom are kind, respectful, and full of insight. This book would not be nearly what it is without their guidance, and if it falls short in any way I'd like to blame somebody else but, alas, cannot. Tim Holman and the fantastic team at Orbit Books USA—I'm truly honored to be a small part of this great publisher. My dedicated readers around the world who inspire me more than they probably know; their willingness to go with me on any journey is very much appreciated (Jos & Co. still have stories to tell, I promise!). My friends near and far, writerly and non-writerly (you should know who you are by now), for their willingness to bust out the pom-poms when I need them most, especially my sushi buddy and con(-vention and -cert) compañero Derek Molata; Winifred Wong-Nicholson and Yukiko Kawakami, who were there when my dreams were in their infant stages, without judgment, and through every dream that followed. And finally to my family, because I've been blessed with a great one.

extras

orbit

meet the author

Karin Lowachee was born in Guyana, South America, and moved to Toronto, Canada, when she was two. Before her foray into fantasy, she wrote three highly acclaimed science fiction novels—*Warchild, Burndive,* and *Cagebird. Warchild* won the Warner Aspect First Novel Award, and *Cagebird* won the 2006 Gaylactic Spectrum Award and the Prix Aurora Award. Both were finalists for the Philip K. Dick Award in 2002 and 2005 respectively. She currently resides in Ontario, Canada. Find out more about the author at www.karinlowachee.com.

interview

Have you always known that you wanted to be a writer?

Yes, I've been writing stories in some form or another since kindergarten and began to think about doing it as a career around grade 5 or 6. In high school I became more conscious of it, and by university it was definitely a goal I was driven to attain. Looking back on it, writing is the only thing that I can remember doing my entire life, consistently and without need of outside encouragement. I've always loved writing, and it's the only thing I can sweat blood over without too much complaint. I have many different interests, but writing is my passion. It's the endeavor that encourages my education, exploration, and edification all in one.

Who or what inspires you in your writing?

The simplest answer to that is the world (or the universe). I'm fascinated by people, places, and ideas, and writing is my way of making sense of it all or examining things that particularly interest me. A lot of writers inspire me as well, from across many genres. Film, history, art, psychology . . . they have always been an inspiration too. I'm also inspired by a desire to get better. Every book I tackle is a conscious attempt to become a better writer, not just to tell a different story.

Your previously published novels were science fiction. How different was it writing a fantasy novel?

I've always written fantasy as well as science fiction, so that change wasn't shocking at all for me. It is a different mindset, though, a different style. I can't write fantasy in the same voice that I do science fiction, so I was conscious of how the book *sounded,* and that was the main difference. The nuts and bolts of it—the research and character building and world building—that's all necessary no matter what genre you write in. It's the same species, different breed.

How did you develop the idea for THE GASLIGHT DOGS?

Since living in Nunavut I knew that I wanted to somehow translate my experience there into a novel or novels, because I found the culture and the experience so unique and fascinating. But I was working on the science fiction series and figured the time would come when I was ready, and my publisher was willing, to have me play in that world. I was given a blank slate to develop an idea and I remembered a book (*Give Me My Father's Body* by

Kenn Harper, with a foreword by Kevin Spacey, oddly enough) when I was up north about an Inuit boy around the turn of the twentieth century who'd been brought to New York. I also had a book I'd found in a second-hand shop in Montreal about the Victorian underworld. And I've always loved Westerns like *Lonesome Dove*. I began to see that these three periods and cultures existed pretty much at the same time and that if I brought them together with some creative license and threw in a little magic, this would be a fantastical world I would want to delve into culturally, socially, and psychologically. It was the perfect combination for me because I didn't want to write a fantasy world that others had written to death (and likely better than I ever could).

You spent some time with Inuit tribes in the north as part of your academic research—how did that influence your ideas for the Aniw and the characters in the novel?

Working among the Inuit of Nunavut influenced me pretty directly. I knew that I wanted to highlight some aspects of what is a great and unique culture that many people are not all that familiar with, but throw my own spin into it as well. There are differences (the Inuit don't have spiritual Dog ancestors, but I developed that idea in order to flesh out the plot of the novel with regard to the Pangani Nation tribes and the Church of the Seven Deities), and I'm conscious of the fact that I'm not Inuit so if I incorporate a specific culture like that into my writing I have to be equally conscious of what changes I make and why. Sjenn specifically was born out of some amalgamation of the Inuit women I'd read about and met when I was in the north, but she is definitely not fashioned after anyone specific. My imagination tends to flesh out all aspects of my writing, and that's part of the reason I love writing speculative fiction.

Do you have a favorite character? If so, why?

Out of all the characters I've ever written, I don't know that I have a favorite, although Captain Azarcon (from the *Warchild* universe) and Jarrett Fawle are on the short list. Maybe I have a thing for captains...Cairo Azarcon, to me, represented a lot of what I was trying to say in that universe about hope and forgiveness and fragility and strength. I'm still discovering Jarrett, but there's something elemental in his denial and struggle to understand what he is; I find that compelling. I became enamored of Sjenn too, just because I've never written a character like her and I think there is plenty more for her to say. Qoyotariz is a character that felt right the second he was on the page, which is rare for me (Azarcon had the same feeling), and that might be because I love writing enigmatic, slightly insane people. He's extremely fun for me.

Empire is a hot topic lately, but the imperial forces in Sjenn and Jarrett's world seem to be much more fragmented than a lot of the encounters between Europe and the New World. Do you think that all encounters between new cultures end in violence, making Sjenn's story inevitable?

The reasons the Sairland-descendent Ciracusans are there are different from what went on in our world (they weren't really off to discover a New World with the intention of conquering or finding riches or any of that), so in a way I've whittled things down a little with regard to Jarrett's people, anyway. I think that violence to some extent is probably inevitable when you have cultures with such a marked difference in technology level, as well as ideals and beliefs. Throw in politics and a few people with ambitions for power and any group of people would find it hard-pressed to live peacefully. If the people are like the Aniw (or the Inuit) and not inherently violent in their day-to-day with each other, then those powers can take advantage of them (like through a forced relocation or cultural infringement), which is in itself another form of violence. I wanted to write Sjenn's story partly because it's a tragedy that's happened too many times in our own world and it can never be examined enough.

What have you found to be the most exciting part of the publishing process so far?

Every part of it is exciting to me. I love the entire process from the nitty-gritty development of the book, to the editorial conversation, to the artwork and the production and everything that follows after. I don't find any of it tedious, probably because I'm still grateful that I get to experience it in the first place and I've consistently worked with truly fantastic individuals, even when editors or publishers change. I love telling stories that are important to me, and being published allows me to reach a wide audience (many of whom contact me and constantly surprise me with their dedication and creativity). There is nothing that isn't exciting about that!

introducing

If you enjoyed **THE GASLIGHT DOGS**,
look out for

THE DROWNING CITY

Book 1 of the Necromancer Chronicles

by Amanda Downum

1229 Sal Emperaturi

Symir. The Drowning City.

An exile, perhaps, but at least it was an interesting one.

Isyllt's gloved hands tightened on the railing as the *Black Mariah* cleared the last of the Dragon Stones and turned toward the docks, dark estuarine water slopping against her hull. Fishing boats dotted Ka Liang Bay, glass buoys flashing in the sun. Cormorants dove around them, scattering ripples as they snatched fish from hooks and nets.

The west wind died, broken on the Dragons' sharp peaks, and the jungle's hot breath wafted from the shore. Rank with brine and bilge, sewers draining into the sea, but under the port-reek the air smelled of spices and the green tang of Sivahra's forests rising beyond the marshy delta of the Mir. Mountains flanked the capital city Symir, uneven green sentinels on either side of the river. So unlike the harsh and rocky shores of Selafai they had left behind two and a half decads ago.

Only twenty-five days at sea—a short voyage, though it didn't feel that way to Isyllt. The ship had made good time, laden only with olive oil and wheat flour from the north.

And northern spies. But those weren't recorded on the cargo manifest.

Isyllt shook her head, collected herself. This might be an exile, but it was a working one. She had a revolution to foment, a country to throw into chaos, and an emperor to undermine with it. Sivahra's jungles and mines—and Symir's bustling port—provided great wealth to the Assari Empire. Enough to fund a war of conquest, and the eyes of the expansionist Emperor roved slowly north. Isyllt and her master meant to prevent that.

If their intelligence was good, Sivahra was crawling with insurgent groups, natives desperate to overthrow their Imperial conquerors. Selafai's backing might help them succeed. Or at least distract the Empire. Trade one war for another. After that, maybe she could have a real vacation.

The *Mariah* dropped anchor before they docked and the crew bustled to prepare for the port authority's inspection; already a skiff rowed to meet them. The clang of harbor bells carried across the water.

Adam, her coconspirator and ostensible bodyguard, leaned against the rail beside her while his partner finished checking over their bags. Isyllt's bags, mostly; the mercenaries traveled light, but she had a pretense of pampered nobility to maintain. Maybe not such a pretense—she might have murdered for a hot bath and proper bed. Sweat stuck her shirt to her arms and back, itched behind her knees. She envied the sailors their vests and short trousers, but her skin was too pale to offer to the summer sun.

"Do we go straight to the Kurun Tam tonight?" Adam asked. The westering sun flashed on gold and silver earrings, mercenary gaud. He wore his sword again for the first time since they'd boarded the *Mariah*. He'd taken to sailor fashions—his vest hung open over his scarred chest, revealing charm bags around his neck and the pistol tucked into his belt. His skin was three shades darker than it had been when they sailed, bronze now instead of olive.

Isyllt's mouth twisted. "No," she said after a moment. "Let's find an extravagantly expensive hotel tonight. I feel like spending the Crown's money. We can work tomorrow." One night of vacation, at least, she could give herself.

He grinned and looked to his partner. "Do you know someplace decadent?"

Xinai's lips curled as she turned away from the luggage. "The Silver Phoenix. It's Selafaïn—it'll be decadent enough for you." Her head barely cleared her partner's shoulder, though the black plumage-crest of her hair added the illusion of more height. She wore her wealth too—rings in her ears, a gold cuff on one wiry wrist, a silver hoop in her nostril. The blades at her hips and the scars on her wiry arms said she knew how to keep it.

Isyllt turned back to the city, scanning the ships at dock. She was surprised not to see more Imperial colors flying. After rumors of rebellion and worries of war, she'd expected Imperial warships, but there was no sign of the Emperor's army—although that didn't mean it wasn't there.

Something was happening, though; a crowd gathered on the docks, and Isyllt caught flashes of red and green uniforms amid the blur of bodies. Shouts and angry voices carried over the water, but she couldn't make out the words.

The customs skiff drew alongside the *Mariah*, lion crest

gleaming on the red-and-green-striped banners—the flag of an Imperial territory, granted limited home-rule. The sailors threw down a rope ladder and three harbor officials climbed aboard, nimble against the rocking hull. The senior inspector was a short, neat woman, wearing a red sash over her sleek-lined coat. Isyllt fought the urge to fidget with her own travel-grimed clothes. Her hair was a salt-stiff tangle, barely contained by pins, and while she'd cleaned her face with oil before landfall, it was no substitute for a proper bath.

Isyllt waited, Adam and Xinai flanking her, while the inspector spoke to the captain. Whatever the customs woman told the captain, he didn't like. He spat over the rail and made an angry gesture toward the shore. The *Mariah* wasn't the only ship waiting to dock; Isyllt wondered if the gathering on the pier had something to do with the delay.

Finally the ship's mate led two of the inspectors below, and the woman in the red sash turned to Isyllt, a wax tablet and stylus in her hand. A Sivahri, darker skinned than Xinai but with the same creaseless black eyes; elaborate henna designs covered her hands. Isyllt was relieved to be greeted in Assari—Xinai had tutored her in the native language during the voyage, but she was still far from fluent.

"Roshani." The woman inclined her head politely. "You're the only passengers?" She raised her stylus as Isyllt nodded. "Your names?"

"Isyllt Iskaldur, of Erisín." She offered the oiled leather tube that held her travel papers. "This is Adam and Xinai, sayifarim hired in Erisín."

The woman glanced curiously at Xinai; the mercenary gave no more response than a statue. The official opened the tube and unrolled the parchment, recorded something on her tablet. "And your business in Symir?"

Isyllt tugged off her left glove and held out her hand.

"I'm here to visit the Kurun Tam." The breeze chilled her sweaty palm. Since it was impossible to pass herself off as anything but a foreign mage, the local thaumaturgical facility was the best cover.

The woman's eyes widened as she stared at the cabochon black diamond on Isyllt's finger, but she didn't ward herself or step out of reach. Ghostlight gleamed iridescent in the stone's depths and a cold draft suffused the air. She nodded again, deeper this time. "Yes, meliket. Do you know where you'll be staying?"

"Tonight we take rooms at the Silver Phoenix."

"Very good." She recorded the information, then glanced up. "I'm sorry, meliket, but we're behind schedule. It will be a while yet before you can dock."

"What's going on?" Isyllt gestured toward the wharf. More soldiers had appeared around the crowd.

The woman's expression grew pained. "A protest. They've been there an hour and we're going to lose a day's work."

Isyllt raised her eyebrows. "What are they protesting?"

"New tariffs." Her tone became one of rote response. "The Empire considers it expedient to raise revenues and has imposed taxes on foreign goods. Some of the local merchants"—she waved a hennaed hand at the quay—"are unhappy with the situation. But don't worry, it's nothing to bother the Kurun Tam."

Of course not—Imperial mages would hardly be burdened with problems like taxes. It was much the same in the Arcanost in Erisín.

"Are these tariffs only in Sivahra?" she asked.

"Oh, no. All Imperial territories and colonies are subject."

Not just sanctions against a rebellious population, then, but real money-raising. That left an unpleasant taste in the back of her mouth. Twenty-five days with no news was chancy where politics were concerned.

The other officials emerged from the cargo hold a few moments later and the captain grudgingly paid their fees. The woman turned back to Isyllt, her expression brightening. "If you like, meliket, I can take you to the Silver Phoenix myself. It will be a much shorter route than getting there from the docks."

Isyllt smiled. "That would be lovely. Shakera."

Adam cocked an eyebrow as he hoisted bags. Isyllt's lips curled. "It never pays to annoy foreign guests," she murmured in Selafaïn. "Especially ones who can steal your soul."

She tried to watch the commotion on the docks, but the skiff moved swiftly and they were soon out of sight. A cloud of midges trailed behind the craft; the drone of wings carried unpleasant memories of the plague, but the natives seemed unconcerned. Isyllt waved the biting insects away, though she was immune to whatever exotic diseases they might carry. As they rowed beneath a raised water gate, a sharp, minty smell filled the air and the midges thinned.

The inspector—who introduced herself as Anhai Xian-Mar—talked as they went, her voice counterpoint to the rhythmic splash of oars as she explained the myriad delta islands on which the city was built, the web of canals that took the place of stone streets. Xinai's mask slipped for an instant and Isyllt saw the cold disdain in her eyes. The mercenary had little love for countrymen who served their Assari conquerors.

Sunlight spilled like honey over their shoulders, gilding the water and gleaming on domes and tilting spires. Buildings crowded together, walls of cream and ocher stone, pale blues and dusty pinks, balconies nearly touching over narrow alleys and waterways. Bronze chimes flashed from eaves and lintels. Vines trailed from rooftop gardens, dripping leaves and orange blossoms onto the water. Birds perched in potted trees and on steep green- and gray-tiled roofs.

Invaders the Assari might be, but they had built a beautiful city. Isyllt tried to imagine the sky dark with smoke, the water running red. The city would be less lovely if her mission succeeded.

She'd heard stories from other agents of how the job crept into everything, reduced buildings and cities to exits and escape routes, defenses and weaknesses to be exploited. Till you couldn't look at anything—or anyone—without imagining how to infiltrate or corrupt or overthrow. She wondered how long it would take to happen to her. If she would even notice when it did.

Anhai followed Isyllt's gaze to the water level—slime crusted the stone several feet above the surface of the canal. "The rains will come soon and the river will rise. You're in time for the Dance of Masks."

The skiff drew up against a set of stairs and the oarsmen secured the boat and helped Adam and Xinai unload the luggage. A tall building rose above them, decorated with Selafaïn pillars. A carven phoenix spread its wings over the doors and polished horn panes gleamed ruddy in the dying light.

Anhai bowed farewell. "If you need anything at all, meliket, you can find me at the port authority office."

"Shakera." Isyllt offered her hand, and the silver griffin she held. She never saw where Anhai tucked the coin.

The she stepped from the skiff to the slime-slick stairs and set foot in the Drowning City.